"An Appalachian coming-of-age novel... intensely lyrical, emotional debut...Keener's vivid imagery and lush, folksy language evoke traditions...the novel succeeds in bringing to life a slice of mountain life..."

—*Publishers Weekly*

"This dark, dramatic novel set in the Appalachians is an impressive and often lyrical debut by a young writer born in Virginia...Rachel Keener shows some serious literary chops; her characters are complex, her plot twists are pleasingly unpredictable and her writing oozes atmosphere. Put this one on your summer reading list."

—*Minneapolis Star Tribune*

"Keener reveals the dignity and sense of community among the outcast and itinerant."

—*Charlotte Observer*

"It has been years since I've read a book as profoundly dramatic in its examination of survival as Rachel Keener's *The Killing Tree*. This is a story of the magic and the meanness of southern mountain people. In one way or another I have known each of them, and Rachel Keener knows them also. Her writing in this debut novel is wonderful."

—**Terry Kay, author of *The Book of Marie***

Available from C

THE MEMORY THIEF

A Novel

RACHEL KEENER

CENTER STREET™

New York   Boston   Nashville

Copyright © 2010 by Rachel Keener

Center Street
Hachette Book Group
237 Park Avenue
New York, NY 10017

www.centerstreet.com

Center Street is a division of Hachette Book Group, Inc.
The Center Street name and logo are trademarks of
Hachette Book Group, Inc.

Printed in the United States of America

First Edition: March 2010
10   9   8   7   6   5   4   3   2   1

Library of Congress Cataloging-in-Publication Data

Keener, Rachel.
    The memory thief / Rachel Keener.—1st ed.
       p. cm.
    ISBN 978-1-59995-112-6
    1. Self-realization in women—Fiction.   I. Title.
    PS3611.E345M46 2010
    813'.6—dc22   2009027277

For Kip, and our gift of ten

The
Memory
Thief

ANGEL

Prologue

The fire stole everyone's attention. The newspapers, the gossips, the farmers from miles away. What they overlooked, what they never got close enough to see, was that the real story was in the smoke. How it hovered low, too heavy to soar. Filled with too many dead things to ever rise.

Weeks earlier I hid a bag of supplies under the tobacco leaves. A little food and water. The money I stole from Daddy's glove compartment. A sweatshirt for warmth. Then I sat and whispered a drunk woman's story to the fields. I called her Momma. But if the night was cold enough, and sleep far away, then the drunk woman's name might be my own. You can call me Angel.

The story was long, but only a few words really mattered. Words like *five thousand dollars. Carolina.* And *rich Holy Roller.* I stamped them in black-and-white letters behind the lids of my eyes. Like a map to someplace I was going. Like a key to who I really was.

With my getaway bag packed, I held a match in my trembling hand. I struck it, and watched it glow against the Tennessee sky. But then I thought of you, and my lips pressed together to blow out that fire. I'd forgotten something. Memories.

I went inside the trailer and tucked a couple in each pocket. Not the best ones, like good report cards or the birthday candle Mrs. Swarm gave me in a cupcake. I left those to burn. What I tucked in my pockets were the answers to what had become of me. To what I had seen and felt. I kept those things because I believed. Because I hoped one day you would ask.

I returned to the matches, read the words across the front of the pack: *Keep out of reach of children.* It had been seven years since the school safety lecture where the dream of fire first came to me. Local firemen got their kicks from showing little kids spectacular pictures of barn fires and forest fires. But the ones that I returned to, snuck back to an empty classroom during recess to see, were the trailer fires. Nothing was left but black ash on the ground. Only a label at the bottom of the page—*Single Wide Trailer, electrical fire*—left any clue. When the firemen showed those pictures, they swore that nothing burns as completely or quickly as an old rusted-out trailer. With the electrical wiring sandwiched in between wood that's not really wood at all, just some sort of stiff paper that's cheaper to make than it is to cut a real tree. And the heat. Pouring down from a steamy Tennessee sun. The rusted metal sucks it in, the cheap walls trap it, and it's ready to burn up quicker than a matchbox.

"In five minutes," the fireman said, "it's all gone. Every picture. Every memory. That's why we're here today. To talk about a safety plan." Their point was about naming meeting places, how to open windows and feel for hot doorknobs. But I sifted through that and started dreaming smoky dreams. Ones where everything disappeared in five hot minutes.

I waited long years to light that match. My own safety plan forming slowly, until it moved and kicked inside me with its own life. And when the moment finally came, I moved my hand smoothly across the front of the pack. Felt the scratch of friction inside my fist. Heard the quick hiss of new fire. And I smiled. Burning down Black Snake trailer was easy. The hard thing was walking away, when what I wanted most was to watch it die.

But I couldn't stay and risk being caught. So I hid in the bacca and thought of you. Whispered old familiar questions. *Where are you?* So much time has passed. *And where have you been?*

Long after the sun had set, I saw smoke still hovering. Unwanted memories burning up the night as I sat whispering with my heart on fire, shivering beneath the Tennessee moon.

HANNAH

I

Things go missing in Carolina. That's what Hannah would remember most about her time there. It started easy, even sweetly, with small things like words. The wasteful parts, whole syllables, disappeared around her. *Charleston* became *Chah'stun*. *Hurricane* became *her'cun*. *Yankee* was *Yank*, only spoken with a snort. Hard *g*'s were an insult. Good manners required a softer tongue.

Comfort went missing next. Hannah's first hour in Carolina left her sweating in a way no powder-soft deodorant could help. Poor Yank, dressed in stinging polyester. That night, after swatting away palm-size mosquitoes, she walked to the water and stuck her face close enough to feel its mist. Sucked in her breath like a newborn ready to yell out a first cry.

Her family arrived with one suitcase each. Father's was everything expected. Clothes, maps, sketches of bridges, and Bibles. Mother's was nearly the same. But underneath her clothes and soaps and Bibles was a small wedding picture. The one where her husband reached under her veil and pulled her out for the kiss.

Hannah had been given the smallest suitcase and told to keep it light. But clothes weren't a challenge. Gray and khaki ankle-length skirts, gray sweaters, long-sleeved blouses, and a few pairs of pleated kool-lots—shorts that were so loose they looked like skirts and fell the required eight inches below her knees. She dug through her nightstand drawer, searching for anything else she might need. There were pictures of her and her friends at Bible camp. Flowers dried and pressed into an album page. A folded-up two-inch triangle torn from a magazine page she found loose in a shopping cart. It hid the checklist: *Top Ten Ways to Know a Guy Likes You.*

Hannah's mother scanned the contents of her suitcase, pulled out a white shirt and replaced it with a yellow one. Then she handed Hannah a trash bag and told her to clear the junk and organize her mess of books. Dozens of them were piled in sloppy stacks around her room.

Those stacks began the day of her sixteenth birthday party. "No more banned books. You're old enough and smart enough, so if it's literature you can read it," Father announced. Hannah shook her head at him, embarrassed by the shock of her friends.

"Like Psalms," Father whispered. "People quote happy ones, yet so many speak of suffering." He handed her a copy of *The Grapes of Wrath.* "Like this," he said.

That winter Hannah hid inside the Mission Room and made up for sixteen years of various versions of *Pilgrim's Progress.* She loved that room. Maps lined the walls with little red flags pinned to all the exotic places her parents had served. Shelves were filled with souvenirs—baskets woven by natives, broken pottery, and a hand-painted porcelain doll.

Babies were the last souvenirs her parents had collected. They spent their youth serving the miserable and poor of the world. But at the age of forty-four they turned up pregnant in the middle of rural Philippines and realized they were more than missionaries. They were a mother and father. And the first thing on their minds was the safety of their own. They left. For the security of a hospital and a doctor. For the steady paycheck and good life Father's PhD in structural engineering could offer. For a little surprise they wrapped in pink blankets and named Hannah Joy.

All the energy they had poured into missions they now focused on building Hannah a spotless world. They lived in a neighborhood that sparkled with money. And drove forty-five minutes into the countryside to the church where Hannah's mother was raised.

They called it Tabernacle. The building's great marble columns and stone archways set it apart from modern, redbrick churches. And the women took it one step further. Their devotion to God and holiness was proven by floor-length skirts, high-collared polyester blouses, and uncut hair.

When Hannah was three, her parents pondered their age. "I'll be sixty-two when she marries," Mother said dryly. And they began to notice how different Hannah was from other little girls in their neighborhood. They watched her struggle to ride her tricycle in gray baggy kool-lots, while other baby girls splashed naked in tiny plastic pools set in their front yards. It didn't hurt them when Hannah couldn't ride the pony at a neighborhood party because her ankle-length skirt kept getting in the way. But it made them see her need.

"I won't conceive again," Mother said. "I'm forty-seven." So Hannah's father took one last flight to the Philippines and came home with Bethlehem Rose, a two-and-a-half-year-old orphan they called Bethie. Now two little girls struggled to ride a tricycle instead of just one.

With only six months between their birthdays, the girls were nearly twins. One pale with white blond hair, the other golden with black hair. Her parents were relieved that Hannah didn't have to start kindergarten alone. Bethie was there beside her. Both of them in plain grays and pastels, their hair in long braids down their backs.

It was at school that the real difference began to show. Letters spoke to Hannah before any of her peers, and she was reading two-syllable words by the end of the first month. She was marked very early by her teachers as *excellent*. And the other students would sometimes call her Nerd *before* they would think to call her Holy Roller.

Not so for Bethie. If the teacher bothered to call on her, it was only to be disappointed. Words never came easy for Bethie. Her parents paid for speech therapy, and when there was no improvement they were told it was a maturity thing. Bethie simply needed to outgrow her stuttering. Mother tried bribing her for smooth words, but by the time Bethie was eight she had switched to punishment instead. When vinegar on a stuttering tongue didn't work, Mother decided not to notice it anymore.

But there was always punishment waiting for Bethie at school. She rode the bus to a long gray building with different teachers and shuffled classes every hour. She wore a white men's-style shirt and a dark gray floor-length skirt every day. Her hair was smoothed back as tight as it could be, her face without a smile. And when people spoke to her, even if it was a curious stranger asking *Gosh, are you hot?* Bethie shook her head coolly, her eyes narrowing in anger.

Hannah tried more. She wore yellow because she knew it complemented her hair. And kool-lots, because even though they were baggy like some joke of a skirt, they at least showed her feet. Hannah's hair was braided loosely, so strands of gold could work themselves free and glow around her face, like an accidental halo.

But both of the girls were teased viciously. Their classmates called them Polyester Pollys. And they never drank Kool-Aid with their lunch. If they did, without fail someone would yell, "Watch out! The Jim Jones girls have gotten to the Kool-Aid again!" When they jogged the slow mile at PE, where everyone else wore the snazzy gym uniforms of shorts and tanks, someone always snickered about them doing the Holy Roller shuffle. And it was true. Nobody can run far in a floor-length skirt. Sometimes Hannah wondered if that was the point.

When Father announced he'd won the lucrative bid to strengthen the bridge that spanned the Cooper River, and that they'd spend the summer in South Carolina, it was the holy *Yes* both girls had been waiting for. It was an escape for Bethie. From all the kids that knew she couldn't speak smoothly. And from the teachers who wouldn't look at her, hadn't looked at her since first grade, when they "socially passed" her to please her parents and let her stay with her sister.

For Hannah, it meant adventure, like in the books she loved. It meant, simply, the gates were opening.

They left behind a house filled with so many rooms they could spend the day without ever bumping into one another. And traded it for a shack on the marshes of James Island. A two-bedroom, one-bath, company-owned box that Father insisted on. He'd turned down the offer of a renovated historic condo within walking distance to the Battery and Rainbow Row. He wanted the mosquitoes. The mud crabs and the culture. He wanted to feel like a real southerner, even if he couldn't sound like one.

Each of them smiled as they unpacked. Hannah and Bethie smiled over the joy of escape. Mother and Father over the excitement of their daughters. Over the pleasure of an extended vacation in a southern beach town. Over the promise of their old life, waiting for them back home.

One morning their first week there, Father rolled a used bike out to the girls, as they sat by the marsh. "You could explore a bit, if you want. The tourist traffic hits the other beaches. And the shoulders are wide, so you could stay on those."

Hannah squealed with joy and ran to the bike. Father noticed Bethie standing behind her. "Both of you girls."

Bethie smiled, but she never sat on that bike. Even if she wanted to, it was always gone before dawn. Hannah spent her mornings on the beach. It was two and a half miles from the shack, and if she set her mind to it she could be there in under twenty minutes. She rarely did, though, preferring instead to take her time and learn the details of her summer home.

Like the pile of oyster shells at the end of a gravel drive that served as the only sign for a motel, a long brick rectangle hidden in the woods that served fresh-catch steam buckets on picnic tables in the front yard. Or the miles of marsh, with its smell that turned her stomach at first, until the days passed and she forgot to notice it. And the palm trees that lined Folly Road, like something from a paradise postcard.

She set her alarm clock based on the tides. And if she reminded herself before she went to sleep, she could usually wake up just before it rang. She'd turn off the clock and dress quietly in the dark. Bethie would lay perfectly still, her pillow touching Hannah's.

Only when the water pulled back from the shore could she find curling starfish, sea urchins, and perfect-circle sand dollars. She'd pick them up carefully and sometimes take them home to Bethie. "Look," she'd say, as she showed her sister. "Treasure's in the low points."

She had packed only two pairs of kool-lots, but that was what she preferred to pedal in so that her feet were free to move. She still wore the polyester blouses, buttoned at her wrists and collar. Hannah had been taught not to care about "pretty." Modesty was the coveted prize. Sometimes the competition could even get catty. Young girls at church would go through fads of wearing head coverings, even though the rules didn't require them for unmarried women. But *pretty* took on a new meaning in that beach town. Golden skin was the standard. When Hannah passed nearly naked people on the streets, her forehead beaded with sweat on a ninety-five-degree day, she knew her polyester confused them.

Sometimes after sunrise, Hannah would relax in the sand and wait for the others. The old lady that walked her little black dog. The man who liked to jog and treated the rock piles, the ruins of old fishing piers, like enormous hurdles. They knew her, too, as part of their usual scene, and always gave a curious but friendly nod. Their arrival meant the day had begun and the world was awake. Hannah would hop on her bike and pedal furiously, letting the wind shake the sand from her. Then she'd ride down to the fruit market, a collection of little tents where fresh produce was sold. She'd pick up whatever Mother had requested, usually peaches or sweet corn. Sometimes a bag of boiled peanuts for her breakfast.

James Island taught her how to eat. Showed her what fruit tastes like when it's still warm from a ripening sun. How fish is meant to be eaten, no more than a few hours from the ocean. Handing somebody a ripe Carolina peach was the same as giving them your best smile. Passing a bowl of shrimp and grits was as clear as any *Love you* could get. Food was a language there.

II

One evening, Hannah was bored after supper. With her parents' permission she pedaled down to the market, even though she'd already been that morning. She was watching people inspect the fruit, how they thumped the melons and squeezed the peaches, when she saw it. A yellowed paper taped to the market tent pole. *OYSTER ROAST! FRIDAY AT SUNSET. FOLLY BEACH. LIVE MUSIC!*

She biked to the beach. In the distance was music. At first, just practice runs on old guitars. A few beats of a drum. Then they started for real, jumpy songs with the moan of a harmonica. There was smoke in the air, and far away the glow of an oyster fire. She pedaled closer, until she felt the good time rippling from them like the waves at high tide. Bronzed bodies were everywhere, and Hannah did not try and blend in. She had lived through too many bad days of school to believe that she could. Besides, she was taught from a very early age that she belonged to a separate and holy people. Compared to holy, separate was always the easy part.

Past the crowd, toward the shore, people worked furiously. They were icing down beers and sorting buckets of oysters. They weren't naked like the others, each of them wearing a black T-shirt with the letters CSM stitched on the pocket. And they weren't listening to the music. Instead they were listening to a woman calling out instructions. "They runnin' outta beer. C'mon now, ice that down and get it to 'em."

Money flew their way—for the buckets of oysters roasted with corn and potatoes, for the Dixie cups filled with sweet tea, for the bottles of beer. The music pulsed louder and stronger, all while the black-shirted CSM team circled the crowd and weaved through them, passing out goodies in exchange for fistfuls of money.

Hannah kept looking back to the woman. Her black skin glistened by the fire. She controlled everything. From the volume of the band—*They need to turn that speaker up*—to the amount of seasoning in the oyster buckets: *Don't get too heavy with that Ol' Bay.* It was her money, too. Boys with young muscled arms were slinging buckets for her and handing wads of cash back. But it was what was behind the table, just fifteen feet back, that made Hannah stand up and take a step closer.

A full moon hung behind her, its glow bouncing off the white tops of each new wave. She saw naked shoulders pushing into the water, cutting through the pull of the waves. They crashed over a boy, and he sank low. She stood, waiting for him to resurface. And waiting some more. Until it was time to return home. She left, uneasy.

Two weeks later she was pedaling down the road when she passed the pile of oyster shells. There was a sign by the shells that day: *Cora's Steampot Motel. Help wanted.*

Maybe it was the way the fire made that woman's skin glisten like the inside of an oyster shell. Maybe it was the thought of all those black CSM T-shirts. Or maybe a part of her was still waiting, wondering if that boy had ever surfaced. Whatever the reason was, Hannah pedaled down the drive and stared at the brick rectangle, a neon sign flashing *CORA'S STEAMPOT MOTEL* in the front window. A smaller one hung on the door. *Rent a Room, Get a Bucket!*

The front desk was empty, except for a little bell to ring for service. She tapped it shyly and waited.

"In the kitchen," a big voice called from inside.

"Ma'am," Hannah called out. "I'm here about the job?"

"Come on back. Shut the door good 'cause I don't want no more flies."

Hannah stepped past the front office, closed the door but kept her hand on the knob. Inside, she noticed the entire middle of the motel was the kitchen. With each side framed by long skinny halls dotted with four doors each. The kitchen was filled with a freezer, a double stove, and two double refrigerators. In the corner of the room was an enormous sink, filled with metal buckets.

The woman from the oyster roast stood by the stove. She looked Hannah up and down and started laughing. "Sissy, git in here. Somebody's here 'bout the job."

A younger woman walked in and burst out laughing, too.

Hannah was used to being everyone's favorite joke. And there in that kitchen, she knew she was ridiculous. With sweat staining her shirt, her collar thrown open in a desperate search for relief, and beige kool-lots clinging to damp thighs.

"Keeps the mosquitoes off at least," she mumbled, looking down at her feet. "Haven't had one single bite since I've been here."

"What she talkin' 'bout? Mosquituhs?" Sissy said, still laughing. The woman at the stove tilted her head to the side, a big grin still on her face.

"You think we're laughin' 'bout your clothes, don't you? We're laughin' 'cause you the most unlikely shrimper we ever seen."

"Shrimper?"

"Yeah."

"I thought you were hiring a maid or a waitress."

"You never eat here, have you?" Sissy asked. "We hand out buckets, but after that everybody serve themselves. We just catch it and cook it. If they need a drink refill, they walk in and git it. They need another bucket? They walk in and git it. We ain't needin' any waitress help."

"Well now, wait a minute," the older woman said, as she peeled a potato slowly. "We don't need a waitress, exactly. But I'm tired of makin' beds up, ain't you, Sissy? And at dinner, there's always somebody that don't know the rules. Leavin' their bucket on the table. And the boys run late with their deliveries, too, and one of us has to run down to the dock to get the catch. If we hired her to pick up those loose ends, maybe we could focus on the cookin' a bit more. Maybe we could finally start servin' that key lime pie you've been wantin' to make and charge a robbery for." She looked at Hannah carefully, and didn't laugh this time. "My name is Cora. And this is my steampot motel."

"I can clean tables very well," Hannah said. "And I've been making my own bed since I was four." She looked them both in the eyes, the way her father had trained her. "It proves you're trustworthy," he liked to say.

"I believe you." Cora nodded. "Put this apron on, and I'll show you the buckets we need rinsed."

"She's gonna git hot with that apron on top of all them clothes," Sissy said.

The apron was a thick, canvaslike material, hanging well below Hannah's knees. It was made to help protect from steam burns and hot water splashes, as the buckets were being prepared and served.

Hannah looked at them. Under their aprons they were nearly naked. Braless under their tank tops, big breasts spreading wide and draping over their stomachs. They wore cutoffs, flip-flops, and long leatherlike gloves reaching up to their elbows.

"Wanna run home and change?" Cora asked kindly.

For a moment, Hannah sounded like Bethie. She stared at the ground and stammered about how the heat didn't bother her. About how her skin was sensitive to the sun. But she could feel them staring at her, and she could nearly see her lies swirling with the hot steam in that room.

"Stuff like this is all I have," she finally said, shrugging her shoulders.

"I gotta T-shirt in the trunk. It's an extra-small, too, that's why I ain't give it out yet," Sissy said, and laughed. "We never had no extra-small person work here before."

Hannah took that prized T-shirt and held it loosely. An old ache returned, as real to her as the burn of steam as she reached across hot buckets for the soap Cora held out. It was uncertainty, that pain that settled in her chest and tightened her lungs. It was the constant wondering, summed up by the simple question her mind was always whispering: *Is it a sin?* Would God still want her if she wore a T-shirt, if the rules of modesty were broken and fresh air cooled her steamy arms?

She thought about Mother, working furiously at home organizing supplies for the children that passed through the downtown shelter. Before they even left home, she had contacted the shelter and asked them what they needed most. Immediately after, she began soliciting corporate donations. And once she settled in and toured the shelter, she started writing letters asking for help from her Yankee friends.

It was her gift, *organizing*. And within a few weeks, the living room of the shack had been turned into a closet. With stacks of pajamas donated from department stores. Diapers from local grocery stores. Little baby blankets from her church sewing circle.

Hannah knew what Mother would say. Standing in the middle of projects to be organized, Mother would give her a memorized, automatic response. She wouldn't have time to consider—even as she worked in her own polyester sweat-box—the ninety-two-degree heat. There were children in the world forced to live naked. What did it matter if she was a little hot?

Hannah held the T-shirt up, saw how it would fit her perfectly. The length falling just to the waist of her kool-lots. She felt the smooth, cool cotton. And imagined how well it would breathe, letting air flow through it and over her skin. The heat seemed to burn more than usual. Like hell sat under her skin.

She thought of Father. As he worked, somewhere downtown, being paid for his genius. She thought of the sermon, about honoring the Sabbath, that they recently attended. Afterward they stopped for gas at a little station where the owner pumped it himself.

"It's not a sin," Father said. "For that man to be pumping gas today. He's doing it because he needs to feed his family." Then he reminded her about David, about how he ate the holy showbread meant only for priests. "God doesn't want his children hungry."

That was Father's gift: *mercy*. He followed all the rules himself. But not only did he manage to pardon when others around him didn't—sometimes he found value in it.

Mother's way was easier. She never asked questions or raised doubts. Long ago, she had swallowed the rules. They were the bones that held her up. But on that ninety-two-degree day, Hannah chose mercy. From the heat. From the sweat. From the polyester that trapped it all inside.

It was the first time she had ever worn a T-shirt. She was

sixteen years old, and how she longed for a mirror at that moment. Looking down at herself, she saw things she normally only saw in the shower. Like the fact that she had a waist. One that was normally hidden in the boxy drape of a high-collared men's-style shirt. But in an extra-small T-shirt, the lines of her body were clear. She was narrow at the center. The hourglass God had designed her to be. And there was something else. Something that made her blush and quickly look away. Only to look back down again. She had breasts. Round, full, womanly breasts. They were still covered. But they were no longer hiding.

She put the long apron on and noticed her skin. The nakedness of her arms, all the way up to her shoulders. They were the color of milk.

"Gonna wash some buckets or stare at that apron?" Sissy called.

Hannah headed to the corner, where Sissy showed her how to take a steel-wool pad and a drop of soap, and scrub the tin bucket out.

"We don't fry nothin' here," she said proudly. "They ain't a drop of hot grease you gotta worry 'bout. Just scrub it, rinse it good, and set it in the rack to dry. Easiest dishwashin' job you'll ever come by."

The buckets were practically clean, having already been emptied of leftovers. There were some bits of corn or potato occasionally stuck to the side. But nothing that required any muscle to remove. Hannah washed them quickly.

"I knew you were good," Cora said approvingly. "Now come over here and let me teach you 'bout the steampot."

On the stove sat two of the largest pots Hannah had ever seen. She watched as Cora filled them with water and seasonings, then laid coils of sausage, little new potatoes, and halved ears of corn inside.

"I'll let that get to cookin'," she said. "Then later I'll add shrimp, mussels, and oysters. It don't take but a minute for that stuff to cook. When the shrimp pinks up and the mussels open, it's time to spoon it out."

Cora rang the dinner bell, a rusted old cowbell that hung from the ceiling on a rope. She gave it three sharp bangs, then motioned for Hannah to bring her some buckets. As she filled them, Hannah smelled the ocean.

"Well, we're set now," Cora said, taking two buckets to carry. She motioned for Sissy and Hannah to pick up two as well.

Five picnic tables, gray with age, sat in a half-moon shape. The tables were interesting enough, with holes cut in the middle of each and trash cans beneath the holes for people to toss shells into. But what really caught Hannah's eye that evening was the tree.

Hannah had noticed them in the distance before, but she'd never been so close to an old twisted live oak. Not like the oak trees of her home, with straight trunks and mitten-shaped leaves. Live oaks were different. With thick squatted trunks, and massive branches writhing and coiling out. Like the way a small child would draw a tree with scribbled curly lines. Most were veiled. Draped with sheets of Spanish moss, gray and weeping. Antiquing the trees to match the town, like another dusty Civil War relic.

"Quit gapin' at that snake tree and drop them buckets down so you can go get more," Sissy yelled.

Hannah jumped, set her buckets down and returned to the kitchen for more. She carried buckets out, two by two, and collected money from everyone that Sissy told her wasn't staying in the motel. But she kept her eye on the tree. And decided that Sissy was right. It looked like snakes. Dozens of them curling out from a center nest. Except the tree was beautiful, in a way that snakes would never be.

Once the tables were full, some ate on the hoods of their cars, pulled as close to the shade of the oak as they could get. Cora went from person to person, saying hello and asking about family and friends. The whole service took forty-five minutes. From tossing the raw shrimp in the pot to serving the last table.

"Only do it once a day, same time every day," said Cora. "I ain't never been nobody's short-order cook. They can eat what I fixed when I fixed it or not. I started it to feed my travelers anyhow. But turned out the locals were hungry, too."

"C'mon, Hannah," Sissy called out. "Number Six checked out a couple hours ago. I'll show you how to git the room ready."

Hannah followed her inside the motel and down the skinny hallway.

"No maid cart. You gotta carry your own supplies and haul the trash and laundry out. But when folks are stayin' here, ain't much to do for the daily cleanin'. Just make their beds and wipe down the sinks and such. It's when they check out that the room gets a good goin' over. And we treat for roaches and sand fleas at every checkout. This is a clean motel. But that don't mean some of our travelers ain't draggin' in their own bugs."

There was a locked closet in the middle of the hall. Sissy took a key from her pocket and opened it to reveal shelves of bleach, a vacuum, glass cleaner, trash bags, and pesticide spray. She pulled out the bleach and gave it to Hannah with a pair of long gloves.

"Best git the worst part out of the way," she said, nodding toward a toilet brush. Hannah pulled her gloves on, trying to look confident.

"Let me know when you've finished that. Shouldn't be too bad, just a man. Much worse with families. The things kids can do to a bathroom would shock most folks. And try not to get bleach on your T-shirt. Only extra one we got."

Sissy unlocked Number Six. Hannah walked inside, turned on the lamp, and looked around. Brown plaid curtains, various shades of mud squared against one another, hung heavy over the one window. There was one bed, standard size, with more brown plaid covering it. Next to the bed was a brass lamp with an embroidered shade, little purple violets twirling across it. It seemed out of place among all that brown plaid, more like something Mother would enjoy making than a motel lamp. A mirror and dresser stood opposite the bed. There was no TV or phone. Instead a card invited guests to a central lobby, across from the front desk, to watch TV or make local calls. There was another card, this one framed on the wall nearest the bathroom.

Welcome to Cora's Steampot Motel, where the rooms are clean and supper is free. This is our home. And for a night or two, it is yours as well. A small scripture was printed at the bottom: *I was a stranger and you welcomed me . . . Matthew 25:35.*

Hannah jerked her head away, like she did when she saw nasty words carved into bathroom stalls. She was used to being around people that didn't know any scripture at all. But she had never been around someone that used it casually, like in a motel greeting, almost as if the words were their own. Scripture was holy, only spoken in church and whispered in prayer. Hannah was amazed that something holy could ever be placed next to common words like *Steampot Motel*. She wondered if that could ever be right. She wished she could ask Mother.

Hannah was overly generous with the bleach, pouring it until she had to use nearly a whole roll of paper towels to dry the floor. She had never cleaned a bathroom before. Never seen Mother clean one, either. That was Inez's job.

Inez was the old lady that Mother hired to clean their house every day. It was a woman's place to clean her home, Mother admitted, and she insisted on that. But with her constant volunteering, and the sewing that always needed to be done for the shelters, she gladly hired daily help. Nobody but Inez had ever cleaned any of the four bathrooms in their beautiful brick home.

Inez was an eighty-year-old widow. She didn't have any retirement, or children to care for her. Mother said letting her tidy the house and scrub bathrooms was a gift to her. "It allows her freedom," Mother said. "She can still earn her own living."

Hannah knelt and inspected the space behind the toilet and the wall, looking for hidden filth. She thought again of Inez, and what she must think of them. Making mess after mess and never cleaning it themselves. Of course Mother didn't lie; Inez's job meant freedom. But as Hannah reached her hand to wipe away scum, she knew Inez's job meant something more. *Humble* was the nice word. *Desperate* the true one.

Cora stood in the doorway. "Smells good and bleach-y. The bedroom's left, but Sissy can show you later how we like it. I've saved you a bucket; you can eat it and then git home quick. It ain't safe to ride that bike in the dark."

After eating, Hannah slipped off the T-shirt and put her blouse back on.

"Keep it," Sissy said, when she saw Hannah hang the T-shirt by the aprons in the kitchen. "You'll need to wash it up before next shift."

Hannah held the shirt in her hand, unsure of what to do.

"I'll git it clean," Cora said. "Don't bother your momma with extra washin'. I gotta run that load of towels from Number Six through anyway. Be careful goin' home. Traffic picks up this time of day."

But it wasn't traffic that worried Hannah as she pedaled home. The sun was beginning to set, and it occurred to her how long she had been gone. She'd never spent the entire day away from home before. As she walked into the shack, it didn't surprise her to see Mother frown.

"Where have you been? Your father is out looking for you. I was against that bike from the beginning, and now I see I was right. It is not safe, especially when you haven't the sense to come home at a decent time."

Hannah looked around the room. There were stacks of clothes piled up to her waist. Bethie was turned and sorting them.

"I'm sorry. I found a job today, helping out at a motel and restaurant. I've been so busy that I didn't think about the time."

"You took a job? Without asking me?"

Father walked in, smiled when he saw Hannah. Mother's jaw was tight, her eyes narrowed, as she studied Hannah. How her hair was tumbling in tangles around her, little curls twisting around her temples. How her face was pink and happy. Maybe even pretty.

"You look unkempt," she hissed.

"It's the steam," Hannah said, her hands going up to her

hair. "They make steam buckets there, and the steam does a number on my hair."

"Go groom yourself."

"Wait," Father said. "Tell me where you've been."

"She has a job. Your father has taken us to eat at the best restaurants in Charleston. We've gone on every historic tour possible. What could you need money for?"

"Nothing. I'll quit."

"Bethie and I could have used your help, you know. I have four laundry baskets full of clothes that I still need to wash and make look like new for the shelter."

"Why do you have a job?" Father asked.

Hannah shrugged her shoulders. "Saw a sign today, and I don't really know why, I just decided to see if I could work there."

"This isn't like her," Mother whispered, her hands covering her mouth. "Maybe we should go home."

"Everybody settle down," Father said, and sighed. "Hannah, you should've called. You worried all of us. You'll wash up all that laundry tonight. But you can keep your job if you want. As long as you go to church, too."

Hannah looked at Mother, standing with her hands covering her face. She hurried over to Bethie. "Tell me where you left off."

Bethie raised her hands, waved them, and curled them in front of her. Hannah took a step backward. "What are you doing?"

Bethie's hands moved furiously, her face like stone.

"Something's wrong with Bethie."

Mother and Father watched Bethie for a moment, before Mother offered a quick solution. "Poor child, you're overworked," she said, shooting a glance at Hannah. "With all this heat, and then the extra burden you've had to carry because of Hannah's absence. Go to bed and rest. Since Hannah likes to work so much, she can finish up here. You'll feel better in the morning."

But Bethie was the same in the morning. Father stared at her, confused, before leaving for work. Mother whispered threats while she cleared the dishes. Then offered bribes. And when none of it worked, when nothing would make Bethie speak or still her hands, she left the room quietly. She returned with one of Father's old T-shirts and a pair of scissors. With one look, Hannah knew exactly what she planned to do.

"Mother," Hannah whispered, as she shook her head. "Don't."

Bethie knew, too, and her hands started moving furiously in front of her. But Mother was strong. She caught Bethie's hands and pulled them behind her. Wrapped strips of Father's T-shirts around Bethie's wrists until her hands were as still as her mouth.

"I'll tell Father," Hannah whispered. "He won't stand for it."

Mother ignored her, pulled a chair near Bethie, and sat down before her. "Just tell me what you're doing. That's all I want. Use your voice, use your words, and I'll set your hands free."

"Bethie?" Hannah pleaded.

One single hot tear escaped the corner of Bethie's eye. It slid down her smooth-as-stone face, shimmered against her golden skin. Hannah couldn't bear it. She ran from the room and threw herself down on the bed she shared with her sister.

The bed was already made. The quilt Mother had designed and carefully sewn was pulled tight and free of any wrinkles. Hannah traced a line of smooth stitches with her finger. She found a snag in one and pulled it until the stitch unraveled. She pulled another, and another. Until an entire patch of fabric fell loose in her hands. She held it over her and pulled each side until it ripped in two.

"Hannah?" Mother called. "Sweep the back steps."

Hannah studied the new bare place in the quilt. She knew Mother would see it. Mother knew every detail of her housekeeping, especially when it involved sewing. She would call Hannah careless. Rough and negligent with their nice things.

"Hannah?" Mother called again.

"Coming."

Hannah decided to hide the fabric until she could sneak some needle and thread to mend it. She pushed it back beneath her pillow. That's when she felt it. Something cooler than the Carolina morning. Something smoother than the texture of worn cotton. She pulled out a book, and her mouth opened in surprise as she read the words printed in block letters: *Advanced American Sign Language*.

Bethie had clearly meant for her to find it tonight when she went to sleep. On the back cover she saw that it was a library book, checked out with her card. Those mysterious late fees, the ones that she had been too shy to protest, suddenly made sense. Suddenly seemed fair.

She ran from the room with the book in her hands. "Mother!"

"Don't raise your voice, daughter. It's not becoming."

"It's sign language. She's been using my card, checking out books on sign language. This one's been checked out for nearly six months. Plenty of time to learn it well."

They walked back to the kitchen where Bethie sat, her hands still tied.

"Bethie," Mother said. "If this is sign language, this thing you've been doing, then nod your head. That's an acceptable sign, I believe, among people like you."

Bethie nodded slowly.

Mother walked behind Bethie, and the T-shirt binding slipped to the floor.

"Why?" Mother whispered.

It was the right question, the perfect question. The one Bethie's hands had waited for all along. Her hands rose slowly and began to move. Her eyes were excited now, her mystery unveiled. For months she had prepared that speech, that answer to Mother's great question, *Why?* She moved her hands carefully before them, in a slow, lonely dance.

Mother walked away before she had finished, but Hannah stayed and watched. She even nodded at times, as she remembered all the days on the bus. The brown eyes that flashed hell when teased. No matter that she couldn't name even one of Bethie's new words; Hannah understood. *No more.* No more *t-t-t-t-eacher* when Bethie needed something during class. No more *p-p-p-present* when role was called.

Later that night through thin walls, the girls heard Mother. "It worries me, this new job that Hannah has. It's not so much the job, I suppose, as it is her boldness. Back home she never would have biked away to some strange place and stayed gone all day long without a word to us. Hannah needs to get back home. With our good friends and our own church. There's nobody like us down here."

"Hannah's fine," Father said quickly. "She's a smart girl. She gets bored sitting in the house all day. If you want to worry over something, look to Bethie. She's pretending she can't talk. Every time she signs it feels like a lie."

"She's not lying," Mother said. "Haven't you been listening to her these past sixteen years? Bethie's not a liar. She really can't talk."

Bethie turned over in bed, so that Hannah couldn't see her face. Hannah flipped quickly through the sign-language book. Then she reached around Bethie, placed her hands before her and made her very first sign. *Good night.*

III

The next day Hannah put on her T-shirt, rinsed buckets out, filled cracker baskets, and tried to do any task that needed to be done before anyone asked her.

She felt hot pride when she overheard Cora and Sissy calling her a fine worker. She was a straight-A student, a Bible Sword Drill champion, and if she was being honest, she'd admit she had the best hair of any of the girls at church. Long, soft, and so blond it was nearly white, it was the reason she refused to compete in the modesty competitions and wear a head covering. But nothing had ever pleased her more than hearing that she was a fine steampot worker.

That evening after dinner service, Sissy took her back to Number Six and told her to vacuum and dust, then showed her how to make a bed with perfectly straight lines and a smooth turndown of the covers. Sissy took a can of insect spray and sprayed under the bed, behind the dresser, and around the baseboards of the room.

"Smell will be gone by mornin'," she said, nodding toward the can of spray. "Any bugs will be, too. We're only half full now. One, Four, Five, and Eight are filled. We try and space 'em out so they won't hear each other. Kids are in Number One, though; ain't much space that can hush that noise."

"Do you and Cora live here, too?"

"Not anymore. One of us, or one of my brothers, always stays overnight to keep watch on the place, in case anybody needs somethin'. There's a pullout cot under the front desk. But we got our own home further from the beach. Out towards Johns Island."

That night when Cora handed Hannah a bucket, she took one, too, and walked out front with her. "Your family gonna stay down here?"

Hannah hadn't told her she had recently moved to James Island. It was her tongue that gave it away.

"Just the summer."

"Your parents know you work here?"

"Yes."

"They fine with it?"

"Father is. Mother worries."

She laughed. "That's what we do. I've got four babies. Grown now, all in their twenties, but still my babies. My boys work shrimp for me. Sissy is my only girl. She grew up by the steampot."

She took Hannah's empty bucket. "Head home. No sense in worryin' your momma anymore today. I'll wash your shirt up for you."

Hannah stood to go but the path was blocked by a pickup that pulled in. Its back was loaded down with nets, coolers, and boys. They hopped out and Sissy met them at the door yelling about how long she'd had to wait for that shrimp. Cora laughed and went inside to grab buckets for them. Hannah eased her bike alongside the truck, and glanced over her shoulder.

She was sticky with sweat and steam, little curls fuzzing up around her face. The cuff of her skirt had come unstitched and was dragging the ground. And she hadn't bothered to tuck her blouse back in. She was almost out of sight, praying to be invisible, when he looked up from his bucket. It was the boy from the oyster roast, the one that had disappeared into the waves.

She guessed that he laughed. Nudged his buddies to look at the Holy Roller on her bike. But weeks later as they sat together on a rusty shrimp boat, he told her the truth. That he saw her hair first, spilling gold light down her back. He never noticed her clothes.

"You seen the mornin' ocean, how it lights up when the sun first touches it? That was you, first time I seen you."

The next morning was Sunday, and to keep her job Hannah had to go to church. Her family had visited several of the large downtown churches simply because they were beautiful. Her mother had stopped outside First Baptist of Charleston and said she must hear holy scriptures read in such a majestic building.

But it was more tourism than worship. Back home they belonged to an independent movement. Their church was not a part of any denomination or central oversight. They had no sister churches. And what that meant was when they were home they had a large, extended family. But anywhere else, and they would always feel like strangers. Even among other Christians.

Hannah wasn't surprised when she woke up that morning to find Mother studying scriptures in a lawn chair by the marsh. Father sat beside her, his head bowed in prayer. Bethie sat on the other side of Mother, a Bible in her lap, but her eyes on the marsh.

Hannah grabbed a chair and pulled it toward them.

"What are you doing?" Father asked.

"Joining you for church."

"No," he said, smiling. "You're supposed to *go* to church. You're brave enough to bike down an unknown gravel drive for a job you don't need. There are lots of churches you can bike to as well."

Mother frowned, but kept to her reading.

"Come with me, Bethie," Hannah said. "We could walk if we hurry."

A car honked as it passed them. Neither girl jumped or seemed to notice. They always drew more attention together than they did apart.

"Are you going to keep this up when we go home?" Hannah asked.

Bethie nodded.

"Would you speak to me at least?"

She shook her head.

"Then you have to teach me."

They walked down the palm-tree-lined road as Bethie pointed to things around them and showed Hannah the signs. She taught her *car* and *sun* and *tree*. Bethie laughed when Hannah confused them. The sound surprised them both. Hannah noticed, and vowed to always make mistakes.

But for most of the walk, Bethie listened. It was what she was used to doing before, with her broken tongue. Hannah talked about her job. Even told her about the T-shirt, her eyes cast sideways to catch Bethie's reaction.

On her bike Hannah had passed several churches, but none called to her like the Lowtide Church of God. Perhaps it was the name *Lowtide*. Her favorite time of day, when nobody was around and treasure was revealed. Or maybe it was the way it looked. Set back off the road with giant live oaks hovering about it, their limbs curling around the roof, Spanish moss sweeping low down the front of the building. It was not beautiful, or historic, like the churches downtown. But James Island engulfed it, marked it as its own.

The sisters stood in the parking lot and caught their breath. The morning was already hot, and under the live oaks swarms of mosquitoes sang around the girls in search of naked skin.

Music started with a boom that made them jump. It was the kick of a drum. The piano started next. And then the clapping. They looked at each other with wide, curious eyes. Their home church didn't have instruments at all. Instead they sang a capella. And in the downtown churches, they listened to quiet choirs and dreary organ solos.

Hannah leaned against a live oak and braced herself for that old twisting pain.

Was it sin?

Back home, sin was clear. Sin was cheating on a test. Sin was when Megan's father left the church altogether and then eventually left his family. Sin was the guy, three streets over from her house, arrested for selling cocaine.

Her mind searched the list of rules fed to her for sixteen years. And she wondered if it was impossible to ever really know *right* without Mother to tell her. With nothing memorized to apply, and with no parent to ask, Hannah walked up to that church door. Not because she thought it was the right thing to do. But simply because she was following her sister. And Bethie was already inside.

She was a white Holy Roller inside a church full of praising black people. She thought of Bethie at school, where she was one of three minority students. She remembered the day she first heard someone call Bethie *slanteye*. The sisters were in first grade when it happened, and the whole way home she stared at Bethie in the backseat of their car. She realized, with some surprise, how different she and Bethie were despite their matching polyester. Bethie's hair was black and sleek, to her white hair that liked to fuzz and twist in any kind of heat. Bethie's eyes were sharply cornered, the angles of them drawn with care and precision, while her eyes seemed to melt into the whiteness of her skin.

"Wish I was a slanteye," Hannah had said in the car that day. Mother turned and slapped her face. Father taught them a new song that night at bedtime. *Red, brown, yellow, black, and white, they're all precious in God's sight.*

Bethie was supposed to be Hannah's polyester twin. So after the slanteye crisis, Mother taught them that neither was white. Neither was Filipino. They were both simply children of the King.

But sometimes, even the King's kids keep to their own. Whites to their sad organ solos. Blacks to their boom-kick. And her family, a whole different type, kept to a capella hymns sung in lawn chairs by a mosquito-filled marsh.

The preaching started. There was no lecture and no peaceful devotional. There was only a *hallelujah* shout, as the preacher paced around the stage yelling out a message with jumpy rhythms. Hannah closed her eyes so she could listen without the distraction of his pacing, or the women down front waving their hands in ecstasy. He was speaking of redemption and forgiveness. Of a holy table, where mercy is served. Hannah smiled. Her father would have enjoyed this sermon.

People started to stand. Some raised their hands and swayed back and forth in time with the preacher's pacing across the stage. The woman in front of Hannah started a high-pitched mumble, her volume gradually building. The preacher ignored her, even as others began to join the woman in their own private conversations.

Something about her shoulders, even through that lemon-yellow dress, seemed familiar. And as her head jerked back, and her eyes rolled to heaven, Hannah realized it was Cora. Broken syllables spilled from her tongue. A mystery chant to heaven.

Hannah ran. Pushed her way out of the pew and through the front doors. And as the door closed behind her, she saw Bethie. On her feet, hands waving in the air.

It wasn't the words, or lack of words, that sent her running. Even the shrill pitch and trembling bodies seemed almost safe. But the thing that didn't, the thing that sent her running to that live oak, was the boldness. That someone would have a private conversation with God in the middle of church. Claim access to his ear with mystery words invented for the two of them. It seemed greedy somehow.

Later, Cora told her it was little tongues of fire being poured over them by the Holy Ghost. But no matter how many times Hannah returned to that church, no matter how much she envied Bethie the ecstasy, the mystery was never revealed to her.

IV

When the sisters arrived home from church, they saw Mother had prepared a picnic. She carried a basket with ham salad sandwiches, peaches, and little square brownies wrapped in foil. Father drove them to the beach, and they carried their lunch close to the water. He wore swimming trunks and a T-shirt, not being bound by the same rules of modesty. After they ate he waded in deep, while the girls dipped their toes in the water. Hannah was jealous of how he looked like everyone else, swimming and floating in cool water on a ninety-degree day. While she sat dying in polyester.

"Ours is a different pleasure, daughter," Mother said softly, guessing Hannah's thoughts. "And it will be your time to enjoy it soon, too. You are sixteen. Only two years from graduating. Not long, and you'll be a woman."

"You said I was a woman when I was thirteen."

She shook her head and grabbed Hannah's hands. "No. It's becoming a wife, having a husband to care for and later a child. Your *own* precious child. My grandchild."

Mother glowed when she said it. Her face lit up like the sun that beat down on them. And her mouth paused to linger and enjoy the sweetness of the words *my grandchild*. But it meant little to Hannah.

"Father said I'd meet my husband at college."

"College," Mother groaned, as she rolled her eyes. "Not a single other girl we know plans for such nonsense. It will fill your head with discontentment. Bethie doesn't want to go. You were raised the same as her. Why do you?"

Hannah remembered all the books she had received as presents from her father. And all of the knitting supplies he gave Bethie.

"You toured that college with us last spring. You said you liked it."

"Not as much as I'd love to plan your wedding and help you organize your own household. Think of it, your *own* household. At eighteen you could have that. There are plenty of good young men at our church. Did you know John Hadley asked to court you last spring? Your father said no, that you were too young. I didn't agree, but it wasn't my place to say. You are older now; you could have more of a say in these matters. And of course, Father and I would take the money we would have spent on college and help you get started in your new life. Think of all the lovely new furniture. A nice house of your own. And Hannah," she said, smiling triumphantly, "think of all the pretty new dishes."

It was vanity. The only one that her parents turned a blind eye to. Even indulged. It began with the porcelain tea set she and Bethie received when they were four. Tiny cups and saucers with pink rosebuds painted across them, the perfect size to fit little doll hands. Bethie was pleased with them and played with them like any child. A fifteen-minute game of pretend before moving on to something new. But not Hannah. She would spend whole days arranging those dishes on their little art table, a pink pillowcase thrown over it for a tablecloth. Each year after that, her parents bought her a new set. They'd pack away the old one, wrapping up pink rosebud saucers in layers of cloth. "We'll save these for your own daughter one day," Mother would say.

Then Hannah would open a new one. She would sit with delicate china cups in her hands and stare at the paintings on them. Garlands of rainbow pansies. Little English cottages nestled by foamy waterfalls. Or beautiful little girls, with braids and ribbons and curled eyelashes. She'd hold the dishes up, and the light would pour through and make the paintings glow. Make their beauty shine down on her.

"Hannah"—Mother laughed softly, that day on the beach—"do you think I didn't notice the way you held the cups to your lips as you stared in the mirror? Children never hide things as well as they think."

Bethie laughed. She looked at Hannah and signed the letter *T.* Hannah laughed, too. They shared a T-shirt secret that made Bethie feel more like her sister than the polyester ever had.

"You still wonder, don't you?" Mother asked. "You wonder whether you are pretty, more than you think of goodness."

"No. If there is any beauty here," Hannah said, looking down upon herself, "it's well hidden."

"That's the point. Or else you end up like Leah."

Aunt Leah was the family scandal, with two divorces by the time she was thirty. Years ago, Hannah found a picture of Leah, taken in the parking lot of a church after a family funeral. Hannah stared at the red face, the swollen eyes. "That's Leah," Mother explained. "We barely knew our great-uncle. She cried like a baby that day, though. Always did like to make a scene." Hannah stared in awe at that woman in black pants, the kind that made a woman look so slim. And at her deep red turtleneck, a perfect match to the shade of her lipstick.

All through her childhood, Hannah had stumbled into hushed conversations. "Looks just like Leah," she'd hear relatives whisper, when they thought Hannah couldn't hear. "Their hair so blond it doesn't look real."

Sometimes at night, when Hannah couldn't sleep, she would close her eyes and think of Leah and her red lips. Leah with her black pants and slim curves. She pretended that picture of Leah answered her heart's question. Of who she might be, what she might look like, if she had only been born to the Presbyterian family across the street.

"Leah was always set on being pretty," Mother continued. "And no matter how hard your grandmother tried to train her, to cultivate her inner beauty, Leah was too selfish. Thinking only of what she wanted, and that was boys. Not a family. Or a good husband. Just lots and lots of boys and good times. Did I ever tell you about when I first met your father?"

"You met him at church."

"He wasn't raised in the faith like me. But he started coming with his grandparents. After he joined the church, he could have had his pick of any girl he wanted. And I prayed for him to make me his wife the way some people pray for money or fame. But it wasn't me that caught his eye. It was Leah. The man in him saw the way she unbuttoned her blouse just enough to make her modesty questionable. He heard her giggle, her teasing 'Hey there,' every time he walked past her. He asked my father if he could court her. And I've never cried like I did that night. It was so awful to have him there in our family home, eating meals with us, taking walks with us, only so he could see *her*. And she did not appreciate him. Only I saw the way she made eyes at common, dangerous boys on the street. Only I saw the way she would pin her skirt, *above her knees*, and hang out by the bus stop waiting for the neighborhood boys. Did you know your father proposed to her? I overheard it all. How lightly she took it. None of us knew it then, but she was already sneaking around seeing that pizza delivery boy. 'I can't,' she said simply. He asked her why. All she said was, 'I want something different.' She left the room and I went to him. He looked so tired sitting on the couch. I sat on the floor, almost kneeling before him. 'She's a fool,' I whispered. We were married six months later. The night he proposed, he told me about his plans for mission work after he finished his doctorate in engineering. 'It's the reason your sister said no,' he said cautiously. I laid my hand on his and promised him, 'I'll hold your hand while you build bridges through cannibal jungles.'

"It was *wanting* that was Leah's undoing. No matter what the doctors said. They only wanted to discuss her childhood, every time I went there. They didn't mention all the chemicals that she had poisoned her body with over the years. They didn't mention the bad choice after bad choice that left her mind in so much pain. Once a doctor stopped me in the hall. 'She doesn't seem to want to get better,' he said. 'We need to find a way. Perhaps if you talked to her.' I didn't. I've never admitted that to anyone until now. But I didn't ask her to get better, and I didn't ask her to try. When I went to get her paperwork, after she did what she did, the doctor was there, a clipboard in his hand. He told me he was sorry. That he had hoped for better. And I told him the truth. Told him more than all his years in college could ever teach him. Some people only do what they want. Never what they should. Never what you hope them to do. They spend their days crying *I want* and *I want* and *I want*. They spend their lives consuming and grasping and swallowing whole whatever is in their reach. Even if it's boys. Even if it's other women's husbands. Even if it's..." Mother stopped and caught her breath. "Even if it's death."

Hannah turned toward the ocean to give Mother time to hide the pain that swept over her face. It had been fifteen years since Leah's suicide. Sometimes Hannah believed she remembered the day of the call. She didn't; she was only one when it happened. But she imagined the ringing of the phone. The way Mother answered, probably knowing what the news would be. How Mother nodded as she listened, her face turning to stone like Bethie's. What Hannah never imagined, what she'd never remember, was what happened behind that stone. All the new fears that were born after the phone rang that day. All the new promises that Mother whispered over her beautiful baby girl.

"The doctor didn't understand," Mother finally whispered. "Hannah, I *need* you to."

"I do," Hannah lied.

Mother sighed and squeezed her hand.

"Father," Hannah whispered, as she watched him. He laughed as a giant wave crashed over him, and waved to his girls sitting on the beach. "It will break his heart if I don't go to college."

"His heart is my job, not yours. Look at John Hadley when we return in a couple of months. Let him see you look at him. He'll know. Think about a family. About babies. Think of all the pretty dishes. And if that doesn't help, remember Leah."

Hannah nodded, and forced a smile for Mother. But her mind begged to know, *What was missing?* When Leah cried *I want* and *I want* and *I want*. She spent her life grasping blindly, for something. Was there a word for the missing thing? Did it ever have a name?

V

Hannah was seven years old the first time she called herself ugly. She was standing in her front yard on Easter morning. Up and down the streets of her neighborhood she saw other little girls twirling bright floral skirts that poofed out at their knees. Their hair was curled and piled with ribbons. Their feet were shiny with black patent. Lace socks, trimmed with ribbons to match the ones in their hair, showed off how tiny their ankles were. Their little hands, some covered in lace-trimmed gloves, clutched baskets filled with treats. They looked like storybook ballerinas, twirling and twirling in blurs of pink and lace. Hannah couldn't take her eyes off them. She caught her breath with excitement whenever a new Easter ballerina appeared.

Hannah was dressed the same on Easter as any other day. Even so, she ran to her room. Twirled around and around, her arms held out, her fingers pointed, just like she saw the other little girls doing. But no matter how fast she twirled, her skirt would not poof. Ribbons did not appear in her hair. And she knew she was not beautiful. As she stared at herself in the mirror, she searched for another word. Too little to know the word *plain*, she settled for something else. That word was *ugly*.

Nine years later, and Hannah was still twirling. Only this time she was inside the Steampot Motel. One of her jobs was to receive the coolers unloaded off the back of Cora's truck, filled with the day's fresh catch. She'd pick them up and take them inside to rinse off the seafood and store it properly.

The boy from the oyster roast was usually the one who made the deliveries. They would talk as he unloaded. About how hot it was, or whether he thought a thunderstorm was coming. She enjoyed his attention, even if it was just weather talk, as he handed her an iced-down cooler. He was seventeen and he was not a *safe* boy. Sometimes he cussed. Sometimes she saw him drinking beer while sitting with Cora.

The moment she gave herself to him was long before they ever touched. It was Friday night, and she was inside the kitchen rinsing buckets for Cora. She heard the truck pull up.

"I'll git it," Cora told her.

Hannah nodded, but listened to see who was delivering.

She heard Cora say, "Hand it out, Sam."

Then she heard him answer, "Where's my pretty Yank tonight?"

The bucket she was rinsing dropped straight into the sink. *Pretty* was the ocean. *Pretty* was the first November snowfall. Or a porcelain tea set. Perfect as God made her, she should've had no use for *pretty*.

And yet, no matter how carelessly he threw that word around, there was a place reserved inside her heart. Waiting for someone, *anyone*, to claim it with that seductive word.

After that day, Hannah worked for his attention. If she saw him sitting out front finishing up a bucket, she'd step outside to take it from him instead of letting him toss it in the sink.

"Workin' you hard, ain't they? Makin' you rinse buckets nonstop."

"We've been real busy," she said, aware that her words were suddenly less Yankee.

"I'll rinse this out for you then."

She followed him inside and watched as he emptied the

shells from his bucket, then soaped and rinsed it. She showed him where to stack it so the hot air could dry it.

Sissy came in and started talking to him about repairs the boat needed. When Sissy stepped out into the yard, Sam started to follow her. Then he turned around and reached toward Hannah.

His fingers twirled through her hair. "Ever pull the husks back from an ear of sweet corn?" He winked at her and left.

If Mother's rules had worked, if Hannah had managed to swallow them whole until they were the very bones that held her up, then she would have run. She would have smelled the flames of hell all around that boy. With his assumption, his *arrogant* assumption, that it was okay to twirl his fingers through her hair. That it was okay to comment on a part of her body. But she didn't run. She didn't even acknowledge the alarm that was going off inside her. Instead, she whispered the words *pretty Yank* to herself. And lingered over the sweet corn at the fruit market.

She invented reasons to be near him. Whether collecting buckets or dodging outside to unload when the truck pulled up. Sometimes, especially if she was going outside, she would slip off her apron. Let him see her in that extra-small T-shirt.

One Saturday the boys didn't show up with their cooler run. Cora told Hannah to bike down to the dock and see what the problem was. When Hannah got there the boat had just pulled in.

"We're goin' fast as we can," one of Cora's boys yelled when he saw her. "I'm runnin' this load back to her. You stay and rinse the coolers, then fill 'em with ice. Sam'll do the rest. I'll be back in twenty."

Sam sat on an overturned cooler, working a net filled with fish.

"Hey, Yank."

Hannah picked up a hose and started rinsing out coolers. Water splashed back, soaking her. She stepped away and slipped off her shoes and socks. There was nothing she could do about her skirt dragging in the water.

"You'd be cooler in shorts," he said.

"Yeah."

"Don't got any?"

She shook her head.

"How come?"

It was the moment she was trained for. When people noticed her separateness she was supposed to become a lighthouse, a ray of hope in a dark world. She was supposed to consider their questions an invitation to open up her heart and tell *why* she followed the rules that she did. It was the whole reason her family lived the way they did.

But Hannah shrugged her shoulders and loosened her Yankee tongue. "Just 'cause."

"It's a church thing, ain't it?"

"Yeah."

"Well good thing for ya'll heaven's got air-conditionin'," he said, smiling. "I go to church, too. With my grandma sometimes. Ladies there don't dress like you, though. Ain't so pretty, neither."

There was that word again. That sweet, sweet word, handed to her like a surprise gift. She wanted to respond in kind. To show him how much she liked his gift. Not knowing what else to do, she thought of her mother when she was eighteen, only two years older than Hannah was now. She kneeled before him, her shoulders next to his knees. Her skirt was tucked beneath her, hiding the long layers of polyester. Her T-shirt showed the milk of her arms and her hourglass shape. And then there was her hair. Unbraided and spilling across her shoulders, down her back until its tips brushed across the water on the boat deck.

He looked down at her, and Hannah believed him. She knew for the first time in her life, *yes*. She *was* pretty. Like an Easter ballerina. Like a porcelain tea set. She reached her hands into the net and began to pull out the treasure inside.

From that day on, Hannah gave up wearing the canvas apron altogether. And she could never be sure when he might appear beside her. Sometimes he snuck into the motel rooms she'd be cleaning. Sometimes he'd pull her to the bed. She'd let him kiss her quickly before running away.

It was easier for Hannah than it should've been. Partly because her polyester life was so unconnected to the Steampot Motel. Her family didn't know about the T-shirt, about bleaching the toilets or sneaking childlike kisses in between her work. And as long as she could do both well, live by the polyester rules at home and enjoy life at the motel, she didn't think she was hurting anyone.

One slow day, after Cora dismissed her from the Steampot, Hannah biked down to where the boat docked.

"Cora need somethin'?" Sam asked.

"No, she's not busy."

He sighed. "Good, cause I don't have any fish to send her."

"She didn't need my help, either. You have some coolers that need washin' or somethin'?"

He shook his head. "We git Mondays off. She uses whatever we caught over the weekend on Mondays. I'm fixin' to head out, though, if you wanna come."

"On the boat?" she asked.

He nodded.

"Will Cora mind?"

"Ain't her boat," he said proudly. "She rents it from my granddaddy during the summers. When school's in, I live back in Columbia. You might even call me a city boy. But I live with my grandparents from middle of May till almost September. Now I'm old enough, Granddaddy lets me drive it while Cora's boys do the fishin'." He held his hand out to her and smiled. "Ever seen the deep water?"

"No," Hannah said, as she took his hand and climbed in. She held her breath and looked away from him as the boat sped away from the land. She had been close to him before, but never so alone with him. She tried to focus on the water, watching it change from murky brown to something cleaner. And as the land slowly disappeared, Hannah discovered the ocean was blue after all. Not a sparkling gentle blue like she had seen in post-cards. But something darker. Something that teased of black.

He cut the motors back and the boat became quiet.

"Let's jump."

Hannah smiled but shook her head.

"Keep your clothes on. The sun and wind'll dry 'em before we get back."

"I can't swim."

He laughed. "We ain't tryin' to git anywhere. All you have to do is float."

"I've never been in the water. Never floated."

"Well you can't come to James Island and not jump in the water. Least once."

He tossed a life ring into the water and jumped. His whole body submerged for several seconds before he rose again. "Jump," he yelled. "I got you."

There was a quick pulse of pain as Hannah's body tensed with fear and cool water swallowed her whole. But it was followed by a rejoicing, as Hannah became numb to polyester and let the ocean pull her long skirt away from her skin.

Hannah started spending every Steampot slow day with Sam. Her parents never knew she wasn't working, but instead, was headed on a boat out to the deep water. It was there that Hannah liked to pretend there was nothing else. Only black ocean water, her, and Sam.

They talked about things she was used to hiding from everyone but Father. Like *The Grapes of Wrath*. She was surprised when he said his favorite parts were the hungry ones. The ones that described what is was like to go days without a meal. Those were the parts that she hurried through, preferring even the dull turtle chapter to that pain.

"They'll either live, or not," Sam explained. "I like that such a big problem, such a big journey, can boil down to something simple. They'll survive it. Or not."

She let him kiss her finally. Really kiss her, without her pulling away. It scared her, though she wouldn't show it. Not just the sin of it. But that sin could be pleasure, too. That sweet tremble that filled her body and made her mind flash with thoughts of the Lowtide church. She wanted to raise her hands high and shout out a whole new mystery language of love.

"Come back tonight," Sam said to her. "Meet me at the boat, around seven thirty."

She ate supper slowly. Knife and fork methodically cutting through cube steak patties and scalloped potatoes. Once, when no one was looking, she held the back of her hand up to her mouth and licked the salt from her earlier swim. For weeks she had done all of the household laundry. Telling Mother that she wanted to help her accomplish the goals for the shelter. When really, she just needed a way to hide the salt and sand that clung to her dirty clothes.

"Hannah," Father said. "Have you given any more thought to what you might major in at college?"

"No. To be honest, I think I should pursue something else."

He laid his fork down. "What do you mean?"

"I'm not sure it's the best thing for me to have more school. I don't see the point."

"You were so excited. What's changed?"

"Let's not pressure her," Mother interrupted. "There's still plenty of time to talk all this out."

Father nodded glumly and started talking about bridge work. Mother rose to serve dessert, but she let her eyes hold Hannah's for a few firm seconds. *Good girl*, she told her.

Later, as Hannah helped wash dishes, she asked if she could return to work for a few hours. "I know it's late. And I probably won't be home till after dark. But I need to go back, just for a little while."

Her mother smiled sweetly as she gently stroked Hannah's shoulder.

"Who am I to say no to another woman? Especially a woman that will soon be running her very own household. Be home by bedtime."

Hannah had expected to go boating. Perhaps watch the sunset from the deep water. But Sam was in a car with a backpack. In the side pocket, she could see a flashlight sticking out.

"Hey," he said, grabbing her hand and kissing her palm. "I'm gonna show you somethin' amazin'."

He offered her a cigarette.

She shook her head.

"Never known nobody half as good as you. Don't drink, don't smoke, don't cuss. Don't wear bikinis. I don't want kids, but if I ever did, you'd be the kind of girl I'd want to be their momma."

Hannah laughed.

"I ain't kiddin'. That's how men get messed up. They marry the prettiest little bikini body they can find. Daddy scooped one up just out of high school, yellow hair like yours. Had me two years later. Then she was gone."

"Something happen to her?"

"She just missed the party is all. Hard to party with a little baby, I reckon."

"You've never met her?"

"Can't know. She could be anybody. Sometimes when I'm out and I see a lady 'bout Daddy's age with yellow hair I'll let her get a good look at me. See if I see anything, a sign of some sort stirrin' in her eyes."

"She might come back."

"What'd be the point?"

Hannah noticed they weren't on Folly Road anymore. Or the James Island Expressway. They were heading through Daniel Island, on an isolated back road, dotted with trailers.

"Where we headin'? Your house?"

"Sort of." He laughed. "You know, you sound different. Keep it up and you'll never fit back in with the Yanks." He pressed the gas pedal and the car surged forward. "We need to hurry. I wanna get there 'fore all the light is gone."

He turned down a road that wasn't a road but a path mowed down by tractors. He pulled over near a ditch and parked by a barbwire fence. From the looks of things, they weren't anywhere. Just a big untended field, with weeds growing up all along the fence rows.

"Climb under," he said, motioning toward the fence. He threw the backpack over and slid under the fence. He held the wire up as high as he could for her, but her hair still got tangled in the barbs.

"You said we were going to your house, right?"

He laughed. "You're scared. Nobody's here but us and a haint or two. And they'll be glad we came. They bound to be lonely."

"What's a haint?" Hannah whispered. But Sam was already running through the field, yelling for her to hurry before the sun set. She tried to follow him, but her ankle-length skirt wasn't made for running. She ran and fell, ran and fell, through a field that was once ripe with cotton. By the time she reached Sam, her palms were stuck with briars, her hair was tangled, and weed fuzz clung to her skirt.

They stood at the top of the hill and looked down. There it was, on fire with the blaze of a Carolina sunset. A mansion. Spreading tall and wide, with gables jutting out of the roof and columns framing the front. It was rotting, but it hid this well. Gray wood glowed orange with light. And live oak trees, centuries old, writhed all around it.

"It's one good thing the Yanks let us keep," he said. "Burned so many others, don't know why they left this one."

"It's that old?"

"Oh yeah. Least a century and a half. Been kept up for years. Was still tended when my granddaddy was a boy. Been abandoned for decades, though."

He grabbed her hand, and they ran down the hill until they were just feet from the front porch.

"What do you think?" he whispered.

"Beautiful. And wild." With Spanish moss twisting off the trees and onto the columns and porch frame. Like a first bite, before the earth swallowed the house.

"It's ours, Hannah. One day we'll claim it. Too rotted to even step up on the porch now. But someday, we'll rebuild it together."

"Yes," she whispered, looking at him instead of the house.

"See the four chimneys? Imagine a home grand enough to have four fireplaces. Slave quarters been demolished for decades now. And cotton ain't grown on this land in who knows how long. But this house has got life to it yet. It don't wanna die, won't admit it is, even as it rots on the frame. It's waitin' on us."

"When will we?"

"When we're ready."

It was a simple answer. One that should have told her *Never.* Or that should have told her *I'm just a seventeen-year-old kid.* But somewhere along the way in Carolina, truth went missing. Hannah heard whatever she wanted. She heard *in a couple years,* or *after college,* or *when your father agrees.*

"Look, look there." He was pointing to the porch ceiling, whole boards missing and sagging low. "See that chipped paint? That's a whole lot newer than the rest of this house. Bet that's from the last owner. Know what it means?"

She took a step closer and looked. She saw dusty chips in a muted, electric blue.

"No."

"That's haint blue. Your people call 'em ghosts. Haints won't cross water. So if they see that blue on your porch, they think of water and won't go in."

"How long will it take? To fix this up?"

"Years. And not just the house. We'd need to get the fields mowed down. These trees need choppin' back. Replant the orchard that must have been here at one point. A house like this is somethin' a man can dream on all his life and never grow tired of."

He pulled a rolled blanket from under his backpack and spread it underneath the largest live oak Hannah had ever seen. It wasn't that it was so tall. Only that it was wide, nearly as wide as the house. With branches scooping and swirling like they were more than just alive. Like they were growing as Hannah watched. They sat on the blanket, ate the sandwiches he brought, and shared a thermos of tea. They were silent, both of them staring at the house until the night was so dark they had to imagine it before them.

Hannah could never explain *why* she let him pull her close under that oak tree. Other than that she wanted him to. And that place made it so much easier. They were in a world of their own, one that died over a century before. They were in a room of their own, too, made of growing branches and covered with Spanish moss curtains. It was all lies, but in that place there were no parents to go home to. There was no God to pray to. There was no husband to wait for. There was only history around them. Their love was the last good thing of a once-great plantation. Nothing else was real.

VI

Good-bye was too easy for him. Hannah's parents were starting to pack the few things they'd brought. Mother was starting to wring her hands, thinking of all the Carolina children that she would never help.

Hannah kept expecting something from Sam. Something as big as the dread she felt when she stared at her suitcase. Something permanent from him, like the gift she'd already given.

But on her last night there, he smiled. And spoke too happily about football camp starting in two weeks. "Wish you could see me play. You think your parents might come back to visit this winter? Your daddy check on the bridge or somethin'?"

She shook her head.

"It's awright," he said. "Always next summer."

She exhaled slowly. That was all he could give her. Next summer. He whispered softly into her hair. "Gonna miss my pretty Yank."

Something thick and hot, like smoke, filled the back of her throat. She choked. He brought her a drink of water and she forced herself to suck in air, her body making little humming noises with every breath.

"It's the moss," he said. "Some people have allergies to it."

The moss did have an earthy scent. But until that moment, she never knew it could crawl down her throat and choke her.

"We won't see each other for a whole year?" she whispered with the first breath that she could.

"That's the rotten luck of kids. But what's a year anyway?

Some day it will take ten years for us to rebuild the plantation."

They used Cora's Sharpie marker to scribble their addresses on the back of each other's hand. He drew a sloppy heart around his.

"Get your suitcase packed," Mother called out when Hannah walked in the door. "We're leaving six a.m. sharp, with or without all your clothes."

She piled it all away. The polyester, the Steampot T-shirt that Cora let her keep, a dried bit of Spanish moss taken from the live oak at the old plantation. She put her suitcase in the trunk and watched as Mother gave her bike to the kids next door.

Driving home, Father talked about revisiting colleges to help her think things over and about securing her place as valedictorian before graduation. Hannah nodded. But she was thinking about life ten years later. She was thinking about repainting an old plantation house.

At home, fall had arrived. The air was crisp and clean, such a change from the heavy heat that still clung to the South. Their home seemed bigger, too. With plenty of space for each of them to hide away. Bethie would have her own room again, where she could study sign language in privacy. And Hannah only had to lock her door to find the strength to write her first love letter.

She began writing about the classes she was taking. About helping Bethie with her homework and leading the four-year-old children's choir at church. About reading *Wuthering Heights* for the first time. After two pages of details, she felt brave.

I've been thinking about our plantation, and the way the sun turned the gray wood orange. I've been thinking of all that chipped blue paint. And how I'm gonna take that off one day. A home that big should have room for anybody that wants to be there. Besides, read Wuthering Heights. It has such lovely ghosts.

Remember the live oak? I've a piece of it here in my room now. I sleep with it under my pillow. It reminds me of you.

I miss you. I love you.
Hannah

It took him three weeks to write back. Sometimes at night, during the wait, she'd grab the moss under her pillow and squeeze till it started to crumble into little bits of brown dust across her palm. She'd squeeze and squeeze and squeeze, trying to shut the words out of her mind. *What if he never . . .*

Bethie brought his letter. Her eyes focused on her sister. She pulled a pen and notepad from her skirt pocket. It was her backup plan for important conversations, one she'd developed after school started. It didn't take long for the teachers to call Mother and Father with questions about why Bethie no longer spoke at school. No longer stumbled over the word *p-p-p-present*, but instead waved her hand wildly to declare her attendance. When she signed her answer in Algebra class, the teacher threatened to suspend her unless she gave a clear answer. So Bethie rose from her seat, walked calmly to the chalkboard, and wrote *X=3, Y=2*. It took her five seconds to write that answer. And if she had tried to speak it, it might have taken her thirty and probably would have come out incorrect. Hannah had noticed that before. They'd do their homework together, Hannah's correct answers marked across Bethie's pages. But if the answer couldn't be spoken clearly and smoothly, as so often it would not, Bethie would desperately grab for something easier. *Three* was difficult. So if forced to speak Bethie would have said *t-t-t-two.*

Who from? Bethie wrote.

"Friend from work."

Boy?

"No."

Says Sam.

"Samantha."

Hannah hid in the Mission Room to read it.

> Scored a winning touchdown last night. Wish you could've seen it. Everybody went crazy over it. Classes aren't too hard, so that's good. I'm not into Wuthering Heights so much. I've no use for Heathcliff. He's all temper and no results. And what the heck you talking about taking down the haint blue? That sounds about like a yankee, ha ha. Wish I could see you.
>
> Love,
> Sam

She folded the letter up and smelled it. And when she couldn't smell him, she pressed it to her lips. She pretended to remember his kiss.

Bethie stood in the doorway. Signed the letter *T* and pointed to her shirt, smiling. *T-shirt secrets.* Hannah shook her head. "Not like that."

Bethie laughed, and Hannah knew she didn't believe her.

"Bethie, why don't you try it on?"

The sisters hid in Hannah's room while Bethie slipped on the extra-small T-shirt. She looked at her reflection and was as amazed as Hannah had been. So many sweet things could be seen. The soft curve of her shoulders. Even the rise and fall of her breath.

Let me keep it, Bethie wrote.

Hannah shook her head. "It's too dangerous. Mother would kill us."

Bethie shrugged her shoulders and wrote back, *She already has.*

Bethie kept the shirt. She'd lock herself in Hannah's room so that someone else could see her, even if it was just her sister, and wear it all afternoon. She played with it sometimes. Rolled the sleeves up, even knotted the front, like the cheerleaders at school. Bethie had her shirt. And Hannah had her love letters.

But Sam had written a note, not a letter. It didn't even take up a quarter of one page. Hannah didn't think about this as she pulled out several pages of her best stationery. She congratulated him on the touchdown. Told him she wished she could have seen it. And then gave him the details of her past three weeks. About trimming her hair, just an inch. Seeing the dead cat on the road. About the cheating scandal at school. After two pages, she found courage again.

> I wish I had introduced you to my father. He wasn't raised in the church either. He wouldn't hold that against you. I think if he saw us together, saw how we feel about each other, he'd understand. He might even help us with the plantation. He would help us get our start. Do you think you could come meet him? Maybe over Christmas.
>
> Love always,
> Hannah

He wrote back quickly.

> Relax, Yank. Our summer was the best. I had more fun with you than any other girl ever. Next summer will be great too.
>
> Did I tell you in my last letter that I'm nominated for Homecoming King? It's because of that touchdown. It was the winning play against our biggest rival. Don't know who I'm escorting yet. I'll find that out tomorrow. But how's that for a great start to senior year? Hope everything is as cool for you as it is for me! See you in Carolina...unless I'm drafted by the pros, ha ha.
>
> Love,
> Sam

Hannah thought about queens. She imagined beautiful girls who wore mascara to curl their eyelashes. Sexy girls who wore short skirts with tall boots. It was clear now that Sam had other happiness. He had football and homecoming queens. He probably went to dance parties and drank beer under the stadium bleachers, like the bad boys at Hannah's school.

Hannah was different. She was locked behind the gates again. Stuck with her floor-dragging skirt and no bike to escape. And her nearly seventeen-year-old heart lied to her. Told her those weeks with Sam were the only time she had ever been happy. Told her he was the only hope.

She waited. A test to see if he would write without the prompting of her own letter. He did not. Maybe he loved her, but Sam loved lots of things. Lost somewhere up north, she was easily replaced.

VII

What began with a Steampot Motel T-shirt, turned into late nights at the high school typing lab. Hannah told her parents she was working on school reports. It occurred to Mother once that Bethie still took the bus home. That she never had reports to type. "If you would just try a bit harder, Bethie," Mother said. "No one expects you to be as smart as Hannah, but it doesn't look quite right to fail, either."

Bethie knew, of course. Hannah tried to convince her that she was doing extra-credit reports for classes where she struggled. But Bethie had spent all her years sitting right behind Hannah. By the time she was in first grade, she had accepted defeat. Hannah would never struggle.

Hannah took a bus to the shopping center. Used what little money she had to buy Bethie two T-shirts, one red and one purple. It was a bribe, but it was love, too.

"His name is Sam. I'm going to go see him. And you're the most beautiful thing I've ever seen, Bethie. You were born to wear bright colors." Bethie twirled around the room in royal purple.

Hannah's "reports" weren't delivered to teachers. They were edited, scrutinized, even researched, for the benefit of Father. He looked over them, asked a few questions, and then signed the bottom of six pages that gave his permission for Hannah to attend a weeklong tour of the best colleges in the Northeast. Sponsored and chaperoned by her school, and reserved only for those students in serious contention for the honor of class valedictorian.

He drove her to the bus station, where a Greyhound was supposedly being warmed up for her and her classmates. He gave her two hundred dollars in cash. He told her he was proud of her. And to remember which colleges were her favorite, so that they could visit them together.

Just as Hannah had expected, he did not walk her inside the station. It wouldn't have changed anything. But later, he would cry as he remembered the way she struggled to drag her suitcase inside. How strangers held the door open for her.

It was the strangers that made him unable to walk her into the station. His heart had always shrunk back from the spectacle his children made when they got on the school bus. All that hair slung over their shoulders and hanging almost to their knees. And braided, it was even worse. It reminded Mother of a halo, but he saw only a noose.

He knew what the inside of that station would be like. There'd be kids with earphones blasting rock music. Maybe swaying their hips from side to side as they listened. They were smart kids, so they'd talk about scholarships and classes. But they'd also talk about dances and dates and new blue jeans. And Hannah would stand by herself, maybe even on the other side of the room. He'd be proud, too, that she didn't blend in. Even as he hurt for her.

There was a memory he hid. Of being sixteen years old and smarter than anybody in school. A favorite of the teachers, like Hannah, but cool, too. With his own prom stories. There was a girl at his school with hair swishing down around her knees and a straight skirt turned gray at the hem from floor dust. She ate lunch alone. Talked to no one in class. And when she passed him in the hall and his buddies yelled out a new *Holy Roller* joke, he laughed.

It was college that changed him forever. For most kids, college was an escape from rules and curfews. For him it was escape from his mother's crying fits and his father's drunken months. He realized, for the first time, that he could build his own life. That it was *up to him* to build his own life. And without the benefit of having a worthy example, he was unsure how.

One late night he took a sheet of blueprint paper and drew overlapping layers. He labeled them. *Degrees, a job, a family.* Each one supported the other, like sections in a bridge. But something bothered the engineer in him. He lacked a formula. There was no fundamental code upon which all things could stand.

He called his grandmother. The one his parents made fun of, with her prairie skirt and head covering, like she was straight out of a Little House book. But despite the way she looked, he had never seen her weep. He had never seen her drunk and broken. When she said, "Hello," he asked her *How? How can I be strong? How do I become something a storm can't bend?*

Grandmother's code served him well for many years. Mother eventually framed that late-night blueprint, his plan for a safe and protected life, and placed it in the family room. And later, as he designed real bridges, it didn't matter to him what his wife wore. But then there was the surprise of Hannah. His pretty baby girl. Set apart for ridicule.

The father in him could not ignore the suffering she would surely face. And so he bought her Bethie. He bought her a green bike. He bought her a bus ticket straight to Carolina.

The ticket was round trip and scheduled to return in one week. The bus was only half full, with just a small seniors group on their way for a tour of the southeastern seacoast. Hannah sat alone in the third row, staring out the window at miles and miles of interstate landscaping.

They stopped the next morning for rest and food. Hannah stood in a corner, drinking a vanilla milkshake.

"Hi, young lady," a man from the seniors group said as he passed by.

"Good morning."

He looked her up and down, nodding his head with approval.

"You seen the pictures of other girls nowadays?" He motioned to a rack of tabloid magazines as he walked away. "Filth."

Everybody else from the bus mingled around, stretching their legs and chatting. A group of women wandered near her, chatting about hairstyles and colors.

"I just want something easier," one of them said. "I hate having to blow it dry every day and then curl it, too."

"My heavens, look at her hair, Barbara," one of them said, and pointed to Hannah.

Her hair had been braided and pinned up when she boarded the bus. But it hurt to rest her head against that thick rope for so long. So during the night she had unwrapped it and let her hair ripple down to her knees.

The women circled her.

"She's like Rapunzel."

"Or an angel."

"How long does it take you to wash it?"

"Does it feel heavy? You ever get headaches?"

Beyond them, Hannah saw a boy about Sam's age. He was with a girl that wore jeans and a high school T-shirt. Her hair was bobbed and swingy. And it made her look young, fun, and happy. Hannah wondered for a moment if she ever looked that way. Even when she was with Sam.

"Sometimes it hurts," she answered.

"Your mother likes it long, doesn't she? I was that way with my girl. I still have the braid we cut off when she was twelve. I cried worse over that than I did her going off to college. Well, one day when you're on your own, you can do whatever you want with your hair."

"She's got a few years before that, though," another woman said. "Can you imagine how long it will be by then?"

"No," Hannah said, savoring her first bold lie. "I'm nineteen. On my way to meet my fiancé." She held her hands up around her collar and smiled. "Mother made the dress. There's light pearl beading around here. Four inches of lace on the hem. Mother's an excellent seamstress."

The women smiled, and they talked of flowers, reception food, and honeymoon trips. At the bus station in Columbia, Hannah found a pay phone and looked up Sam's number. His father answered and told her Sam was getting ready for a game that night. She went to the women's restroom and dressed for him. Her skin tingling with joy, as it felt the smooth cool cotton of her black CSM shirt once again. She washed her face and smoothed her hair. And when she noticed how her hands trembled, how unsteady her feet seemed, she found a vending machine and bought a bag of shortbread cookies.

She returned to the pay phone and called a cab. When the cab arrived, her voice shook as she told the driver to take her to Columbia High. And when she saw the word *HOMECOMING* painted on the entrance sign, her fist opened. Spilling her cab money across the floor.

In all her years of school, she had never been to a football game. Never heard the drums of the marching band thumping and clicking wildly. Never pushed her way through a revolving gate, or handed her ticket to a man wearing maroon face paint. She was smart enough to know that none of the commotion was about her. Yet she still couldn't shake the fear that someone would ask her to leave. That everyone knew she did not belong. That she was not from Carolina. Did not go to Columbia High. And wasn't really about to get married to Sam, their star football player.

She didn't know where to sit. There were numbers and a letter on her ticket. But as she stared up into packed bleachers that stretched toward the stars, she had no idea where L42 was. So she stood apart, her shoulder leaning against the gate, her arms crossed in front of her.

She didn't know Sam's jersey number. And as boys with helmets and shoulder pads poured on and off the field, she could not find him. Soon the crowd was on its feet and the boys were running wildly and everybody was screaming and clapping. In the middle of all that noise, with the drums and the screams and the cheers, Hannah heard one thing: "Yay, Sam!"

She looked at the far end of the field and there was a boy holding a football. He was jumping and slapping high fives with his teammates. The cheer came again, from one of the girls down front: "Woo-hoo, Sammy!"

Number forty-seven. Now, with his number, the game had meaning. Hannah watched him run. Watched him catch the ball. She found herself whispering prayers for him. That he would score. That he would win. That somehow he would know that she was watching.

At halftime Sam marched out on the field, still in uniform

but with his helmet off. His arm was around a girl in red. She won queen and he won king. And with their crowns teetering on their heads, they kissed quickly while the crowd went *Awwwww*.

Hannah turned away. Not because of the kiss. Or the crown. But because with his helmet off, she could see his face. And he was *happy*. He was satisfied. He was a teenage boy having the time of his life. She didn't look in a mirror often, but she knew her face never looked like that.

After the game, she waited for him to leave the locker room. Most everyone else had already left. Only Hannah and a few cheerleaders remained. She heard them talking about a homecoming dance that was starting.

As the players came out, a few of them looked at her and nudged each other. Hannah wished that she had worn her hair smoothed and braided. She could feel it tangling and fuzzing from the night air.

"I'll be darned, but would you look at the size of that bug," one of them said.

"Where?"

"Over there." He pointed at Hannah. "That bug caught in that big web of hair."

"Awww. Let's cut it free. 'Fore some spider gets it."

"Stop it," Sam said, stepping out from behind them.

"You seen anything like that before?" one of the boys asked.

"No," he said, not looking at her. "But the dance has started. We're already late." He turned to one of the cheerleaders. Hannah recognized her as the girl with the red dress. "I forgot somethin' back in the locker room. Catch a ride with Bo and I'll see you there."

"Awright," she cooed. "Don't be long, though. I don't wanna dance with nobody but the King."

He laughed and returned to the locker room while Hannah waited. When he was sure they were gone, he came back.

"What in the world?" he said, smiling. "What are you doin' down here, Yank? I didn't think your daddy would be bridgin' again till next summer."

"Thought I'd surprise you. Saw you play tonight. You were amazing."

He hugged her. "Gosh, I missed you."

She stayed there in his arms, her head against his shoulder, until he pulled away.

"Your folks know the game's over? You need to call 'em or somethin'?"

She shook her head. "I was hoping we could go somewhere."

"Wish I could. But I've gotta go to the homecomin' dance. Wouldn't be right for the King not to show up."

"I could come with you."

He laughed softly. "This ain't your type of thing."

"It might be."

"Nah. You're a boatin' girl. A deep water Yank. You ain't meant for silly high school dances."

"You're worried what those boys will think. The ones that were laughing at me."

He held his palms out in surrender. "We ain't on the island anymore, Hannah. This is high school we're dealin' with here. My senior year. My last homecomin' dance, and I'm King. And I'm supposed to go with the Queen, that's practically in all the rule books. I'll hang out with you a bunch next summer. But if I show up with you instead of the Queen, they'll eat us alive."

Hannah backed away, shaking her head. She tried to take a deep breath, and when she couldn't she closed her eyes so that she wouldn't see him, standing there but wanting to leave. She remembered kneeling before him on the boat, working on the nets and believing that he was right. Believing that she was pretty. She tried desperately to feel that way again. To be his pretty Yank just once more. She grabbed fistfuls of hair and spread it across her shoulders. She prayed the moon would shine upon her and make her glow. "Like sweet corn," she whispered.

She looked at him then, and remembered the feel of the old cotton field beneath her. The live oak twisting above her. She remembered Sam, like the ocean. Freeing her from polyester. Freeing her from everything she thought she was, everything she was supposed to be. "I'll change for you," she begged. "I'll be a queen for you." She blinked her eyes and saw the picture of Leah. So pretty and curvy in her black pants and red turtleneck. So very queenlike with her red apple lipstick.

He shook his head. "We're different. No point pretendin' we ain't. We never went anywhere public together, even on the island. We went to the deep water. To the plantation. We went under them live oaks."

"But I gave you everything."

He nodded his head slowly. "It was a big deal for you. I should've thought 'bout that, before... But it ain't such a big thing to the folks that I know. I'm sorry, I just got caught up in that night. With that house. Them oak trees. And you, lookin' like some golden antique yourself, with your hair and your long skirt. Like you was somethin' the Yanks left behind, too."

"I gave you my whole life that night."

Somewhere behind the stadium a car honked its horn.

"I ain't growed up enough to give my life away."

The car honked again.

"Look, I'll write you," he said. "I'm so late, I gotta go. Call your folks to pick you up. There's a pay phone down by the bleachers. I'm glad you got to see me play. Always wanted you to."

"I know I can," she cried, as he kissed her on the cheek. "Let me show you. I can be a queen."

He ran off toward the parking lot. Before he was out of sight, he turned around and waved with a friendly smile. He called out something that she couldn't quite hear. It sounded a bit like *I'm sorry*. But by the way he shrugged his shoulders and smiled as he ran from her, it looked more like an easy *Good-bye*.

She paid a cabdriver one hundred dollars to take her to Folly Beach. It was after midnight by the time she arrived. But she remembered the path from before. That sandy public-access trail, with the sea oats nearly blocking the way. It was cold. The wind wrapped around her until she shivered. And it was dark. The moon was bright enough to show her the caps of waves, but not the crabs that were scooting around on the sand. She dragged her suitcase to a dune and sat on top of it.

It was the first time she'd ever heard the ocean. Before, she'd always been distracted by looking at all the colors and counting off the patterns of the waves. But staring into that black wall, she heard power. What had always seemed like a *shhhh shhhh* lullaby was really a war cry. Water delivered blow after blow to the shore. She sat there all night, until the war cry echoed inside her heart.

When the sun rose, she went to Cora's Steampot Motel and rented a room for the price of daily labor. Cora thought it was strange. Sissy told her as much. But both of them pretended to accept her lie about Father returning to finish up loose ends and out-of-town company showing up for a visit.

"There just isn't enough room for all of us and my cousins," Hannah said.

It hurt her to hear deliveries pull up. And it hurt her again to hear the new shrimper laugh at her *mermaid hair*. Ridicule wasn't new. But once, not so long ago, she had been called pretty.

At night she sat at a picnic table under the snake tree with Cora and Sissy and listened to them talk about men and raising babies.

"You have a man?" Sissy asked her.

"No."

"Ever had one?"

"No."

"She's lyin', Momma," Sissy said, a sly grin on her face. "Look at 'er. She's lyin'."

"Leave her alone," Cora said. "Just 'cause you like to share your business with everybody don't mean she wanna."

"I'm not lying."

Sissy giggled. "Was it Sam? We ain't blind, you know."

"Hush," Cora said. "Her people would stone 'er."

"Yes," Hannah said, as a tear ran down her face.

"Aww, what's wrong?" Cora said. "He not good to you?"

"He doesn't love me."

"He's a little boy. Can't love nobody but hisself right now."

Cora put her arm around her. "But you. You're a woman. You never been allowed to be a baby girl."

"It hurts sharp," Sissy said. "But another'll come along one day and ease that pain."

"There's never supposed to be *another*."

Cora laughed softly. "Said somethin' like that myself once," she whispered, and looked at Sissy. "About your daddy." She turned to Hannah. "Poor baby girl, you're more right than you know. But honey, we lost the garden a long time ago. Devil's done twisted this earth as crooked as a live oak. We livin' in the snake tree now, and there ain't much that goes the way it oughta. On the chance that it does, it's so God can whisper one more testament of his presence to a dyin' earth."

"Amen," Sissy whispered.

"My husband was killed," Cora said. "Loadin' freight down in the harbor on the big boats. Somethin' wasn't stacked right."

She held up her hands. "They put a check in these empty hands. Some kind of apology or maybe just best wishes. I threw it across the room. Stomped on it. Even put it in the oven once with the gas turned on. I didn't want to be a check-holdin' widow any more than you wanna be a Yankee Holy Roller. I just wanted to be his wife. That's the way my life, how'd you say it? Was *supposed* to be."

Hannah nodded.

"I learned, like it or not, that's who I was. A check-holdin' widow. And as I stared at that check, I began to see it different. It wasn't the thing that took my husband from me. Instead, it was the last thing that he would ever give me. I had four babies, and I had to make it count."

"So here we are," Sissy said. "Twenty years later. Momma raised us in that motel. We had a home and a business, all because she decided to turn the gas off and get that check back out."

"Wasn't as easy as Sissy likes to say. She's my baby sunshine,"

Cora laughed. "It was hard on 'em. I ordered the kids to sleep outside under the snake tree when the rooms were full and the late-nighters were watchin' TV in the lobby. It was a sad sight to look out there and see their hot faces peekin' in the windows, the boys' dirty hands—little boys' hands is always dirty—wavin' at me. It hurt me, but we needed the rent money bad. And now there's a real sweetness to it. They was wild, all four of 'em. But they laid under that tree all night for me. They never once acted up. I can't imagine how hard that must've been on 'em." She shook her head. "They'll break for you. If that's what they think you need. They'll lay under a twisted snake tree and never once cry *Momma*."

"She don't tell it right," Sissy said. "We was good kids, for one. None of that wild bit that she likes to talk. And we was happy ones, too. Sometimes at night, if no renters were here, Momma'd have all our cousins come and we'd have the biggest sleepover. We'd eat cheeseburgers, not a shrimp to be found. We'd jump on all the beds, run races down the hall, turn out all the lights and play hide 'n' seek. Sometimes Momma'd pretend she couldn't find us and start hollerin' that she'd have to eat all the ice cream herself and, oh mercy, we'd come flyin'..."

"Our point is," Cora said, interrupting Sissy, "we livin' in the snake tree now. Things ain't how they oughta be. Won't be till Jesus himself comes to uproot us all. Till then, you gotta make do."

They fed her sweet tea and key lime pie all week long. And at night, she would lay in Number Four and think about snake trees, falling freight on big boats, babies breaking themselves. But the thing she thought of most, the thing she whispered into her pillow like a sweet lullaby, was the thing Cora first whispered. *You poor baby girl.*

When the week ended, the cabdriver drove her down to Folly Beach for one last look before driving to Columbia.

She lingered. Searching for something different. The piled rocks of old broken fishing piers were the same. The war cry still matched the beat of her heart. The people, staring at her four-foot-long hair whipped around by ocean winds, seemed the same.

Still, though, something was different. And though the cabdriver honked his horn, Hannah could not leave until she knew what it was. She took off her shoes, felt the deep chill of the ocean. Dipped her hand in the water, to scoop up a shell. Brought her hand to her mouth to taste the salt.

And then she smelled it. Not like before, with the smell of salt. She could smell all of it. The dead fish and the clean live ones. The rocks being pounded into sand. The bait that had been discarded at dawn. The nylon of summer swimsuits. The oil of old shrimp boats.

Something stirred within. Like a storm inside her body. Like hot snakes twisting in the sun. She was working to build a new universe. From her blood and bones and tissue. It wasn't that she felt a baby. It's that she could feel the *making* of one.

She faced the ocean, her arms wrapped tight around herself as she whispered, "Poor baby girl."

ANGEL

I

Inside my left front pocket is a picture. Daddy's back is turned, but if you could see his face you'd see love. Real as any of us ever knew. You'd see pride, too, as he gently scrubbed that car. You'd understand why he called it Baby. Why he used to joke that it made up for the fact that Momma didn't give him a son.

It was a 1970 Chevy Chevelle that shot little bits of fire from its muffler. It was green, but not rich like grass or yellow like tobacco. It was an in-between shade that Daddy called Money.

Momma took that picture on a hot September afternoon. We were all outside in our cutoffs, Momma and Janie wearing bikini tops. I was a bare-chested five-year-old with nothing to cover.

That afternoon he parked like he always did. As close to our trailer as he could get without splitting the tin walls.

"Bring me buckets," he yelled.

We hurried inside to start the shower and fill up anything we could find. A mixing bowl. An empty milk jug. The little plastic bucket that Momma kept her curlers in. We carried them to him, careful not to spill any water and encourage the rust that crawled across our tin home.

"Bring 'em quicker," Daddy ordered. "If the sun sets, there'll be water spots."

We worked as fast as our skinny-girl arms let us. We didn't talk or laugh. We didn't even stay to watch him pour the water over the car. We carried water, over and over, to the front door.

"Bless him," my baby mouth whispered.

Like he had sneezed. Or given me a gift. I learned the words from Mrs. Swarm before she served a farmhand supper. *Bless this food, Lord.* But I found the desire by my grandma's grave. *Let's pray over your troubles,* the preacher comforted us. There were many things I did not yet know about my daddy. But there was one thing no one needed to teach me. He was trouble.

Momma slid from the trailer as Daddy polished the car with a soft piece of deer hide. She wore red lipstick, her shirt knotted up in front. She leaned against the car, showing herself off. I hid behind the corner and watched her. Leaned my body against the trailer. Matched the angles of my shoulders, the arc of my back, to hers.

"Woman, git one smudge on this car and I swear I'll…," Daddy began, before Momma stood up and yelled, too.

They argued over that car more than where the money went. More than over all the hours Daddy spent gone, long after farm work was done.

"Weren't for me, wouldn't be no car," Momma liked to say. "It's been as much home as any you give us."

She was right. We lived in that green car the first half of summer, after Daddy lost his mechanic job and the peach crops didn't need any more workers. After two months of not paying rent, the sheriff showed up with a piece of paper covered in big words that no one in my family could read. "What it means," the sheriff hollered, "is if you don't have the money, you have to git." With nothing but old clothes piled in the trunk and my green baby blanket clutched in my fist, we left Daniel Island. "It's awright," Momma whispered to herself. "Promise land's waitin'."

I was the baby, and a small one, too. So while Janie slept

curled up on the backseat and Momma and Daddy leaned their bucket seats back, I snuggled into a ball on the car floor. When morning came, Momma would drag me from the car to pee in a ditch by the road, my legs too numb and confused to move.

We crossed state lines twice. Daddy found weekend work at old garages. Just enough for gas money and a little food to keep moving. We entered East Tennessee, on our way to the big city of Memphis. But in that part of Tennessee we didn't pass any cities. Just miles and miles of land with barns and old houses scattered across it. Occasionally we'd drive through a hub with gas stations, grocery stores, and a local diner. But it would quickly end and we'd drive back into empty land.

Daddy coasted down hills in neutral to save gas, but our tank was nearly empty. Out of desperation he turned down a dirt road with a hand-painted sign staked at the corner: *Swarm Tobacco. Established 1893.*

Tobacco as tall as Daddy and healthier than Momma waved like a welcome banner. It led us to Swarm house. A place more like a king's throne than anything else.

Daddy said he felt like saluting, the way he was taught the month he was in the army. Momma said she felt like praying, the way the preacher did over Grandma's grave. Janie mumbled a cussword, because at ten that's as big as it gets. And my hungry-baby eyes wondered if we were still on earth at all, or if Carolina had been the end. Maybe everything beyond was the heaven preached at Grandma's grave. If so, I doubted they'd let us in.

The Swarms walked out, one in overalls with a slick bald head, one in a gingham apron with gray hair tied back in a braid. Daddy told them about being raised in the fields. About running tractors since he was knee-high. Momma chatted with Mrs. Swarm about me and Janie.

I hid behind Momma's leg like I always did. Momma joked that I was more shy than a broke-down dog. And told how when we'd stop for gas, I'd tuck myself into the floor of the car so nobody could see me.

"Must be good at hidin'," Mrs. Swarm said. "That's somethin' to brag over when you're a kid, ain't it?" She peeked behind Momma and winked at me. "Might as well stay for supper. No place within miles to feed these babies."

"We got groceries in the car."

It was a lie. The money had run out so long ago I couldn't remember the last time we'd eaten anything more than stale snack cakes from the gas station.

"Your babies look pale. Give 'em a break from that car for a few minutes. Let me fix 'em a plate and run it out."

In all my years on Swarm farm, I never went inside that home. Long ago, Mr. Swarm had been robbed. Somebody stole his granddaddy's shotgun and his grandmother's engraved silver goblets.

"Who'd ever want a goblet that says Swarm anyhow?" he'd ask, every time he told the story.

Swarm house rules allowed only family and friends inside. We had many names on that farm. Bacca farmhands. Folks from Carolina. People living in Black Snake trailer. But we never confused any of them for the word *family* or *friends*.

That first day on the farm, Mrs. Swarm made trips in and out of the house carrying bowls of stewed beef, plates of cathead biscuits, and pitchers of milk and tea. We sat around a picnic table underneath a giant sycamore tree. The trunk as wide as Daddy with his arms stretched out. The leaves as big as my head. I looked all the way up, at the shaggy bark peeling off in chunks and wide strips, showing raw wood beneath. A trail of ants marched down the trunk. When Mrs. Swarm stepped inside to bring pie, I pointed them out to Daddy.

"Ants is killin' that tree."

Daddy looked and then shook his head. "Hurts to grow. Bark's gotta yield to a risin' trunk."

Mr. Swarm said the tree was famous.

"Biggest one in the state, they say. I don't set too much by it, though. Look out that way, beyond them fields. Think of all the trees nobody's lookin' at. One of 'em's bound to be a big ol' sycamore."

The land looked like my green baby blanket when Momma shook the dust from it. But in the distance, mountains circled. We weren't *in* the mountains. But we would never be far from them.

They watched us eat that day. Saw how I used baby fingers to pick up biscuit crumbs and tuck them in my mouth. Saw how Momma pushed the food around her plate, like she didn't know what to do with it. Food never mattered much to Momma. She preferred a good smoke and a cheap drink. Her bony knees poked out from tanned-as-leather legs. Knobby shoulder blades humped up beneath her bikini straps and showed off her heart-on-fire tattoo. And her cheekbones never needed the flame-pink blush she smeared across them. No one could miss them, those bones that sharply divided her face and always made her look sick. Especially when she smiled.

Momma's bones are what made Mr. Swarm insist we move into the trailer in the first place. When Daddy said no, Mr. Swarm whispered gently, "Your family could use the break."

Mrs. Swarm nodded. "Joe ran power an' water out to it two

years ago, when we thought the men might wanna cool off in it. That was before they stacked it full of old parts. Turned it into another one of our sheds. But I bet we could have it empty for you by sundown."

It wasn't being used by anybody but rats, and the old black snake that hunted those rats, until we moved in. Mr. Swarm bought the trailer because it was a good deal. Two hundred bucks at a farm sale. They carried it home on the back of a hay wagon.

Before harvest, no one could see much of our trailer from the main road for all the thick yellow leaves around it. When I started kindergarten in early August, kids whispered that me and Janie appeared like magic every morning. The leaves would part and we'd step through to the waiting yellow bus. Words like *bacca fairies* and *tar ghosts* swirled around us at school. But the name that stuck, the one that followed us until we each dropped out, was Girls of Old Number Nine.

Old Number Nine was a king's tobacco. A type of Burley crop that grew so tall the tips would drag the ground as Daddy carried staked plants, his arms held over his head. That was why everybody called it bacca. It was big enough on its own. It didn't need our extra letters.

I knew paths through the bacca that seemed to stretch to the mountains. If Momma and Daddy started to fight and the few dishes we had started to fly, me and Janie would run. If it was midsummer, the leaves would be so high we wouldn't have to do anything but push through them. And if it was early we'd crawl. Our hands and knees dragging through the fresh spring dirt.

If things were really bad, we'd spend the night out there. Sometimes in the mornings, we'd get on the bus without ever going home again. We'd wear the same clothes as the day before, only dirtier.

When a teacher would ask if things were okay, I'd think of my family. How if Daddy came home late, he always said he was working the fields. Even if it was the middle of December. If Momma's lip was busted, she said she fell over a cinder block. And if Janie got off the bus with purple marks all over her neck, she said she had the chicken pox. Again.

"Yes, ma'am. Things are fine."

Lies were the same as mercy to us. Even if everything wasn't okay, even if nothing was, we could pretend different. Sometimes when a lie would slip off my tongue, easy and warm, I'd think about Mrs. Swarm's God. How maybe he heard my first cry and agreed with my tears. How maybe he gave me the only gift that could soothe a hard life, a lying tongue to sneak through it with.

School never helped me, like the bacca and my lies did. So I went to eat a hot meal. To listen to the pretty music the teacher played during art time. To stare at all the colors inside a new crayon box. So clean and perfect I hated for other kids to touch them with their greasy hands. But I didn't go to school to learn. Because I remembered the black snake, and the waste of its hard work.

It was four and a half feet long, a legend on Swarm farm. It killed more farm rats than any pack of cats ever could. But that first night in the trailer, Daddy slapped a hoe on its neck. I ran my hand across its new skin, slick and inky as oil, and thought of all the shedding, all the growing it had done before Daddy came along.

By the time I was eight, I couldn't read anything but my own name. Even that was memorized. I didn't know the sounds letters made, just that when I saw *Angel* spelled out, it meant me. I had blond hair and the dumb eyes of a baby calf. Teachers whispered, "She's an innocent, bless her heart," as they huddled together on the playground. I didn't know what it meant. Only that they treated me differently. Never spoke sharply. Never kept me in at recess if I hadn't finished my papers.

Then one day Mr. Swarm saw me trying to hold the front door open with one hand and pull myself up with the other. All while carefully keeping my legs from touching Daddy's car, parked twelve inches away. Black Snake trailer floated on cinder blocks, stacked three feet off the ground. Sometimes I'd just stay outside and hope somebody would come along to pull me up.

Mr. Swarm walked over to a pile of scraps, old fences, and tractor parts sitting at the end of our trailer. He pulled out two cinder blocks and stacked them together. Then put one more in front of them.

"Just made you a set of steps outta farm trash." He laughed.

That day Mr. Swarm taught me something my teachers hadn't. Good answers were out there. And there was no telling where they might be hiding.

By the end of second grade, I was reading on a first-grade level and digging through all the trash around me. I looked at everything, even the silly dot-to-dots our teacher liked to call art. I listened to everything, even the old DAR women who came to brag how their dead great-granddaddies fought in some war. I could never be certain where my next cinder-block tower would come from. The one that would help me up. Lift me to a higher place.

II

I wish I could show you Janie next. I wish I had tucked her, along with the other memories, safe inside my pocket. So I could hold her up to the light between us and make her shine again. Like she must have once, so many years ago.

Momma and Daddy liked to pretend it was the State's fault. That somehow the State ruined Janie after it took her for a few months when she was a baby.

"She used to be the best girl," Momma would sob on a bad whiskey night. "Sweet baby, never cried when her diaper was wet. Slept through the night right from the beginnin'. Some Nosy called the State, though. Said she was too skinny. That lady came with her clipboard, had the nerve to open up my fridge and look in my cabinets without askin'. Took Janie that same day. Didn't see her for near six months. Till Daddy got better work and we could show off all the new milk in the fridge. When Janie came home, though, she was different. Was a danger in her eyes. No tellin' what was did to make her that way."

Momma and Daddy liked to threaten that the same thing was going to happen to me, was going to ruin me, too, every time a teacher sent a note home for them to stumble through.

"You gittin' lazy at school?"

"No, Daddy."

"You mopin' round like a broke-down dog?"

"No."

"Keep it up and the State'll come. Give you to strangers.

Gave Janie to a gook family. Ain't no tellin' what they done to her all them months. Made her eat dog and such."

Once, I asked Janie about it.

"They're lyin' 'bout the dog part," she said. "I was just a baby, but if I ate dog I'd know it. You hear me, Angel? I'd know a thing as big as that."

I nodded. Janie always spoke with the force and grit of a strong cussword, even if she was just saying hello. That force alone made me believe her. And compared to my own baby voice and to Momma's hoarse whisper, I wondered if it was the gook family that taught her how to do that. And I wished they'd teach me, too.

In spite of being ruined by the State, it was Janie that taught me the important things a girl needs to know. Like how to dance sexy. How to swallow a strong drink. And how to be a thief and a sweet little girl at the very same time.

Her dancing lesson came late one summer night when I was prowling through the bacca. I heard noises coming from an old shed on the corner of Swarm field. Laughter. Cusswords. I crept up to the side of the shed and peeked through the slats.

I saw Janie. Dancing in the middle of every farmhand I knew except for Daddy. She was singing Elvis, like Momma did whenever she felt sexy. The farmhands were passing brown bottles around, reaching out and tugging at her bra straps. Yelling *whoo-eee* if they got the job done, before she tugged it back. But my eyes kept returning to Janie. Beautiful fifteen-year-old Janie. The way she slid her hips in circles, the way her flat hair was curled and teased like a dark crown on her head.

I followed her home that night and finally named the smell around her. The one I'd wondered about for months. It was dead flowers. Like the ones Mrs. Swarm refused to water at summer's end.

The next morning I opened Janie's underwear drawer. Tried her black bra on. Looked in the mirror, at the way the cups dangled on my flat chest. I tried to slide my hips in circles. Whispered Elvis.

Janie walked in and saw me. My first thought was to run. Because she'd know I spied on her and cuss me good. Then I saw her smile. She walked over to me, joined in the song.

"Like this, Angel," she said, as she slithered so sexy around the room. "Move your body like this."

We spent the morning singing Elvis and being sexy.

"You're too young now," Janie said. "But look at this." She pulled out a sock from her underwear drawer. It was filled with money.

"One day soon, you can do this, too. An' if we put our money together, you and me, we could git out of this place, easy. We could make more than Daddy in a week, the two of us. You're too little to know it now, but men are gonna love you for that white hair of yours."

We practiced in the bacca. The two of us twisting and sliding up and down the rows. In her mind, Janie was dancing herself as far away from Black Snake trailer as she could get. I was just dancing to be like Janie. After harvest, we went to the barns. We kept warm humming Elvis and dancing for each other. When winter ended, I could move like a woman.

One night that spring, Janie went to the dancing shed. I knew what she was doing, and I wanted to come with her. She told me I wasn't old enough.

"I know all the right moves," I begged. "See, watch this."

I let my face melt into what Janie called her naughty smile.

I kept my shoulders still as my hips began to move round and round.

"You ain't old enough," she said.

"But think of all the money we could git," I tried.

She shook her head. "Soon. But not yet. You're just ten years old."

"I turn eleven tomorrow."

"Well, look at you," she said with a smile. "Almost a woman after all." She hugged me. "Listen, I'll buy you somethin' good with the money I earn tonight. For your birthday, okay?"

I nodded sadly and watched her walk across the field. Toward that falling-down shed, where men and money waited. The next day, though, I didn't think about my birthday. Something much more important than me was taking all of the attention. Daddy's car.

It wouldn't start. It sputtered, clanked, and smoked. But it would not start.

"Needs a real mechanic," Momma yelled. "Not a man that tinkers on tractors."

Daddy slid out from underneath it long enough to yell back, "Woman, you need to git more money from 'em. You know you could if you scared 'em enough."

It was The Birthday Fight. The one they had every year. About the money and where it all went. Whether they could demand more. But that day the fight was worse than before. It was Saturday; there was no escape for us in school. Momma and Daddy had started drinking early. And then the car died.

Momma stormed out of the trailer when she heard the gears grind and then *bang* as something misfired. She yelled at Daddy about how he had ruined the one chance life had given them.

"Had one good chance to make a go of it. And all we got left is a broke-down car. We had a fightin' chance in this life, handed down like a gift from heaven. And you blew it. Just like you always do."

He threw a wrench at her. Missed. She threw it back with good aim. We could hear him groaning as he dug in the car for more weapons. Me and Janie were sitting on the couch sharing a box of dry cornflakes. Janie turned to me as she grabbed her purse.

"The bacca," she whispered. "Run, Angel!"

Hand in hand we ran through muddy fields. We stopped for breath and listened. Heard Momma scream and ran farther. Until it was quiet, and we knew that we were safe.

It was a spring night. I'd been ready for bed, dressed only in an old T-shirt and underwear. Sitting on the ground, I started to shiver. And sob. Janie rolled her eyes and cussed.

"Sorry, Janie. Don't know why." Momma and Daddy fought like that all the time. Maybe I cried because it was my birthday. Or maybe it was that I knew what the fight was really about. The word they used was *money*. But all I heard was *Angel*, yelled over and over.

Janie pulled a bottle out of her purse. Took a long drink and handed it to me. "This makes it better," she whispered. "Drives 'em out of your head. It'll drive the cold out, too. Happy birthday, Angel."

It took some practice, but Janie was a good coach. I slept well that night. I found warmth. I felt safe, too, more than ever before. And from that night on, whenever I'd find Momma or Daddy passed out drunk, I'd slip the whiskey from their hands. Pour just enough to not be missed into an empty coke bottle. Then, if it was summer, I'd bury it in the fields. Winter, I'd hide it in the barn. Like a teddy bear, or a best baby doll. Something to get me through the darkest nights.

I never ran out of whiskey, because Janie taught me how to be a good thief. Under her watchful eye, I took whatever was in reach. She taught me how to escape if I was caught. Like when a teacher caught me sneaking snacks home in my pocket. "Next time, tell her you want to mail 'em to the hungry African kids you saw on TV. Teachers love that kind of thing," Janie told me. She taught me how to be sweet and good around the Swarms, so that they wouldn't ever suspect me of thieving. "Open up your eyes wide, don't let 'em ever squint, it looks like you're plottin'. And find ways to say things like 'Good mornin',' 'How are you,' and 'God sure gave us a lovely day.'"

Her lessons began that first supper under the sycamore tree, when I was five years old. Janie whispered in my ear, "If we ever gonna git anything good in this world, it's gonna be 'cause we're smart enough to take it when nobody's lookin'."

Then she took my spoon and tucked it in my pocket.

"Leave that till later."

While Momma and Daddy chased out the rats and unloaded old farm equipment from the trailer, Janie pulled the spoon from my pocket.

"Feel how heavy." She placed it in my hand. "That's real silver, Angel. Daddy can sell that easy at any pawnshop. We just gotta buff out them marks there." Neither one of us could read the marks. But years later, I remembered that spoon. It said *Swarm.*

"These people are richer than they know," she said. "You keep your eyes open. You keep fillin' your pockets. And when Momma starts bearin' down on you like she does, you hand her that spoon with your best smile."

"How do I know what to take?" I asked.

"Whatever glitters," she said. "And don't take it all. That's what people expect a thief to do. Leave somethin' behind, and they'll think they just misplaced the rest of it."

"Are we thieves, Janie?"

She shrugged her shoulders. "We sure ain't Swarms."

More than dancing, even more than drinking, thieving came easy to me. Maybe it was because the small TV we had worked only when it stormed, and even then only picked up two channels. Or that our radio played fuzzy country music, but only if we held it high over our heads. Maybe it was because whenever I handed my gifts to Momma, her face would melt into something soft, even gentle, as she held the treasure in her palm. But my eyes were drawn to anything that glittered. Like the pocket change a farmhand left sitting on a fencepost. Like the silver thimble Mrs. Swarm left on the front-porch railing.

Or like Mr. Swarm's gun, that day he left it outside the old barn. Farmhands complained a copperhead nest was inside. Mr. Swarm killed the snakes and proudly carried the bodies through the fields to show the farmhands. I stayed behind in my hiding spot in the bacca. My eyes feasted on the bit of sun that flashed off the metal. Off the handle, the color of maple leaves in the fall.

I carried it home tucked in my waistband, my T-shirt pulled over it. Momma swore when I handed it to her. Then she giggled and kissed me.

She wouldn't let Daddy pawn it. Even when he lost a week's wages in a round of farmhand poker. We lived on stale crackers and flat coke the whole week and he promised he could get a hundred dollars for it, but she wouldn't let go of that gun.

She kept it next to her ashtray, on an overturned bucket that she used as a nightstand.

Just the sight of it made me close my eyes and hold my breath. It pulled me toward it, like metal to a magnet. It promised something strange. Something like *peace*.

Sometimes I couldn't fall asleep for thinking about it, there in the next room. Its outline a darker shade than the black of night. But behind the promise of peace, I sensed something else. I didn't know what to call it, except fear. That the gun lied just like the rest of us did and there wasn't any peace. Or maybe it was hope. That something even better waited. That couldn't be stolen. Or pawned. Or lay by a dirty ashtray on an overturned bucket.

Momma came to depend on my gifts. Just as Daddy handed her part of his wages every Sunday, I was expected to deliver a prize to her. That was what she called the change, the thimble, the broken radio I returned home with. They were her prizes, and I was her thief.

I never left her empty-handed. Sometimes she'd forget the days and run out of whiskey. Then she'd demand her prize early. First she'd threaten me with a switch or a smack. Then she'd cry and beg. Ask why I wouldn't help her like a good baby should. Janie would bring me something then. She was always trading kisses for cigarettes with the boys at school. And trading cigarettes for lipstick and perfume with the girls. She'd sneak up behind me and put a shiny tube of lip gloss in my hands.

"Look here, Momma," I'd whisper. "I was walkin' in them fields today and look what I found out in that bacca. Who would've ever thought somethin' so pretty would be stuck there in that dirt?" She'd step forward and smile, hold that tube of gloss up to the sun, and watch it shimmer.

After Janie left me, I learned to set rules. Once a week. On paydays only. That was when I'd give Momma her prizes. Anything else, anything left over, went to a stockpile for the low weeks. A little brown bag tucked inside the front cinder block and filled with bits of stolen treasure.

Even with my nice stockpile, I never stopped taking from the Swarms whenever I had a chance. Not even after I heard Mr. Swarm fire a farmhand over that missing gun. Or after I heard Mrs. Swarm sobbing about the silver picture frame she had carried out to the porch to polish. She turned her back for a quick phone chat, and it vanished. Not even after Mr. Swarm slumped by his tractor and died.

Daddy ran home to Black Snake trailer after he found Mr. Swarm dead. It was the only time I ever saw him cry. I was seventeen years old, but I could still feel baby prayers sitting inside my mouth. *Bless you, Daddy.* He sat on the hood of his car and sobbed until his body shook. Mumbled how Mr. Swarm's lips turned purple.

Momma turned and looked at the trailer.

"They gonna kick us out quick now," she said. "His boys ain't liked us being here anyways. And they ain't plannin' to farm."

"He was closest thing to a daddy. Taught me everything he could in these fields."

"He wouldn't let you in his home for a drink of water on a hundred-degree day," Momma snapped. "And now we're gonna be kicked off this farm in a week, I guarantee. What about this week's work? You been paid yet?"

Daddy shook his head. "It's just Tuesday. Only worked two days since last pay."

"Well, he owes you then. You git back there 'fore they find him. Git his wallet. Take what's there."

"I can't," Daddy sobbed.

"We ain't got enough for gas money. That's assumin' that car will even start. You gotta go back."

"Can't see him like that. Woman, his lips are turned purple!"

"Angel? Git over here." Momma pointed to the rows of bacca. "Walk straight until you find ol' Swarm. Git his wallet and take the money. An' if you see anybody, don't say nothin' 'bout him being killed over. Let his own kin find him."

I took a step back toward the trailer. "But he's dead, Momma. Can't rob him now he's dead."

"If we don't got food to eat, the State'll come for you. That's why they took Janie. Now go git us some money."

"I already paid you for the week."

"But these are emergency times, Angel," Momma begged. "I'll give you back that charm bracelet you brought home last week. You gotta go right now, find that dead man, and bring me money. And any other prizes you find, too."

I found him slumped by his tractor. His hands loose around a wrench. His lips were purple, just as Daddy said. His eyes open but staring down, like he had watched himself fall. I felt inside his pockets and pulled out his wallet.

Sixty dollars were inside, along with receipts from old auctions and calling cards for wholesale buyers. I tucked the bills inside my bra. Slipped off his wristwatch. And as I put his wallet back, I found something else. A silver pocket watch. *Swarm* engraved across it. Inside there was a picture of Mrs. Swarm when she was young. *To my groom* printed in tiny square letters across the bottom.

It was one of the few things I wouldn't let burn in the fire, but kept inside my right pocket. It was one of the things I hoped could make you see Janie. Could make you see how much she must have loved me to have given me the gift of thieving.

When I tucked it in my pocket, I imagined holding it up for you, to let sunlight catch it. I imagined how our eyes, drawn to anything that sparkles, would enjoy the show. I thought of the right words. Ones that would finally tell you my story. They went like this:

Robbed a dead man once. His money was Momma's prize. But I kept this. I kept the love.

I imagined your story, too. Your very own right words, as you repeated my lip-gloss lie.

I was walkin' in your fields today and found you out in that bacca. Who would have ever thought somethin' so pretty would be stuck there in that dirt?

III

Daddy didn't say good-bye when he left, soon after Mr. Swarm died. He spent days tuning up his car for one last getaway. I watched him and knew exactly what he planned. Knew exactly where he was hiding the whiskey money he slipped off Momma as she slept.

He started his car one morning and drove away. I walked out into the bacca, dug a hole, and buried the money I'd just stolen out of his glove box.

Two weeks passed and Momma cried when she realized he wasn't coming back for her. I knew then it was time, finally time, to run from Black Snake trailer. For good. I dug out the bag of stockpiled treasure from inside the front cinder block. I emptied it before her as she lay sobbing on the couch. I would never need to steal for her again. Never need to space out her prizes.

"Look here, Momma," I whispered. "More prizes than you ever imagined."

She sat up and fingered through it. Pulled out the change, an empty Zippo lighter, and some eye shadow. She tossed a Mars bar back at me.

"That ain't treasure. Money's what I need. How come you can steal candy and makeup but not money? Your sister could."

"Momma, you got somebody you can call. Don't you?" I asked. Momma was married to Daddy, but she had her own escape plans that she liked to toy with from time to time. Other men, new sideways lines, one after the other.

She nodded her head, but wouldn't look at me. "You think I should leave with him?" she whispered.

"Yeah."

"You're right. You'd be better off."

When she said that, her face broke up, her cheekbones sliced through the darkness and cut my heart. I wished that I could say, "Take me with you," like a good daughter should. Or maybe just beg, "Don't go." But no matter how nice it would have been to whisper those words, I couldn't make myself. That night, lies didn't flow easy and warm like they were supposed to.

And so I did the only good thing I could think of. I reached back in the bag of treasure. Pulled out a turquoise and silver ring she had overlooked and dropped it in her palm.

Her eyes grew wide and warm. Her face softened and became nearly happy. "You've always been a good daughter."

The next morning, I stood in the middle of Black Snake trailer as she stuffed her trinkets and clothes into a tiny suitcase. She looked up and tried to comfort me.

"Don't worry, baby. We livin' in America. The State won't let you git hungry."

"What do you mean?" I whispered, feeling a spark of old panic.

"When they hear you're livin' in this rathole trailer by yourself, they'll come for you. They'll git you a real place to stay. Some food and nice clothes."

"I ain't gonna let them take me."

"No point in fightin' 'em. It took two big policemen to pull baby Janie out of my arms. But in the end they walked right out the door with her, easy as pie."

She walked over to the fridge and opened it. "If you try, you can make this last a week. The Swarm boys are gonna be clearin' this trailer out soon anyway. They'll call the law for you when they see you've been left behind."

Momma's boyfriend pulled up on a motorcycle. I stepped outside and watched her climb up behind him. She turned to me and shrugged her shoulders.

"Well, bye, baby."

"Bye, Momma."

The motorcycle pulled away and I saw she forgot her cigarettes. The box still flipped open, laying on top of the cinderblock tower. Next to them was the only good gift she ever gave me. A brand new pack of matches.

I picked them up. Paced the trailer to find the most rotten spot. A place where the sun had burnt and warped the fake wood and tin until it was ready to burn up quicker than a matchbox.

I wanted to be certain, though. And so I stepped into the bacca. Pulled out the gas can I stole from Daddy's trunk. Emptied it over the walls. Over the door. Lit that first match before remembering you, and all the things I wanted to show you.

I went inside and filled my pockets. And afterward, as I lit that second match, I thought about last words. About whether I should say good-bye to the tin rectangle that I had spent so many nights running from.

I thought about flipping it the bird, the way Janie always did as she walked away from it on her way to catch the bus. I thought about screaming a curse, the way Momma always did before she threw a dish. But then I remembered Grandma's grave. And as I threw that match and watched the flame spread quickly, I knew that I was burning more than sorrow. More than the years of dead things that had framed my life. I was burning down trouble.

"*Bless you,*" I whispered.

Then I walked deep into the bacca, where I kept watch over the smoke that hovered low. I saw the little bits of fire that shot up into the dark sky. Working so hard to escape the dead things below. I thought of you, and the journey before me. "Carolina," I whispered to the tall bacca. "Holy Roller," I cried to the Tennessee moon. And after one more long drink from my whiskey bottle, I closed my eyes and let my mouth whisper, with numb lips, "Five thousand dollars."

The sound of screaming sirens woke me. I saw red and blue lights bounce off flat bacca leaves. Somewhere men were yelling orders to each other. The smell of hot tar swarmed over me and I knew. The bacca was burning.

I held my sleeve over my mouth to breathe and crept as close as I could to the flashing lights. Policemen, firemen, and the Swarm boys were all working madly. Hell was behind them. Acres and acres of blazing red fire.

When dawn came, I saw the ash on the ground. The firemen were right. Nothing burns as quickly, or completely, as a rusted-out trailer. There was nothing left. Not a dirty ashtray or a broken dish. Not a pass-out couch for drunks. Not my sister's letter, the one she wrote before she ran away.

Then I noticed something else. The black ash didn't end. It stretched far and wide. It replaced everything that should have been green and growing. Nearly half of the farm was ruined. Every field behind the trailer, every barn and parked tractor, had burned during the night.

Flat on my belly, peeking through the bacca, I listened.

"Lost more than half our yearly income. Plus Daddy's barns. His best tractors. Ain't no insurance, Daddy dropped the policy years ago."

"Son, let me ask you a few questions about the family you said was livin' here. They good people?"

"Daddy never said one way or the other. They worked these fields for years. We told 'em to move on a few weeks ago, though."

"When's the last time you saw 'em?"

"The man left a couple weeks ago. Saw the woman leave earlier on a bike. Didn't see the young one go, though. Oh, you don't think she was inside?"

"Doubt it. What I am wonderin' about, though, is that burned-out hull of a gas can sittin' there by the road. I want the fire chief to come investigate this."

"You think she—"

"You kicked her family out, right?"

"Yeah."

"And her momma took off without her."

"Yeah."

"Ain't much trailer trash won't do. Especially the young ones."

"When I catch her, I swear I'll—"

"You won't have to do anything. Law will do it for you. Nobody likes a firebug."

I edged my way backward. Then turned slowly and walked away carefully. It was easy for me. I knew how to turn my shoulders *just so* between the leaves. I knew how to find the spaces between the plants. When to duck and crawl because I needed to be lower. I grew up in the middle of that great bacca field. No one ever knew it, really knew it, the way I did.

I walked through acres and saw the corners of Swarm house rising up with pride. Then I saw flowers, Mrs. Swarm's joy, brittle and matted around the windows. Boxes were stacked on the porch. Moving vans lined the driveway, as daughters-in-law shouted commands of which van to put which box into. Dividing the spoils. I turned my eyes back to the proud bacca, and felt shame for that house. Once it had been something to salute. Something to pray and cuss over.

I didn't reach the road until midmorning. Still more acres lay on the other side, but a large *For Sale* sign stood in front of those. They were chopping up the farm. It made sense. Swarm farm was the largest one in that half of the state. Only kings needed that much land. Our king was dead.

I touched the leaves gently. Soon those plants would be cut and staked and dried and carried to auction outside Knoxville.

It hurt to think I would miss those auctions. I had gone every year since we'd first come to Black Snake trailer.

I went to mourn and pay last respects. I'd look at all that dead bacca and wonder how I'd survive the empty fields waiting back home. Nothing is as lonely as a cold barn on a winter's night. Everyone else just sighed relief and counted money. The warehouses were lined with golden-brown wilted leaves. Numbers were shouted, farm names swapped. Crates measured, graded, and weighed. And the smell. With no wind inside the warehouses and all that ripe bacca, all the tar, hanging heavy around us. The men, women, too, dipping and chewing and smoking and spitting. Sampling goods from other farms and then spitting it out to make room for more. Daddy said when the auctions were over they'd go back through and sweep the floors. Gather all the bits of bacca that lay dried and scattered like gold dust. Box it into little round cans and call it snuff.

No matter what it was to other people—a drug, a cash crop, an honest living—to me, that bacca was home. More home than Daddy's car. More home than Black Snake trailer. But somehow I'd finally outgrown it.

I stepped through the fence onto Old Route Two. A road used by tractors more than cars. Anybody *on their way* used the highway. And anybody on Route Two lived for bacca. They grew it. Chewed it and spat it out their truck windows. Rolled it and smoked it. Bought and sold it. Carried green gold off in the back of their trucks. There were no cities built around Route Two. There was only land, rippling like my green baby blanket, and filled with thousands of acres of bacca. In the distance, mountains locked everything in. Like a giant fence.

I crossed over Route Two and into the fields on the other side. I walked the edge of the bacca and hid quickly when anyone passed. Two cop cars drove by slowly during the day. So did the Swarm boys.

I spent the whole day walking, and once evening came I settled for the night in the fields and glared at the mountains, somewhere in the darkness. They were still so far away. There were already blisters on my heels, but my journey to you was only beginning.

When the sun rose the next morning I didn't start walking. I sat in the bacca and waited. Until I saw a truck coming that I didn't recognize. One that I knew didn't belong to the Swarm boys. I walked out onto the road. Held my thumb up the way I'd seen Janie do once when she wanted a ride into town and Daddy wouldn't take her.

The truck slowed to a stop.

"Where you headed?" asked a man about Daddy's age. He had a graying beard and a tractor-supply hat on.

"Towards them mountains."

He nodded his head, and I opened the door and climbed in. I tried to not look scared. I remembered Momma storming out of the trailer and throwing dishes at Daddy. I remembered the look in her eyes, meaner than the black snake had ever been.

"What you so grumpy 'bout?" He reached between his legs and brought an empty Pepsi can to his mouth. Spat a long stream of golden bacca juice into it.

I shrugged my shoulders and looked out the window.

"You runnin' away, ain't you? Pretty girl like you walkin' down the road alone. What's wrong, Daddy won't let you have a boyfriend?"

"Ain't runnin'."

"You from them mountains?"

"Gonna find out."

He laughed and swore under his breath. "You a little crazy?"
I shrugged my shoulders. "Maybe."

The truth: I wanted to touch a mountain. After staring at
them my whole life. Jealous that they were bigger than the
bacca. Jealous that they were louder. Yelling out their presence, while the bacca only whispered. I wanted to touch a
mountain and feel something great.

The rest of the truth is that I found a map. Inside Daddy's
glove box. A dollar sign was drawn over the Carolina mountains. I looked at that sign, traced it with my finger, but didn't
see the word *Money*, like I was supposed to. I saw your name.
Strange letters that I don't know and couldn't read.

"Which farm you from?" I asked, noticing the tar stains on
his hands.

"Tucker. You?"

"Grigsby."

"Well you must've walked a good ways, then. That's a few
hours west, ain't it?"

I nodded.

"I guess that's the big farm in these parts now. Since Swarm
is closin' down." He shook his head slowly. "You heard of
it? Shame what's happened there. That land's been in the
same family since it was took from the Cherokee. One batch
of bad sons and it's chopped up and sold in pieces. Did you
know somebody's already lookin' it over? Wanna make it a
quiet country home. Don't wanna work the land. Drove up
and asked my boss to lease it and work it. Otherwise it'll lay
untilled. First time ever, Swarm farm won't be a farm. It'll just
be a place somebody lives. Mr. Swarm would die twice if he
knew. He always set such a high standard for farmin'. He was a
gentleman farmer. A dyin' breed. You know?"

"I guess," I said and nodded. But that trucker was more right than he'd ever know. Mr. *Swarm was a gentleman*. All the rest of us, all of the people stuck waiting beneath his sycamore tree, hated him for it. And waited for our moment of revenge.

The day he died I returned to him. After giving his money to Momma, I hid in the bacca just a few feet from him. Daren, another farmhand, came by. He didn't realize Mr. Swarm was dead at first, and asked whether he should start digging new fence holes. When he saw Mr. Swarm's face, the purple lips, he swore under his breath and turned around and ran. He stopped, though. I saw the bacca leaves grow still and knew that he wasn't running anymore.

Daren came back and stood in front of Mr. Swarm. He looked around in every direction. Then reached down into Mr. Swarm's pocket and pulled out his wallet. I had left a five-dollar bill behind.

But Daren didn't know Janie's lesson, and he tucked the five-dollar bill in his pocket. "You won't be needin' this no more," he said. He walked to the tractor. Lifted the hinges on the seat. Pulled out a pistol.

I cussed inside my head. That pistol was worth more than the money I'd grabbed out of Mr. Swarm's wallet.

"No more snakes for you to have to shoot, neither," Daren said, as he tucked it in his pocket. He opened a toolbox that sat on top of the tractor. Thumbed through it roughly. Put a few things in his pocket before he walked away.

I knew then, that Mr. Swarm was right about us all along. Every farmhand cussed about not being allowed to step on the Swarm front porch. It seemed unfair. Arrogant. Hateful. We were the ones that made him a King. Our backs, our hands, our lives, given to raise his golden treasure. But in the end, Mr. Swarm was right.

There are only two kinds of people in the world. The first are Swarms. People that eat inside the farmhouse. People that drink from silver goblets engraved with a royal name.

As for the rest of us, we are all stuck beneath the sycamore tree. Waiting for the king to come and bring us paychecks. Waiting for the queen to come and bring us pie. We drink our tea from paper Dixie cups. We rob dead people without a second thought. We are not to be trusted. We are not to be welcomed. We are thieves, every last one of us. Even the sweet little girls.

IV

As the trucker drove Route Two we talked about farms, bacca crops, and the coming harvest. I was careful not to reveal the truth. Of how much I really knew about bacca. Or that I was once a girl of Old Number Nine.

"My stop's up the road," the farmhand said. "I'd let you come but my woman wouldn't like it. You're dangerous pretty." He reached his hand out and ran his fingers across my thigh. He was shy at first, like he expected me to swat him away. But I didn't, and he let his hand rest just above my knee.

"Could you drive me a bit further? Maybe to them stores up the road. The one that sells candy in the barrels?"

"This ain't my truck. An' I'm due in the fields."

"I could pay you."

"A kiss?"

It would be my first. I had watched Janie with boys on the back of the bus and farmhands in the back of the barn many times. She never drew the line that I did, connecting boys she kissed to Daddy. Once he had been a farmhand chasing Momma to the back of the barn. Promising her a way out. But unlike Momma and Janie, I knew the truth about that line. It went sideways. Never up. Never out.

Once my own breasts filled up black bras and my own hips became worthy of a dance, I was invited to those back corners. Even chased a few times. But I had no use for sideways lines. So I sat at the front of the bus. And ran from the barn corners to the bacca.

The farmhand parked in front of the stores.

"You can git your candy now"—he laughed, as he leaned toward me—"an' I can git mine."

The muscles in his mouth pulled forward, like he was drinking a coke on a hot day. I saw the stain of bacca on his chin. Felt the scrub of his beard, the firm wetness against my lips. I closed my eyes and enjoyed the smell of bacca all over him. Sweet and peppery, like at the auctions.

"I could change my mind and take you home with me," the farmhand said.

I shook my head and stepped out of the truck. As he pulled away I raised the hem of my shirt and wiped my mouth. It was over. And it had been easy.

The row of stores was built out of old barn wood, with sagging front porches and hand-painted signs. One was a general store. The front was filled with barrels of hard candy and taffies and brown bags to stuff. The back had shelves of groceries, a rack or two of clothes, some magazines and books. When I was little we'd go there after payday. Daddy would go through the car magazines. Momma would try on clothes. I'd clutch a sweaty dime in my palm, one stolen off a farmhand and hid from Momma, and pace in front of the candy barrels.

The next store was an antique and hardware shop filled with tractor parts and seed for the locals. A few antiques for any tourist that might have taken a wrong turn off the highway. Mainly blue mason jars, and iron skillets labeled *Probably Civil War era*. Retired farm tools with magazine clippings of flower beds framed next to them, to show how a person of style could prop an antique plow blade between rows of petunias.

I'd never been in the last store. The Biscuit 'n' Gun Shop. An all-in-one stop for hunters. Where they could get ammo or a new rifle, a hunting license, and a pork chop biscuit.

I went inside the general store first. Ran my hand over the full barrels of candy, then headed to the back where the magazines and books were. I found a map of the entire southeast. Sat down on the floor and let my finger trace the short line between me and the mountains.

"Can I help you?" the cashier asked. She was Momma's age. Skinny and tired like her, too.

I folded the map and placed it back on the shelf. "I'm lookin' for a day's work. I can clean or watch the store. Been in here plenty of times growin' up. I know how the candy barrels work." It was a good lesson Daddy taught me during our journey out of Carolina. He earned our food and gas money by drifting from one odd job to another.

"Don't hire out day jobs."

"Know if the antique store does?"

"If you really needin' work, go to the Biscuit 'n' Gun."

"They hirin'?"

"Always. Worked there a few times myself." She winked at me. "Tell 'em Marcy sent you."

Inside the Biscuit 'n' Gun the walls were lined with dead animals, their chopped-off feet holding up the guns that killed them. Glass-topped counters were filled with rifles, handguns, and boxes of shells. Pictures of men holding their kills were framed around the register. In the back was the food counter. A small chalkboard listed the biscuit menu and prices. Men huddled around a stack of pictures, comparing recent kills.

An older man walked toward me. "You want a biscuit you go to the back, honey. Just gun business up here."

"Marcy sent me. I'm lookin' for a few hours' work."

He laughed and softly slapped my shoulder like we were old friends. "Send my thanks to Marcy." He turned to the men. "Boys, it's been a month. But this joint will open again tonight. Come at dark for beer, cards, and her." Someone let out a long whistle.

"Be back at nine," he told me. "Pay's fifteen bucks, but you can keep whatever else you make. If you're still here in the mornin' you can run the biscuit rush."

I stared at him, hoping for a reason why I should say no. "Will I be in charge?" I asked.

"I'm just payin' you to be the somethin' pretty that these boys come to drink and watch. Whatever else you do is up to you."

"Any cops comin'?"

"None that'll admit to it the next day." He laughed.

I shrugged my shoulders and nodded. I hurried to the antique and hardware store, went to the back where the bathroom was. Closed and locked the door. I stared into a foggy brass mirror. The words *Probably Victorian, $10*, taped to the bottom. I saw my round brown eyes, my pale skin, my hair that glowed. I hadn't changed. Hair, face, skin, was all the same. It was what I'd lost. Black Snake trailer. Momma. That green car parked out front. My home was ugly. With it gone, I looked in the mirror and saw pretty for the first time. Maybe it was instincts. Or maybe it was just hope. But I felt certain of one thing as I stared in the mirror. Pretty can be very useful.

I walked out of the bathroom and lingered over the antiques. Sifted through a box of old kitchen tools. Tried on old rings, most of them brassy bands with an empty hole in the center. The original stones had disappeared long ago. I stared at the shelf lined with blue mason jars. I reached for one, felt the weight of its thick glass. I held it up to the light, looked through, and watched the room turn blue.

The front door opened and a farmhand walked in. He asked the man up front if he could see the parts catalog, and the two men started talking about placing an order to fix a broke-down tractor. I walked past the jars, on my way to the general store to look at magazines, when I saw them in the corner. Velvet banners framed in gold. White tigers and red roses painted across them. I stepped closer. Ran my hand across the cheap velvet and shivered as I whispered, "Elvis."

I remembered him, from a little tent inside a Carolina county fair. Momma bought pink cotton candy that day and she gave me and Janie each a bite. Janie whined for more, and Daddy yelled no, so I didn't ask. They were counting money. Each of them digging in their pockets. Momma made me hold a stuffed bear that Daddy had won. The bear was almost as big as me and probably heavier. I had to lay down my green blanket on the ground so that I could use both hands to hold it. When they counted enough, they smiled and walked away holding hands. I picked up my blanket and put it in my teeth. Ran behind them carrying that bear.

They stopped in front of a velvet banner booth. There were white tigers and red roses. And the one Momma cried over, it made her so happy. Elvis. With blue velvet eyes and black velvet hair.

"It's gonna look so good over our couch, baby," she whispered to Daddy.

He nodded. "Well, git it then. If you want it so bad."

We walked away with Elvis. And then me and Janie rode the carousel. I chose a pink pony. She chose a purple one. We went round and round giggling. But when the ride was over, Momma was crying and alone. Elvis was ripped in two, laying in the dirt.

Momma grabbed Janie by the hand and started running toward the gate. I ran behind them. Janie kept turning around, making sure I followed.

"Wait, Momma!" I yelled.

She stopped and knelt in front of me. "Listen up, girl, when somebody finds you here today, you tell 'em this, 'I've lost my momma.' And when they ask you what her name is, you say, 'It's Momma.' And when they ask you what your name is, you say, 'Angel Ray.'"

"But my name's Angel Mosely."

She shook her head, as tears streamed down her face. "Oh baby, be a smart girl today. Git yourself lost. Git away from us." Then she ran, pulling Janie with one hand. The two-piece Elvis in her other. I dropped the bear I was supposed to carry and ran as hard as I could. I dove in Daddy's car the minute I saw the door open. Daddy whipped me good over that lost bear.

From that day on, the sight of Elvis, the sight of black velvet and red roses, would always remind me. I had a chance.

One small chance in the middle of a Carolina county fair. It was handed down like a gift from heaven. That moment that I could have escaped Black Snake trailer. Escaped all the things I'd later ache to burn down.

Oh baby, be a smart girl today, Momma begged.

But I wasn't smart. I was scared. And so I ran. Not to Momma. Not to Daddy. Or even Janie. I ran to that green car. Like it was the only thing that could save me. Like it was the only thing that mattered. Like somehow I knew the truth about that car. And how more than anyone else on earth, it belonged to me.

V

By the time the sun set, the Biscuit 'n' Gun was nearly full. The old man showed me a back room, where there was a laundry basket of things left behind by other women. Sequined bras. A tube of red lipstick. A hairbrush. An old bottle of Giorgio that had been refilled with water to try and soak up leftover scent. Four-inch red heels, size nine.

I flipped my hair upside down and teased it till it piled across my shoulders and down my back in a wild swirl. I took the lipstick and smeared it across my mouth. Rubbed a bit between my fingers and across my cheekbones. I stood in front of the mirror and slid my size-seven feet into those heels. Stuffed tissue into the toes to try and make them fit. Then I knotted my T-shirt in the front, the way Momma always did. So my belly showed as smooth and flat as a high-summer bacca leaf.

"Boys," the old man called out, as he helped me onto the counter. "I give you Angel."

Just as I chose not to go to the back corners with farmhands, I chose to let them stand me up on a biscuit counter. Men were still swapping pictures. They were passing guns, too.

Testing sites as they aimed long barrels at random spots in the room. Sometimes at my swaying hips.

I passed out beers. My heels made little *clink clink* sounds as I walked up and down the counter to hand out cold cans. When I wasn't serving beer, I was supposed to dance. My hips slid in circles and the men shouted lust. I thought about how Momma would have loved to be a fifteen-dollar dancer at the Biscuit 'n' Gun. The only difference was that she would have done it to feel pretty. I already knew I was. I did it for money. I did it because I could.

"She really is an angel," a drunk man yelled. "Look at all that hair."

White hair that Momma promised, threatened, and hoped would darken as I aged. But it was still as white at seventeen as it was at three. I wore it long, halfway down my back. People assumed it's why I was called Angel. I never bothered telling them the truth.

About how the first time Daddy saw me my arms and legs were twisted and fighting. Momma said I had the worst colic she ever saw. And the pain of it made me curl my limbs and punch and kick with anger.

"Scrawniest legs I ever seen," Daddy would laugh. "No more meat on 'em than a chicken bone. You was all curled up and twistin'. Just like that live oak everyone in Carolina fusses over. The one named Angel Oak."

When the beer ran out, the music was turned off and the old man helped me off the counter. He paid me, then led me to the back room where he locked me in, *for my own safety*, since I didn't want any extra business.

In the morning I served biscuits to the same men I'd danced for the night before.

They grabbed breakfast before heading over to the hardware store to pick up whatever they needed for the coming harvest. A few of them stopped to talk about their bacca. Held their hands up to show how tall. Behind the counter my own hands ached to rise in pride. *This tall. A king's tobacco.*

"Two pork chop biscuits, please," a man said. "An' a coke."

Someone yelled behind him. "Get that truck moved. You swore it'd be gone by dawn. Nobody else can git in to park. They're fillin' up the ditches."

I handed him biscuits. "Goin' now," he said over his shoulder. "Just grabbin' biscuits. See you in a few weeks."

"Park better next time."

He laughed, shrugged his shoulders, turned back to me. "Big trucks get no respect round here. If it ain't a tractor or a pickup they got no use for it. Where's Maude? She usually serves up the biscuits. Don't know that I trust yours."

"She cooked 'em," I said. "Went home and let me serve 'em."

Through the window I saw two cop cars pull in and park in front of the general store. After a quick flash of panic, I remembered who I'd been just the night before. They called me an angel. A sexy Elvis dancer. I remembered the lesson I'd learned staring in the bathroom mirror. I was pretty. And I could use it.

I ran to the man I'd just served biscuits and put my arm through his, like we were old lovers.

"So you drive a big truck? I'd just love to see it."

It was a rare sight, but sometimes big trucks would drive Route Two when they were breaking freight laws and didn't want to pass the weigh-in checkpoint on the interstate. Whenever I saw one I'd stare at it with wonder. Unlike the tractors and pickups, the big rigs were always in a hurry. On their way to someplace better.

He nodded and tried to pull back, but I tightened my grip. "Give me a ride, cowboy, please?"

"Where you headed?"

"I need to get to the mountains."

Two men in uniform stepped out of the cars and walked toward the general store.

"I've got money, or maybe you want somethin' else."

"You're right," he said. "You need to get to the mountains."

With the police inside the general store, I hurried to the truck. Pulled and climbed my way inside. There were dozens of knobs and switches and little gauges. It was more like the way a kid dreams of rockets, or draws his own spaceship. I huddled low in the floor of the truck, and begged the trucker to hurry up and leave. My heart was pounding. My mind playing tricks and telling me jail was a place worse than biscuit counters. Worse even than Black Snake trailer.

He laughed softly, but didn't smile. He was younger than I imagined a truck driver should be. In his early twenties, not much older than what Janie would have been. He was built smaller than the farmhands. His muscles used to turn a wheel rather than lift crates of bacca. But even with him sitting, I could see that he was taller than any man at Swarm farm. He dressed differently, too. Instead of camos or overalls, he wore clean jeans and cowboy boots. A plain black T-shirt.

"You want one of the biscuits?" he asked when we were on the road.

I shook my head. "Where we going?"

"I'm haulin' pipes outta middle Tennessee into North Carolina."

I climbed into the seat and looked out. I had never been so high above the bacca. It was several feet below, passing by in a green blur. It didn't look big and safe anymore. It looked more like a garden than a crop. More like a row of beans or a hill of potatoes. Something simple and weak.

I noticed a handwritten note, taped to his steering wheel. As he adjusted his hands, the writing became clear. *I cry out to the Lord, he answers me from his holy mountain. Psalm.*

I turned away and leaned against the window. I was tired from my long night, and after an hour of listening to the roar of the great truck, I fell asleep.

"Look up," he said, his hand gently shaking my shoulder.

I opened my eyes, and slid lower in my seat. My hands rose to touch my face and hide whatever I could. Never, not even curled up on the floor of Daddy's car, had I felt so small. No matter which direction I turned, land was above me. Land pressed down on me, like it knew how strong it was. Like it wanted me to know, too.

"Don't be scared. You were right to come here."

"How do you know?" I whispered.

"'Show yourself to me, on top of the mountain'. That's what God said when he wanted to give Moses the ten commandments. When the Devil wanted to tempt Jesus with the glories of the earth, they stood on a mountain. Big things, *holy* things, happen here."

Outside my window, the guardrail was all that separated the road from the sky. Clouds were within reach.

"If they're so great, how come you leave 'em?"

He shrugged his shoulders. "I want it to stay special."

I nodded and thought of summer nights, with the bacca all around me. I'd look at stars in a black Tennessee sky. Sometimes they were so warm I almost didn't need the whiskey.

In eighth-grade science I failed the astronomy unit. Not

because I couldn't do the work or learn the material. But because I *wouldn't*. That first day, when the teacher started talking about how stars are just balls of gas that shoot out light, I laid my head down so I couldn't see the poster she held up. Of a star sliced in half so we could see the dull insides. I put my hands over my ears so I couldn't hear her description of what makes a star shine. And I refused to look at the sky charts. To learn the names. To trace out the picture of some hunter and his giant belt.

They were *my* stars. They shined to keep *me* warm. Not because a gas made them. I saw whatever picture I wanted, not what someone long ago decided I should see. Sometimes I saw my own reflection. White hair studded with stars and streaming through a black sky. Sometimes I saw Black Snake trailer. And I stacked star upon star until I built a cinder-block tower high enough to escape.

Sometimes I saw you. With your own starry hair streaming behind. Moonbeam eyes staring down on me. You were a stranger. Yet lying flat in the bacca, sometimes your stars seemed to move close. Almost seemed to reach for me.

"Well," he said, as the truck came to a stop. "You're high enough here. No need to climb on any more counters."

As I stepped out of the truck, I wondered what you would say when you first saw me. Or when you saw the things I'd saved for you in my pockets. What does a Holy Roller think of a half-naked daughter that danced on a biscuit counter? Without any excuse other than *I'm pretty*? Or because I can? What does a Holy Roller think of a daughter who robbed a dead man?

My name is Angel. But there's a joke that Daddy loved to tell: Even the Devil was an angel once.

VI

The mountain had one main street, lined with shops and restaurants. I walked down the sidewalk, peered in windows, and guessed I was standing in a tourist town. Most of the shops featured the mountain's best hobbies. Skiing, fly-fishing, and hiking. There were shelves of hiking boots and racks of thermal-lined clothes. Walls of fishing rods and canoes hanging from the ceiling on thick wires. There was mountain "gear," too. Compasses and pocket knives and canteens. All of it promised the thrill of "rugged survival." And of course, every tourist town needs souvenirs. Shot glasses painted with foggy mountaintops. T-shirts with pictures of rainbow trout ironed on them. Snow globes with little plastic skiers inside.

At the end of the sidewalk was a path that led away from the main street and into the woods. A sign next to it said *Scenic*. I followed it to an overlook and discovered that though land was still above me, there was much more below. I was high above the bacca. Above the foothills that I could see far in the distance, like ripples on a baby blanket. I was high above all the ashes I'd left behind. For a girl once too small to crawl inside her trailer without help, it felt good to look down on something.

I spent my first few days shaking snow globes as I explored each shop slowly. I even ate at a restaurant once, instead of sticking to my plan of cheap foods like chips and coke. And at night I walked the path marked *Scenic* and settled under the trees close to the overlook. There I could see dozens of lights, tiny sparks of homes and businesses on the earth below. I named them all. Grouped them together and searched for pictures.

But the mountains were cooler than I had planned. I was closer to the sun by miles, but the night winds were something even whiskey could not defeat. Soon I grew tired of washing up in store bathrooms. The store workers were tired of it, too. I saw how they glanced at each other when I walked in *again* to shake a snow globe, use the bathroom, count the money in my pockets, and consider buying a big fleece blanket. But I always bought snack cakes and beef jerky instead. No amount of cold, no shiver of my skin, could be worse than an empty belly.

Besides losing Janie, the pain of a hungry belly is what I remember most about her running away. The night before she left, I found her cussing about how her jeans didn't fit right anymore. I looked at her, saw the strain of her belly against the waistband. Saw the black bra she ripped off, cussed again that it was so tight it hurt.

"What you lookin' at?" she said, rolling her eyes. "You a Holy Roller too? You wait. Give or take a few years, you'll be standin' same as me."

There was a boy. There was *always* a boy around Janie. But one had a plan for her. Recognized her special talents. He'd park outside all the big farmhouses in East Tennessee while Janie snuck inside. She filled his trunk with engraved things. Silver carved up with family names. The treasure of tobacco kings.

She put a good-bye letter under my pillow, then left with him forever.

Momma and Daddy had no plans to follow her. Till Momma discovered Daddy's paycheck was missing. They cussed her, the baby in her belly, the farmhand she was running away with. And then they taught me the words *family emergency* and left me alone for days.

With them gone, I liked Black Snake trailer even less. That night I dragged my baby blanket out to the bacca for the company it offered, rather than the safety. And I returned the next night. And the next.

Groceries were our luxury. Only after gas money, car repairs, cigarettes, and whiskey did we buy food. The cheapest, since there was little money left. Cornflakes, macaroni, cans of ground-up potted meat that Momma liked to pretend was ham salad.

If it had been winter, I would've been fine. With my government breakfast and lunch pass, I kept a stock of smuggled snacks stashed in odd places around the farm. But that stash always ran dry by mid-June.

I thought of breaking every Swarm rule and knocking on the farmhouse door. Maybe even stepping inside as I cried about how we were out of food. But I couldn't risk somebody finding out I was alone, giving me over to the State to be raised by *Lord Knows Who*.

One night when the whiskey was gone, I couldn't sleep for hunger pains. I reached for a bacca leaf. Smelled it. It was a scent that changed with time. Started with the dirt smell of new fields. Moved to the fruit of ripe bacca. Ended with cans of spit, smelling like apple cider with the punch of whiskey.

I took a bite, spit on the ground like I'd seen Daddy do thousands of times. Took some more to chew. Ignored the fire in my mouth and tucked it in my bottom lip, like a seasoned farmhand. Spat and took more to chew. The fields started to blur. My head felt heavy, and I liked it. The easy drunk. Like fields of whiskey were growing all around me. I reached for more and sometimes forgot to spit. My hands shook so that I couldn't find the leaves anymore. My head was so heavy I couldn't lift it from the dirt. I was beyond drunk. Vomiting in the dirt. Over and over till my fists punched the ground, sick from the fight of it all.

I woke up to the sound of Daddy's car the next morning. Laid in the bacca while they sat on the hood and smoked. They giggled about the look on Janie's face when the cops showed up. They joked about the way Janie tried to run when the cops opened the trunk. Saw it full of family guns and silver from all the big local farms. Momma and Daddy sat in that green car, not twenty feet over from Janie, and waved as she was handcuffed. They called out *Hello* like any good parent would. They called out that she'd deliver her baby in jail.

I watched them from the bacca as they slapped each other high five. "You see the look on her face?" Daddy asked, while Momma giggled. My fists found the ground again. Punched silently over and over. Sick from the fight of it all.

After that summer, though, I knew the rules of hunger. About spacing out food, never eating until I was completely full. Always hiding a bit more than I thought I might need. It carried me through many weeks of empty cabinets. And gave me the courage to get through cold nights on your mountain. In a way, that cold, that fear of hunger, was a good thing. It reminded me of the whole reason I was there. During the day I'd get caught up looking down on a small earth below. Imagined I could burn it down, too. But at night the chill that covered the mountain reminded me I was small. Warned me that winter was coming. I laid awake and made survival plans. Drawn with lines that went up and up and up. Like a map of the mountain.

Our last name was Ray. I knew that much. I went to a store and swapped a five-dollar bill out for quarters. Then I found a pay phone with the phone book still attached. I snuck back at night, when the streets were quiet and peaceful, and started making my calls.

Ray is a common name. And there were many ways to spell it. *Ray, Rae, Reigh*... I counted a possibility of thirty-six phone calls. Put a mark by the first one, dropped a quarter in the slot and dialed the numbers with my trembling hand.

"Hello?" a sleepy voice answered.

I stayed silent.

"It's too late for pranks—"

"Wait."

"Who's this?"

"Angel Ray."

"I think you've got the wrong number."

"I'm lookin' for my family. I found your name, Eva Ray, and I thought—"

"This isn't a family home, honey. It's an upholstery business. Eva was my great-grandmother. Ray is my dog. Sorry. Hope you find them."

I made six calls each night. A few times, the people that answered were friendly. They'd chat about how good it was that I wanted to find my family. How sad it was I lost them. Most of the time, though, people just hung up on me. I kept calling. Down the list I moved, night after night. And I cursed the tears that filled my eyes after each hang-up.

There were six numbers left to call the night the lovers came to the overlook. It had happened before once, during the day. I had been dozing under a tree and woke up to the sound of them laughing. I opened my eyes to see a young couple, not much older than me. They were rich. With their clean jeans and tucked-in shirts. Tennis shoes that looked brand new and so comfortable. And the jackets they wore, not heavy enough for winter, but perfect for a windy mountain day.

I looked down at myself. My dirty cutoffs and sweatshirt. Beef jerky wrappers scattered around me. A whiskey bottle in my hand.

"You livin' here?" the girl asked, shaking her head. "Cops could show you where a shelter is. His daddy's one, maybe he could take you..."

I ran away. And avoided the overlook during the day. But one night the lovers returned. I heard them kissing and giggling. I grabbed my things and edged deeper into the woods. Until I couldn't hear them anymore. Until I saw the moon shining down on a big old sycamore and felt home all around me.

Sometime during the night the rain came. I scrambled to my feet and started to walk back toward the scenic path. I wanted to return to town and sit beneath an awning for the night. Soon it was pouring, and I had to hold my hand over my eyes to see clearly. I kept walking straight, the same way I had come. But I was numb with cold. Numb to how long I had really been walking. And to how far away the path suddenly seemed.

The rain stopped before dawn. But there were no lovers' giggles. And no passing cars. All I heard was the *drip drip* of leftover water falling from the trees. I laid on a pile of wet leaves and waited for the sun to rise and show me the way.

When morning came, I retraced my steps until I returned to the big sycamore.

Only this tree, with its matching wide leaves and shaggy bark, had lichen growing down the side. A grayish green mat. And I didn't remember lichen from before.

I felt panic as the wind suddenly blew stronger, like before rain. I learned something important that day, as the last bit of leaves fell from the trees and the animals scurried for food. Winter comes early in the mountains. It never measures itself by months or weeks. It comes whenever it wants.

I also learned that Mr. Swarm was right about something else. The mountains are full of giant sycamores. I went from tree to tree, my eyes always searching for wide sharp-tipped leaves and shaggy bark. Whenever I found one, I rested beneath it. Marked it with a broken branch so that I would know if I returned. I never did; each tree I came to was new. And though panic grew inside me, so did awe. I ran my hands across the hurting bark, and wondered if I was the first in years, maybe decades or even a century, to lay eyes on those great trees. We were so far from the scenic path. So lost on the mountain.

I should have been more prepared. I'd spent years of my life searching out hundreds of bacca acres. Learning how paths doubled back without warning, or eventually emptied out by old barns or broke-down tractors turned over in ditches. I'd spent years not being lost in a place where any other child would be. Anytime I needed a map, a way to track myself in the bacca, I'd jump to see which mountains fenced me in. If my eyes saw a flash of the close green ones, then I knew I was in the west fields. If the mountains were a faraway blue, I knew I was close to Black Snake trailer.

But standing on the mountain was a whole different thing. I had risen above fences. So I drew crooked lines and circles, one after the other, between the sycamores. I looked to the sky for help. But stars were replaced by clouds. Old ones moved away with the wind. And new shapes formed above me each morning.

Days passed, and I tried to circle back again, always feeling that I had just missed the path. As food ran low, I watched the squirrels eat acorns and felt jealous. It rained again. Too tired to walk, I sat and shivered through it. Let the rain soak me as I dreamed of the overlook. Not so I could find my way to the stores, shake a snow globe, and get warm. And not so I could trace pictures of lights in the dark. I dreamed of the overlook and what it would feel like to step over the stone wall. I dreamed of clouds, and how good, how soft, they would feel as I sailed through them.

Maybe I was only half awake, or maybe I was dying, but soon my thoughts no longer came as ideas. I didn't make plans. I didn't whisper wishes. I only saw visions.

Like Momma's gun, the handle the color of red maple, laying in a stack of wet leaves. I reached for it, pretended to turn it over and over in my hands. It was sexy. Like Momma leaned against that car. Like me on top of a biscuit counter.

I saw Janie, too, after she ran away. I saw the look on her face, the look that made Momma giggle, when the cops showed up. I turned into the bark of the sycamore and sobbed. Yelled *I'm sorry* to Janie. She always hated it so much when I cried. "You've gotta be tougher," she used to say with her strong gritty voice. "Can't run very fast if you're always cryin'."

I reached into my back pocket, where I kept my strength—a little red ring of plastic. I closed my fist round it, until I almost felt warm again. Until I felt my tears dry up and knew that Janie would be proud.

I earned that red ring the hard way on the day the milk spilled. The day I learned Momma and Daddy could hurt me. But they never owned me.

Daddy's car had died. He had tried to get it running all week. It would start at first, sputter, then die. But by the end of the week, when he turned the key there was only a click. And then nothing.

"I could fix this with some money," Daddy yelled. "Woman, git the money. It's ours by rights."

Momma sat on the couch, nodding. "What you reckon I oughta ask for? Fifteen?"

"We could buy a whole new one and a motorbike, too." He smiled.

"How will I git there?"

"If I can git it runnin', will you go?"

He pawned her gun, promised to buy it back with the money she'd bring home. Bought just enough parts and gas to rig it to Carolina. I remember the day she left. How she kissed me on the forehead. How I jerked back in surprise, and then hated myself because I did.

"I'm gonna tell 'em she's sick and dyin'," Momma said, as she pulled away.

Daddy smiled. "Be back in two days, baby."

It took four days, and Daddy paced and yelled and pointed his finger at me like I'd done something to keep Momma away. The day she came home, I was laying in the bacca wondering whether we'd make the farmhand picnic. Every year right before the harvest and auctions, the Swarms held a picnic under the sycamore. The tables would be loaded with chicken and ham, all kinds of pie. It was as close to Christmas as our family ever came.

I heard the car pull up, got as close to Black Snake trailer as I could without being seen.

"Woman, where the hell you been?"

"Weren't there," she said, her hands raised, palms up.

"You go to Lizbeth's?"

"She wouldn't even open the door for me. I scrubbed that woman's toilets on my hands and knees, and she acted like she never knew me."

"So that's it, then," Daddy said. He sat down on the hood of the car, his head in his hands.

"Lizbeth told me where they used to live. I went there, then went next door and told 'em I was lookin' for the Holy Roller family. They said they moved years ago, but a few months after the man called 'em. Sent 'em a check to ship an old bike. He'd given it away, but wanted it back again. Said somethin' bout bikin' in the mountains come fall."

"Where'd they send the bike?"

She shrugged her shoulders, pointed to the mountains in the distance, whispered, "Somewhere near Boone."

We went to the farmhand picnic. Daddy wore his nice jeans, the ones that didn't have a Skoal ring burned into the back pocket. He shaved his face and slicked his hair back with water. Momma wore a see-through sundress. It was white cotton and she made sure her bra and panties were a matching hot pink. I wore cutoffs, tried to knot up my shirt but couldn't get the tie to stay. So I pulled the collar open a bit, to make sure everyone knew I was finally wearing a bra.

We sat six to a table. Me and Momma and another farmhand wife on one side. Daddy, a farmhand, and another little girl on the other. The Swarms were busy passing platters of chicken and biscuits. Plates of corn on the cob. Mrs. Swarm brought a half gallon of milk and a pitcher of sweet tea to our table. She blessed the food and we all started to eat.

"Car won't ever be fixed now," Daddy said through gritted teeth.

"You seen that sycamore, Daddy? I bet it's growed another foot."

"I bet this trip killed it for good, too," he continued. "Hundreds of miles on a half-dead car. All for nothin'."

"Well, if we had done it my way," Momma said, "we wouldn't be in this mess. We could've bought somethin' that wouldn't die. We could've bought land. Or our own business. But no, you had to buy somethin' that would wear out. Somethin' that you could show off and be the big man. How's it feel now? We ain't got nothin'. No money. No car. Just her."

Daddy raised his arms to stretch, like he was shaking her words off. But I could tell from the flush on his face that he felt every word. He looked at me. Reached across the table for my glass of milk.

Something hit me. And as I blinked wet eyes, I saw milk dripping onto my T-shirt. I cried, "Momma." But in an instant, forks returned to plates. Daddy started talking to the other farmhand about the differences in tractors. Their speeds, digging strength. Others started passing plates for seconds, laughing about how there'd be no room for dessert. I sat stone still, my face covered in milk and tears.

I didn't know if it was real. No one else seemed to think so. But then I remembered the shock in their eyes. How the little girl across from me gasped. How her momma shushed her. And I remembered how Momma's head turned away, to stare at mountains when I cried out for her.

I reached my hand up and touched the sticky wetness.

"Why Angel, you've spilled your milk all over you, sweetheart. Let me get you somethin' to clean up with," Mrs. Swarm said.

I felt her apron, warm from the heat of her body, as it wiped across my face.

"Just a little milk. No big deal. Nothin' to cry so hard over. I got more," she whispered.

I reached out and grabbed that plastic red milk cap. Held it, tight and sweaty in my palm, until the picnic ended. When Momma got drunk later that night and sobbed out the details, about five thousand dollars and the pregnant preacher's wife, it felt familiar. More like an echo than a memory. Like something I had spoken long before, returning again with Momma's voice.

That night my hurting heart clenched tight. Till it was more like a fist than anything else. I kept that milk cap underneath my mattress so that all I'd have to do at night was reach my hand down and feel it. And I tucked it in my pocket before I burned Black Snake trailer.

But lost on that winter mountain, I knew I had made it as far as I was going to go. In the end, though, I was finally *Somewhere near Boone*. And if I blinked my tired eyes just the right way, I could almost see you, sitting there in those wet leaves.

I held the milk cap out. "This is a piece of a war," I whispered. "A hard one, fought inside me. One that finally ended with the truth that I belong to someone else. You. With your starry hair streaming behind you in a Tennessee sky. You can make the very stars reach out for me."

HANNAH

I

Hannah didn't fall through the porch of the old plantation, like Sam once predicted she would. Instead, her feet carefully stepped over the empty places that dropped six feet to the ground below. And she passed easily through the front door, though the handle was lost long ago. The house was dark inside even when the sun was strong. Trees covered the outsides of the windows and dirt covered the insides. The house was cold, too. Even on warm fall days, heat wouldn't go where light refused to.

Hannah counted ten rooms on the main floor and looked up a broken staircase to guess of many more. Her suitcase was missing, left behind on Folly Beach or in the back of the taxi that drove her to the plantation. But she never once thought of it.

Instead she pulled down old curtains, the hems gnawed by the same gray creatures that scurried around her at night. She pulled her hand across dusty velvet and marveled at the softness of it. She took off her clothes and let dirty polyester fall to the floor. Then she wrapped that velvet, decades old, around naked skin. She shivered with pleasure at its softness.

She explored her new home, and found a hand pump on top of an old well that she used for water. In the old orchard she dined on fallen peaches, well past harvest, that lay on the ground and had begun to rot.

Something lived in the chimneys of that home. Especially at night, she could hear it, scratching, beating, *living*. She waited, her eyes open, and eventually saw an owl fly out; it had a wingspan of three feet. The other gray creatures, the ones that now wallowed in her polyester, scattered. The owl flew perfectly, under arched doorways and fallen beams, until it escaped out a broken window.

Other things lived in that home, too. Haints. They were all around her. Sometimes they called to her. Other times they sang. Either way they always looked the same. White blond hair falling down their backs. Polyester clothes hiding pale skin.

One was ten years old. She sat on a box in the corner of the room while her mother brushed her hair.

"Some day you'll be a mother, too," the mother said. "And you'll brush your little girl's hair, just like I'm brushing yours. Hopefully she won't have as many tangles."

"When?"

"Stop squirming. When you're much older. Right now you're still mine."

The child giggled. "I just turned ten."

"Still too little," the mother said.

"Will she have long eyelashes? Like a teacup princess?"

"If she does, don't ever let her know."

And then they would disappear back into the rotting walls. Hannah waited for them every night. She'd sit wrapped in molded velvet and pull her fingers through her hair. Until she could feel the brush that moved in the mother's hands.

There were others, too. A girl, looking the same as the ten-year-old child, only older. Sadder.

"Mother?" the girl called.

"Yes, child. What's the matter?"

"Something's wrong."

"What is it?" the mother asked, looking worried.

"There's blood."

The mother smiled and took the girl's hands. "How wonderful!"

The girl started to cry. "I don't understand."

"You're thirteen years old. You're a woman now."

"But why is there—"

"It only means you will have babies one day."

Hannah had it memorized. Her mouth mumbled the words like a favorite passage from one of her books. And when she got to the part where the mother said *you will have babies one day*, she laughed loudly. But the walls of that plantation hadn't heard laughter in decades and didn't know what to do with it. The sound bounced unclaimed from room to room.

She was not afraid of the haints. She called out to them. Brought them peaches from the old orchard. Decorated their corners with red and yellow leaves and carefully arranged clumps of Spanish moss.

She spent week after week in her new home, caring for her new family. The smells of rot and mold didn't bother her. Neither did the taste of rusty water or browned peaches. She liked her velvet corner. She never planned to leave.

But then one day, after so many safe days inside her tomb, light poured in. She pulled her velvet closer, wrapped it around her face, and closed her eyes. She heard a scream and clutched her curtain tightly. Something clawed at her. Pulling and tearing until the curtain split open and she felt cold air across her naked skin. She saw horror on the faces around her, and watched them stumble back in confusion.

Fists raised above her. She turned herself into the corner, but the fists came down on her. And the screams cut her.

Someone came running. Poured himself over her, around her, until the fists stopped. "What are you doing?" he yelled.

"Look at her!"

Hannah reached for her curtain and saw it was thrown to the middle of the room. She tried to pull her body low to the ground, but discovered she could no longer lie flat for the new swell beneath her. And so, with a naked stomach filling the space between her and the rotting floor, she crawled. Hand over hand, skin pulled across splinters. Her eyes fixed upon velvet.

Somewhere in the room was moaning and weeping. A shrill scream, that made Hannah long to cover her ears. It was like a colicky newborn that nothing would comfort. Like an abandoned baby that no one would help.

II

Father carried Hannah into their old shack on James Island. He laid her gently in bed and left the room without speaking. Mother came to her, sat by the bed with a list in her hand. Mother stared at the paper, never once looked up, as she read off each question. *Who. When.* As Hannah answered, she thought of deep water. *The Grapes of Wrath.* And the beautiful plantation.

"His name was Sam, and it happened two weeks before we left," she said.

Mother nodded slowly. Then held up her hands to count silently. "You're going to have a baby in about four months."

A funeral began in their home. Bethie guarded the door, shook her head to the mailman that wanted to deliver a package. Her father answered the phone and whispered lies about reinforcing bridges over the Cooper River. Then he paced, his heavy steps giving a *boom boom* percussion on the hardwood floors. Mother wailed all night. On and on with no relief.

Day came. Hannah could hear Father.

"We'll move west after she has it and say the baby is ours. She can move on with her life and always be the baby's sister."

"I am sixty-one years old." Mother laughed bitterly. "I am not Sarah. You are no Abraham. And this baby is certainly not our promised land."

"Well, the boy should know. She'll be eighteen in a year. We were married then. Maybe, with our help, they could make a go of it."

"No," Mother hissed. "For seventeen years I've turned a blind eye to you. I let you give my baby dirty books. I listened while you challenged her to question *why* she followed the creed we live by. This is your mess. I'll clean it up; that's what a mother always has to do. Clean up messes. But now it's your turn to look the other way."

That night Mother brought her a plate of supper. A turkey sandwich and sliced pears.

"I'm not hungry."

"Doesn't matter in the least," Mother replied, forcing the plate into her hands. "Time you stopped thinking of only yourself."

Hannah no longer shared a room with Bethie, who was ordered to sleep on the couch in the living room. She spent her days alone, hiding her stomach beneath piles of blankets on her bed and eating the trays that were carried to her.

"Get up," Mother said one day, setting a tray of food by her bed. "Go for a walk. It isn't good for you or the baby to be in bed all day."

Hannah waited until the sun was beginning to set. Then she walked out of her room. It was the first time she'd done that, other than to step quickly across the hall to the bathroom. She walked through the house and felt new pressure in her feet. The added weight in her hips. She caught herself against the wall and realized walking required new skills.

She found Bethie by the marsh, took her hand and pulled her away. Together, they walked to the beach. Hannah's skirt was pushed low so that her stomach could swell over it. Her hemline dragged in the marsh sand. Her breasts spilled out of the edges of her bra. There was no modesty anymore. Her body displayed sin like a prized trophy. And as the cars passed by, she knew what they were thinking. She even whispered it to herself with their soft southern tongues. *Bless her young heart. A knocked-up Holy Roller.*

Winter was dark at the ocean. With stronger winds and bigger clouds. Christmas passed. Then Valentine's. But Hannah moved through these months without complaint. Her body grew bigger and her heart felt cold.

"I'm sorry, Bethie," Hannah said one night, as they walked. "I've messed your life up, too. You should be at school."

Bethie shook her head, put her arm around Hannah. Sometimes they would sit on the dunes and count waves until they could no longer see them. Hannah reminded Bethie of the grocery-bag lesson their father taught them when they were little. He would fill a bag full of various objects. Like candy. Or money. King crowns. He would have them reach their hands into the bag and pull something out. Only if they said the right thing could they keep it.

Hannah pulled out a dollar bill. "I'm a child of God, more precious than money," she'd whisper, as her father nodded.

Bethie pulled out candy. "I'm a child of G-g-g-g-od, and that's sweeter than c-c-c-candy." Once Hannah pulled out a seashell. She held it in her hand, unable to think of the correct answer. Her father helped her. "You are a child of God. The crown of creation. More glorious than the ocean."

The baby moved within her. She talked to it. Even stroked it through her belly sometimes. But she didn't own it; it would never be hers. Mother said it was meant for someone worthy. Someone that waited for a baby and couldn't have one. "Just like our Bethie was a blessing to us when we couldn't have more children," Mother explained.

Most of the time, Hannah accepted Mother's words. She didn't try to imagine the baby's face. She didn't wonder what color its eyes would be. She only thought of the words Mother told her every day when she brought the breakfast tray. *Soon this will all be over.*

There was one night, though, that Hannah lay in bed watching the skin of her stretched stomach. Something knotted up. A tiny hill upon the mountain of her middle. She guessed a knee. Maybe a foot or hand. "I'm not better than the ocean," she whispered. "Maybe you can be."

That was the first time she thought of keeping it. She didn't know how to be a mother. How to teach modesty and all the other things she failed. She only sensed that a growing baby was something very close to holy. Despite her own filth, a promise bloomed within.

"Father," she whispered in the dark of night. "Come to the water."

It was freezing that night. Little bits of icy rain falling around them. But she was always hot, with the weight, with the memories.

"What?" he asked, his eyes shifting around the night sky, scared to look at her.

"I want to keep it."

"What?"

"I want to keep it."

"You're not married."

"I want this baby."

He shook his head sadly. Pulled her as close as he could get her to his chest. He sobbed.

"It would be selfish."

"Why?"

"I know it's been hard to grow up the way you have, but if this baby is a girl, can you imagine how much harder her life would be? Being raised by an unwed mother and still having to wear skirts to the floor and a noose of hair around her neck? She would be an outcast."

"I'll leave the church," Hannah sobbed. "I'd even let her wear pants."

Hannah cried as Father whispered "I'm sorry" over and over in her ear. And she cried more when he told her about the wonderful family Mother had found. A woman, married for fifteen years, with no children of her own. A preacher's wife that had prayed for years for a child just like the one within Hannah.

"When we get back home," he said, "nobody will know. Mother's already talked to that lady you used to work for. She's agreed to help deliver you, off record. And the barren woman will say it's hers. A few more weeks and you'll be home again. It will be like this never happened."

Exhausted, Hannah could only nod. But the next night she woke Mother.

"Come swimming. No one will see us."

"Have you lost your mind? It's the middle of the night. It's not even summer."

"You've never been, have you? If you could just feel it, Mother, feel the water everywhere that your clothes should be. It's so special. I want to share it with you. I want to share it with my baby."

"It's not your baby," Mother hissed.

Hannah went alone. Stripped her clothes off by the dunes in the middle of the night. The cold bit her skin as she pushed her body into the water. Her balance was thrown off by her new shape, and the waves tossed her playfully. The burn of the cold soon eased into a sweet numb that made her feel sleepy. The baby moved. And Hannah smiled sadly.

"I've had this much at least," she whispered.

Her body felt more weightless than it had in months. The bright moonlight bounced off the skin of her stomach. Someone yelled, but she ignored it, and let her mind go as numb as her body.

Someone else was in the water. Grabbing her, dragging her to shore. Her heaviness returned, and she felt the struggle of someone working hard to pull her to the dunes. Blankets were wrapped around her naked body. Arms wrapped around the blankets. Hannah looked up to see Bethie crying over her.

The next day, dark clouds rolled over the ocean and hovered over the coast. A storm settled in, more dense and dark than any spring storm a local could remember. Hannah looked out her window and saw the marsh water rising nearly to the back porch. It made her feel caged, all that water coming up to the back door and her knowing that on the other side lay the ocean.

Early that night, pains began. And though she cried with fear, Mother smiled and even laughed sweetly. "It's almost over, daughter. We'll be home soon."

Father set out in the storm. His car plowed through deep puddles and violent winds. By the time he returned, the house was beginning to shake. Hannah heard old wooden boards groan with the heavy effort of staying put.

She screamed when the pains came. And she screamed again when the window above her broke. But the water felt good. The rain streamed over her bed like a cool baptism.

Cora was there. Lifting her legs and mumbling instructions. She said something to Hannah. Words of encouragement or faith. And then her tongue lit up with fire and she shouted to the heavens. Hannah screamed, too, but never stopped listening to that sweet mystery language. Through every broken syllable, every nonsense word, Hannah heard only this: *You poor baby girl.*

And then the storm inside her body stopped. "A beautiful baby girl," Cora announced. She laid her across Hannah's chest. For one tiny moment, Hannah's baby was all hers.

"You," Hannah whispered to her baby, even as Mother stepped forward. "Better than the ocean. As close to holy as I'll ever get."

III

Three days after she gave birth, Father carried Hannah to the car. Bethie rode up front, in between Mother and Father. Hannah was too weak to sit up. She lay down in the back and watched the clouds pass by above her. She wanted to sleep. She wanted to die. But neither seemed easy enough.

Crossing the state border hurt worse than the birth. Carolina held everything. The ocean with its low tides. Her first love. Her daughter. She screamed so that Father broke out in a sweat, Bethie sobbed, and Mother yelled, "Get control of yourself!"

"Keep going," Mother insisted, when Father hinted at stopping to rest. "She needs to get home."

Mother turned to Hannah. "You've answered all their prayers. For years that woman has begged God for a baby. Your sacrifice made it possible. You should be so proud."

"What of mine?" Hannah moaned.

"Your what?"

"My prayers."

Late in the evening, Father pulled over at a hotel, even though Mother wanted to drive through the night. They fell asleep quickly. Father in a recliner. Hannah in one bed. Mother and Bethie in the other. Everyone woke up feeling better, refreshed in the morning. Eager to put the past behind them. To start again, new and clean.

Except for Hannah. The sheets around her were wet with blood. Her eyes wouldn't stay open for more than a moment at a time. Her skin was damp and cold.

"We've got to take her to a hospital," Father cried.

"No," Mother whispered. "No, there can never be a record. We promised…"

"But she will die!"

"And she'll die if there is a record."

Father ran from the room, but returned quickly with a doctor carrying a black bag. Hannah never remembered the exam or what the doctor said was wrong. She only remembered how Father handed him a stack of cash.

They stayed in the hotel for two weeks. The doctor came

back to check on her and Mother handed him cash every day. Hannah swallowed handfuls of pills. And when she could finally hold her eyes open, she looked out the window next to her bed. She saw mountains.

She had passed through them before, but they were always a part of the journey. One more thing to hurry and get through. She'd never paused long enough to feel them, how heavy they could seem, especially lying sick in bed and looking up.

"These are the Appalachians," Mother whispered when she saw Hannah's opened eyes. "Some of the oldest mountains in the world."

Hannah didn't speak.

"Think of all the history this land has seen. Think of the families that have found protection here. From wars. Famines. From sin."

Mother walked over to the window and pulled the curtain back so Hannah could see more. "Look how high they rise. Like Jacob's ladder."

"When are we leaving?" Hannah whispered.

Mother shrugged her shoulders. "Maybe we won't." She kept her back turned as she spoke. She stared at the mountains so that Hannah wouldn't see the fear that had gripped her. Over how easy it was for her daughter to fall prey to the world.

Mother and Father were scared. And every scared person needs a place to hide. The mountains were perfect. Not just because of the land. How the clouds settled over the top, or how sometimes the trees grew so thick they hid the sky. But because of the people, too. If ever there was a place where people liked to keep to their own, it was the mountains. Neighbors could live within walking distance for years, but never know each other existed.

"What about our home?" Hannah whispered.

"All we need is each other. All we need is a chance to make a fresh start. We don't need a brick house. We don't need a fancy neighborhood."

They built a fortress. It was the first step in Mother's plan. If the gated neighborhood up north had failed to keep them safe, then surely a castle on top of a mountain would.

Mother returned to her sewing. But soon, her daughters had enough clothes. Her husband had enough socks. And there was so much time to think. About babies, and how busy they can keep you. About babies, and how much sewing a new one requires.

There was plenty of time, too, for Mother to notice Hannah. How despite the new home, despite the return of her girlish shape, Mother's promise had not come true. Hannah was not the same as she had been before.

Mother wanted a distraction. Something that would absorb her family, keep them busy, and protect them from their secret memories. She convinced her husband to draw up plans for a major home expansion. She opened up the kitchen. Added a Great Room. Took down a wall and built two new wings of bedrooms. She called the tourism board and listed their address as a mountain retreat. Then she visited shelters. Street corners. Church charity closets. Anyplace where she could find desperate people. She lured them to her home with promises of work, food, and shelter.

Through it all, Father remained in his study. He focused on his drawings. New and complex designs that he mailed away to patent attorneys and sold for crisp checks with large numbers typed across them. When his trembling hands made new drawings difficult, he finally went to the doctor. He accepted the sentence of Parkinson's. Returned to the chair in his study and passed his days in silent thought.

But for Hannah, at least, Mother's plan seemed to work. She settled into her new routine and stretched herself toward a whole new level of piety. She stared at the bridge hanging in Father's study until she felt it rise within her. Until it was the very bones that held her up. She spent her days tending guests and mumbling old prayers from her childhood. She quit the color yellow. She decided there was something redeeming about the colors gray and black. She hated the golden halo of her hair. She worked hard every morning to pull it back tightly. She watched closely as Mother taught her how to tie on a proper head covering.

This new submission, this new zeal from Hannah, was a victory for Mother. But there was one detail of the plan still missing. Hannah was isolated, just like she had been when she was three years old. Her modesty set her apart even from Bethie, who would never cover her head and was looking more and more like just another mountain hippie with every week that passed. She wore chunky knit purple sweaters, and patchwork scarves that she sewed together and then draped around her waist. Her hair was still long, but loose now, or with just one small section braided.

Mother heard the guests whisper about Hannah. About how odd it was for such a young and pretty girl to dress so plainly, so severe. Mother ordered a new dress code for all female hotel staff. It included long black skirts and gray tunics. Aprons and head coverings. Soon Hannah was surrounded by a dozen polyester twins.

Hannah may have blended in, but there were some things that polyester twins couldn't fix. Like the crying. At night, she

woke to the sound of babies. Sometimes it was just her. She'd
wake herself up screaming into her pillow. But other times, it
wasn't. She'd sit straight up in bed and listen, as she went over
and over each guest who was staying at the hotel.

It was Hannah's job to check them in. It was her job to
notify the workmen when a guest requested a crib or a cradle.
If she woke up to the noise and remembered a baby, she'd lay
down and sleep again. But if she couldn't, if she knew there
were no babies on Bedroom Hall, then she'd dress quickly and
step out of her room. Usually, all that met her was the silent
hum of a sleeping hotel. The quiet kitchen crew getting an
early start on the workers' breakfast. The sound of heat or cool
air being pumped into the building. But sometimes, she'd hear
the cry again. She'd hurry downstairs. Run through the Great
Room to the front porch. She'd listen and know: *Somewhere*
there's a baby. She'd run through the woods until she came
to the edge of the mountain. The sun would start to rise, and
she would see all the land that stretched for hundreds of miles
below her. She'd realize there was a whole world living and
growing. It seemed a brand-new discovery each time: a whole
big world carrying on without her.

It was Father who brought up school. Not *college* like before.
But there was a little school, down the mountain. It offered
courses like pottery and watercolors. Some business and tech-
nology classes, too. Mother didn't approve. If it was up to her,
she'd never send her daughters out into the world again.

"Remember," Father told her. "When you first convinced me
to turn this into a hotel. You said they'd never marry. Not with
Bethie unable to talk. Not with Hannah, now that she's..."
He shook his head. "Your point was that they would have to
take care of themselves. I agreed. I wrote the check that built

this place. Don't you think once we're gone, it'd help if they had a bit more education? They'll have to compete with the rest of the tourism industry. Who knows what that will be like in thirty years?"

Hannah was signed up for Business Administration 101. And when Father picked her up after her first class, he showed her a surprise in the trunk of his car. It was the green bike, straight out of Carolina.

"I sent for it by mail," he said. "I remembered how you loved it before. I thought now that you're starting to get out of the house, you might want to explore."

Hannah thanked him, but she never used it. She was scared of what she might find. Of all the things that lay at the end of gravel roads. She was pained by the color green. The shade that first wrapped the baby. The baby Mother said was never hers. The baby that everyone, but her, seemed to have forgotten.

If only I could, Hannah thought sometimes. If only she could forget the sound of her first cry, the quick rise and fall of her little chest as she sucked in air. If only Hannah could forget how full she felt as she held her. How empty she felt as Mother walked away.

The pain was distracting. The memory was crippling. Hannah earned a C minus in her business class. The only reason she didn't fail was that her small school needed all the tuition money it could bring in. Teachers didn't give Ds or Fs, simply because parents didn't like to pay for failing grades.

"Try pottery," Father said. "You've been out of school for a while. It takes time to remember how to think academically. Try art instead."

Hannah did, and she fell in love again. It was the mud

that she found irresistible. That something could start out dirty. And with enough pressure, with enough force, change. Become *something*. Maybe not pretty, because that word scared her. She'd stare at her creations—vases, bowls, a little dish for Father to store paper clips in—and she'd see *value*.

Everyone noticed the difference in Hannah. How she came home from her pottery classes shining, so close to the way she used to look. Father wrote another check and had a potter's workroom built for her at the end of the hotel. Sometimes Hannah wouldn't go to bed; she'd spend the night pounding her fists against mud. In the morning, Bethie would go to the workroom while Hannah slept. She'd carry out any vases, bowls, or jugs and proudly show them to Mother and Father. Over breakfast, everyone would talk about the miracle of it. How all this time, Hannah was an artist. All this time Hannah had a gift. And if she hadn't taken that one little class, if they hadn't stayed on the mountain, they would have never known.

While Mother and Father were admiring Hannah's art with the guests, Bethie would sneak back to the workroom and take the babies. Dozens of little muddy dolls with blank clay faces that Hannah formed during the night. They were laid in a shallow bowl that was in the shape of a loose rectangle. Mother admired that bowl often, said it looked like an antique dough tray. The kind made of wood and used long ago for kneading.

Only Hannah and Bethie knew the truth about that bowl. How it really was a cradle. Only Hannah and Bethie knew that the plates and vases were just afterthoughts.

Because, finally, Hannah had a way to pretend she was full again. There was a way to imagine the rise and fall of tiny little lungs, breathing for the first time. All she needed was found in the mud. Perfect little clay babies.

IV

Hannah repeated the basic pottery class over and over, so that she could watch other people pound the clay and watch strangers respond to her creations. The teacher took an interest in her. Called her an artist instead of a student. Gave her a set of paints and encouraged her to embellish her dried pottery.

Hannah returned to her old pieces, the ones scattered around the mountain hotel home, and began to paint them. Guests frequently would gather at the door of the workroom to watch her. She had a messy technique that splashed colors dizzily across the clay, across her apron.

Mother stood with the guests and watched. It made her uneasy. All those blurry images. All those clashing colors. She stared at the paintings on the pots, and felt the same way she did the first time Bethie signed to her. There was a message hidden there. A warning of some kind. One that she would never understand.

"I'd love a pot with flowers," she said to Hannah. "Imagine a nice vase, painted with mountain wildflowers and filled with them, too."

Hannah said yes, but she never painted the flowers. Instead she painted swirls in clashing shades and waves. Mother thanked her, pretended she could see mountain wildflowers somewhere in the picture. Hannah's teacher called the technique Hannah's Mist. It was the best description anyone had given that cloudy design, that reckless mixing of odd colors. People were drawn to it. They would turn each piece over and over, convinced that *somewhere* hid a purposeful design.

"Is something there?" a guest would sometimes ask. "The way these colors meet here...it's almost as if you were drawing something...but I can't quite tell what..."

Hannah always shrugged her shoulders. But her eyes would rest against the piece and stare at all the colors. There was the golden of a Carolina sunrise. The green ripple of a baby blanket. The pink skin of a screaming newborn.

"You should sell them at the artisan's fair," her teacher encouraged her. "Your pieces are quite striking."

Father thought the idea was wonderful. He rented her a little booth and bought her shelves to display her work. She sold several pieces those first few months and took a few special orders. Over time, she became a local celebrity. People started coming to the fair just to stop and look at Hannah's table.

It was something new for Hannah, to be known and celebrated instead of mocked. For the first time in her life, looking different, being different, was a part of what made her successful. People didn't just talk about the pottery, they talked about *that long-haired Amish-looking girl with the pretty pots.* The long hair, the long black skirt, the sad eyes, the headcap, all of it worked together with her pottery. All of it fit the image of what people expected, of what people wanted to see in the rare *true artist.*

Hannah's family soon learned something new about mountain people. Though they keep to their own, they are also fiercely proud when one among them does something remarkable. They ignored her Yankee tongue and adopted her as a true Appalachian. Her work became something to collect. Conference room tables at all the best businesses in town displayed a piece of Hannah's Mist, often filled with ripening fruit. Housewives placed her work across their fireplace mantels. Brides-to-be who were in the know always registered for at least one piece of Hannah's pottery.

Hannah was financially independent. She stayed with her parents, not because she had to but because she couldn't think of anywhere else she would have liked to go. Her parents celebrated her success. Just as they had indulged her love for tea sets when she was a baby, they indulged her pottery. They called her gifted and blessed. When they went to bed at night, both of them knowing that Hannah was still working feverishly in the workroom, they smiled at each other with new peace. "It's going to be okay," Father whispered. Mother nodded. "Yes. It's all going to be okay."

And then Hannah met Daniel. The first day he saw her, she was running late. A lady had placed a special order for a set of twelve dinner plates. The agreed exchange time was Friday afternoon at three. Hannah had worked late into the night every day that week. As the sun rose on Friday, she fell asleep. When she woke up it was two thirty in the afternoon.

She jumped to her feet and carefully packaged each plate, wrapping them individually before boxing them up. She ran down the steps and cried out for the hotel driver to come quickly.

She was out of breath, running through the fair with her arms full of pottery. Her headcap was off, her hair was unbound. Golden chaos spilled all around her. Her hands were covered with mud. Green paint was smeared across her chin. She still wore her pottery apron. Once white, it was now covered with its own mist. A wild rainbow of colors that suited her better than anything she'd ever worn.

She came to her booth. Dropped the box gently on the table.

Daniel walked over, peeked inside the box.

"New pieces?"

She nodded.

"Can I look?"

"They're already sold."

He laughed. "But can I look?"

She shrugged her shoulders and he opened the box. Unwrapped a plate and held it up next to her.

"I get it," he said, as he glanced at her paint-covered apron. "It's you." He looked at the other pieces on the shelf, then back at Hannah. "You're the picture hiding in this paint."

He had come to the fair because it was his mother's birthday. He had no idea what to buy her, but he knew that his law partners often bought their wives things from the artisan's fair. He had seen Hannah's pieces brought into work. Secretaries wrapped them carefully for the partners' wives. They all turned the pieces over and over, studying the designs. Like looking for pictures in the clouds.

He bought his mother a vase that day. And she loved it so much it gave him a reason to return. Over the next year, for every holiday, every birthday, Daniel went only to Hannah. He was her best customer.

"Can you do something just in blue?" he'd ask. "Nothing else, just blue."

She'd always say yes and take the order. But when it was time to deliver the piece she'd hand over something different. It would have started out blue and only blue. But by the time she finished there would always be an edge of green. A touch of gold.

"It didn't look right otherwise," she'd apologize. "I understand if you don't want it."

"No, it's perfect."

One day he asked to see her gallery. "It's my parents' fortieth wedding anniversary and I'd like something special. Like I've never bought before."

"I don't have a gallery."

"Is there a place you store your work? A place where maybe you keep back pieces that you like for yourself?"

"That'd just be my home."

"Great," he said. "When can I come?"

V

"Welcome," Mother said, standing behind the front desk. "Reservation name, please?"

"No ma'am, I'm here to see Hannah Reynolds."

"What?"

"The artist? She rents a room here. Or maybe..." Daniel paused as his eyes searched the old woman.

"One moment, please," Mother whispered. She turned around, pretended to look through paperwork, and fought the urge to raise her hands in blank surprise. *There was a man.* And he was all grown up. Wearing gray corduroys and a thermal shirt. With a bit of stubble for a beard. He had called her *ma'am.* He had asked for *Hannah.*

Another woman walked up to the front desk. "Mrs. Reynolds, the guests in room three are requesting the off-season discount. They said it was guaranteed at reservation time, but didn't show up on their receipt."

"Mrs. Reynolds? You're Hannah's mother?" he asked.

Mother turned around. "Yes."

He reached his hand out to greet her. The surprise of it all made her hesitate for an awkward moment, until she put her hand in his.

"I'm Daniel Phillips. A friend of your daughter's."

"Nice to meet you." She motioned for Tabby across the room and waited for her to join them. "Tabby, if you'll please show Mr. Phillips to the Great Room and offer him tea and coffee service. I'll try and locate Hannah." She watched him walk away with her sharp, busy eyes. She searched him out for any evil intentions. She willed that he was good. She willed that he would be careful. *So careful* with her daughter.

Hannah was busy in her workroom. The door was closed, and it was a firm rule of the house that if the door was closed Hannah's privacy was to be respected.

"Hannah," Mother said, as she burst through the door. "A man is here for you."

Hannah blushed and Mother noticed. "No," she whispered. "He's not here for me. He's an art collector. He wanted to see all of the pieces we have here. He's looking for something special." She stood up from where she was working, didn't bother to rinse her hands before she walked toward the door. "Please don't worry. He's not here for me."

"Wait," Mother said. She went to Hannah. Pulled off her headcap, unbound her long braid and smoothed the length of her hair. She twisted fuzzy pieces down around Hannah's face, until the old halo shone again.

"Oh, daughter," Mother whispered lowly, as Hannah left the room, "yes, he is."

Hannah found Daniel in the Great Room. He was standing by the mantel with a piece of her art in his hands. It surprised her. There was a clearly marked plaque on the mantel. *Do not touch the pottery. Thank you for your cooperation. The Reynolds Family.* Mother ordered that plaque after a guest broke one of her favorite vases.

She knew Daniel saw the sign. He was standing right by it. And yet there he stood, holding her vase up to the light, turning it slowly round and round as he studied the paint. Like he already owned it.

"Your mother has something similar to that already," Hannah said.

Daniel turned toward her and nodded. "But I like how you used so much green in this one. It might match my office." Hannah was looking at the vase as he spoke, but Daniel wasn't. He was looking only at Hannah. It was the second time he had seen her with her hair unbound. She was standing in front of the Great Room window, and the last bit of sunset fell over her shoulders. Made her shine.

"Would you like a tour? I could show you the different pieces that decorate the house. There are some bowls across the dining table that might interest you. I made them last year and matched them enough so that they are clearly a set. But I also made certain that each one would always be a bit out of place among the others. I think they are some of my most unusual work, and I haven't ever shown them at the fair or offered them for sale until now."

Hannah was surprised that he shook his head no even as she spoke. She had never wanted to sell those bowls. She could still remember the way the clay felt inside the rim of each one. She could still remember the pictures inside her mind as she painted them. She had worried all night about what she could offer him that would be special enough, unique enough, to justify the trip up the mountain. The bowls were her best pieces.

"I want to see where you work," he said.

"I don't have anything there you'd like. Most of it's unfinished. Much of it I'll destroy before I finish."

He shrugged his shoulders. "I'd still like to see it."

No guest had ever set foot inside the workroom. Hannah locked the room whenever she left and carried the key inside her apron pocket. Daniel noticed the way she was wringing her hands as she held them behind her back. "I'll keep your secrets," he said, and smiled.

She led him up the stairs. Inside the room, Daniel smiled again when he saw all the colors splattered across the floor. Years of mist, layers of drops and mistakes, swirled across stone tile. Hannah watched with interest as he stepped carefully around the swirls of color on the floor. As though even the mistakes, the spilled paint, the dust of old mud, were somehow special.

Daniel looked at the pile of broken pottery. The corner where Hannah would toss a dried piece that didn't satisfy her. He looked at the potter's wheel in the corner. At the large metal box with a three-inch pipe coming out of it. The metal baker shelves, lined with dozens of drying pieces.

"Those are unfinished," Hannah said, when she noticed he was looking at the shelves. "Most of them special orders. Seems all people want these days are plates and sushi sets."

Daniel noticed a piece sitting alone in the corner, near the potter's wheel. It was empty and looked like a tray of sorts. Almost a long rectangle, but with rounded unbalanced edges, and a shallow well in the center. What struck him most about the piece, was that it wasn't painted. It was only covered with a standard glaze. The clay, the shape of it, had to speak for itself.

"Look at this," he said, as he walked over and picked it up. He ran his hands into the well of the center. "What could this be? Why didn't you paint it?"

Hannah was silent.

"It's so different from any of your other work. So…what's the word I'm looking for…so *bare*? What do you use it for? Does it hold supplies or something?"

"No. It's just a piece for me. It reminds my mother of an old dough tray."

"But you didn't let her have it," he said. "You kept it here, instead of giving it to her."

Hannah nodded.

"Because," he continued, "if you give this to her, she'll set it out in the hotel. Place apples in it. Or maybe little tea bags and coffee stirrers. And so you keep it here, empty in the corner. Where no one can see how beautiful it is."

"Yes."

"I want it." He held the tray tightly against his chest. "I'll take the bowls from the dining table for my mother. This one's for me."

"What would you do with it? Perhaps tea bags and coffee stirrers for your office?"

Daniel pressed his hands into the well of the piece and shook his head. "No. You were right to keep it empty. That's where the beauty lies." He looked at her. "Can I have it?"

She nodded, her eyes staring down at the floor. "Yes."

As they left the room, Father was coming down the hall. He stopped to introduce himself. And, since dinner service was beginning soon, invited Daniel to stay.

During dinner, Hannah stared at her plate. When Daniel spoke to her, asked her about the pieces that decorated the buffet table, Hannah whispered replies. But as he talked with Father, she snuck glances. And she couldn't help but like the way he agreed with Father. Liked the outrage they shared over a proposal for a new mountain highway.

"How long have you known Hannah?" Father asked.

"More than a year. My mother collects her art. I do keep a few pieces for myself, though."

"What do you like about her art?" Father asked.

"Henry," Mother whispered, and shook her head. But Daniel smiled.

"Nobody can solve it. None of us can ever know what she was thinking when she made it. When you look at most art, you can usually guess the artist's thoughts. Perhaps just by the color choice, or the choice of shape. But with Hannah's art, especially pieces like this," he said, as he held up the cradle, "all we can know is that there is something vaguely familiar about it. Somewhere there in the shape of the mud. Somewhere in the confusion of the color. It's like looking at one of my dreams. Everything seems familiar, but still so far away."

Hannah watched Daniel carry her cradle out the door. Watched as he put it on the seat next to him. She liked that he didn't put it inside his trunk.

"We all like him," Bethie signed.

Hannah shrugged her shoulders.

"Maybe he'll come back."

"He won't," Hannah said. "I showed him all my pieces today. There's nothing left for him to see."

"You gave him the cradle."

"Yes," Hannah said, and sighed.

"He'll be back."

Two weeks later, Bethie's promise came true. Daniel returned without an invitation. He carried a cracked plate from his mother's collection.

"How long will it take to make a new one?" he asked.

"I can throw it tonight, but I'll need to let it shelf-dry before I fire it."

"I want to watch."

"Sometimes I leave the door open so the guests can watch. Mother has set hours for that. Tuesday and Thursday afternoons. Would you like me to wait until then?"

He laughed. "No, I don't want to wait."

"But Mother has a schedule for guests—"

"I'm *your* guest, not hers. And I don't want to stand outside the room, watching with a bunch of . . . of tourists."

Hannah laughed. "You almost said Yankees."

It was the first time he had ever heard her laugh. The sound of it, the effect it had on her sad eyes, amazed him more than her pottery.

They went to the workroom. He walked in after her and closed the door behind them. When she went to grab her apron from a hook near the door, she propped the door about six inches open. "Seems a bit stuffy," she explained. She walked over to a box and began cutting out some clay. "I don't know how to do this. I've never had a guest in here before."

"Just do what you always do, but tell me about it."

Hannah walked over to the metal rectangle that sat on the counter and put the clay inside. "This is a pug mill. It twists the clay together, mixes it, and pulls most of the air from it."

With her back to him, Hannah talked about the different types of clay. How the white clay could be used straight from the box. How she liked to work with different clays at different times, depending on her mood and what she wanted to make. Daniel was surprised at how much she talked, never looking at him, always watching the clay. She said more to him as she worked than she had in the entire time they had known each other.

She took the clay over to a work surface and pushed it down and over. "I'm cow-head wedging," she called out over her shoulder, and laughed again. She held the piece up to him and motioned him over. It was a slightly bumpy, triangular piece. "See the cow head?" she asked. And he nodded as she pointed to different spots on the piece that she thought looked like ears and eyes. "My teacher taught me to look for this shape as I wedge. It means I'm working the clay correctly. Mixing it well."

She shaped the clay into a small loaf. Took a wire and sliced a piece from it, rounded it with her hands. "Now we're ready to throw your mother's plate."

She carried a bucket of water over to the wheel, sat down on a stool, and began slapping the piece of clay from one hand to the other. "Everything here starts as a cylinder. The jugs, the vases, the bowls, the plates." She held the piece of clay in her hands and looked up at him. "And if this clay isn't centered well on the wheel, it won't work. A piece can only be as strong as its center."

She threw the clay firmly onto the wheel. As it began to spin, she dipped one hand into the bucket of water and pressed the other into the clay. She kept adding water with the one hand, and pushing up and down with the other.

"But how do you know," Daniel asked, "if it's centered right?"

"By the rhythm. I feel the spin of the wheel," she said. She put the palms of her hands around the edge of the wheel. "This wheel is centered, and I want my clay to feel the same way. So I feel this wheel, I feel for the rhythm of it. And then I put my hands on the clay and keep working until they match."

Hannah stopped talking then. She was focused on the shape of the clay, on the pattern of her hands. Sometimes she whispered things. About how she wanted the clay a bit thinner. Sometimes she told the clay what it was, or what it should be. "You are a plate," she whispered.

Daniel watched her face as much as he watched the clay. She was so easy to read, so open before her work. He saw her love for the clay. He felt her desire to see it beautiful. He wondered about the gentle sadness that veiled her eyes.

When she was finished, she felt awkward, embarrassed. It was just occurring to her that she had worked before a close audience. Instead of one fenced safely in the hall. It felt odd to be so visible, after so many years. She had grown used to hiding on that mountain. She had grown comfortable in her somber polyester. But as she stared at the formed plate on the wheel, and thought of how long he had watched her while she was unaware, she couldn't help but remember. All those nights of washing steam buckets, that long canvas apron hiding her CSM T-shirt. All those times she turned around to see Sam staring at her while she worked.

And now there was another. Standing across from her, watching her blush as she mumbled an explanation of the drying process. Even as she spoke, she wondered for the first time in years whether or not she was pretty. A part of her, the older and wiser part, hoped that she wasn't. But there was still something left behind from the girl she used to be, that bicycling James Island Holy Roller.

"Thank you," Daniel said, after she told him when he could pick the plate up. "I'll see myself out while you finish up." He walked through the door, and Hannah couldn't resist the urge to call him back.

"Wait."

He turned toward her.

"Does your mother want it glazed simply, the same as the original?"

He stared at her and nodded slowly, his arms crossed in front of his chest. "I wish for once you'd paint to order."

"Why? She wants something different?"

"I do," he said, as he turned to leave. "I want you to paint yourself. Just as you are now, across that plate."

After he left, Hannah went to Bethie's room, where there was a mirror. She saw the mud smeared from her hands to her elbows. The bit of mud smeared across her neck. She saw her forehead, damp with sweat from the effort of her work. She saw her hair twisting into golden fuzz around her face.

She repeated his words. "Just as you are now." It wasn't a common gift. Like a smooth line about sweet corn. Or like an arrogant, casual touch. Daniel made *her* the compliment. She alone was the pretty thing. Just as she was.

VI

Hannah made another plate. When it was ready, she dragged the mirror from Bethie's bedroom into her workroom. She stood in front of it and studied herself, as her hand began to reach for paints.

She grabbed gold for the stubborn halo she saw. Black for the polyester. White for her skin. Brown for the mud on her hands. Green for her memories. And blue for the haints that always seemed to be looking over her shoulder.

And then she painted to order, for the very first time. When she was finished, she held up the plate and saw herself. All the things that make a portrait—eyes, lips, mouth, and hair—none of it was distinct. Instead, she relied on colors and their location. The gold covered the full-circle edge of the plate, for her hair was long and overwhelming. The blue splashed randomly across the surface, for no one knows where haints come from or where they go. She traced a silhouette, complete with the flowing drape of long polyester in wispy lines of black. And then she added green. A perfect circle of green, right in the center of the plate, right in the heart of the black silhouette.

When it was dry, she wrapped it together with the plate for Daniel's mother. She wondered what Daniel would think when he saw it. Would he know it was her? Would he care?

Hannah had the hotel driver deliver the plates to Daniel's office at the arranged time. And then she waited. When Mother came that evening to tell her Daniel was in the lobby, she felt victorious. She had painted to order. It had brought him back.

It's enough, Hannah warned herself. It was time to end the game, especially since she was winning. Especially before he hurt her.

"Tell him I'm too busy," Hannah said to Mother. "He doesn't have an appointment, and I have no pieces ready for him yet."

"What are you doing?" Mother demanded.

"Finishing this order. And then I have two new sushi sets to make. Sushi, can you believe it?"

"Hurry and dress yourself. I'll have Tabby press a new sweater while you wash up. Daniel is waiting."

"Tell him to leave."

Mother's eyes narrowed, she held her hands out palms up. "But he is your chance, Hannah. Your only one. You are grown up now. Others may not come. He is a decent man and he's taken an interest in you—"

"But I'm not."

"You're not interested?"

"*Decent.*"

Hannah turned her back, so Mother couldn't see her face. How it twisted into something painful and wounded. They hadn't spoken of it in so many years.

Mother walked to her, placed her hand gently on Hannah's back. "He will never know, Hannah," she whispered. "You shouldn't think of it, not even once. I worked hard for you, daughter, to make it as though it never happened."

"But I do," Hannah said, choking back her sobs. "Think of it. All the time. Don't you?"

"Even if I did, I wouldn't let my heart be blind to new blessings. Don't refuse the second chance God has offered you. Now go to him. Groom yourself and then go to him."

Hannah sighed. "Send him here." She brought her hands to her face and smeared a bit of mud across her chin. "He likes me best this way. Send him here."

That night Hannah taught Daniel how to wedge clay into a cow head. And Daniel taught her how to be alone with him, talk with him, and feel almost comfortable. She was still afraid, of course. Of him, and the pain he could cause her. The lies he could tell. She was afraid of his happiness, and that he knew how to find it on his own. She was afraid of the bridge she had built inside her. And how shaky it seemed whenever he was around.

Slowly, carefully, something began to bloom on the mountain. Mother started sewing soft yellow sweaters. She hid the headcaps that Hannah had grown fond of. Bethie made sure to fill all the vases around their home with flowers. She tied Hannah's hair back with one of her patchwork sashes. And Father, more exhausted and shaky with every day that passed, managed to leave his study whenever Daniel came to visit. Hannah watched them sit together on the porch and talk of ordinary things. Like weather and politics. She thought of Sam, and how Father liked everyone. How he would have liked Sam, too.

Hannah was careful. A true, deep water Yank. She stayed on the mountaintop. She made Daniel come to her. She ignored the invitation that came in the mail to an office party at his firm. She ignored the messages he left at the front desk for her during the morning, asking if she wanted to meet him in town for lunch.

But Daniel kept showing up in the Great Room. Mother came to him once, determined to protect Hannah. Determined to thoroughly sound out his intentions. She pulled him into the library, and bluntly asked him why.

"I'm here to see Hannah, of course."

"But why do you keep coming back? Your art collection is full, I'm sure."

"No, there's one piece left I must collect." He looked her squarely in the eyes. He was one of the few, one of the only, that could do it without having to look away.

"But you're one of the most successful bachelors in town. You could have any other woman. A modern, beautiful woman. So I have to wonder, why on earth do you want my Hannah?" He shook his head as he turned to go. "How could you not know?" he asked. "She's been yours all this time. How could you ever wonder?"

Wonder. It was the same word that came to him, whenever he thought of Hannah. After the other women in his life that had come and gone, Hannah seemed like a new creature altogether. Like a beautiful secret waiting to be revealed. She made him believe that he would never grow bored of her. That he could never fully understand her. He hadn't so much as seen her naked ankle, and yet when he looked at her before that potter's wheel, whispering gentle words to her clay, she took his breath. This thought of her, the mystery of her, interrupted his thoughts, his work, his peace. He only had to close his eyes to see her and be filled with wonder.

He had touched her, only once. They were walking toward the front door to sit on the porch. She reached for the doorknob and so did he. He let his hand fall over hers. She jumped, pulled her hand back as though he hurt her.

"Sorry," he said quickly, as he pushed the door open.

He was old enough, perceptive enough, to see the challenge of loving her. And to enjoy it. He kept his distance, and whenever doubt crept upon him he remembered the plate. She had painted to order for him. He was the first. He was the only.

"Come to dinner with me," he said one evening. "In town. My mother could join us. She thinks you're quite the celebrity."

"No," Hannah said. "I have too many orders to work on. Let's just eat with the guests. Shari is making lasagna tonight."

"But we always eat here. Besides, there's a new gallery opening about twenty minutes away. A painter. I thought you'd enjoy—"

Hannah shook her head. "Please don't."

"Why?"

"I don't want to leave this mountaintop. I don't want dinner out. I don't want to see a new gallery. And I don't want to meet your mother."

"What are we, Hannah?" he asked calmly. "I keep coming here. I can't make myself stay away, but I don't know if you want me to come or not. I have no idea what we are supposed to be."

"That's what you like best," Hannah said lowly. "Remember? *Nobody can solve it.* That's what you told my father you liked."

"About your *art*."

Hannah sighed. "There's no difference between me and my art."

"That's fine. I think I've made it clear that I *love* your art."

Hannah turned to walk away, the bridge within her swaying wildly. "You need to leave now," she said coolly. She went to her workroom, but the clay wouldn't do what she told it to. She threw it to the floor and went to her bedroom.

Mother came to her. "What's wrong?"

"He wants to take me off the mountain."

"Of course he does."

"I can't."

"Why not?"

"It's not safe. Besides, I can't meet his mother. She'll see right through me."

"Nonsense. You're surrounded by guests and workers, and none of them have guessed."

"But her son likes me, so she'll study me closely."

"Is that all? Just likes?"

Hannah shook her head. "He thinks he loves me. But he doesn't know me."

"And how do you feel?"

"Like a liar. Sometimes I want to tell him. Just so he'll be warned and know to escape."

"There's no reason to tell him. But even if you did, what happened was so long ago. You were young, and you made the same mistake that many young people do. The only difference is you got caught. I doubt your past would matter to Daniel nearly as much as you think."

"Then I would hate him."

"Why would you say such a thing?"

"Because it matters, Mother. *It matters.*"

"Why can't you just allow yourself to be happy? This man is my promise to you come true. Maybe we can all finally have peace together."

"Oh no, not together," Hannah whispered bitterly, as her voice broke. "Somewhere there's a baby."

"Shhhh, not a baby. Somewhere there's a girl that is happy. Somewhere there's a girl that is loved. She's growing up and moving forward. She's having a *wonderful* life. Why can't you do the same? Go to him at his office tomorrow. Tell Daniel you were wrong. Tell him you want to meet his mother. Show him that you are willing to be loved."

"Once," Hannah whispered. "Back when I used to think that Sam and I would be together forever, I wrote him a letter and told him I wanted him to meet Father. He wrote me back, 'Relax, Yank.'"

Mother laughed dryly. "Daniel is no Sam."

"You wouldn't know."

"Oh, but daughter, I do."

Hannah sat up in bed. Mother nodded slowly. "Yes, I met him once. He was so defensive. 'I'm just a kid,' he kept saying. Like that excused him from everything. He never once looked me in the eye."

"But why did you go to him? Because Father suggested we marry?"

"Because we needed to find you. When you didn't return after a week like you were supposed to, Father went to your school demanding answers. He explained to them how you were attending the senior college tour. He wanted to know what the delay was, and when you would return. When they told him there was no such trip, he refused to believe it. Nobody could convince him that you had lied. When a secretary suggested he contact the police and file a runaway report, he jumped across the desk at her screaming, 'My daughter is not a runaway!' The only way they could get him to leave was to call the police on him."

"I wasn't a runaway," Hannah said lowly. "I meant to return, until I found out..."

Mother shrugged her shoulders. "Doesn't matter what you *meant*, Hannah; we imagined the worst. We knew, just knew, that someone had lured you with a fake trip. We called the police and told them about the college trip that you had believed you were going on. The trip that someone had set up and tricked you into so that they could lure you away from any protection. To do Lord knows what to you. They believed us at first. They searched records at the bus station. They ran your picture in the paper under the headline *Have You Seen This Girl?* They interviewed dozens of kids at your school.

They focused on a certain group. I never knew of them until those police interviews. Kids that chased you and Bethie to the buses every day. Called you Polyester Pollys?"

Hannah nodded.

"Why didn't you tell us?"

"You should've known," Hannah said.

"We knew there was teasing. But that you and Bethie had to hide in the janitor's closet to escape them? That they threw cups of Kool-Aid at you? When I read those reports, I started to wonder. Maybe you really were a runaway. And then the police brought me copies of the bus schedules. Told me to review them to see if there were any locations that we had family or friends that you might go to. There was only one thing that caught my eye. A tour of the Atlantic coast. Beginning in South Carolina and working its way back up through North Carolina and Virginia. It left the same day you had. It all made sense then. You were happier on James Island than I ever remembered. With your job and that green bike."

"So how did you find him?"

"We went straight to that little place you used to work. The steampot place. I found your old boss and asked her if she had seen you. She told me how you had stayed with her when there was too much company at our home on the marsh. She said she thought I knew, thought I had sent you. That's when it all started to unravel. She was hesitant to talk to me. I could tell she didn't like me one bit. Didn't respect me, or our ways."

"She just sees things differently."

"I begged her as a mother to help me find you. I told her I knew you were in danger. *I knew it.* And begged for any way that she could help me find you. She wrote something down on a piece of paper, and then looked me in the eye. 'Your daughter is a good girl,' she said. 'But she's a baby yet, and when you find her, for once in your life, you treat that child like the baby she is. You hold her. You comfort her. She done got her heart broke for the first time. For once in your life, be the momma she needs.'"

Mother covered her mouth with her hands and shook her head. "I went crazy that day. I could've been arrested, too. I took the paper from her hand and then I slapped her as hard as I could. Father had to drag me away, and she followed, yelling, 'Lady, I forgive you already. 'Cause there's a hurt comin' your way that's a world darker than any hurt you just gave me.'"

"A prophet," Hannah said.

"Perhaps. But she loved you. That's why she agreed to help you later. She hated me, blamed me, but she loved you."

"What did her paper say?"

"*Go see Sam*," Mother whispered. "A part of me knew exactly what trouble you were in. Such awful words for a mother to read. *Go see Sam*." Mother shook her head and laughed softly. "Of course your father was still expecting the best. Cora gave him Sam's mailing address, and the whole drive to Columbia he spoke of how maybe you had gotten another job. Maybe Sam was your new employer. Maybe you were just out in search of new adventures, tired of your academic routine. But then we found Sam. So young and already with that unmistakable mark of rebellion in his eyes. It was clear to us both then, Sam was something altogether different than a green bike or a new job. Altogether more dangerous."

"He wasn't so different from me, Mother. It took us both to make that choice."

Mother leaned closer, stared hard into Hannah's eyes. "I know about the promise. Such lies he told you."

Hannah shook her head. "He never promised me anything."

"A house. He promised you a house, and with a house comes a life. That's why you ran to it. That big rotting house. That place you lived in, filthy and alone, like an animal, for weeks. Father could never understand it, but I know why you ran there. It was all you had left, wasn't it? After Sam had taken everything else."

"He was just a boy," Hannah whispered. "And he wasn't raised to believe like I was. I should have been stronger. You'd spent so many years teaching me to be stronger. But when it really mattered, I wasn't. I was the same as him. I was as weak as him."

"No child, you are not the same. You loved him. And he didn't even want to help us find you. We told him you could be hurt. We told him you could be dying. But he kept twisting his hands and denying that he even knew you. Father threatened to call in the police, to name him as a suspect in a missing-person case. That's when Sam started spilling it all, about boats and deep water and Cora's motel. None of it helped, though. None of it returned you to us. Until I interrupted and asked the right question. 'What did you promise her?' He shook his head and swore he'd never even spoke the word *marry*. 'But you still promised something, didn't you?' I demanded. He nodded. 'Just to fix up a house. An old abandoned house.'"

"Did he take you there?" Hannah asked. "Did he see me, the way I was?"

Mother shook her head. "I shoved a pen and paper in his hands and made him write directions. He doesn't even know that we found you. He never bothered to check. We never spoke again."

Hannah looked at Mother's face, and marveled at how easily stone can break. There were deep lines across her forehead, lines around her narrowed eyes and her tightly set mouth. "My, how you hate him."

Mother closed her eyes and bowed her head. She sighed. "He hurt you. But *we* were the ones punished."

"I'm sorry," Hannah whispered.

"If you really are," Mother said, "then you'll stop the punishment. Don't pass it on to Daniel. Let the hurt Sam gave you end with us. Discover the difference between Sam and Daniel, between what you once thought love was and what it could be, what it is."

Hannah lay back against her pillow. Mother leaned and turned off the lamp by her bed. She stood to leave the room.

"He called me pretty," Hannah said.

"What?"

"He gave me more than the promise of the house. He called me pretty, too. And it was a gift that I'd always wanted. I was used to boys laughing at me, chasing me with scissors and trying to cut my hair. Sam was different. He was the only person in my entire life to ever call me pretty. It doesn't matter so much now. But for some reason, at sixteen, it meant everything."

Mother breathed deeply and turned her back to Hannah as she stepped toward the door. She paused with her hand on the doorknob. "He had that much right, I suppose. You are pretty," she said, the words catching in her throat and sounding more like a choke than love.

Hannah closed her eyes and felt the war inside her. Between the pressure to move forward and the desire to savor guilt, and remember the one perfect moment she'd had long ago.

Everything swirled together, like paint on dry clay.

VII

Tucked away inside a sleeping hotel, Hannah spent the night comparing Sam and Daniel. She paid all the attention to detail that any true artist would, and began in the most obvious place. With what she saw.

Sam was an island boy, if only for the summer. His skin was browned, his hair was streaked gold by the sun. He was bare-chested and barefoot as much as not. His body very lean, built of long, thin lines. He wore a hemp-rope necklace. Turquoise beads were strung across it. He was always smiling, showing his perfect rows of teeth. His eyes, she couldn't remember the color. But she remembered their message. He was happy. Easily happy. And she thought him very beautiful.

Daniel was raised on the mountain. He wore hiking boots, even with his work clothes. Unless it was a court day, khakis and polos in the summer or cords and thermals in the winter were as dressed up as he got. His face wasn't browned like Sam's. But by the time Hannah saw him in the evenings, the shadow of his beard was apparent. His body was grown up—his shoulders squared, his arms muscular. There was a thickness to his build that a boy would never have. He shaved his dark hair close to the scalp. A no-frills kind of cut that required no grooming. But it accented the lines of his face. The swift rise of his cheekbones. The brooding that hovered over his brow. He didn't smile easily, like Sam. He saved his smiles and gave them away sparingly. Hannah never thought to call him beautiful. She called him striking. She called him intimidating. She called him strong.

Hannah reached her hand up to her head, felt the rope

of hair beneath her. She thought of all the things she had felt with Sam. Such beauty, such fear, mixed together. Like the feel of his hand reaching out that first time, grabbing a handful of her hair. The feel of the deep water pulling away the polyester from her skin for the very first time. The feel of running and falling through an old cotton field on her way to the mansion that would always belong to them. The feel of his hand reaching out, pulling her to him underneath that old live oak. The feel of an electric fence. The pain. The numb. The rejoicing.

She *hadn't* felt with Daniel. Other than the one time he reached for the doorknob when she had. Their hands had touched, and his had lingered for just a moment over hers before she pulled away in fright. Everything else was a mystery. She had known him now for much longer than she had ever known Sam. And yet, she knew Sam's touch but could only wonder about Daniel's. What his hands might feel like running through her hair. What that shadowy beard might feel like as he pressed his mouth to hers.

Hannah smiled in the dark, remembering what Daniel had said: *I've made it clear that I love your art.* In another time, in another state, love was something to hide. Love was a sloppy heart drawn with a Sharpie across her hand. Love was a fistful of Spanish moss tucked underneath her pillow, crushed into dusty bits as she waited for a letter. Love was pledging herself, all of herself, if only Sam would want her just a little bit. Love was a Greyhound bus ticket, a wannabe teenage bride. Love was a broken heart. A war cry learned one awful night on the dunes of Folly Beach.

Hannah closed her eyes and dared to face the memory of who really pulled her close under a tree on a dead plantation.

He was seventeen years old. Just a boy playing dress-up at his favorite playground. A motherless little boy, playing Confederate hero.

Downstairs the workers were beginning their morning routines. Hannah heard them and went to her wheel. She worked with fresh energy, one hand dipping in water as the other applied a steady pressure. She was making something new, only she wasn't sure what it was yet. She didn't talk to this piece, never told it to be a plate or a vase. She only felt its rhythm, perfectly centered within her hands, as she guided it into an unknown form.

She let the wheel stop and continued to pull out the clay. Until before her sat a sloppy rectangle of sorts, with a well in the center, and low sloped sides. Her mother would have been pleased. Another antique-like dough tray. Perfect for apples and tea bags.

When it was ready, she filled its empty center with paint, nearly every color she had or could mix to create. Only when she stared at the finished piece did she finally speak to it. She gave it the message, the one it was supposed to carry in its center. She spoke of love. No longer satisfied with sloppy hearts, war cries, and fistfuls of moss, she gave love a new name.

"Love is like mud. Only as strong as the shape you give it. Love is like paint. It can color over all the empty places." She whispered lowly, "If you drop it, Love will break you."

When the piece was dry, she placed it in a box. Then she went and dressed herself, found her best yellow blouse. She unbound her hair from its tight braid. Waves, perfect like the ocean, spilled down her back.

The hotel driver dropped her off at Daniel's office downtown. And as she walked into the lobby of his office, she couldn't avoid her fear. What if he didn't want her there? Around his friends and his staff and his clients? What if she was wrong, and he was just like Sam? Wanted to keep their relationship hidden high on the mountain, a new form of deep water?

The receptionist was staring at her hair. She could feel her hands trembling, the tray inside the box she carried began to shake.

"Can I help you?" the lady behind the desk asked.

"I'm here to see Daniel."

"Mr. Phillips?"

"Yes."

"Do you have an appointment?"

"No."

"Is there some type of emergency?"

"No."

"Then we don't accept walk-ins. Mr. Phillips is a very busy man. You'll have to make an appointment. Let me pull his calendar. What type of consultation do you need? A will? Criminal? Custodial?"

"No, ma'am. I'm not a client."

"Well, you still need an appointment."

"Maybe I could wait?" Hannah asked, looking at the couch behind her. She saw a shelf built into the wall above the couch. It was filled with her art.

"Listen, honey," the receptionist said and leaned forward. "I've been here ten years for this reason: Everyone, *everyone*, has got to come through *my* desk to get to Daniel. And unless there's an emergency, like *I just killed somebody and I gotta go tell the cops*, then I don't let anyone by without an appointment. No matter how long they wait. It's what gets me the nice Christmas bonus."

"Oh," Hannah whispered. She started to turn and go, but hated to leave without seeing him. "Do you think, maybe—," she said, and blushed.

"Yes?"

"Can...love be an emergency?"

The receptionist shook her head. "We don't handle domestic cases."

Hannah laid the box on the receptionist's desk. "This is for him."

Outside, she walked up the street and found a pay phone. She called for the hotel driver's return. As she waited, she walked and looked in the windows of the shops. At all the ski gear and hiking tools. At all the sweatshirts and trinkets for tourists to carry home. She walked to the end of the street, to the famous scenic overlook. She followed the path to the end. And, as always when she saw the world below, she wondered at how it all kept going.

"Hannah!" she heard someone call out behind her. "Hannah!"

She smiled, but she didn't answer. She knew he would find her. And this time, with this love, she wanted to be the one sought.

When he took her in his arms she felt his strength surround her. She felt the chill, the one she carried like a trophy inside her heart, start to thaw. She pulled her tired eyes from the world below her, and looked only at him. For the first time, she dared to hope on Mother's promise. Everything, *someday*, might be okay.

"Yes," Daniel laughed softly before he kissed her. "Love is an emergency."

VIII

Hannah's pottery brightened. She chose reds and oranges far more than she used to. Green was rarely the center anymore. Blue was a hazy memory.

She accepted fewer special orders and began creating more things for herself and for Daniel. And even on lonely nights, when she hadn't seen Daniel in days because he was locked away working on a heated trial, she resisted the urge to return to old habits. She did not build clay babies. She did not search the mountain for the crying that sometimes still woke her.

When Daniel asked Father for his blessing to propose, Hannah knew. Even before Daniel had so much as whispered the word *marry* to her. She knew by the joy, the absolute radiance, in Mother's eyes. She knew by the way Father spent more time in the Great Room instead of locked away in his study. She knew by the way Bethie raided Mother's lace collection. She sat gently fingering it and telling Hannah, "You'd be so lovely in this."

Hannah had never thought she'd be *golden* again. She never thought she'd be the one to please her family so well. The one on whom they pinned their pride and staked their hopes. No longer Hannah the Ruined, she was something new. Something altogether lovely. She was Hannah *the Bride*.

Daniel asked her in her workroom. The place where their love first took shape. And when he said it—*Marry me, Hannah*—her past, the ugliness, took on new meaning. Because without the pain of Sam, Hannah wouldn't have found the love of Daniel. And in that moment, when he said those words—*Marry me*—the love was worth the pain. The love was *equal* to the pain.

She spent three months making her own wedding dishes, while Mother sewed her gown. In the end, everything matched. The dishes were simple but perfectly formed. The gown was nearly unadorned but made of the finest white silk and trimmed in handmade lace.

Hannah winced over the white. An old reflex, a habit of savored guilt. Bethie saw and shook her head. "White is for new love. White is for miracles. Like you. Like me, too." Bethie pointed to her own new outfit. A breezy white cotton skirt. A pink T-shirt and sandals. Bethie had replaced her blacks and grays, after her miracle happened. After her tongue finally grew up and she began to talk. Bethie wore rainbow colors. Bethie cut her hair to just at her shoulders and got a job at the hospital downtown. She never wore gray again.

Mother came to her room, just after she had finished dressing for the ceremony. Hannah sat quietly on the bed as Mother kneeled before her and adjusted the lace of her hem.

"You may choose something," Mother said. "It is a wedding-day tradition in our family, passed down from generation to generation. You may choose anything you want from your father's house to take to your new household. Perhaps you want your grandmother's silver tea set?"

"I want the bridge."

"What?"

"The bridge. The one in Father's study, that he drew in college. I want that."

"Really," Mother said with an amused smile.

"You used to make me and Bethie stand with our noses

to it. You pressed our faces against it and told us to pray that the bridge would become a part of us. Hold us up forever and ever."

"You can't have it," Father called from the doorway. "Perhaps you would like the sitting chair from my study. It's nearly one hundred years old."

"Why not the bridge?"

"I don't want your wedding prize to be something untrue."

Mother glared sharply. "Don't start. Not today." She hurried past him, to make sure everything was ready for Hannah's entrance.

"Hannah," Father whispered, as he took her in his arms. "My wedding gift to you is this: There is a bridge. Built *for* us. All along, we were just supposed to walk across."

Hannah noticed how badly Father was shaking, how weak his grip seemed. She led him to the bed and he sat down. She sat down beside him.

He patted her hand. "You're a good girl. Always have been."

Hannah started to cry. "Don't," she whispered.

"We've worn ourselves out," he sighed. "Trying to build our own bridge. Today is your chance, Hannah. There *is* a bridge builder. It's not us."

Mother returned and pulled Hannah to her feet. "It's time."

Hannah looked to Father, panic in her eyes.

He offered his arm to her. "Oh, it's not so hard," he said, and smiled. "The first rule is *Believe*. The second is *Love*."

Hannah stepped outside then, and the rule of Love covered the mountain that day. Mother and Father, the tension that lived between them, melted as they stood together and watched Hannah. She was beautiful. Not just her hair, which radiated the light of the mountain sunset under her long veil. And not just her milky skin, like porcelain, from all the years of hiding behind polyester. But Hannah's face, the happiness that glowed across it, was beautiful.

"We did all right after all," Mother whispered tearfully, as she reached for Father's hand. "It was hard. It was so hard, but just look at her today. She's happy."

Father nodded and wiped the tears from his eyes. "She's going to be okay, in spite of us."

When the minister announced Hannah's new name, when he declared to the family around them that she was Mrs. Daniel Phillips, Hannah stepped out of her old name. She decided that maybe Father was right. Maybe she should try walking, instead of building. Maybe, Mrs. Daniel Phillips could have a good life. A husband. Children.

They spent their honeymoon on the mountain. Daniel had wanted to take her far away, but she begged to stay. More than anything, Hannah told him, she just wanted to be *home* with him. She didn't need to run away to celebrate.

So Daniel took her to his home, a small mountain condo near the ski lodges that overlooked the winter slopes. He held her through the nights while she lay sleeping in his arms. Sometimes he thought of her childhood, the bits and pieces she shared with him. About the dark days, locked within the gated neighborhood. About the horrible days doing the Holy Roller shuffle at school. Sometimes he hated his in-laws for it all. And yet he couldn't deny that it had all worked together somehow to make Hannah. Beautiful, fragile, mysterious

Hannah. Whose eyes had a shadow of sadness pass over them at the most surprising times. Like when he suggested just a weekend at the beach. "You don't have to swim," he told her, when she said she couldn't. "We could just search for seashells. We could just count the waves."

He lay awake and dared to wonder about that shadow that appeared without warning and vanished just as suddenly. Whatever it was, she was his now. And so was that sadness. Maybe she wasn't strong enough to defeat it. But he promised himself—he pledged to his sleeping bride—*he was.*

IX

They bought a house down in the valley, at the end of a long gravel drive and built against the base of the mountain. It looked like a great white ship, one that was about to be swallowed, doomed even, by the green wave swelling behind it.

The first thing Hannah noticed when she saw it was the flowers. So thick she suspected they were more than an ornament. They were a disguise, for age or rot. Hydrangeas, up to her waist, stood shoulder to shoulder around the porch. Jasmine vines twisted messily around the railings, and window boxes overflowed with dizzy rainbows. It was a wild garden, and all of the things that make a home—the walls, the doors, the tire swing out back—seemed to rise by accident.

"What a mess," Daniel said.

"It needs us," Hannah whispered.

It needed their marriage, their love. All the babies they would surely fill it with. It needed them to take it from the sadness of neglect and make it what it was supposed to be. A home. A restored historical mansion.

Daniel bought it for her, even though Mother warned it might be too big, too much work for one woman to manage. The first thing Daniel did was hire a crew to renovate one wing of the house into a workroom for Hannah. She kept up with her art, but there were other things to keep her busy, too. She had her own nest now, and there were weeds to pull, old floors to strip, varnish, and wax. So many errands to run. She spent her afternoons practicing to get her license, driving up and down the long gravel drive.

They agreed to wait a year before starting a family. And as their first anniversary approached, the expectation of it, the significance of it, was heavy on both their minds. Daniel started reviewing his investments. He increased his life insurance policy. Hannah scrubbed and scrubbed their home, and wished she had paid more attention to Mother's knitting lessons.

But on the night of their celebration, Daniel knew they would be okay. He had planned well for them. And Hannah knew that floors would always get dirty again, and that clothes could be bought as well as made.

Their love that night had new meaning. It was more than pleasure. It was creation itself. A promise between them. To fill the rooms in that great empty house. To multiply their love until it surrounded them in the form of little round faces, tricycles, and dimpled knees.

Of course it was supposed to happen at once. That was the way it happened before. *Just once.* But the month passed by. Then two more. Hannah mentioned it to Mother, who reacted calmly. "It took me over twenty years to conceive you. Who are we to rush God's time?"

So Hannah waited. And waited. And then still waited. She

prayed *Please* and begged *Soon* and promised *I'll do anything.*
Daniel tried to ease her worry. He'd run his hand over the skin
of her stomach. "Cheer up, our baby might already be on its
way."

But a year and a half passed, and Hannah was not pregnant. She made a doctor's appointment. Her first exam since
the one in the hotel.

"What happened to you?" the doctor asked after the
exam.

"What?"

"You must have had one of the worst cases of infection I've
ever seen. Was the placenta left inside you? I don't see how you
escaped death."

"I have no idea what you're talking about," Hannah whispered.

"Look, you don't have to tell me," the doctor said kindly,
as he laid his hand on her shoulder. "But whatever happened
to you has left your reproductive organs terribly scarred. I'm
afraid, my dear, you need to explore other options."

"What?" Hannah whispered.

"Adoption. Surrogacy."

"What are you saying?" Hannah choked.

"You will never conceive."

The doctor saw the look on Hannah's face and called for
the nurse. "Bring a Valium!"

Hannah left the doctor's office and drove straight up the
mountain. She collapsed in Mother's arms. "It's because we
sent her away," she cried. "How could I deserve a new one? We
sent her away."

Daniel found her that night. He held her as she told him
pieces of the truth. She had been sick long ago. It had scarred

her organs. She would never conceive. She cried *Sorry* all through the night.

Each time he answered her. Each time he said the same thing. "You're enough for me." And though she wanted to with all her heart, Hannah could not whisper back the same thing.

They began their life together as a childless couple. Just as he promised early in their marriage, Daniel stayed strong. He fought against that desperate sadness that threatened to swallow his wife. He found ways to be close to her, to watch over her. He fired his secretary. Begged Hannah to "rescue" him by helping him out at work. He let her answer phones, type up notes. He took her shopping on his lunch break.

He rented a new booth at the artisan's fair. After their engagement, she had stopped taking orders and stopped attending the fair. But he took her back, watched over her as customers swarmed her again. He went to the workroom with her late at night. Stayed up with her as she worked with a fury, throwing paint across the mud.

But in spite of his efforts, something was missing from Hannah. From their marriage. Before, there had always been the hope between them. The inevitable promise. The discussions that began with the words, *When our baby comes . . .*

With hope gone, new introductions were needed. Hannah stared at their great big house and no longer felt excited to own such a perfect nest. Instead she wondered, Who really owned who? Entire rooms remained unfurnished. And despite the parties Daniel began throwing, the crowds and wine and music he filled their home with, it seemed more empty every day.

They kept to certain corners. The workroom when Hannah

needed to escape. The bedroom for sleeping and love. The kitchen and breakfast room for food. The small den off the breakfast for lounging. But there were no sleeping babies to carry to the dozen other rooms. No toy-filled Christmas mornings to need the great room for. Even her art brought Hannah little pleasure. It hurt her to think that she could create anything except a child with Daniel. Winded from so many years of wanting, Hannah decided she had only pretended to have found a home.

Home. When she thought about that word now, and all the ways that she had failed Daniel, one memory always surfaced. She was seventeen years old, just a baby herself, laying inside a shack on the marsh. Her baby was with her, though. *Welcome home*, she wished that she had whispered.

Late one Friday night, it happened. It started when the phone rang.

"This the Phillips residence?" a man asked.

"Yes," Hannah said.

"Don't know how these things are done."

"If you have a legal emergency, then call the after-hours number of Brooks, Goodman and Phillips. My husband isn't on call this weekend, but somebody will get you in touch with an attorney."

"Don't need a lawyer."

Hannah waited.

"There's a baby. Heard through friends you can't have any. Thought you might want it."

Lightning. That was what Hannah felt. She remembered a storm back on James Island when she was pregnant. She was craving honeydew and had walked down to the market when the clouds turned dark. Everyone ran to their cars. Hannah ran, too, her hips aching with new weight, one arm across her heavy breasts. In one second, she was soaked. Lightning blinked and someone behind her screamed. She dropped the fruit, forgot about her painful breasts, and ran faster. Until a flash of white heat, as bright and painful as any vision could be, stretched the length of the sky and ended at her muddy toes. She stopped. Rubbed her eyes and looked at the new glowing, blurry world around her. She crouched low, near the mud and water, felt the relief of her hips and turned to look for the lost fruit. God was going to kill her for her sin. Or not. She might as well taste the honey.

"Whose?" Hannah whispered into the phone, looking around her at the new glowing, blurry world.

"My fifteen-year-old baby girl's," he sobbed.

Hannah sucked in her breath as Daniel's hand grabbed her shoulder. She sank to the floor, whispering promises.

It was clear that Daniel did not approve. And she knew why, though he'd never admit it. It was because of the weeks after the doctor. The weeks she spent in bed and wouldn't move. The weeks she begged him to leave her. To find another woman that could give him children. He had asked her to consider adoption during those dark weeks. "There's still a way," he had begged her. "Lots of little babies out there that need us." But she would always shake her head. "No, there's a reason, Daniel. A reason I'm not supposed to have a baby."

"I thought you weren't interested in adoption?" Daniel asked her. "You seemed so set against it, but now…"

"He chose us," she whispered to Daniel. "Don't you see? I didn't look for this. This family, this baby, chose me."

Hannah arranged a meeting at a local café. And over coffee that grew cold, she sold herself. She gushed about their home as though she'd never felt it owned *her*. She talked about their ten acres as though she had never wanted to escape into the mountain behind it. As though she'd never prayed to be lost and never found. She only spoke of the best details, like the tire swing out back, just waiting for a child. Or how they'd paved the drive, making it the perfect half-mile tricycle trail. She told them about Daniel's good salary. About how she would quit work tomorrow to prepare for the child. And then, without blushing, she told them how much she would inherit one day from her parents. Private schools would be no problem. They could pay for the baby's college tomorrow if they needed to. They could go to Disney once a month if they wanted.

Through it all, Daniel sat silent, only nodding occasionally as Hannah talked. But then the girl's father spoke. About how relieved he felt, and how it could only be God's will that he found them. About how God was going to use them to heal his family. Hannah watched as Daniel leaned forward in his chair.

"How did you hear about us again?" Daniel asked.

"Mutual friends," the man said.

"Their names?"

The man hesitated, Hannah saw the worry in his eyes. The suspicion in Daniel's.

"It doesn't matter," Hannah said quickly. "We're here together because we all want what's best for the baby. Names don't matter."

She grabbed Daniel's hand and squeezed, privately begging him to hush. In the car ride home she turned to him. "I know why you're worried," she said. "I know you're thinking about before, about how I was after I went to the doctor. But don't you see this is different? Daniel, there's already a baby! We just have to take it."

"It's just strange. We don't know these people and they want to give us a baby."

"Stop it. Stop acting like this wasn't meant to be."

Daniel shook his head. "It wouldn't hurt to make some calls. I know people that could get answers. Secretly, of course."

"This is a miracle. This is the miracle I've waited on. Don't you ruin it. I'd never forgive you."

At home Daniel paced the empty room next to theirs, the one that they had stepped into the day they bought the house and proudly called Our Nursery. Hannah grabbed the phone and a J.C. Penney catalog. She ordered a boutique sleigh crib in vintage cherry.

The next day the girl's father called and asked to visit their home. Hannah wanted him to come right away, but he said he had to work and would call back in a couple of weeks to schedule the visit. To pass the time, Hannah spent her days shopping. She forced herself, difficult as it was, to pass over the sweet things like blankets and tiny socks. She decided to be disciplined. She would buy only the most necessary things. A rocker. Baby monitors. A little gift basket of lotions and creams.

Daniel smiled tightly when he walked in and saw the sleigh crib against the wall and the rocker in the corner.

"We have to show them the baby is already ours," Hannah explained. "Will you paint the room?"

Two weeks passed, and the family didn't call back to schedule their visit. Hannah focused on paint colors instead of the days that were passing by.

"Which green did you want?" Daniel asked.

Hannah stared down at three rows of paint chips, arranged neatly across the kitchen counter. She shrugged her shoulders. "I don't like green."

"Look at this one. It's called Lichen. It's not too bold. I was thinking it would work for a boy or girl's room. The mother hasn't found out what she's having."

"Don't call her that," Hannah whispered. "I'm the mother."

She lingered outside that day, not wanting to go in and wait for the phone to ring. She pretended to weed roses that the landscaper had tended the day before. She was on her knees in the dirt when she glanced up at the house. An enormous piece of mountain history. And from where she knelt, the house looming over her, the window to Our Nursery just above her, she felt it. The house was laughing at her.

She hurried to the garden patch. Took a quick breath and grabbed the electric fence. Hot pain shot through her body. At first it hurt badly. But then it changed, just as it always did. She discovered it as a girl on the single-strand fence Mother had put around their garden to keep the deer out. The pain went away and left behind a sweet numbness. This time Hannah held it longer than ever before. She cried out with pain, but when she stood up she felt in control, and blissfully numb. She yelled at the house, "Shut up!" and then walked inside and sat by the phone, watching it the rest of the day.

She never told Daniel the phone call came. That the father cried and said his daughter wanted to keep her baby. And they were going to let her. They were going to *help* her.

"How wonderful," Hannah lied.

Another week passed, and Daniel was worried. "Listen," he said. "If this doesn't work out, it doesn't mean *never*. You know that, right? There are lots of places we can adopt. It will take some time, longer than this would have, but I know an attorney over the mountain that could speed the process up. Just, you know, in case we don't get this baby."

Hannah laughed. "I can't believe I forgot to tell you. He called. His daughter was feeling ill. Started vomiting every morning. They want to wait to visit until she's feeling better."

"Good," Daniel said, as he hugged her. "Come to work with me today. I sure could use your help. I'm so behind on filings."

Hannah smiled, but she shook her head and mumbled an excuse about a vase she wanted to make. The truth was, she couldn't wait for him to leave. She couldn't wait to watch his car disappear into the mountain. To know that finally, she could begin her morning, her beautiful new morning routine. The one for just the two of them. Her and Baby.

Perhaps it was the sight of that empty crib, just across the hall from her own bed. Or maybe it was the sound of silence, the sound of *empty*, from the baby monitors that Hannah listened to throughout the day. But every morning, as soon as Daniel left, Baby took over that house. Just as surely as she had once taken over Hannah's body.

She announced her arrival like any baby would, with an awful morning the day after the final phone call. Hannah ran to the toilet. Weeping as she vomited. In spite of everything the doctor had said, she went to the pharmacy to buy pregnancy tests. She spent her afternoon peeing on sticks, waiting for lines that would never appear.

It didn't matter that the tests said no. Her sick mornings persisted. Soon, she began to depend on them. She ran her hands over her large painful breasts. And she need only close her eyes to smell honey filling the house.

In one last, brief flash of fear and sanity, she ran from the house and bought paint. *Haint Blue* paint. Daniel was so happy when he saw the room. "So it's a boy, then."

The blue didn't work, and Hannah spent long days in Our Empty Nursery, rocking and feeling blissfully nauseous. Dozing sometimes, and dreaming in pinks and blues. "Shhhhh," she would wake and whisper to the clay baby she had laid in the crib. Sometimes she'd reach to turn up the baby monitor's volume and listen closer. That was when she heard her, just like all those nights on the mountain. The ones that sent her running through the woods, searching blindly. Hannah listened again. And heard her panicked cry, loud and clear.

Hannah rose from the rocker. She ran from the room. Finally, she accepted the truth she'd avoided all along.

Abandoned babies always cry out for their mothers. They never stop.

X

"We have to find my baby, Mother. I heard her, she's in trouble."

Mother took a deep breath, and remembered one of her rules. A good mother never shows how scared she really is. A good mother is calm in the face of her child's panic.

"Shhh, be still. Shhhhhh."

"She needs me. I heard her!"

"Shhhh, daughter, settle yourself. You are overwrought."

"It was a miracle!"

"Easy now. Your mind is playing tricks. Let Tabby bring you tea."

"It was a miracle. You of all people should believe me!"

"Shhh. Come, sit. Let's not talk now. We'll talk when you're calm."

"Was Jacob calm after he saw the ladder? Was Lazarus calm when he walked out of death? What about Jonah? When he went into the great fish, was he calm, Mother?"

"That is different. Come, sit and drink your tea."

"Why is it different? Your life's work was teaching me to believe in the miracles of old. I believed, I still do. So why won't you believe now? If ladders can rise to heaven, if the dead can rise, then why couldn't I have heard my daughter over a baby monitor? Am I not allowed a miracle, too?"

"What did you hear?"

"She's trapped in the snake tree."

Mother turned and saw Daniel walking down the length of the front porch.

"Hush that talk. Here comes your husband!"

"But I heard her!"

Mother grabbed Hannah's hands, and made one last desperate attempt at fixing things. "Go to the library and gather yourself before your husband sees you. I'll take you to her. Go now, before Daniel sees you like this. Hide yourself until you're composed."

Mother stepped into the hall. As she waited for Daniel, she tried to calm the panic that swelled inside her. Over the wild look in Hannah's eyes. Over the despair in her voice. She had seen it before. She remembered it well. It was Leah's look. The same expression, the same panic, right before Leah did what she...*No*, Mother thought. *I won't let it happen.* Surely there was still something to do. Something that could fix it all. She heard Daniel's footsteps in the hall. *I can do it*, she thought. *I can still save my Hannah.*

"Mrs. Reynolds?"

"Hello, Daniel, always good to see you. Hannah is resting in the library. She was terribly tired. She must be overworking herself for the artisan's fair. I'd suggest a weekend away for the two of you sometime soon."

"I didn't come here to see Hannah."

"Oh?"

"I came for you."

"Well, it's always good to visit with you, Daniel."

"I want some answers."

"Oh?"

"About a night, just a few weeks ago. Our phone rang, it was a man with a baby...but Mrs. Reynolds, you already know all about that, don't you?"

XI

"Shhhh, Hannah," Mother whispered from the doorway of the library. Her eyes were tired, and she leaned her body against the door for the support it could give her. But her voice was confident and calm, as she promised, "I can give you peace, daughter."

It was night now, and Hannah lay across the couch, her face buried into a corner pillow. Her shoulders rose and fell with the rhythm of her sobs. The tea that Tabby brought her hours before sat cold and untouched on the table beside her.

"Daniel's gone," Mother said. "He agreed to let you rest here tonight. You can return to him tomorrow, after you've seen her."

Hannah turned her face toward Mother. "What?"

"I can prove to you that she is all right. I'll show you that she is no ladder to heaven. She is no Lazarus. She's just an ordinary girl, the kind that doesn't need a miracle."

Early the next morning they drove to James Island. Mother promised Hannah that she would see her daughter. "But we mustn't let her see us," she warned. "It would violate the agreement I made years ago on the day she was born. She is happy without us. They have raised her well. Rest your eyes upon her and find peace. But do not disturb her. You must not bring her your grief."

Mother held a slip of paper in her hand with an address scribbled across it. They turned down a side street, just ten minutes from the marsh. Mother pointed to a house, a perfect cream-colored house with a red door and palm trees circling the drive. They parked just across the street from the house. Mother handed Hannah a pair of binoculars.

Hannah looked through them and smiled. There she was, sitting on the front porch of a fine house. Hannah felt glad, even as she choked back sobs. For so many years she had imagined that moment. And finally, there was Baby, a straight shot through the fuzzy binocular lens.

"Oh, she's pretty," Hannah whispered. Baby had light brown hair. Golden skin that glowed beneath her sundress. Hannah was happy to see that dress. Happy to see her round knees at the edge of the chair, her legs tucked under her so casually. She looked closer and thought maybe she even saw tan lines. A white mark around her collar. Maybe she had gone swimming before.

"What's she doing?" Mother asked.

"She's painting her nails."

Hannah watched her for nearly twenty minutes. Long enough for three coats of polish. She whispered any detail she saw. Searched for any little scrap of information. So that she could know what was real. So that she would never forget. She whispered things like "She likes iced tea. No lemon." And "She's right-handed." Long after the girl went inside, Hannah sat, still looking through the binoculars. Just in case she came back.

Mother's hand gently pushed the binoculars down. "It's time to go now."

"Wait," Hannah said. "I didn't see her face that good. She was looking down. Maybe she'll come back out."

"She seemed happy, though, didn't she?" Mother asked.

Hannah nodded. "She looked so safe...and bored...and young." Hannah wiped the tears that suddenly poured from her eyes. "Mother, she satisfies me."

Mother reached for Hannah's hand. "Good."

The girl came back out and Hannah quickly raised the binoculars. Watched her walk down the porch and get in the passenger side of a little gray Volkswagen. She rode right past Hannah. Never once looked over.

"Look at me, Baby," Hannah begged. They had only shared eight months together, and Hannah couldn't help but feel greedy. She would have done anything to share one more moment. Even if it was a glance as Baby drove past her, on her way to something better.

"Where are you going?" Mother cried, as Hannah opened her car door and started walking away quickly. "Hannah!" she yelled.

Hannah stopped and turned around. "I want to peek inside the house. I want to see the woman that raised her. I won't let them know..."

It was a slow walk up to that house. Not because they were

parked far away, but because of all the things Hannah thought of. About Mother, and how once she had taken that same walk. Up to the house of a stranger, so that she could give Baby away.

A woman opened the door. Her bangs fell below her eyebrows, and she was constantly pushing them out of her eyes. But her smile was soft and gentle, and she was at least fifteen years older than Hannah. Hannah imagined how that must have pleased Mother. How much more deserving that woman must have seemed.

"Somethin' I can help you with, honey?"

Hannah nodded and looked past her into the house. They had money. Not as much as Father, but still enough to line the floors with rich hardwoods. To have fresh flowers on the dining table. A piano in the corner. On its edge was a framed family portrait. A man and woman, their arms hugged around the girl from the front porch. The girl's smile was so real and sweet.

"You sellin' somethin'? I don't really need anything," she said, as she started to shut the door.

"My mother brought you a baby, years ago," Hannah said.

The woman's mouth fell open. She started to shake her head and Hannah hurried to finish. "I don't want to meet her. I just wanted to tell you thank you, because she looks so happy. You did a fine job. Do you think...would it be too much...since she's already left...do you think I could see her room? Just a quick peek?"

"This ain't part of the deal," the woman whispered.

Hannah shook her head. "I'm not going to speak to her or anything like that. I just want to see the place she grew up."

"A thousand dollars," the woman said. "That's what the

deal was. You all could park your car and stalk us all day. But you weren't supposed to come knockin'. Do you know that my husband would kill me if he knew I'd made a deal with crazy people? That I agreed to pretend our daughter was theirs? I did it for college money, but he wouldn't care. He's due home any minute now, so you gotta go."

"Wait," Hannah whispered as the woman closed the door in her face. "You mean it isn't her?"

Hannah sat in the car the whole way home thinking about the two of them. How both of them were such liars. Hannah's lies about deep water and T-shirts. Mother's about Baby and where she had gone.

When Mother finally parked the car that night, Hannah did her best to please her.

"Thank you, Mother. You've made it all better now." They walked inside together, Mother's arm gently wrapped around Hannah's waist. But the lie sat heavy on Hannah's tongue, and she shivered when she stopped in front of the Great Room window. She studied her reflection in the glass, blinked her eyes, and saw Aunt Leah with her slim curves. Leah with her very own golden halo of hair. She took a step closer, until she heard Leah, too. Pounding out a new war cry within her. She nodded her head.

I want...I want...I want...

ANGEL

I

"Thought you was dead," a man whispered above me. "You ain't, are you? Can you move?"

My eyes, trained to find anything that glitters, saw the silver canteen that flashed on his belt. I wanted to reach for it. But my arms wouldn't lift when I told them to. He followed my gaze, unscrewed the top of the canteen and held it to my lips.

"I was trackin' bear. Saw you against this tree and thought you was dead. It ain't that unusual. Tourists come down to hike, can't find their way out. Start walkin' crazy circles and such, either starve or freeze. From the looks of it, you were gettin' close yourself. I bet you'd of been gone in a day or so. How'd you end up out here? We're a good day's walk from town."

He laid his coat over me, and the shock of sudden warmth pulled me into a deep sleep. When I woke up I was being lifted onto the back of an ATV. A policeman drove and the bear-man rode behind him and held me like a baby. We raced through the forest. My eyes blinked as dead gray limbs flashed overhead. I slept again, and woke up as they wheeled me into the hospital.

The policeman started asking me questions.

"I need to report a missin' person," I mumbled.

"Someone else up there? You wasn't alone?"

"Me."

"Excuse me?"

"I'm the missin' person."

I spent the first two days asleep in the hospital. And when I woke up they asked more questions. *What is your name?* Then they asked where I was from. I remembered hell burning behind Black Snake trailer. Acres and acres, glowing red with fire. Police cars, their blue lights flashing against flat bacca leaves.

"Can't remember a thing," I whispered.

Some of them heard it for the lie it was. Looked at me with narrowed eyes and tight lips when I said it. One nurse even warned me, "They'll bill you as Jane Doe if they have to." Others treated me with pity. Like I'd lost my mind on the mountain. These nurses did more than bring me vitamins, bags of sugar water for my IV, and hospital meals. They bought me dessert from a vending machine with change from their own pockets. They marched happy people, wearing pastel name tags that read *Volunteer*, by my bed, "in case I needed a friend." They'd whisper sweetly, sad smiles on their faces, "Honey, you 'member who you are yet?"

I'd shake my head no and nibble the candy they brought.

They ran a story about me in the paper:

> BOONE, NC: Authorities are seeking information concerning the identity of a young woman discovered in the mountains last week. She was found alone and disoriented in the forest, several miles outside of Boone. She appears to be in her late teens, five feet four inches, with long white blond hair and brown eyes. If you have any information regarding her identity, please contact local authorities.

I imagined sliding that little piece of newspaper across our family dinner table. *Nearly died tryin' to get to you.*

There was a knock at my door.

"Know your name yet?" a policeman asked, as he walked in. "Ever been over the mountain, to Tennessee? They're looking for a blond girl, about your age, set fire to a farm. Burned half of it down. That wouldn't be why you can't remember your name, would it?"

"Never been to Tennessee," I said.

"I'm gonna go make some calls about you. I'll be back tomorrow and we'll chat some more. You rest up now."

As the door closed behind him, I pulled the IV out of my arm. Put my cutoffs back on and prepared to leave. But just as I put my hand on the knob, someone was coming in.

It was the volunteer again. My "friend" in case I needed one.

"Oh," she said, surprised. "Your IV fall out? That happens sometimes. You lie down and I'll get a nurse to tend to it."

I cursed under my breath but returned to my bed. The volunteer reached for my hand when the nurse had to prick my arm to find a new vein. But I jerked away from her. "It don't hurt," I mumbled.

When the nurse left, the volunteer sat at the edge of my bed. "I can only imagine how scared you must be. And if you're in some sort of trouble, if that's why you can't remember who you are, then I want to let you know that I can help you. There's lots of reasons for why people make the choices they do. I don't know why you were out there alone, or what you were running from. But I'd like to help make you safe again. I've got lots of resources at my disposal."

"I just want out of here. Can you do that for me?"

"Will you go home? Back to wherever you were, before you got lost on the mountain?"

I shook my head. It was the reason I struck the match.

Not to burn the memories until they looked as worthless as they were. The candy that Daddy collected. The dishes that Momma threw. The bucket where the gun used to sit. That was all sweet extra.

The real reason I burned that trailer was so that no matter what else happened I could never go back. I might get lost on a mountain and almost die. And there might be a moment when I'd think about Black Snake trailer, how warm it could be come winter with just a tiny kerosene heater set in the center. And that moment, that imagined warmth, was the reason I burned it. It was one thing, maybe the only thing, that I could promise my future. No matter what, I would never have to run from Black Snake trailer again.

"Winter's coming, honey. I can tell you're scared. I can see you don't wanna run back into that cold forest. Just say the word and I'll help make you safe."

I hated her, even though I knew it made me more redneck than Black Snake trailer ever did. I winced at the thought of that word, *redneck*, a curse I'd heard many times over the years, just like *trailer trash*. Those words meant many things, but they all started with land. How we didn't own any. We plowed it, planted it, picked it, and helped sell off its goods. But we did not own it and neither would our children's children. Land was a right reserved for the farm kings. A right reserved for those born of DAR blood. For those that could hang signs on the corners of farms: *Established 1893*.

I never doubted I was trailer trash. Knew it from my cutoffs and my black bras peeking out from my knotted-up T-shirts. My clothes were given to me from a closet at school, or left behind from Janie. But I'm the one who chose how to wear them. I'm the one who tied knots, whenever it served my purpose, to show off my belly.

Redneck. The word I really feared, the one hissed at Momma. Once, a new super grocery opened up forty minutes away, just off the highway. The gas station was close and stocked almost everything our kitchen needed. But Momma heard Mrs. Swarm, and then another farmhand's wife, mention the super grocery. So one day she drove us up to see.

Everything was shiny, especially the bright new buggies waiting for shoppers to fill with their food. Old women with green aprons stood behind carts and passed out samples. We took their crackers and spreads and nibbled like real ladies would.

Something came over Momma. A wanting, or maybe a hope. She lifted me high and stuffed me down into a buggy, so she could push me the way other mothers pushed their babies. But I was eight, and my long legs dangled halfway to the floor.

We went up every aisle slowly. Momma stumbling over the words of all the new foods.

"Angel," she whispered. "They even got the Chinese food here." We stared at bottles of soy sauce and cans of water chestnuts. "Ain't nothin' you can't eat now. If it's a food in this world, then it's here in this store."

She put soy sauce in the buggy. And a taco kit. And something so wonderful I never dreamed it could exist. Star fruit. I held it in my grubby hands, knowing at last what it was I had hungered for my whole life. I closed my eyes and imagined stars sitting on my tongue.

At the cashier line I noticed Momma's bones more than usual. She stood differently. With her shoulders pulled tight and her arms folded over her body. Then she raised her hand over her eyes to look out the window and sighed loudly.

"Oh dear. Looks like the weather man was right. I do believe a rain cloud is coming and I've forgotten my umbrella."

"But Momma," I said, and laughed. "We ain't got no umbrella."

Someone giggled behind us. Momma looked down at the ground and I knew from the burn in her face that I'd messed up. Maybe even hurt her. I just wasn't sure how.

"Five twenty-two," the cashier said.

Momma never carried a purse. She pulled a five out of her front pocket. Then reached into another. And then another. And then her last one. She shook her head.

"Damn it," she whispered to the ground.

"I got it," a woman behind us said, as she held out a quarter.

She was everything we were trying to be. With smooth blond hair cut short to make it swing cheerfully with every move. Soft pink lipstick and matching nail polish. Leather purse on her shoulder, probably filled with good money. And sitting in the front of her buggy was a well-scrubbed baby, wearing a clean new sundress and matching bonnet.

"I forget my purse all the time, too," the woman said sweetly.

Sticky goodness surrounded us. Flowed from the sugary sound of her voice that made it clear she'd never hurt anyone. Never tossed a dish at her husband. Never passed out drunk. Never slapped her baby's mouth or demanded an early prize. And her boldness, her assumption that help was wanted, made it clear that she'd never been hurt, either. That she'd lived a life so safe she could afford to let her strength flow down to people like me and Momma.

I hated her because she was so perfect. Because she'd never been hurt before. And I loved her, too. Because I knew she was good. I wanted her to lift me up and put me in her buggy. Put a brand-new pink sundress on me and make a fuss over tying my hat just right.

Momma just hated her.

"To hell with your free food." She jerked me from the buggy. My long legs got stuck getting out. My shoe popped off. Showed my mismatched socks with holes all over the toes.

"Git your damn shoes on. And git you a pair of decent socks next time."

"Star fruit?" I whined. "How 'bout we just git that?"

She walked away and I ran behind her. But before we left, someone whispered the truth. "*Redneck.*"

It wasn't my socks. Or that Momma didn't have a purse or an umbrella or enough money. They called her redneck because she didn't know how to accept kindness. It made her angry. Made her cuss at her baby and run with shame.

Later that night, she cried over her whiskey.

"She didn't look at me, Angel. She looked at the cashier, at her own baby, at the quarter in her hand. Her words lied, said, 'We're the same, me and you.' But not her eyes. Her eyes called me everything her mouth wouldn't."

That day in the hospital I looked up at that kind volunteer, at her black eyes and warm brown skin, at the pretty patchwork scarf tied around her shoulders, and I hated her for trying to help me. For acting like she wanted to fix all that was broken inside me.

"Sorry," I hissed. "Daddy taught me long ago not to trust a gook. What you wanna do, feed me dog or somethin'? You best just git out and leave me be."

She did, and then I whispered "Redneck" to myself. She was dressed too nice. With her starched blouse and patent flats. With her smooth black hair, cut into a silky bob. And she saw me too honest. My fear, my danger, before my angry eyes. She offered the thing I needed most, and I cursed her for it. I wasn't raised to expect kindness. You didn't keep me long enough to teach me any different.

II

When the volunteer returned just an hour later, I sat up in bed, ready with new insults for her. But I didn't say them. Because behind the volunteer was someone new. Someone that I couldn't take my eyes off. Someone that silenced me, made me forget all the Black Snake curses I had planned to yell.

She was old, with long gray hair covered by a black veil. And a skirt that dragged across hospital dust. The words, the map, I had memorized deep in the bacca fields started flashing before my eyes.

"Are you a Holy Roller?" I whispered lowly.

She answered me with a cold stare, her mouth set tight and not moving. Her eyes swept over me, searched my face, my body. She came back to my face and reached her hand toward me. Let it hang in the space between us.

I jerked back. Her hand dropped quickly and she cleared her throat. "I'm a businesswoman," she said with quick syllables that could never be learned in Carolina. "I have a resort at the top of the mountain. There is always work to be done. As long as you work, room and board are provided."

"Don't like charity."

"You and I agree. You'll work for everything you're given. And you can leave anytime you're ready." She handed me a piece of paper. "This is my business card. If you agree, let me know and I'll settle your hospital bill this afternoon."

I let her card fall from my open hand onto the sheets. But the door was closing behind her and she missed my insult. The volunteer picked the card off the bed, handed it back to me.

"You need someplace to work *and* live. She runs a bed-and-breakfast on the top of this mountain. You can see the whole world from her view."

"She's a Yankee."

"Turns out they're not so bad," she laughed. "She doesn't pay money, but you'll have a room and all your meals. You'll have a safe place to stay as long as you need. I know her well."

I imagined all the mean words I could yell to say no. But then I remembered cold mountain winds. I remembered watching the squirrels eat acorns and feeling jealous of their full bellies. I remembered the glow of dozens and dozens of acres, burning up the night. And most important, that the policeman was coming back soon.

"Just say yes. Nobody needs you to say thank you."

I nodded but couldn't bring myself to look at her. She picked up the phone, made the call.

"The police will be back tomorrow morning," the volunteer said. "You should leave today. There's a staff exit on the basement level. My car is there. I'll take you."

One hour later, I was sitting in the backseat of a black Oldsmobile. It was unlike any car I'd ever been inside. It was so quiet, without the roar of muscle that Daddy loved to hear. And there was so much room. I looked at the floor of that backseat, and wondered how many five-year-olds could fit in it. At least two or three. Especially if they were like me and small for their age.

We drove through town, past the scenic path that had nearly doomed me. Then the car turned onto a side road, narrow and winding. We twisted our way up and up and up. Until we were at the very top and I slid down in my seat.

The volunteer opened my car door and helped me out. I stepped onto that firm mountain ground and looked around. I didn't know what I was supposed to do, or if it was safe to stay. I only knew one thing: I wished that you could see my view.

Before I burned Black Snake trailer, I chose things for you. Each with a story. And each offering an excuse. Something I could hold up, maybe with anger or maybe just sadness, and say *This is why* . . .

But that first day on the mountaintop, I reached for a brochure from a stack on the front porch. I looked at the snapshot, how it captured the view before me. The sky that rolled forever. Not just a ceiling of blue, but walls, too. And a floor like a blue rug pushing out from the land. In the middle of clouds rose a red castle built of perfect polished cedar. With odd, unpredictable angles that left me guessing what the rooms hid inside.

I thought of books then. Growing up, I didn't just hide the snacks bought with my free government lunch pass. I didn't just hide whiskey in an old coke bottle. I hid books, too. Sometimes they were borrowed from my school library. Sometimes they were stolen from unzipped backpacks on the bus. And underneath those bacca leaves in summer, and hidden in cold barn corners come winter, a new life waited. I read anything I could find. Vacation guides, fairy tales, inspector novels, and biographies. I learned my *right words* from them, far more than from my teachers at school.

Momma smacked me whenever I talked like my books. Whenever I said "I absolutely refuse" instead of saying "I ain't gonna."

"Don't you get prissy with me, Miss Smarty-pants. Think you get a few As in school and suddenly know more than your own momma?"

So I hid the books. I made certain I talked like trailer trash. And I whispered my right words only to the bacca, only for you.

Besides the good words, I studied pictures. Sometimes of castles in the clouds and royal feasts. "Nothin' but lies," Daddy said, if he happened to see me with a book. When he said that, he seemed fatherly. Like he believed he broke my heart. But what was lies to Daddy was *mercy* to me.

I folded the brochure and tucked it in my pocket, not for excuse or explanation, but for the surprise it might bring you. Maybe you thought you knew the paths and limits of this world. The ditches from the fields. The kingdoms from the trailers. I did, too, until I saw the mountaintop and realized there was a richness I'd never imagined. Or maybe you were like me, and thought mercy and lies were the same thing. *Look,* I dreamed of saying as I held the brochure up. *A castle in the clouds just like in my books. Sometimes lies surprise you. Sometimes they turn true.*

I rang the bell. The old woman answered. She looked down at my backpack.

"Is this all of your things?"

"Yeah."

I tried to look her in the eyes as I spoke.

Mr. Swarm told me once that I could spot a biting dog by whether it looked me in the eyes. He said a dumb friendly one, the kind that would hop in any farmhand's truck, would lick my hand while staring at nothing in the distance. But a biting dog would look me in the eyes. Give a warning that he might be little, or even starving, but he could still hurt me.

I was a baby when he said it. Watching him chase a stray dog out of the bacca. But I learned it. Practiced it like the survival lesson it was. From that day on, I looked people square in the eyes. Maybe I was a little girl. Or maybe I was a pretty young thing dancing in red high heels. I could still hurt you.

But I could not hold the old woman's gaze. The effort of trying embarrassed me. I brought my eyes up, and then down. Up, and then back down. Her eyes were too busy, in contrast to the stiff poise of her body. They weren't hard, or cold, or even heavy with feeling. They were searching.

"We require a uniform. One has already been delivered to your room. Other basic items, like a toothbrush and comb, I will send as well."

I nodded.

"You will earn them."

"Yeah."

"Come, I will give you a tour of the house. And explain our rules."

The angles outside were a disguise. Inside the rooms were open and connected, each one swelling into the next without any need for doors or division. There was a great room, with half-empty bookshelves that stretched into the open cathedral ceiling. And a large fireplace, surrounded by cane-seated rockers. Next was the dining room, with a table built to seat thirty. I ran my hand down the wood. Across knots and deep scratches.

"I bought that at an estate sale outside of Asheville. The

seller guessed it was nearly one hundred years old. Made from American chestnut. All but extinct now. This table is probably the only American chestnut you and I will ever see."

"Bet with all them scratches you got it for a real bargain," I said.

She shook her head. "I bought it for the scratches. For dead wood dented by elbows of generations upon generations of families. For the crumbs of past meals ground into the markings."

She pointed to a closet in the room. "It's full of supplies. Anything you'll need. Polish, cleaners, and brooms. Extra aprons in case yours gets soiled. We all eat together, here, every night at six thirty. Afterwards, you will clear the table. Pay special attention to silence. Our guests like to lounge and read in the Great Room before the fire. It is tiresome to hear the clatter of dishes."

As we left the room she turned suddenly and stood before me. Her eyes fixed upon my face.

"Tell me of your table."

"What?"

"Did it have ... scratches?"

Stop, I ordered my hands, as they reached for the memories in my pockets. A reflex, from the pent-up hunger inside me. From the constant waiting for someone, *for you*, to ask about details. Like the wood of my family table.

"You're right," she said, turning quickly. "Most tables aren't worth discussing."

We walked through a carved archway that opened to the kitchen where three women were cooking. They looked up and waved.

"This is Jill, Anna, and Shari. You won't be needed in here, unless of course one of the other ladies is ill or absent. Carry on, ladies. It smells delicious."

The wood above the back archway in the kitchen was carved: *And having food and raiment, let us be therewith content . . .* I whispered the words, confusing like poetry. Pretty like it, too. As we walked into the next room, I saw the words again. Carved upon the cedar beam that spanned the ceiling.

"This is the small sitting room and your daily responsibility. Tidy it as needed. Clean it thoroughly every evening before bed. There's a chess set under the cabinet. Learn its pieces. Each night inspect it to make sure they are all there. There are also books of local photography. Make certain these are accounted for as well. As for other entertainments, television and radios are strictly forbidden. But clean books, particularly true ones such as these photographic journals, are allowed. And, of course, good conversation among our guests, perhaps with an apple dumpling and a cup of tea from the kitchen, is always encouraged.

"This is a mountain sanctuary. A place of refuge and peace from the world below us. If you see guests in this room, and other duties have been attended to, ask if you can bring them anything. We have handwoven afghans in the Great Room closet. Other journals and books are in the library next to the upstairs office. Fresh-baked snacks, coffee, tea, and milk are always available in the kitchen."

At the top of a wide staircase, two halls branched out and were divided by an open space that viewed the Great Room below.

"These are the Bedroom Halls. Guests on the right. Staff on the left."

She took a key from her pocket and opened a room.

"This is yours. Rest here until dinner. Afterwards you will clear the dishes and straighten the small sitting room."

It didn't glimmer. Or flash the way coins did after a farm-hand set them on a fencepost. But my eyes found the bed in the corner of the room and would not move.

"Rules of the house: Never go in anyone else's bedroom for any reason. If there is an emergency that you feel requires breaking this rule, find me first and we'll break it together. We hire male and female, but you will never do the same work. You'll never have reason to be alone together. Any violations of this rule result in immediate dismissal. Do you understand?"

"Yeah."

"No cursing. No singing vulgar songs that you remember from the radio. Be quiet around the guests. Don't try and converse with them, just ask if they have any needs. If they show an interest in talking to you, be polite but not overly engaging. Your work here is not social, it is functional. As you clean, be as quiet as possible. We use brooms always. Never vacuums. Guests come here from their cities and their jobs for the silence. It's the only way they can hear the mountain. It's the only way they can hear themselves. We charge the most expensive overnight rate on the mountain, and are nearly always fully booked. People pay a premium for the silence. Understand?"

"Yeah."

"All work is finished at nine o'clock, and you must return to your room. Once in your room, you may stay up as long as you wish. Now, meals. Breakfast and lunch aren't communal meals like dinner. Many of our guests request breakfast trays to be delivered through the slot at the base of their doors. You will help deliver these. Shari from the kitchen will direct you. Workers' breakfast is served at six o'clock sharp in the alley behind the kitchen. We haven't marked the alley room on guest maps because it is the place for workers to gather for breakfast, lunch, and any short breaks. There aren't tables and few chairs. That is because your first two meals are brief. Nourish yourself with the food offered and then continue your work. Dinner is different. There is dessert and lingering and conversation. But we work throughout the day. All of us. It's the reason we can all be here comfortably. You are allowed two other nonmeal breaks between breakfast and bed. There is a master list of all worker break times hanging in the alley. Your name will be added before morning. If during your break you need something to drink or perhaps a snack, return to the alley and Shari can help you. If you need to rest, return to your room. Sitting rooms are for the enjoyment of guests only. There is, however, a check-out system for books. In each sitting room there is a leather-bound catalog. Inside is a list of materials that guests have signed out. If you wish to take a book to your room for the evening, you must wait until just before nine o'clock to give all guests the opportunity to sign it out first. If by five till nine an item has not been signed out, you may do so. But it must be returned before your six o'clock breakfast. Since the small sitting room is your responsibility, you will also need to monitor the sign-out catalog for materials in that room. If something has been checked out for more than three days, please notify me. Don't ever ask a guest about the materials yourself. That's it for now. If you have questions, ask. If I'm not available, ask Shari. It's a simple life here. Follow these rules. Do your work neatly and quietly, and you may stay as long as you wish."

It was a full bed, the size that me and Janie used to share.

Only this one was high off the floor, with what looked like two mattresses stacked together. There was a wooden headboard, carved with a lacy pattern, at the top. And four posts rising toward the ceiling from each of its corners. Lace, thick and stained the color of tea, fell from somewhere beneath the mattress all the way to the floor. It hid the wires and springs and bolts that held the bed together. An ivory quilt, simple but thick, covered the top, with two pillows tucked beneath. And propped against the headboard, a small square cushion made of matching tea-stained lace.

"Is this satisfactory?"

I thought she had left. I thought she had finished her list of rules and closed the door behind her. But she was standing in the hall, the door halfway closed, her hand still on the knob.

She had watched me step toward the bed. Watched me peer under it to see the metal bolts and make certain it didn't float. She had watched me run my hand down the smooth quilt, pick it up between my fingers to test its heaviness. She watched me stare at the lace throw pillow. Raise my hands to my mouth in awe, as I wondered whether to cuss, pray, or salute.

I nodded.

"Your uniform is in the closet. Change before dinner." I listened for the door to close. Sat down at the edge of the bed, my back stiff, my feet braced firmly against the floor like I was ready to run.

The first night in Black Snake trailer, me and Janie slept on the floor. I woke all through the night, worried the rats would come back. Worried the dead snake would return. But after so many nights curled up on the floor of Daddy's car, it was sweet luxury to stretch my legs. By the end of the summer, we slept on a mattress that Mrs. Swarm threw out. Daddy dragged it to our room, and we jumped on it like little girls would. When summer ended and the nights grew cool, we could feel the chill sneaking up through that thin metal floor and into our mattress.

Janie dragged six cinder blocks inside. She spaced them underneath so that the mattress was several inches off the ground. If we laid still enough at night and held our bodies in just the right angles, then it wouldn't sag and dip between the blocks.

Someone knocked at the door. "Dinner in ten minutes."

I walked to the closet and found a floor-length black skirt, a gray tunic, and a white apron with a matching headcap. I dressed slowly, unsure of where everything went, how it all fit together. Even in a Tennessee winter, I'd never worn so much. I wished for a mirror as I struggled to pull my hair into the headcap. The girl in me, the one that watched Momma lean so sexy against that green car, cursed that outfit. Even though I knew it was a costume. Something I had to wear, had to hide myself in, until I found better.

At the dinner table an ivory card was placed before every seat. Names were handwritten across them. And silver flashed everywhere. Forks and spoons and knives circled every plate. I wondered how many of those Janie would have tried to steal.

The old woman nodded and pointed to my seat. I sat as others, guests and uniformed workers like me, came to the table. An old man, not as straight or poised as the woman, shuffled into the room. He sat down at the head of the table. His hands shook as he unfolded his napkin and laid it across his lap. The old woman reached down, helped smooth the napkin. Motioned for the kitchen women to begin dinner service.

The guests were served first. Each dish presented, described, and then spooned onto individual plates. The women worked quickly, and soon I had a plate of roast chicken and vegetables. A bread basket was passed around.

"Lord, we ask thee to bless this food," the old woman said. Others whispered *Amen*, and everyone began to eat. The old woman began to cut up the old man's food. She placed the fork in his hand, helped wrap his fingers around the handle. He dropped it. She picked it up for him, wrapped his fingers around it again.

Guests were talking about hiking. About how beautiful the mountains were in fall. They planned an afternoon picnic by a waterfall nearby.

"I'm Tabby," the woman next to me said.

"Angel."

"So, what're you in here for?" She laughed. "It's the joke we tell all newcomers."

"Oh."

"I mean if we hadn't messed up somehow, we wouldn't all be desperate for room and board."

"I'm not here for long."

"We all said that once. You'll change your mind. Sure, the routine here is borin'. The silence will drive you nuts. The clothes are shameful, they're so ugly. But it's safe. You wake up knowin' what to expect. Go to bed warm and full, and most importantly, go to bed alone. I didn't have that luxury before I came here."

"I just need a place to stay for a while."

"Runaway?"

"Yeah."

"You're our first. We've got battered wives. Addicts. Homeless bums. And hookers like me. Nice to have you, Runaway."

"Thanks."

"The old woman means business about her rules. But in time, we'll teach you the secrets. We have a bit of fun in spite of her."

"Who's he?"

"The old man? Her husband. Stroked out a few years ago. He keeps to himself, reads all day long in a study at the end of Bedroom Hall. Supposedly, he was a genius once. There's a book of newspaper stories about him. Now he just shuffles and reads."

Our eyes met. I held his gaze and noticed that unlike his wife, his eyes weren't busy. They were just sad. They rested against mine.

Women emerged from the kitchen, served coffee and passed a plate of sugar cookies. As the guests drifted into the Great Room, we began to clear the dishes. I turned around and found the old man standing next to me. He reached a shaking hand out. I thought he was trying to introduce himself, so I reached my hand to meet his.

"My name's Angel."

But he grabbed my hair. Held it up so that the light could shine across it.

"Sorry, couldn't fit it all under the cap."

The old woman hurried over and grabbed his arm. "I'll help you to your study." She turned to me as he walked ahead of her through the door.

"Angel?" she asked.

"Yeah?"

"Your bed...the quilt on it, on every bed here, is hand-made."

I looked at the ground.

"Perhaps, you'll learn how. I can always use another seamstress."

I cleared the dishes. Mopped the floor the way Tabby showed me. Then we straightened the sitting room together. After our chores were complete, Tabby led me down Bedroom Hall.

"He lost a daughter," Tabby said about the old man. "Sometimes he cries out for her before the old woman can hush him." She stopped and put her hand on my shoulder.

"Listen, Angel, if there's somethin' you need, somethin' you can't do without, I'm the one to bargain with around here. I've got ways around all of her rules. And I always like to give my new customers a welcome present. So name your poison. What do you need?"

"There is one thing...," I whispered lowly.

Later that night I couldn't sleep. I had never been more comfortable. My body full of healthy food. Wrapped in soft blankets. But my mind was busy like the old woman's eyes. Going over every little piece of my day. From the new brochure down in my pocket to the old man holding my hair up to the light.

The moon was nearly full, and its light spilled in from the window. I noticed a carving above the door. The same as in the kitchen. *And having food and raiment, let us be therewith content* . . .

Whispering the words over and over didn't help me sleep. Neither did trying to make a plan for finding you. I went to the closet. Reached inside for the whiskey that was Tabby's welcome present. I drank from it and returned to bed soothed by the familiar burn in my throat. I closed my eyes as the room spun pleasantly around me. "Tell me of your table," the old woman said.

It was a trailer floor. I sat a cupcake on it once, while Janie sang and Momma lit the candle with her cigarette lighter. It was the brown earth of a bacca field. I hid snacks from school under the baby spring leaves. They could last me till mid-June.

I shifted in the bed until my body found its familiar angle, the one that kept my old mattress from sagging between cinder blocks. *Tell me of your table*, she repeated. *Did it have . . . scratches?* Yes. The day the milk spilled. I sat at a graying picnic table beneath a famous sycamore tree. The table was scarred and weathered like an old barn. I looked up and saw bark peeling off the tree in slabs. I wiped milk from my face and called the tree Sister. Bark yields to a rising trunk. It hurts to grow.

III

Within a week I finished my welcome whiskey. After one sleepless night, I became one of Tabby's customers. Money was as important at Red Castle as any other place. None of us earned real cash. But we all had things we wanted to buy and things to offer in exchange. The alley was our marketplace. As we stuffed meals into our mouths we whispered desires. Cigarettes for some. They'd pretend to enjoy a hike when all their chores were done. But they walked just far enough to keep the smell of smoke from reaching the house. Magazines for others. Dressed like pilgrims, some of the girls still longed to know the latest fashion and gossip. Lotions and lip gloss for Shari. Her hands and lips chapped from kitchen heat. One girl just ordered candy. Bubble gum and Kit Kat bars. The men ordered the same as me: *Whiskey, please.*

Tabby jotted down our orders on a scrap of paper and handed it to the mailman each Friday. He'd tuck a parcel underneath a garden rock for her. She paid him in her own way. And we paid her. Each of us shared a portion of our loot, so Tabby enjoyed everything. Cigarettes, magazines, lotions, candy, and whiskey. We also gave her our break times as we covered her chores for her. And we'd lie for her.

"Where's Tabitha?" the old woman once asked me.

"Her stomach wasn't feelin' right. She ran up a few minutes ago to lay a cold washcloth to her head. I think she may have the milk allergy. Seems every time she puts cream in her coffee that happens."

"Let me know if she doesn't return."

But Tabby was on a date with the gardener. Shari had packed them a picnic basket. I had loaned her my cutoffs. She wore them beneath her gray tunic and long black skirt. In return, I sipped whiskey and slept again.

My days of work were easy. Mop a floor, dust some shelves. Make sure my apron was never spotted with food or dirt. The rules were easy, too. Rising at dawn wasn't hard when hot coffee and pastries, sometimes fruit salad and eggs, were waiting downstairs. I gained weight. Always skinny like Momma, I soon had to squeeze into my cutoffs every morning. But I always wore them, unless Tabby needed them, beneath my long black skirt. I kept my pocket treasure close.

It was easy to keep quiet, too. The rule of silence was a welcome one. I nodded as guests filed past, but never tried to choke out *Good mornin'*. And I didn't have to tell anyone why I signed the Appalachian Ancestry book out from the sitting room. I searched the index, looking for the history of a family named Ray.

During my first two weeks there, I rarely saw the old woman. Most of the daily management was left up to Shari. But one morning the old woman came to me as I dusted the sitting room.

"Follow me."

She led me to the library. Sat down and pointed to a chair for me. She pulled fabric from a basket on the floor.

"Can you learn?"

"What?"

"If I showed you the stitches, would you pick it up quickly or struggle? It's best to answer this now before we waste each other's time."

"I taught my own self to read. Years after the teachers gave up."

"It's a simple stitch. I'll be doing all the actual quilting." Her fingers lined up the edges of two squares of fabric. She pressed patterned sides together while I knelt before her, watching as she sewed a straight row of stitches a pencil's width from the edge. "This is piecing," she said. "A perfect place for a beginning quilter to start."

And that's how our mornings together in the library began. After breakfast, and after I delivered trays down Bedroom Hall and dusted the small sitting room, she would find me.

Fresh fabric always waited for me in the basket. I wasn't quilting. Or making long hems of lace, the way her old fingers did. But I was still creating. Taking scraps that were nothing alone and putting them together to make something new. To make something warm.

"You know many people on this mountain?" I dared to ask one day.

"Can you work *and* talk?"

"Long as I don't look up."

"Very well. I know a few business owners that I purchase supplies from."

"I'm lookin' for a family named Ray. They live on this mountain, or around it somewhere."

"I don't know them."

"Where should I start?"

"You should pray."

I looked up. My sewing fell to my lap.

"Please attend your stitching," she said.

"Yeah."

"Have you never?" she asked, minutes later.

I thought of Daddy. "I've prayed a few times. Didn't help none."

"Then recite the line carved above your door until your desire to find something God has not brought subsides."

" 'Havin' food and raiment let us be therewith content.' "

She nodded. "Angel, everybody comes here wanting. The guests want peace. The workers want refuge."

My stitches were crooked. I ripped them out and started over.

"I call this a mountain sanctuary, and that is my goal. But I know the truth. This place, it's the House of Wanting. Everybody's aching like you. Everybody's searching like you. My hope is that with time those words above your door will become real. They will bring you peace, even through your wanting. They will remind you that a full belly and warm skin are tender mercies from God. Who are we to ask for other happiness?"

That day, my question opened something between us. From then on, she didn't comment on stitching patterns anymore or the scratchy feel of new fabric. Instead she asked about my life at Red Castle. If I had noticed the pattern of frost on the alley windows in the morning. If I enjoyed the apple strudel that Shari had baked. If I knew those apples were raised in the back orchard. If I had studied the book of Appalachian birds in the Great Room.

"This summer you might see a great horned owl," she said. "Magnificent. Most live their whole lives and don't see them. This mountaintop is their hunting ground."

She spoke of new seasons like there was no doubt I would be there. And though my mind fought her, answered her, *I'll be long gone, lady,* I couldn't deny how her words warmed me. Couldn't deny how sweet it was to have plans made for me. To be expected, to be *wanted,* in the coming months. She promised to teach me how to garden. So that I could earn my keep in the summer, because quilting was winter work. And in the fall she would teach me how to can and freeze the harvest.

Sometimes she spoke of her childhood up north. Of her grandmother's bread recipes that Shari now served on the chestnut table.

"Why'd you leave?" I asked. "Didn't think folks up there ever wanted to come down here."

"I'm a runaway, too," she said, and laughed softly. "I passed through these mountains on my way home, and found myself reconsidering what *home* meant for me, for my family. Is it where your house is built? Or is it where your family is safe?"

"I've only been to Tennessee. And then the other Carolina when I was…"

"But look at you now, child," she interrupted softly. "You're here now." I looked up from my stitching. "Come, we should focus on this new bolt of fabric for the quilt backing," she said. "I'll show you how to baste the layers together so they don't slip as I quilt them together. If we work with diligence, we can have a good start by lunch."

It always happened like that. She would speak warmly about future plans for me. About summer work and spring plantings. But if I hinted of my past, she interrupted me, refocused me on our work together. Sometimes by whispering the carving above my door.

It's not that I wanted to tell her my story. The one saved just for you. She was a stranger, and I didn't want to empty my pockets for her. But there were other things I found myself wanting to tell. Things that teachers at school knew about me. Things that the Swarms themselves saw. Sometimes as we sewed and she talked of plans for me, I'd find myself wanting to interrupt her. Tell her something easy. Like, *I was raised real poor.* Or maybe, *Daddy was a hard man to live with.* I tried it once.

"Sorry," she said, before hurrying to answer a call she said came from the kitchen. I shrugged my shoulders and sat alone, making small, straight stitches.

That night, with the help of cheap whiskey, I whispered it in my room. I knew the truth, what her *Sorry* really meant. That she didn't want to be my sounding board. That she was too busy with the demands of her popular resort. Her *Sorry* was the same as covering her ears and singing *la la la* to block out unwanted noise.

I drank more whiskey and tried again. That time, I heard what I wanted. *Sorry.* Because maybe the things I'd lived through were more than sad or scary. Maybe they were wrong. Something even a stranger should want to apologize for. Sure, I was trailer trash. But once, I was a little girl. Your baby born in Carolina and wrapped in a green blanket.

I fell asleep and dreamed of you.

I was running through the bacca. It was midsummer and the leaves were high and strong. You were chasing me, laughing. I hid behind tall plants and watched you pass by. Watched you worry over where I was. I didn't cry out for you, or wave my hands through the bacca. Life was sweet enough, just knowing that you were looking.

IV

The next morning, I traded Tabby all my breaks for the next two days for one conversation with her mailman. I flagged him down in the road before he reached the mailbox.

"You deliver to this whole mountain?"

"Where's Tabby?" he asked.

"She's sick. I'm lookin' for the Ray family."

"But I got Tabby's things. Who's gonna pay me?"

"If you help me, there'll be big money for both of us. More money than you'll ever earn deliverin' mail and whiskey."

"Slow down," he said. "What's this all about?"

"I'm lookin' for my family."

"And what am I supposed to do about that?"

"My mother's last name is Ray, and she might be a Holy Roller. She's got money, and if you find her, you'll be rewarded. Look, all you gotta do is keep your eyes open. You walk up to homes all over this mountain. You see names and addresses that nobody else does."

"Yeah." He nodded.

"Find her and we'll both be rich."

Four days later he told Tabby he had a lead. A family was looking for a baby they had given up for adoption, eighteen years ago. He had delivered a package to them from a company called Finding People.

"All he knows so far," Tabby said, "is that their house is huge. And they got a cross on the door. And they're lookin' for a baby that would be your age. Now the name wasn't Ray, but what if your mother got married? It just might be your folks, honey."

I spent that night laying things from my pockets across my bed. Like a time line. Like a story told in pictures.

"It was a boy," Tabby told me two days later. "They're lookin' for a boy."

I wrote *Sick* next to my name on the chart in the alley. Went to my room and fell across my bed. Stared at the carving above my door until I could trace the letters perfectly, my eyes closed.

"Pray," the old woman had said.

Maybe she was right. Daddy was trouble, so my baby lips prayed over him. Black Snake trailer was trouble, so I prayed as I burned it down. I was trouble, too. I found my whiskey bottle beneath my mattress. Took a sip though it was only noon, closed my eyes and tried. *Bless me.*

Someone knocked on the door.

"Yeah?"

"Why aren't you working? You have obligations," the old woman called.

"I'm sick."

"Very well. You'll be needed tomorrow, though. We begin Christmas."

At first, Christmas at Red Castle didn't seem like a holiday as much as it was a production. Bedroom Hall was booked solid by people seeking holiday peace. We cleaned more, carried more trays, and had to help in the kitchen frequently. Families took short walks through the soft mountain snow and returned to order trays of Christmas cookies and warm cider. And then one day after supper, the Christmas tree went up.

It was a real tree, cut from the mountain. Nearly twelve feet tall and six feet wide. It stood in the corner of the Great Room, just before the entrance to the dining hall. There were no lights for it, only handmade ornaments. Many of them quilted lace, and I recognized the patterns of the old woman's skilled fingers. Some of them were childlike, initials and dates scribbled on the back.

Guests were busy hanging the ornaments, while I stood against the wall and watched. The old woman appeared by my side. "I'm sorry," I said. "I'll go clean the sittin' room now."

She shook her head and handed me an ornament made from the scraps of fabric we had just worked with. "Hang this."

I'd never had a Christmas tree. But I knew how beautiful they could be because of Swarm house. The Swarm tree was always covered in large rainbow lights and tinsel. When I was little, I thought they put it in the front window for people like me who didn't have a tree, but needed to see one.

Momma taught me the truth.

"Look at them, showin' off that tree. Bet they spent a hundred dollars on decorations. Bet that's a real crystal star on top. That's why they put it up front and open them curtains. They want everybody to know just how good they got it."

The old woman watched me as I found the loop at the top of the ornament and opened it. I saw how the branches were pulled slightly through the loops of others and did the same to mine. But it was too heavy and the branch too small. It bent forward and drooped in front of another ornament.

"Oh," I said, as my face flushed. I started to remove it.

"No, it's perfect," the old woman answered.

I hurried to the sitting room, but I worked slowly that night. I forgot to straighten the cushions and didn't bother to count the chess pieces. I kept returning to the Great Room entrance, just to look one more time. I held my broom and swept and swept the one space on the floor that let me see the tree, until curfew was announced. Then I walked to Bedroom Hall, my hand on my skirt, pressing against the place where my last pocket was. I hurried into my room and pulled out that final memory. My happy one.

It was a small bar of soap. Broken, but the crumbs were held inside the wrapper. The words *Holiday Inn* stamped across it. It smelled like crushed flowers. But when I held it to my nose I only thought of the good Christmas.

It was during one of the winters that Momma had a secret boyfriend. Whenever Daddy took off for the night, Bobby drove up in his yellow pickup. Momma would send us outside to stand guard.

"You hear your Daddy's car comin' down the road, you run quick and tell me. He'll kill us all if he finds Bobby here."

Christmas came and Momma wanted to celebrate for the first time ever. We didn't have a tree, but she hung a string of lights off the edge of Black Snake trailer. They blinked on and off through the night. She took us shopping. Bought us each a candy cane and a little bell necklace to wear around our necks. Gave up her whiskey money to buy Bobby a bottle of cologne.

"He's takin' us away," she whispered, as she hid the cologne beneath our couch. "He's got money, and he's gonna take us all away."

On Christmas Eve, Daddy was out. Bobby pulled up and we all piled into his yellow pickup.

"Merry Christmas," he laughed. Momma jumped on his lap and they started kissing and sighing like the big kids that sat at the back of the bus. He drove us to Gatlinburg.

That year there was a rich girl in my third-grade class. She had written an essay about her trip to Disney. She spoke of spinning rides and ice cream, castles and princesses. As Bobby drove us into Gatlinburg, I looked at everything around me. My eyes never missing anything that blinked or shimmered. I wrote my own report and imagined reading it to my class.

My Best Vacation Ever
by Angel

My best vacation ever was to a place called Gatlinburg. It took a long time to get there. At least an hour, but probably more. I saw a store with a sign that said Feed the Black Bears, two dollars. I saw chairs that hung from a wire and could lift and carry you up to the mountain top. I saw a place called the Mountain Fudge Factory. The sign said they sold 15 types of fudge. In the window, a man was making taffy. He pulled on a rope of blue candy as long as my arm. We went to a hotel next. It had a pool inside. You could swim in the winter or in the rain and never get cold. There was a machine in the hallway too. If you pressed a button, ice would shoot out. And another machine next to it. It was full of candy. Gatlinburg is the very funnest town in the whole wide world. When I grow up, I want to live in that hotel.

Bobby booked two rooms. One for him and Momma, one for me and Janie. Then he piled a bunch of quarters on the bed.

"Git your supper from the machine. Just leave us alone."

The room had two beds in it. We could jump back and forth between them without ever touching the floor. There was a TV, too. With dozens of channels, all of them clear even though it wasn't storming. We watched *Little House on the Prairie* for the first time. Giggled at the way those girls yelled *Ma* and *Pa*, instead of saying *Momma* and *Daddy*. Janie held a sheet around her head.

"How you like my bonnet, Laura?"

We went swimming next. We didn't own swimsuits, so we jumped in wearing our long sleep T-shirts and panties. Janie was a teenager. But she splashed in the water same as me, her black bra showing beneath her wet shirt. When we were hungry, we dried off and returned to our room. Divided the quarters evenly between us.

Janie bought a Mountain Dew, a bag of Fritos, and a Snickers bar. I bought a grape coke, a bag of Cheetos, and M&M's. And later that night after swimming again, we split a pack of orange crackers with peanut butter in the middle. It was the best Christmas dinner ever.

Once we finally turned out the lights and decided to sleep, each of us in our own bed for the first time ever, I saw Christmas lights flashing outside.

"Merry Christmas, Janie," I whispered.

She laughed. "Wish every day was."

In the morning, we woke up to Momma pounding on the door. Janie rolled out of bed and let her in.

"Your daddy's waitin' on us outside."

"Where's Bobby?"

"Didn't like him as much as I thought. Now git up, Daddy's waitin'."

I saw the way she held her body tight. Like the bones that jutted from her skin hurt her. I saw the swell of her cheek, the skin stretched and purple beneath her eye.

We climbed into Daddy's car.

"Janie," Momma said to Daddy with a roll of her eyes. She told him a story about Janie running off with a boy from the back of the bus. About chasing Janie and finding her in the hotel with a bad boy.

"He knocked me around a bit. But I knew how to run him off," she said, pulling the gun out of her bag.

"Next time," Daddy said, shrugging his shoulders, "just let her go."

Janie closed her eyes tightly and slid a bar of soap into my hand.

"Smell it," she whispered. "Smells like Christmas."

V

I stood inside my Red Castle room, smelling Janie's Christmas soap. Someone knocked.

"Yeah?"

"We have work to finish," the old woman called.

It wasn't unusual. Lately she often had extra tasks for me once the other workers were in bed. Sometimes I waited long into the night to sip my whiskey, fearful that she would come for me. If I stayed up late working with her, she gave me extra rest during the day out of the sight of other workers. She hid me in the library and let me rest on the couch.

We had finished making quilts and began a new pattern for aprons. It was my job to attach the pocket. That night I picked up the apron I had started earlier and began a row of new stitches.

"I thought we could make ornaments tonight. There are some bare places on the tree."

She showed me a snowflake pattern, and I watched as she attached tiny pearls to soft velvet.

"Cut this pattern. I'll do the sewing."

From my quick glances up, I noticed fresh snow was falling and sticking to the window.

"We had so much snow when I was growing up," she said. "That's why I like this pattern. It might start falling in October and last till May."

"I was born near the ocean. It don't snow there. And in Tennessee, if it snowed it usually just skimmed the ground. There were a couple of real good ones, though. Once snow came all the way up to the front door of our trailer. That meant it was real high, too, 'cause our trailer wasn't planted to the ground like a real home."

"Finish your pattern."

"Yeah."

When I finished, I handed it to her but she didn't give me more velvet. Instead she stood up, laid her snowflake to the side. "I have an extra wool coat. Your clothing is enough for quick trips outside, but tonight you will need more. Come."

She got the coat, then led me out the alley door and past the back gardens. There was a trail into the forest there, made smooth by the men of Red Castle for the guests to hike. Snow covered it, but we could still tell where it began.

"That's how you know it's really snowing," she said. "It takes more to cover a forest ground."

The moonlight glowed on the snow, and I could see the old woman perfectly. The sideways glances she kept giving me. But soon I forgot all about her and remembered the bacca.

It had been months since it had hidden me. But those dark woods, with twists and bends, with paths glowing of moonlight, reminded me of home. I saw myself, just a baby, laughing and running through the fields, my hair lit up with moonlight streaming behind me. I saw myself, just a baby, hiding beneath bacca leaves. Clutching my blanket and waiting for stars to move.

"I git why you didn't wanna go home," I whispered.

"Not even my husband knows I come out here. There is something special about a mountain, with only a moon to guide you through it."

"Tender mercies, like you spoke of before. As good as food or raiment. Mine was only the bacca. Just like this mountain trail, only with stalks and leaves growin' over my head."

She turned to me. "No food?" she whispered. "No raiment?"

I shrugged my shoulders, and was careful not to look at her. "Just bacca."

She sighed. "My prayer is that you've found more here."

I nodded. "The food is good. My clothes are warm. But I still wonder—"

"Remember what I said before, about not wanting what God has not seen fit to provide."

"But it wasn't him that said no."

"What do you mean?"

"Somebody else got in the way."

"But what about *now*...I'll never let you hunger." She turned to me and grabbed my hands firmly. "Oh child, you will never be cold again."

Her promise, her strength as she grabbed my hands, took my breath. She was just an old woman, a stranger. Yet she offered something Momma and Daddy never had. Perhaps it was just comfort. But it sounded like safety. Like the rustle of tall bacca leaves in the wind. Like a promise that harvest would never arrive, that my fields would always be full.

I followed her back to Red Castle. We walked without speaking or looking at one another. I handed her my coat and walked toward Bedroom Hall.

"If you're not tired, we could finish our sewing," the old woman called out. "Or perhaps you'd like a cup of warm cider. Angel?"

"I am," I said without stopping or turning around, "tired."

"Tomorrow then."

I nodded, raised my hand to wave good night. But we never shared that cup of cider together. Because later that night there was another knock at my door. I assumed it was the old woman again and I was already sipping sweet whiskey. I lay quietly and pretended to sleep. Something slid under my door.

"Mailman brought this today," Tabby whispered. "Said you'd want to see it."

I stared at the thin paper on my floor, sat up in bed and took a quick gulp of whiskey for courage. But it didn't work. I trembled as I walked to the door, as I reached for the envelope. Addressed to Mr. and Mrs. H. Rey. I trembled as I held it up to the moonlight pouring in from the window.

"*No*," I whispered.

I ran to my closet, found the crumpled business card the old woman gave me at the hospital. I held it next to the envelope. The addresses matched. But something was different. Something burned.

Names. At the bottom of the business card in little black letters: *Mr. and Mrs. H. Reynolds.* But on that envelope, hand-written and stamped out of New York, important things were missing. Letters vanished. *Mountain Top Lodge. Care of Mr. and Mrs. H. Rey.*

I paced the floor. Surely it was a mistake. Some careless person must've addressed the envelope. But then I thought of the old man, holding my hair up with awe. I thought of the old woman's special interest in me. Teaching me things she taught none of the other workers. Finding reasons to spend time with me, to laugh and talk together. I thought of that moment when she first came to see me in the hospital. How, for one quick moment, I thought she could be the one. I had asked her, "Are you a Holy Roller?" But she shook her head, and in a hard Yankee tongue that could never come from Carolina, called herself a businesswoman. Handed me a card with her name, *Mrs. Reynolds . . .*

I opened my door, peeked around the corner and up and down Bedroom Hall. It was three hours past the worker curfew. I crept down the hall, not knowing where I was going but hungry for answers. I walked past the stairs and library until I stood outside the old man's study, a room no one was invited to, a place no one but the old woman ever cleaned. I took a breath and pushed the door open.

The room was black with darkness. I bumped into the corner of a desk. Felt my way to the window and pushed back the heavy drapes. My eyes adjusted to the room and used the light from the window to look around. I saw the desk, the one that bruised my hip, huge and messy in the middle of the room. I saw maps framed behind it. Stacks of books, the titles I couldn't read for lack of light. Couldn't find anything that said

Rey on the desk. I turned toward the window again. Saw the picture frames centered around it.

There was a strange drawing scribbled on a sheet of notebook paper. With lines stacked across more lines. And words like *Wife, Family, Work, Unity of thought, Unity of purpose*, carefully centered across the lines. I stared at that picture. I had no idea what it was supposed to be. But maybe I was supposed to be there, somewhere on one of those lines. Maybe somebody got in the way...

I thought of Momma. The way she laughed as she described the *old Holy Roller woman*. How all these years I doubted her. Wondered whether I could ever trust the story of drunken trailer trash.

"I was cleanin' the toilet," Momma told me, the day the milk spilled. "On my hands and knees scrubbin' when I heard the doorbell ring. Preacher's wife was in a bad mood that day. She needed to cuss, but wouldn't go ahead and shout somethin' bad and git it out of her system." She laughed. "I don't blame her for being in a bad mood, though, 'cause the front porch was trashed. Biggest storm I can remember passed through that night. Your daddy and me was just in a little ol' shack, too. We huddled down in the tub together 'cause that's what the man on the news said to do. We heard Janie cryin' in the bedroom and argued over who had to go git her. But somehow we made it through the night okay. I showed up for work the next day and saw a palm tree had been lifted up by its roots. Smashed through the front porch. That old woman didn't care, though. She charged up them steps and rang the front door bell all the same. The preacher's wife groaned loudly. I crawled, close as I could, still scrubbin' so I wouldn't seem like I was snoopin'. 'Here she is,' the old woman said when the door opened. 'It's a girl.' That old

woman's gray hair was loose and tangled all the way to the floor.
A little cap sittin' crooked on her head. She was scary-lookin',
like a crazy nun or somethin'. She tried to shove a bundle out,
but the preacher's wife backed away. 'The baby?' the preacher's
wife said. 'It's too early. Has she seen a doctor?' The old woman
shook her head. 'Take her. Say you found her on your doorstep.
Or that you had her on your bathroom floor. She's yours now.'
The preacher's wife took another step back. 'I wanted to tell
you, Ms. Ray,' she said. 'I was gonna call you later today, in fact.
There's been a miracle, you see. Doctors said never, but God said
yes.' The old woman held the baby out again. 'Please, I have to
get back to my daughter,' she said. 'You don't understand,' the
preacher's wife said. 'I can't take this baby. I'm havin' my own.'

"They started to argue. The old woman nearly shoutin'
through gritted teeth. The preacher's wife tried to stay polite.
'I really wanted to tell you before,' she kept sayin'. 'Had no idea
it'd come so early. You should really get it to a doctor soon.'
But the old woman wouldn't leave, and finally the preacher's
wife started to shut the door. 'Ever think this baby is your
gift? That it's the reason I've got my own on the way?' The
old woman started to weep like nothin' I'd ever seen. 'I'll pay
you,' she begged, as the door shut. 'Five thousand dollars!' The
preacher's wife kept on shuttin' the door, though. And that's
how I knew for certain she was the craziest lady I'd ever met.
Shuttin' the door in the face of good money. Desperate money.
I wasn't crazy, though. I knew opportunity when I saw it. I
ran out the back door, around the side of the house, and met
that old woman in the yard. 'Five thousand dollars,' I said, as
I reached for you. The old women seemed like she was gonna
say no. And then she reached down in her apron. Pulled out
a stack of money."

Momma turned up the whiskey bottle. It was empty. "Go git under your daddy's pillow. Bring me what's there."

I shook my head. "You told him I was the one that did it last time."

She tried to sit up but couldn't. "Git in there and bring me what's under his pillow. Then I'll tell you somethin' funny." She started to giggle. Rolled over onto her side. I brought her the half-empty bottle from under Daddy's pillow.

"It was so hot," she laughed. "Ain't no heat like Charleston's. It'll bake you quicker than any oven. But that Holy Roller was scared to show even the tiniest bit of skin. Her face drippin' with sweat. She wouldn't unbutton her collar. But she sold her baby without even blinkin'."

"You didn't buy me. You got paid to take me."

"Darn straight she sold you. And I paid her what she wanted most."

"What?"

"The right to be rid of you for good."

"And then Daddy bought the car?"

"Yeah." She laughed. "Old woman handed me the cash. Said, 'A thousand for you. But the five is hers. Take care of her with it.' I looked down and counted as she walked away. And I'll tell you now what I never told nobody." She turned the whiskey bottle up, laughed as she took a drink.

"There was six thousand dollars. Not five like Daddy always yells. I went straight home, but before I went inside, you better believe I hid that extra thousand under the porch. And handed Daddy the five. Like that old woman said, that thousand was for me. When somethin' caught my eye, maybe a pair of jeans or a new pair of sexy boots, I could buy it without askin' your daddy. I never told him, not even when we ran out of money and couldn't pay the rent. Or when that sheriff showed up and kicked us out. That money was mine. My prize."

"And he bought the car with my five."

Momma nodded. "Your first crib. You know he never once asked me before he bought it, only barely thanked me. Left me at home with two cryin' babies and went and got that car. You spent your first night out in it. You had the worst colic of any baby I'd ever seen. Born early, not a bit of meat on you, your legs were all twisted and kickin' with pain. Our house was just two rooms. None of us could sleep for you. I tried walkin' you. Tried givin' you a warm bath. Tried bottle after bottle but nothin' helped. Daddy picked you up. Laid you on the porch. But we could still hear you screamin' and the nights were still cold. So I took you to the car. Wrapped you up in your blanket and laid you in the seat. Come mornin', you'd worked it all out. You never cried like that again."

She sobbed suddenly. "It ain't been easy, you know. Sometimes I think about that day and wonder if we all wouldn't have been so much better if I'd just kept on cleanin' that toilet. Wouldn't have the heartache of a car that keeps breakin' down. Wouldn't have the worry of another mouth to feed." She started to weep. I helped her stretch out on the couch. Pulled her legs from under her, straightened her neck so she wouldn't get a cramp in the morning.

"Go bring me a prize," she slurred, as she started to fall asleep.

"It ain't due yet," I said.

Her eyes were closed but her hands were still tight around that bottle when she whined, "But I gave you a home when nobody else would."

VI

Stars fall sometimes. Without warning, light plunges in wild streams before disappearing. I read once in a fairy tale that I was supposed to make a wish when it happened.

But I only wished on *living* stars. Not the dying, falling, disappearing kind. The kind that disappointed me. Sometimes I'd build a perfect picture. Draw glittery eyes and reaching arms. Then something would change. A star would fall and my picture would collapse. You'd disappear all over again.

I returned to Bedroom Hall and knocked on the old woman's door. "Ma'am?"

After a moment, the door opened slightly. "This is against house rules, Angel. You're never supposed to leave your room after curfew without—"

"But there's work for us to do."

She started to protest, but peered from behind the door and saw my face. She nodded. "Very well. I'll come to the library in five minutes."

In the library I laid out a picture. Of a slick green car with a muscled man washing it. There was a bare-chested little girl holding a tin full of water behind him. Five years old and nothing to cover. I stared at the picture and tried to remember the speech I had rehearsed for so many years. But the words wouldn't come. All I could think about was how that car belonged to me. My first crib.

"Mrs. Rey?" I whispered when she walked in.

She bowed her head as she sat down across from me. We sat in silence for several minutes. I waited, watching her, until finally she answered, "Yes." She looked up then, tried to smile. "It's no accident that you are here, Angel."

"I left Tennessee to find my mother. And instead I found you. The one that got in the way. Where is she?"

"I found *you*, Angel. First in the newspaper. A story about a young girl lost in the mountains. The right age, the right build, the right hair color. I sent my Bethie to see you. Why do you think the same volunteer kept showing up day after day? Did you really think she just wanted to be your friend? She watched you. Heard the things you cried out for in your dreams. And reported it all back to me."

"The gook?" I whispered in disbelief.

"She's Filipino. She's your aunt. She lives down the mountain. After she told me the things I needed to hear, I knew I had to see you. One look and I knew. You were the child."

I watched as tears filled her eyes. As she started to speak and then stopped, because she didn't trust herself not to weep.

"Is she dead?" I asked.

"We lost her years ago."

"And I look like her?" I cried.

She nodded again. "So much."

"And you're the one that sold me?"

"Yes."

"Did she want you to?"

She shook her head. "There are so many things I must explain."

I held my hands up in the air between us. "I don't want your excuses."

"Let me just—"

"What about me? Don't you want to hear what you did? I've

carried it all, here in my pockets, like tourist souvenirs. Just so one day I could show her. Give her back a piece of everything you took away."

"I turned your past over to prayer years ago. It's your future I need you to trust me with. Whatever happened, whatever fills your pockets, give me a chance to replace it. I'll give you new treasure."

I slid the picture over to her. "This was my daddy. He's the one that taught me how to pray."

She stared at the picture, but I wanted more.

"Pick it up," I growled. I wanted her to see me, a five-year-old baby girl. The one she gave away. "You bought that car, you know. It's how I learned about love. I'd watch Daddy's face, the way he looked at it, the way he called it Baby. That's how I learned what love looks like."

"Forgive me," she groaned. "Please."

"No," I said, as I grabbed for the picture, held it tight against my chest.

I stared out the window behind the couch, as the old woman wept. The sky seemed darker than ever before. Like every star tumbled at once and left behind a perfect sheet of black. A place where a mother could never be born. A place where a daughter would always be lost.

"Turns out Daddy was right all along."

"No, that's not what love is supposed to look like."

"He was right about you."

"What?"

I smiled. "'Woman,' Daddy used to shout. 'If you scare her enough, she'll give more money.' They spoke of you, nearly every day. They hunted for you. Cursed each other for not knowin' how to find you. Because they wanted one thing. Because to us, to my family, you are only good for one thing."

I looked at her as she waited for me to speak. My eyes went dry. My throat tightened so sobs could not escape. And my face twisted into something ugly. Something mean and cruel, that belonged at Black Snake trailer. "*More*," I whispered.

"Money? You think money will fix you?"

I nodded.

"I want you to stay. I'll pay you to stay."

"No."

"I'll pay you ten thousand dollars to stay."

"You'll pay more, and you'll want me to leave."

"Where will you go?"

"I want twenty-five thousand dollars."

She sighed loudly. "But where will you go? What will you do?"

"Live," I whispered.

"And you think money is all that's needed to do that? What about after it's spent? How will you live then?"

"I've turned profits dancin' half naked on a biscuit counter. I did it for the money, but the woman you gave me to would have done it for free."

"You'll end up right back in the trailer. Is that how you want to live?"

"Livin' was always the easy part. It was the not dyin' that was hard. My momma had this gun, kept it by her bed at night. Sometimes I couldn't sleep for the way it called out to me through the night." I looked at her, the misery across her face. I felt a surge of victory. "You want to know what it said to me?"

"I already do," she cried loudly. "Every word it spoke, I know by heart. And money won't make it hush, Angel."

I laughed softly, even as tears dripped down my face. It was a trick I'd seen Momma do so many times. It used to confuse me the way she could sit on our couch and laugh and cry at the same time. But as I sat before that old woman, I finally understood. It wasn't that Momma was crazy or didn't know what she really felt. It was that she felt the joke of her life, the hurt and anger over it, all at once. Like me, sitting there before my grandmother, the woman that sold me away. I was angry and sad, too. But the joke wasn't lost on me, either. About how all the bad things in my life had so perfectly trained me for one thing: how to get *More*.

"Ain't been a year since I robbed a dead man. Momma made me, 'cause she thought that dead man owed her. Now you're the one that owes me. And if I have to, I will wait for you to kill over dead."

She pulled a checkbook from her pocket. Wrote the right numbers, signed the right name. "We'll go to the bank tomorrow. It's too late tonight. Return to your room, and in the morning I'll help you set up an account for twenty-five thousand dollars. But once you leave here, do not return for more. This twenty-five is my final payment where you are concerned. Do you understand me?"

"Don't worry," I said, as I left the library. "You're finally rid of me for good."

I returned to my room, sat down on the bed, and stared at the check. I tried my best to feel happy. I let my finger trace the numbers. I let my mind imagine the spending. The clothes. The food. Shiny silver buggies filled to the top with star fruit.

Just an hour earlier, I had been poor. Redneck, too. But as I sat, holding that check and dreaming of all the ways I could spend it, I couldn't shake the feeling that I would leave that mountain poorer than when I arrived. I'd lost the hope of you.

I fell across the bed, let my hand drop to the side. I pushed against the mattress in search of that bottle that always brought relief. I held it up before me, tried to find the strength to return it to the mattress. Whiskey was what I needed to escape Momma and Daddy. It was what I needed to feel warm, when night winds were my bedtime blanket. There in that bed, with Momma and Daddy far away and so much money in my hands, I made a promise: *I don't need whiskey anymore . . .*

But I was born a liar. And so I brought that bottle to my mouth, over and over in the dark. Because no matter how safe I was, no matter how rich or warm, whiskey was the only thing that silenced the noise. Of a thousand drunken screams. Of a hundred dishes being broken. Of Janie crying alone somewhere in jail. Of her baby being handed off to strangers, just like I was.

I put that bottle to my lips, found silence, and fell asleep. It was just a quick fix, that quiet whiskey numb. Some new noise would usually reach through the whiskey and startle me awake. Sometimes it was a tractor starting before dawn. Or maybe an animal running through the bacca. Once I woke up to a crashing noise. Heard leaves, just a couple rows over, being stamped down. I hugged my knees to my chest and scooted close to the plants. A baby's effort to hide. The noise came closer and I cried, thinking a mean stray dog, the kind that would want to look me in the eye, was hunting me down.

But then something leaped, just out of my reach. And then leaped again. Deer. A whole pack of them running through the bacca. Leaping between the rows. It was all over in a couple of seconds. Their speed, their soft brown hides that Daddy liked to rub his car down with, vanished, and I was alone.

I tried to tell Janie about it later. And the only word my baby mind could think to describe it was *Fireworks*. Because it was beautiful. Because it made me feel hot and scared and happy all at once. Because it was over in a flash.

That night at Red Castle was no different. Something ruined my whiskey quiet. A new noise that didn't belong in the middle of my night. Like the sound of fingers snapping. And then there was a voice. I sat up in bed and hugged my knees to my chest. I scooted under the covers and hid, like a broke-down dog. I reached for my whiskey, as the echo bounced inside my head.

Click. Click. Click. And then a whisper. About something sad. Like a thousand regrets. Like a hundred apologies. Like a deep sigh and shrug of old shoulders... "For your own good."

VII

Morning came and I lay in bed, foggy from the night before. I was no longer an employee of Red Castle, and I welcomed the liberty of extra rest. I missed breakfast in the alley. And when it was time for lunch, I didn't bother dressing in my uniform. I slid on my old cutoffs and sweatshirt. Grabbed my check and prepared to leave.

I turned for a last look. At that bed, that beautiful bed, with its lace and handmade quilt. At the carving above my door, which I'd never be able to understand, never be able to own. I reminded myself of the new treasure in my pocket. Twenty-five thousand dollars. I reached for the door.

But then something happened. Something that made me fall back and look nervously around the room. That made the old fears of my childhood swarm over me. Fears about monsters waiting. About feet that need to run and can't.

Daddy had come across Janie in the fields. She had a picnic spread for a farmhand date. But all the food was Daddy's. The pimento cheese he loved. The baloney and crackers he craved. The coke that we all preferred to drink flat before we'd drink the limestone-filled water.

He didn't say anything when he found them. But when he went home he opened the fridge and saw that she had left him nothing. Except the stale cornflakes Momma liked, and the potted meat and canned sausages that we pretended was ham. He remembered the way he caught her feeding his crackers to that dirty farmhand. He ran to his bed, looked under the overturned bucket that served as a nightstand. It was where he hid his collection. Some men, like Mr. Swarm, collected silver. Other men collected pocket knives. Daddy collected sugar. Pieces of hard candy, flavored like cherries or limes. Half-eaten candy bars, because, unlike Momma, he knew to savor luxury. To draw it out a bit, make it last as long as it could.

That day after finding Janie in the field, he turned the bucket over. She was too smart to take it all. But even I knew that he counted his sweets. He stood over the little pile humming out numbers, stopped and growled lowly. Picked up the bucket and threw it against the trailer wall. Janie had stolen four bits of Daddy's best prize.

The next day, when we got off the bus, her dog was laying in the road. A bullet in his head. Black blood pooling under him on the ground. The dog wasn't really hers, in the way it would have been if she had bought it or raised it or even fed it. It was hers because it picked her. Out of everybody else on that farm, that dog stayed by Janie. It'd run to meet her when we got off the bus. It'd wait outside the trailer for her in the mornings.

She named him Underfoot. Because that's what Momma always cussed when she saw the dog run toward Janie. "That girl's always got that damned dog underfoot." There wasn't spare food to feed him, and we guessed he lived off farm rats. There wasn't room in the trailer for him, either. He slept under it most nights. But Janie loved him. Loved that out of everyone else, that dog said she was best. Never before, with her dead-flower-smelling, trailer-trash ways, had anyone called Janie the Best.

When we found him that day, Janie started sobbing and shaking. My baby mind couldn't decide what to do, couldn't understand what had happened. Until Daddy's voice called from the bacca.

"Figured you'd prefer dog like them gooks taught you. So I got you a fresh one. Now you and your farm trash can eat him instead. And you can leave my pimentuh cheese and cherry suckers be."

Janie walked over to Daddy, standing there in the bacca, and she hit him harder than I ever dreamed a skinny girl could. It knocked him back, he lost his balance and fell down. I remember thinking, *Do it again!* I remember thinking, *Do it harder!* But she just stood there. Amazed, like me, at how strong she really was. She had knocked our daddy down. The big man of Black Snake trailer was laying flat in the bacca. With a cut lip, a gash an inch long streaming blood.

Soon, though, I stood there by that dead dog and knew fear I'd never imagined. Because Daddy was on his feet again.

Daddy was moving again. And this time, it was Janie that fell to the ground.

They were real fighters, the two of them. They didn't just share the same blood, they shared rage. The difference was this: Daddy was used to being strong. He was used to standing over skinny girls with bloody lips. He didn't hold back, dumbfounded, amazed by his strength like Janie did. He didn't give Janie a chance to find her feet. A chance to take another swing.

I wanted to get away. But I couldn't leave Janie. And of all the things I saw that day, the one thing I can't forget is her feet. I don't remember the way her face looked after. The tooth that must have been laying somewhere in the dirt. I can't even remember what Underfoot really looked like, whether he was an old yellow dog or a red hound. But I'll never forget her feet. The way her shoes, old scuffed red pumps that she liked to wear with cutoffs, went sailing through the air as she kicked. Her feet were working hard. Like she thought she was still standing. Like she thought she could actually get away. They were kicking and shaking and rolling from side to side while Daddy stood over her. They were trying to do everything my baby mouth was screaming, *The bacca, run!*

But then they slowed down. Covered in the red mud of that dirt road. And then they were still. Only moving with the rest of her body, by the force of Daddy's blows. I'd been scared before, when I first saw Daddy stand back up and walk out of the bacca. But that day Daddy taught me a new lesson. Even when I think things are as bad as they can be, *I'm wrong.* Things can always get worse. Especially if you need to run, like Janie did, but can't.

"Daddy!" I screamed. "I'll git you some food!"

He didn't stop.

"How 'bout biscuits, Daddy? You want some chicken? Pie?"

I was crying so hard, screaming and slurring my words as my mind worked to build a king's menu.

He slowed down and I begged, "Please, Daddy. Anything you want I can steal for you. Swarm fridge is full to bustin' with stuff and I can git it if you'll just stop killin' Janie. I'm the best thief you'll ever meet, I swear. I can git you anything you want in the whole wide world, Daddy. Just stop killin' Janie."

When he disappeared into the bacca, me and Momma dragged Janie home and laid her in bed. I waited under the sycamore that night. Yelled at the top of my lungs for Mrs. Swarm to come out. When she did I cried that Janie had fell into a pit of old barbwire and was cut up real bad.

"Let's get her to a doctor, sweetheart," Mrs. Swarm said.

"No," I whispered, remembering what Momma had promised would happen if anybody ever found out. "We just need some medicine. For bad cuts. Some bandages and ointments. Any aspirin if you got it."

She nodded. "Wait here. I'll be out in a minute."

Three weeks later, Janie seemed almost better. But she never went back to school, even though I begged her. Even though I knew she missed the hot lunch and the swapping kisses for cigarettes.

"I'm too scared to," she finally admitted.

"There's nothin' to be scared of at school. Why, that's where you're safest," I insisted.

She shook her head and I saw her wince with the pain of

moving her neck muscles. "I'm scared of what might be waitin' for me when I git off that bus. How I might be expectin' love to come, like the way Underfoot used to, and git a monster instead."

It was Janie's words that returned to me, like a warning, when I tried to leave my room at Red Castle and couldn't. Her voice was there with me in the room. She reminded me it was dangerous to hope on love, to look for love, because you never know when a monster's waiting.

I pulled the knob again and again, and knew for certain that it was too tight to turn. I banged my fists on the door and screamed for help, as I remembered Daddy's good lesson. Even when my mother is dead, even when I know I'll never find her, things can always get worse. Especially if I need to run and can't.

VIII

There is a fire that burns hotter than a steamy Tennessee sun. Angrier then a tin box trailer in the middle of a July drought. And painful as one of Daddy's whippings. Like something the old woman would warn me about, that fire's name was *Want*. Its cure? Whiskey.

I was sick. Locked in that room for three days without a drop to soothe me. It had been years since I had gone so long. I lay on my stomach across the floor and watched the crack under my door, waiting for shadows to pass by. They never did, except in the morning, when a tray of food for the day slid through the slot in the door. I lost my voice screaming for whoever dropped it off. "Let me out!"

But soon, I couldn't hold still long enough to keep watch. And I was so tired that I only wanted to lay in bed. Wrapped in layers of tea-stained covers, my eyes squinted shut as I tried to force sleep. But instead of sleeping, I shook. Kicked my legs from one side of the bed to the other. I bolted up, paced the floor to try and work the trembling from my body.

"Room service," someone called. The voice sounded happy and warm. I started to cry, covered my mouth with my hand. A tray slid through the slot in the door.

I lifted the lid and saw perfect-circle pancakes. A little puddle of whipped butter that melted slowly across them. I took a bite, but it sat heavy in my mouth and my tongue didn't remember what to do. Neither did my jaws. I couldn't chew or swallow, so I gagged.

Heat swarmed me. It crawled over my skin and out of my pores until I peeled off all my clothes. Until I ran to a cold shower. Until I knelt and vomited into the drain. I crawled back to bed, naked and shivering but still hot.

I cried *Whiskey* to an empty room. Hell answered. Hell whispered across my skin. Made me tremble and shake and moan, until I gagged and then vomited in my bed. Until I rolled away from the mess onto the floor, hit my head on the corner of the nightstand, and blacked out.

When I woke up, it was dark. I was weak, and my head throbbed. But the fire seemed cooler. I stayed put on the floor. That hard pressure supporting my body felt good. Felt strong.

"Angel, are you awake?" the old woman called through the door.

I lifted my head as high as I could, but laid it down again with exhaustion.

"Help me," I cried.

"I am."

"I'm gonna die if you don't let me out."

"Did you think I didn't know about the whiskey? That I didn't see all the empty bottles that you hid in the trash cans outside?"

I sobbed, but covered my mouth so she wouldn't hear me.

"You're going to be so much stronger, so much clearer. You're going to be who you were meant to be all along."

"Let me go," I begged.

"Never. I let you go once because of the trouble I thought you brought. God's given me a second chance. Brought you back to me. And this time, I will never let you go. Not like this."

I spent the night on the floor. The throb in my head from falling turned out to be mercy. The pain of it distracted me just enough from my craving to help me rest a bit. To help me stop gagging. To help me drag my body to the slot in the door and wait and watch for shadows.

When morning came—my fourth day without whiskey—I saw black filling the space where there should have been light. I heard the clatter of a plastic tray being slid through the door. I moved quicker than I had in days. Maybe ever. I grabbed the cold hand on the other side, held on tight, and wouldn't let go.

"Tabby," I called, and knew how my voice sounded. Scary and sick.

"Angel, you're gonna get me so fired."

"Help me."

"Can't do it, honey. I got the good deal. Old woman's closed the hotel for the season. Sent away the workers with nice bonus checks. She only let me and Shari stay. Only I can come up here every day to bring you your tray."

"She's keepin' me prisoner. Some kind of sick game ... You gotta help me git out."

"She's payin' me more money than a lot of college-schooled folks. I can't ruin that."

"Help me, Tabby—"

"This is the best deal I'll ever git, Angel. And it ain't like you have it so bad. She's orderin' Shari to cook the best food she can dream up for you. In a few days I'll be deliverin' you some fresh clothes. An' she told me I could pick out somethin' nice and young. Modest, she said, but pretty, too. Not like these old black skirts."

"She's killin' me ... Walk away and my blood's on your hands."

"I gotta go," she said, as she tried to pull her hand back.

"Wait, Tabby. I got somethin' to trade ..."

She paused, let her hand rest easy in mine. "I ain't lettin' you out, but I'm always open to a good bargain. I know you've got the need for strong drink. I'll help you if it's worth it to me."

"Twenty-five thousand dollars."

Tabby laughed. "You've lost your mind."

"I'm her kin. She done give me a check for twenty-five thousand. And I'll sign it over to you. But for as long as I'm in here, you bring me whiskey. Start with three bottles."

"You've really got twenty-five—"

"Yes. But I'd rather have whiskey."

We shook hands between the slot in the door. And the next day I opened my tray to find the food was gone. Only a few crumbs were left from where the tray had once been loaded down. Instead, beautiful like surprise flowers in the middle of the plate, were three perfect bottles. It had been days since I slept. And when I tried to stand up to drink, I couldn't. I sank to my knees and used my teeth to twist the cap off. Hot whiskey poured into my mouth. I turned the bottle up high until it ran out of the corners of my mouth and down my neck. Already I felt stronger. I felt the peace of being still, as my muscles relaxed and the tremble disappeared. I closed the bottle and set it on my nightstand.

But it wasn't five minutes before I opened it again, even though I felt guilty. Even though I knew I was breaking the most basic rule of Black Snake trailer: *Don't take too much*. It was something I'd remind myself whenever I came across Momma passed out. Her mouth would be open. She'd be snoring. Sometimes spit or vomit would be pooled beside her. I'd pull that bottle out of her hand and pour a bit into my empty coke bottle. But always just a bit. Never enough for her to notice. It's not that she would have cared that I was drinking. That I was an eleven-year-old drunk. I was a careful whiskey thief simply because more than anything else, more than anything I could ever steal, whiskey was Momma's favorite prize.

I found an old tray of food from the day before. Ate the cold chicken and potatoes. Ate the little cup of banana pudding. Never once did I gag. Never once did my mouth go dry and close up with a craving for something that burned. I fell asleep in bed, clutching the bottle tightly to my chest like a best baby doll. Like a green baby blanket.

I woke up the next afternoon. Realized the vomit was still in my bed. I stripped the sheets off and went to inspect the tray that had been pushed inside sometime that morning. I ate the eggs and biscuits. Poured a bit of whiskey into the coffee. And spent the next few hours wishing the old woman would return. So I could lie and say, "You were right. I'm strong like never before."

I was happy when it turned dark outside and gave me an excuse to go to bed. I wrapped myself in that quilt and finished that first bottle of whiskey. I let each sip sit on my tongue until my eyes watered with the burn. I adjusted my pillow but it still didn't feel right. It was too big. Too comforting for what I was used to. I pounded my fists to try and make it smaller. I covered half of it and pretended the other half was being used by someone else. Janie. Sometimes, back at Black Snake trailer, I'd wake up and her long dark hair would be all tangled up with mine. There'd be a soft little nest of white and black swirled in between us as we slept.

When I was really young, and before the farmhands found her, she used to whisper stories in the dark when we couldn't sleep. She never made them up, they were always *almost* real. About our day, about our life. Only they sounded better, prettier somehow, with the words she chose.

"Once upon a time," she whispered in the dark one night, "there was two sisters named Janie and Angel. They followed tractors through the fields, watched magic seeds dropped down into rows. Them seeds started to grow. Taller and taller, till they made a big green castle in the fields. It was a magic place. Only princesses were allowed."

I'd giggle, and she'd hush me so I wouldn't wake Momma and Daddy. And then she'd ask me to tell her a bedtime story, too. I'd always repeat something that I'd heard at school, something read during storytime.

"Not *Snow White*," she'd complain. "Make it 'bout us."

But I couldn't pretend the way she could. I couldn't find the right words, the pretty ones, that bedtime stories deserved.

That all changed that night I was locked away in Red Castle. I rested on a half-hidden pillow and sipped whiskey. I turned in the bed, until my body was the perfect angle to keep a mattress, one held up with cinder blocks, from sagging low.

"Once upon a time," I whispered to the darkness, "I had a princess sister. She handed me a brown bottle. A magic one. It was my first thick blanket. It was a full belly and peaceful sleep. It became the *Hush baby, things'll be awright* that I needed to hear. It was my childhood lullaby. One I can't outgrow. It sounds like bacca leaves wavin' in the wind. Like Tennessee stars, singin'."

IX

I walked over to the stage in front of the bed. I wore my black bra and panties. My long white hair was teased into a crown. I twirled around to show myself off. Nearly spilled the bottle in my hand.

I looked down at my body. Ignored the ribs rising higher than my breasts. Ignored the hip bones that jutted out as I swayed back and forth. I pinched my face until I was sure color returned. I smiled and hoped my cheekbones didn't cut through any happiness. Didn't make me look hungry or sick.

I arched my back the way Momma always did. Men appeared all around me. They were eating biscuits, drinking beer, and aiming their shotguns at my hips. I took a long sip of whiskey, took a deep breath, and danced. *Whoo-eee*, they yelled, as they clapped.

I twirled around the bed. Tossed my long white hair over

my shoulders. "It's why they call me Angel," I lied. My brown bottle was empty. I threw it across the room and laughed as it hit the wall and shattered.

"More!" the men yelled. I nodded as I opened my last bottle. After all my years of trying, I was Momma leaned so sexy against a green car. I was Janie, dancing in a shed and smelling like dead flowers.

Boom! Boom!

I turned to the noise. Fell as I walked toward it. Hit my head on something and tasted blood in my mouth.

Boom! Boom!

It was coming from my door.

"Angel?" someone yelled.

I crawled back to my stage but couldn't find my bottle. Someone had stolen it. I looked at the men in the crowd. Their mouths full of biscuit crumbs. I looked at the slot in the door and wondered if old hands had somehow reached through.

"Which one of you took my whiskey?" I yelled. My head hurt. I brought my hand to my face and felt wet blood. I remembered Momma's face, twisted, ugly, and yelling for whiskey. "Tell me who took my damn whiskey!" I reached for the dirty dishes that were stacked on a tray in the corner of the room. I picked them up and threw them at the men, at the slot in the door. I smiled at that old familiar sound. Of something breaking. Of something being ruined forever.

There was knocking again. Someone yelled for me to go to bed. I ignored it as I searched for my whiskey. I looked under the bed. In the shower. Behind the dresser.

"More!" the men yelled.

I looked in my bag. Under the covers. I couldn't catch my breath. I couldn't hear anything but the *boom* on the door and the shout of the men all around me. I picked up the tray and threw it against the wall.

I curled up on the floor and sobbed, "More." Cried "Whiskey" until my body trembled. The heat swarmed over me again. Like the Tennessee sun rose in the middle of that room. I tried to open the window to cool off the room. But I couldn't push the lock. I yelled for the men to open my window. To give me whiskey.

When they didn't come, I turned toward them, furious. But they were gone. I was alone, surrounded by piles of broken dishes. By the blood that dripped across the floor. By that lace bed, covered in vomit.

I ran back to the window and leaned hard against it. I stared at the stars outside and pretended to know them. Pretended to name them. But just as I started to draw your picture with sloppy drunk hands, something else caught my eye. Blue. There in the window, just a slight tint of the glass. I remembered the antique and hardware store in Tennessee. The shelves of blue mason jars. How I had picked one up, held it toward the light so I could look through it at a new blue world.

"Careful," the old man working the front called out. "That's older than your great grandpap, I bet."

"Sorry," I said, as I set the jar back down.

"Don't worry 'bout it. You like 'em?"

I nodded.

"Most people pass 'em by. There are so many fakes out there now. Prettier than these real ones, too. People don't care so much for what's real as for what's pretty these days."

"Why are they blue?"

"Keeps the bad out," he said, as he shrugged his shoulders. "Ever seen a woman can food?"

I shook my head.

"Take the lid off. See that old seal? Most of it's rotted by now, but that jar wasn't made to toss loose change in, be stuffed with smell-good cinnamon sticks, or even sit on the shelf in this antique store. Long ago, before these shoppin' centers full of tin cans, a woman had to work hard to make her food last past its season. She had to work hard to keep it safe, stored inside jars. There was one thing, though, that was easy enough. Start with blue. It keeps light and heat out of the jar. That stuff can make food rot so that it would kill a person."

"Blue keeps the bad out," I whispered to the window inside Red Castle. I studied it. The clear pale blue. After a childhood lived out in green, it seemed to glow like a promise. Like sweet peace.

"Blue's keepin' me from you," I cried to the stars on the other side. "I'm too bad to git to you."

I backed up all the way to the wall on the other side of the room. I closed my eyes and ran. I ran as hard and fast as I could. Like a baby running into the bacca. Like a black snake running from the hoe aimed at its neck.

I never stopped.

BETHIE

I

It didn't take much to remind Bethie of her sister. Sometimes it was something as small as a stack of T-shirts on a department store shelf. She'd stand and let her hand touch them softly. She'd hold one up over her own T-shirt and remember days on James Island, nearly eighteen years ago, filled with sweet sister secrets. She'd remember that though Hannah was buried away somewhere, she was still *alive.*

But alive is not the same, or nearly as good, as *together.* Hannah was gone. Maybe forever. And all Bethie had of her were memories of T-shirts, and the promise of a redneck girl staying with Mother on the mountain. In Hannah's old room.

And then one day, Dr. Susan Vaughn called to invite Bethie for a visit. She said yes before the question was finished, and agreed to come the very next morning. As she drove to the hospital, she remembered the last moment she shared with Hannah. How dirty the jail cell had been. How incoherent Hannah was. Bethie tried to communicate with her. She resorted to old tricks and tried signing, hoping Hannah would grab onto those signs like the secret language of their youth. But Hannah only cried as she shook and mumbled broken sentences about sweet corn. And velvet corners. About the color blue.

Bethie wondered as she left the jail feeling so helpless, if that was what her own mother felt that day on James Island when she had refused to talk. She drove from the jail straight to Daniel and Hannah's home. She needed him to tell her it was going to be okay. He was an attorney, after all. She needed him to tell her that he could fix it.

She found him sitting on the couch, his head in his hands.

"Daniel," she called from the open front door.

He looked up at her and shook his head, clamped his hand over his mouth. She saw the strain in his face from holding back his grief. She went to him, put her arms around him, felt him sob against her shoulder. He pulled away and nodded toward the hall that led to Hannah's workroom. "All her pottery," he whispered hoarsely.

Bethie followed him to the workroom door. It was the one place Hannah never fully left. Standing inside her workroom was almost the same as standing next to her. Hannah's energy, her love, her mysterious sadness, all of it pounded down into the mud that lined the shelves.

But that day, something was different. Orange dust was scattered across the room. Orange pebbles, orange rocks... orange shatters everywhere. Daniel walked in and picked up half of a loose rectangle.

"This was my favorite piece," he said. "She gave this to me the first time I visited her workroom, up on the mountain."

Bethie stared at the piece and remembered it well. It was the old cradle, the one Daniel carried away. It looked like it had exploded.

Daniel sat down in the dust and wept. "It's all ruined." Bethie watched as he took a box from the closet in the hall. Picked up all the pieces from his favorite works and lay them gently inside the box. He carried them out, shut and locked the door to the workroom for good. Years of Hannah's work, years of the art she and Daniel loved, lay broken on the other side.

"Can you get her out of jail?" Bethie asked him. "We can help her, if you can just return her to us."

"She won't even look at me," Daniel said. "She's lost somewhere, inside her own mind. She keeps mumbling nonsense. I tried over and over to get her to speak to me. But I don't think she knew I was there. *She didn't even know I was there!*" He shook his head, panic in his eyes. "How am I supposed to help her like that? How?"

"I don't know," Bethie cried.

And she still didn't, even as she drove toward the asylum determined to somehow help. She checked the map and tried to shrug off the memory of Hannah's first day in jail. It was a skill she had learned over time and polished on a daily basis. She'd take a deep breath, raise her shoulders, give her head a slight shake, and push the air forcefully out of pursed lips. With the air went her heavy thoughts.

She replaced the thought with a sweeter one. About her own wedding day. Hannah helped her zip her dress. She adjusted the lace around her veil.

"Remember that time I said I wanted to be a slanteye?" Hannah asked.

Bethie laughed. "Yes."

"I meant it." Hannah turned the mirror that stood by the closet toward her sister. "Look at you. You are so beautiful, Bethie." The two sisters stood in front of a long oval mirror, one of them pale with glowing hair, the other golden with hair the color and gloss of wet ink. Bethie leaned her head against Hannah's shoulder.

"In a way you are," Bethie said.

Hannah laughed. "How?"

"No one else on this entire earth knows as well as you what it's been like to live in my skin."

A car honked its horn as it passed her. Bethie looked down, saw how slowly she was driving. She sped up and set the cruise control. She was only an hour away. She glanced in the rearview mirror, and had that pain of loneliness that she always felt when she saw the empty car seat. Little Corbin was home with his daddy for the day. They were probably digging in the backyard sandbox. Or maybe going to the pizza shop for lunch. She always thought it odd that she could spend all her days with that child, rock him to sleep every night, be driven to a frazzle by his constant wants and demands and tantrums, and then miss him when he wasn't near. Miss him whenever she spotted his empty car seat. She reached her hand down to her tummy. Felt the firm rise beneath her waistband. It was too soon for the new baby to move, but already she was rubbing the skin of her belly with anticipation. Longing for the day she'd feel that first turn or swish. Longing for the day she'd feel something entirely new to this earth taking hold within her.

It wasn't that she romanticized babies. She knew firsthand the work, the total exhaustion, they brought with them when they entered the world. But she also knew, better than most, how important it all was. *Life* within her. The tending of that life. And the protecting.

She hadn't known how to dress for the visit with Hannah. The doctor advised subtle colors, and she wondered why. Hannah had never seemed sensitive to color before. But the doctor was very clear with her instructions. *No Reds. No Purples. No Yellows or Oranges.*

One thing was for certain, Bethie didn't want Hannah

to know she was pregnant again. The day she told her about Corbin had been hard enough.

"I'm pregnant." They were at lunch with Mother, and Bethie surprised them all by blurting out her news. She had guessed, or hoped, that Hannah already knew. She was nearly six months along by that point. But Bethie would never forget the shatter that spread across Hannah's face. Or the way Hannah's teeth bit deeply into her bottom lip. Bethie saw blood.

Mother saw it, too, and started talking fast. About redoing the wallpaper in the foyer. About installing a garbage disposal and all the plumbing challenges it presented. About plans for new tile. Everywhere. The bathrooms. The kitchen. The laundry room.

"Hannah?" Bethie had whispered, tears welling up in her eyes. "I wanted you to know. You're going to be an aunt. We're going to have a baby in our family."

Hannah leaned over the table and vomited.

Oh, how Bethie was angry that day. As Mother half-carried Hannah to the car. As they let the door fall back on her on their way out. She was the one having to waddle for all the pain and pressure that was settled in her hips. She was the one having to heave herself into the car, the hot backseat no less, because Hannah felt nauseous. She sat back there, the window rolled down, and whispered hate to the mountain wind. Later she'd remember her words and blame them on hormones. How they make you say things you don't mean. How they make you do things that embarrass you. But the truth was, she was sick of the game. That old family game that made *everything*, even her own blessed pregnancy, somehow all about Hannah.

"No," Bethie whispered, as she drove toward the asylum. She would not tell Hannah she was pregnant again. She would not tell Hannah that the baby's heartbeat was much faster than Corbin's had ever been. That Mother promised a fast heartbeat meant *girl*. That Mother sewed a lace gown, complete with the tiniest lace booties.

If Hannah noticed that she'd gained weight, she'd laugh and say she never lost the baby weight from Corbin. But then Bethie winced and wondered bitterly whether it was safe to mention Corbin. She would always wonder if he had been the trigger. It had only been two weeks after Bethie announced her pregnancy that Hannah ended up in jail. When it first happened, when Bethie first learned what Hannah had done, she felt guilty. She felt a sharp sense of responsibility. Maybe her joy broke her sister down.

The next thing she felt, though, was something more true than guilt. She lay in bed and felt Corbin swishing inside her like the magic bean he was. She started sobbing. Not because she was sad. Not because she felt guilty. But because in the end, *it was right*. It was right that Hannah was locked away. It was right that Hannah was in a dirty jail cell mumbling crazy words. She deserved it.

Bethie started having nightmares. She mentioned them to her doctor. "It's hormones," the doctor assured her. "From a biological perspective, it's just your body's way of preparing you to be up all night feeding a little one." She didn't tell him what they were about. How she saw herself carrying her baby to the park. Or to the store or the library. She walked looking down on a sweet blanket filled with love. But when she looked up it was always the same. She was surrounded by thieving monster women. With reaching hands and guilty eyes. Women like her sister. Like her mother.

"No," Bethie whispered out loud again. She would not

mention Corbin to Hannah. She glanced wistfully at the empty car seat and wondered at her little one's amazing ability to distract her from *this*. If Corbin had been there, he'd have been yelling for her to roll down the window. Then roll it back up. Then he'd howl in protest. "*Up* means 'down,' Mommy!" She'd have popped in a CD. They'd sing a silly song together about the letter *D*. And just as her mind would be tempted to think about Hannah, Corbin would yell for Goldfish. *Not* the orange kind. The rainbow kind. *But wait*, she'd have to wonder as she reached for his snack, *does* rainbow *really mean "orange"?*

Bethie smiled. There were bad days with Corbin. Ones when his daddy worked late or when Corbin didn't nap. There were even some bad months. Like last winter, when Bethie felt like she measured life not by days but by ear infections. One after the other, an entire feverish winter of antibiotics and no sleep. And Bethie loved it. She remembered attending a playgroup. All the whining that the other mothers seemed to do. Bethie smiled at them, offered short words of sympathy she didn't feel. She had Mother to thank for it. Because of her, Bethie knew what a bad day really was.

Bethie slowed the car, and looked to the left where a stone fence appeared and stretched up the road ahead. She turned into a gated drive, where she had to show her license to the gatekeeper. He told her to wait a moment while he called in her information. After he hung up the phone, he returned her license, raised the gate, and motioned her forward.

She drove down a wooded driveway, trees and laurel shrubs planted on either side. It seemed peaceful enough, she thought. So much better than that dirty jell cell. She drove further and saw the green field that stretched to meet the stone wall. And for a moment, looking at all those trees and all that green, she had hope. Maybe Hannah was better. Maybe she spent her days walking in the woods. Maybe she read light poetry, sitting in a lawn chair on that great green field.

The driveway emptied into a parking lot, where the spaces were clearly marked for doctors or visitors. It wasn't until Bethie parked that she paid any attention to the building.

She'd imagined it many times. Usually like a prison. With bars and wires, protected by armed guards. Sometimes, she imagined it like a hospital. With red brick and straight sides. What she didn't expect, though, what she never imagined, was that the building would look like a monument, like a stone memorial, rising out of a groomed green lawn. With its marble carvings over the doors. And its slate stone sides. With its ornamental angles, its L-shaped design. It was just another death trophy, like any other you'd find at a nice cemetery. Only bigger. And with people wandering the halls inside.

She came to another gate and another guard. This time Bethie walked through. She handed her license and waited through another phone call. Then a door was buzzed open, and Bethie walked inside to a small lobby.

"Bethlehem Parker?" a lady called out from behind a desk.

"Yes."

"This way, please."

Bethie followed her to a conference room.

"Wait here, and a doctor will be with you shortly."

Bethie sat at a round cherry conference table. It was polished so well that she could see her own reflection in it when she bent forward. She saw the number eleven. Two vertical lines that creased in perfect unison between her brows. Wrinkles, still mild enough to appear only if she laughed too hard or worried too much.

There was a knock as the door opened. Bethie sat up straight, smoothed her shirt with her hands. Tried to relax her brow as she faced the white coats entering the room.

There were three doctors, two men and one woman.

"I'm Dr. Vaughn," the woman said. "I hope you had a nice trip here."

Bethie nodded and looked at her. She had short gray hair that nearly matched the styles of the men next to her, except that her bangs were swept messily across her brow, down into her eyes. She had glasses, too, that kept sliding down every time she looked at the papers in her hands. She always pushed them back into place, sometimes when they didn't even need it.

"I did," Bethie said.

"We're so glad you came. Your sister has been working hard lately. There is still so much progress to be made, but she is doing just that. Finally making progress. That's why we called you."

"What do I do?" Bethie asked. "To help her?"

It was the question that had been on Bethie's mind for years. How could she help her sister? Long ago, she tried by hiding all the clay babies that filled Hannah's cradle. She tried by encouraging her sister to think of Daniel, to welcome him. But none of it had worked. She thought of how she'd found help herself. Of how she had once been a bitter, silent, and scared girl. But she'd never told Hannah the truth she'd finally learned. Never mentioned all the conversations she'd had with their ill father about bridge building. And whose job it really is. She doubted whether Hannah would have listened to her, anyway. It was strange, the difference in them as they grew. Hannah had been Father's star. Yet as Hannah entered womanhood, she became more like Mother with every passing day.

Dr. Vaughn took her seat, leaned forward and put her elbows on the table. She looked at Bethie kindly. "I'm glad you want to help. How about we start at the beginning. On the day that *it* happened, your sister was very ill. We believe, as the court obviously believed, she had a psychotic episode. That was the only reason the court allowed her to come here instead of prison. The hallmarks of psychosis are hallucinations, delusions, disorganized thinking... and, of course, bizarre behavior."

Bethie nodded anxiously.

"What I'm trying to tell you, Bethie, is she wasn't herself that day. Sure, it was her body, her hands that did what she did, but not her mind. She was sick. She was psychotic. Hollywood would have you believe that the word only describes ax murderers and serial killers. Not true. It means, simply, Hannah broke from reality that day. Lost touch with consequences. Lost touch with *truth*. And there's a reason that people become ill like that. Just like the cold germ gives people runny noses, *something* caused Hannah's break from reality. Our job here is to untangle all the reasons for it. To help find all those *somethings* that are making her sick and teach her to cope with them so that her mind won't need to break from reality ever again."

Dr. Vaughn leaned back in her chair and thumbed through a stack of papers inside a manila folder. "Hours of watching her," she said, "here inside this folder. But no big answer yet. Not what you're hoping, not what you came here wanting me to hand you, anyway. You see, our treatment of your sister has been complicated by the fact that she suffers, has suffered perhaps for many years, from some type of dissociative disorder."

"What's that?"

"Well, the most famous type, the one Hollywood loves, is

dissociative identity disorder, which used to be called multiple personality disorder."

Bethie's face showed her alarm. Dr. Vaughn shook her head. "Don't worry, that's not what Hannah has. Dissociation, in general terms, deals with a disruption of memory, of awareness and identity. There are four main types of dissociative diagnoses, but there is so much yet unknown about the human mind. And so, as with many psychological illnesses, there is a fifth diagnosis, a catch-all of sorts for when doctors recognize dissociative symptoms but can't fit them neatly into one of the four specific diagnoses."

Dr. Vaughn flipped through the manila folder again. She pulled out a stack of papers two inches deep and held it up. "All this," she said. "Nothing. During the early days Hannah wouldn't admit who she was, where she was, what she did, what was done to her. These notes are full of Hannah dissociating herself from her past, from her present, in spite of our efforts to help her mind refocus itself."

The doctor raised her hand in a sweeping motion from side to side. "Her room... We've stripped away certain things, distractions, if you will, like color, like visitors—I'm the only doctor that makes in-room visits—so that other, more important things might surface. But then we added something. Something that led us to call you."

"What was it?"

"A chair." Dr. Vaughn pulled a few pages out of the folder and waved them proudly for a moment. "That chair is why we have these."

"What do those say?"

"Progress," she answered, as she leaned forward and looked Bethie in the eyes. "Your sister is making real progress, Bethie.

Talking to that chair in a way she hasn't before. She's told us all about having the baby, and then how she had to pretend like it never happened. How she was basically forced, by your family, to dissociate herself from the memory of it."

"I can't believe she told you," Bethie said. "She's spent so many years pretending, hiding. You know she never even told her husband. I never thought she'd tell anyone. Especially not an empty chair."

"To her, it's not empty."

Bethie nodded, new worries evident across her face.

"Oh, it's not an unusual treatment at all. It's a simple technique, really. Something used to help people release unspoken burdens. Like after a divorce, for example. A person can sit in front of an empty chair, imagine their spouse across from them and say anything that still haunts them. Void themselves of curses they long to utter. Rid themselves of leftover love."

"But you said Hannah doesn't know the chair is empty."

"She may know, somewhere within her mind. But for now it helps her to believe otherwise. She is giving voice, finally, to her regrets and desires. She is being *heard*, and that can be a very healing thing."

"What can I do to help her?" Bethie asked again.

"We want your sister to remember *more*. We think she's ready to face what she's done, to talk about it, and finally begin real healing. If she can own her past, all of it, then we can begin the work of teaching her to cope with reality. You've been witness to so much of her life, your presence might trigger new memories. You see, unlike others we might have called, Hannah owes you nothing. No obligation as a daughter or wife. There'll be no guilt in this visit, no judgment. Just sisters enjoying one another's company again."

"Okay," Bethie said. "I can do that."

"There are some rules, of course, that we'll need your strict adherence to. Don't talk about faith, or hope, or future, all of those unseen things that Hannah's mind loves to torture itself with. Talk about yourself, your life, your memories together. Concrete things that Hannah doesn't have to question or ponder or pray for."

Bethie nodded.

"We'll be there, in the presence of the intercom on the wall, if guidance is needed. If you have a question, call out to us. She calls us Legion."

Bethie looked at them strangely.

"I know it sounds odd," Dr. Vaughn said. "We've all grown so familiar with the name now. We even call ourselves that sometimes." She laughed. "It's from the Bible. It means *many*."

"I know," Bethie said.

"Now, if you'll just sign the releases here on the clipboard, we can get started with your visit. Remember, if you become frightened or need a break, just call out to us. We're always listening."

Bethie signed the papers, promising her cooperation, and her confidentiality. But her mind began to pulse that name: *Legion, Legion, Legion.* It meant much more than *many*, and she wondered if they knew that.

It meant a story about a man so wild no one could subdue him. So lost he spent night and day in the tombs crying out and cutting himself with stones. Until the day Legion was sent away from him. On that day, the man stopped being crazy. On that day the man was healed.

"Are you okay?" Dr. Vaughn asked her. "Would you like a glass of water?"

Bethie looked up quickly from the stack of papers. She could feel hives blooming over her skin. Stinging welts that sometimes spread over her neck and chest when she was emotional. "Oh," she said, nervously touching her neck, "I'm fine."

"Are you...are you pregnant?" one of the men asked.

"Yes."

"Whew," he said, smiling. "That's a hard question to ask because the only other possible answer is, *No, I'm just fat.*" He laughed, and Bethie forced herself to chuckle softly. "Listen, Bethlehem, we don't want to put any extra stress on you or your new baby. This is a difficult situation for you; all of us understand that. What you're experiencing, there on your skin, is just a symptom of the emotional stress you must be feeling inside. If you want to cancel, or take some time to relax and think things over, we'll understand. You don't have to do this. We'll still find a way to help Hannah."

"No. She's come all this way," Dr. Vaughn said quickly. "And we need her!" Her face flushed pink as she turned to Bethie. "I'm sorry. But if I may...do you mind if I speak a bit more personally?"

"Please," Bethie said.

"Your sister's case means a lot to me. To all of us, I'm sure, but I'm the one who's been going to her room for so long now, sitting on her bed while she ignores me and sees whatever she wants. I know her. And I can feel a change happening, a stirring within that room. And even outside that room, I've spent so many days and nights drinking coffee and watching her on the monitor. Recording the moans of her dreams, her silent daytime agony. I've never really had much hope for her. This place," she said, and she waved her hand around the room again, "it's a last stop for so many here. And if you'd asked me not so long ago, I'd have agreed that it was Hannah's last stop, too. But something is happening. We are at the edge; I feel it. There's a chance for her. I believe it with all my heart."

The men looked away, embarrassed. But one of them spoke as he stared out the window. "I respect your comments, Susan, but these are your personal feelings and not at all a professional diagnosis. It's your choice, Bethlehem. We're doctors; we don't rely on visitors to heal our patients."

"Doesn't matter," Bethie said, her eyes holding Dr. Vaughn's. "I'm not going home. I'm supposed to see my sister."

"What do you mean?" he asked. "'Supposed to'?"

"Just that I've spent my whole life behind her. I used to think it was because she was better than me. Prettier. Smarter. More lovable. I used to think her greatness pressed down on me like a boot on my forehead." She stood up and handed the clipboard back to Dr. Vaughn. She pulled at her shirt, till the collar rose and covered most of her hives. "But I was behind my sister because I needed to back her up. A part of me always knew she'd fall." She smiled softly and forced her eyes to hold back tears. She walked to the door and opened it. "Let's go see Hannah."

They led her to an elevator and told her to proceed to floor six and register at the front counter. Bethie stood inside the elevator, waiting to rise to Hannah's floor. She whispered, "Legion, Legion, Legion." Only this time it was more than just a story. It was a prayer. She felt the floor rise beneath her, knew she came closer to her sister with every second. *Legion*, she prayed. So that the story could be Hannah's. So *the many* would be sent away. So that Hannah, finally, would be healed.

II

The hallway glowed with the sick blue of too many fluorescent lights. Bethie sat with another clipboard and more paperwork to complete. She didn't see any patients. She didn't hear them. She saw only door after door down a long hallway. All of them shut. All of them without windows.

A janitor's cart wheeled by. With her pregnant nose she could smell the mingling of old Clorox with the mildew of the mop. She could smell the dirty water that was sloshing around in the bucket. When her stomach lurched, she looked up and searched for a distraction. Her eyes found a picture on the wall across from her. It was a cheap hotel painting. Every corner filled with some element of a glossy paradise. A sailboat. An ocean. An innocent child with a sand bucket in her hand.

A woman walked toward her. "Bethlehem?"

"Yes."

"I'm ready to let you in."

Bethie rose, felt her legs tease her with the thought of buckling. Or running. But she pushed them in front of her. Step after step down the long hallway, all the way to the very last door. The woman used a key to open the door. Bethie stood behind her.

The woman motioned her forward. "Just you."

Bethie sucked in her breath and held it. She let the hives sting every inch of her skin and didn't fight it. She felt her old stutter, long since beaten back, swim forward and threaten to freeze the tip of her tongue. Then she stepped—slowly, slowly—into the great white room.

At the time, there was too much adrenaline pumping

through her. Too much sting racing across the skin on her neck. Too much banging inside the walls of her heart. Too much prayer inside her mind. She didn't care about the details or worry over them. Like the white cinder block of a room. That perfect square that was around her sister. Without one picture. Without even one glossy idea of paradise. Or like the open bathroom corner. With its metal toilet and open stall shower. Such an insult to the modesty Hannah was raised to revere.

No, the adrenaline rushing through Bethie's veins, the boom throbbing inside her heart, focused on one thing. Hannah. With her shoulder-length hair. With her too-thin shoulders rising beneath a white tunic. With her milky skin, paler than Bethie remembered.

"Hannah," Bethie whispered. "Hannah? It's me. Bethie."

Hannah looked at Bethie, coolly, vacantly. Bethie stepped toward her. She reached out slowly, touched the cuff of her sleeve, and choked back a sob. "Sister?"

"Go," Hannah whispered. "Get out of here."

Bethie shook her head. "I came to visit you."

"Go."

Bethie sighed, pushed the air out hard between her pursed lips. She remembered what Dr. Vaughn had told her. To focus on the simple, happy times of their past together. She decided to try again. "Guess what I remembered the other day? All those times we snuck over to our neighbor's house when we were little. Just so we could watch that tiny TV they had in the garage. Remember how we'd fight about whether to watch the motorcycle show, with that cop always driving fast and dangerous, or that cartoon with the little orange people? What was that called? I can't remember for the life of me. Mother never found out about that. She still brags about us never owning a

TV. She has no idea how many shows we watched, all because the Franklins never locked their garage."

Hannah didn't move. She hardly breathed. Bethie watched her silently for a minute and couldn't decide whether Hannah had heard her or not. She shrugged. "I don't think I'm doing this right, Hannah. I'm supposed to visit with you, chat about old times together. But what I really want is for you to look at me. I'd love to see your face. Don't you want to see me?"

Hannah turned toward her, her eyes wide and scared. She shook her head slowly. "I'm not supposed to," she whispered.

"What do you mean?"

"They don't let me," she said, and pointed to the camera on the wall. "I'm only allowed to see her now," she said, as she pointed to the empty chair. "Everything else is supposed to be what's real. Just these white walls. Just this empty room. I'm not supposed to see visions anymore, except the ones they want. So I'm sorry, Bethie, but you gotta go now. I don't want to get in trouble."

"But I'm—"

"Shhhh," Hannah whispered, as she covered her ears with her hands. She closed her eyes tightly. "When I open my eyes, you will disappear."

She opened her eyes, saw Bethie, and quickly shut them. Opened her eyes. Then shut them tightly. Again. And again.

"What are you doing?" Bethie asked.

"Making you disappear. I've learned how, finally. Things might appear whenever they want, but I've learned if I focus enough, if I close my eyes and try hard enough, I can do it. I can see what's real."

She opened her eyes, saw Bethie.

"I'm still here. I'm not a vision." Bethie noticed the tremble in Hannah's lips, the fear that spread across her face. "Let's just talk. Like we used to."

"If you're not a vision, there's only one more thing you could be..." Hannah ran and stood behind the empty chair in the corner. She angled the chair until a chip in the white paint that exposed a little circle of blue faced Bethie.

"What are you doing?" Bethie asked. "Legion brought me here. Didn't they tell you? Legion?" Bethie called out. "Tell Hannah I'm real. That you brought me here." She waited for an answer, but the intercom stayed silent. "Legion?" she called out once more, and then shook her head. "Damn it, Hannah, just touch me. You'll see I'm real."

"The real Bethie never cussed," Hannah said triumphantly. "Except with her eyes."

Bethie laughed bitterly and held her hand out. "Just put your hand in mine, like the way we used to walk to the bus together when we were babies."

"That won't prove anything. Haints aren't afraid of flesh and blood."

"What can I do?"

"See that blue?" Hannah said, as she pointed to the small circle on the empty chair. "If you're really Bethie, alive and in the flesh, you can touch it without fear."

Bethie looked at the empty chair. She didn't understand the test. She didn't know the story about the chipped blue paint on the old plantation. But she walked to the chair and laid her palm over the blue. "I am not a vision. I am not a haint. I'm your sister."

Hannah nodded slowly, as she stared at Bethie's hand covering the blue. Quick tears sprang from her eyes. "Bethie," she cried.

Bethie walked to Hannah and hugged her carefully. It

wasn't the way she had dreamed it. The joyous crashing of arms around one another, the laughing into each other's tangled hair. Hannah stood very still, while Bethie wrapped her arms around her and gently held her. Like a mother holding a sick child.

"I've missed you," Bethie whispered, when she gained control over her voice.

"I'm sorry. It's been so long. But I still should have known you. I don't know why—"

"Shhh," Bethie said. "It's all right."

Hannah pulled away quickly. "Talk to me." She didn't say it friendly. Like from one sister to another. And she didn't say it rudely. Like any other lonely Yank might. She said it hungrily. Like a baby needing milk. Or else it will cry. Or else it will scream.

Bethie started with simple, sweet memories. Like how they played with the porcelain dolls together in the Mission Room. Hannah sat, hugging her knees to her chest, bottling up every word that spilled out of Bethie's mouth. Sometimes she repeated them softly, and marveled at how good it felt. To feel something brand-new inside her mouth. Someone else's words. *Real* ones.

Hannah memorized the shape of Bethie's mouth as her words fell out. She memorized the rise and fall of her tone. Bethie's punchy syllables, a clue to days long past, when every sound she spoke was a struggle, a giant effort to release. Hannah loved it, just as she always had, when the strict rhythm of Bethie's words melted into something smoother, more musical, as she laughed.

Bethie was telling a story about the time they made apple butter in the fall. Bethie had turned up the stove's heat when Mother wasn't looking. She was tired of waiting and anxious to taste something sweet. But she scorched the whole batch. Bethie laughed softly, and Hannah smiled as she listened.

"We ate it burnt," Bethie said. "Remember? We pretended we liked it, so Mother wouldn't feel bad."

Hannah nodded.

"Ten minutes left for visitation," Legion called out from the intercom.

Bethie had to look away from Hannah's face. From the knowledge they both had in that moment. That it might be years before they saw each other again.

Hannah covered her face with her hands and moaned. "I wish I was a slanteye."

Bethie laughed loudly. "What a thing to say right now."

"I mean it," Hannah said firmly. "If I was a slanteye, I would of escaped it."

"Escaped what?"

"Being Leah."

"You *aren't* Leah."

"You don't have her in you, like I do. All growing up I heard what people said. She's *in me*, Bethie. And I'm ruined now. Just like Mother said Leah was. Once she was in that hospital, Mother said there was no return for her."

"You're not ruined."

"Look at me! Look at this place!" Hannah cried out. "I *am* Leah. I *am* ruined."

"No," Bethie said, her eyes screaming cusswords like they used to on the bus. "You're not ruined. You're *empty*. There's a real difference between the two."

Hannah shook her head and looked toward the wall.

"You think I don't know?" Bethie whispered darkly. "Oh, sister, did you miss my childhood so completely? Were you that lost in your perfect days, your smart, pretty, glory days? From my first memory of speaking, I felt the *ruin* inside my mouth. From that first taste of the vinegar Mother poured over my tongue—remember? From that first taste, how do you think I felt about myself? *Ruined.* I couldn't even say my own name. I couldn't even tell the bus driver *my name.* And all the things that girls, girls like you, took for granted, I had no hope for. Things like giving a class book report. Making a phone call to a friend. Meeting a boy, and shyly whispering *Hello.* All of that was *ruined* for me. So I quit. I forced my tongue to be still. I forced my mouth to be empty. And I felt like you do now. I felt ruined." Bethie stepped toward Hannah, searched her face, until their eyes met.

"Sorry," Hannah whispered.

"Shhh," Bethie said, as she laid a finger gently over Hannah's mouth. "I'm about to tell you something very important. Everyone thinks I outgrew it. What did Mother call my years of signing? The 'Rest Period.' Everyone thinks that Rest Period gave my mind and mouth time to catch up to one another. Time to grow and develop without stress." Bethie shook her head. "You're all wrong."

"Then what?" Hannah asked.

"Do you remember the waterfall, way off the trail? I used to walk there at night. Nobody was around. Nobody could see me. I would sit by that waterfall and hear the roar of free water tumbling easy and powerful off the mountain. One night, I opened my mouth to speak, for the first time in years. The waterfall was too loud, so I couldn't hear my words. But I felt them. Big and clumsy and full inside my mouth. The Rest Period hadn't done a thing to help me. I kept going back. And since I couldn't hear myself, I paid attention to the way my lips and tongue worked together. To the way some words rolled out like silk. While others seemed to cling to the backs of my teeth. And I kept going back, every night."

"What happened?"

"I was never one for learning scripture like you. You could remember whole passages to my short *Jesus wept* verse. But words from Job returned to me by that waterfall. *He stretched out the north over empty space . . . He hung this whole earth on the face of Nothing.*"

Bethie reached for Hannah's hands and grabbed them. "Don't miss it, sister. Emptiness is the miracle canvas. The whole earth, everything we see, every word I speak, all hung on Nothing."

"Miracles?" Hannah laughed bitterly and shook her head. "Not for me. Not after the choices I've made. And certainly not in this place. I believe in the miracles of *old*, Bethie, just like we were raised to. But I'm no patriarch. I'm no prophet. And even if I were—if I were Jonah and this place was my great fish—all my prayers would never get me out."

"Jonah," Bethie said, and smiled. "Just like my old Hannah. You still focus only on the achievers, on the ones that score points and make As. Like patriarchs and prophets. You've overlooked some of the best miracles. Jonah's story isn't just about a prophet getting out of a fish. It's about a doomed city. What about their miracle?"

Hannah shook her head.

"They were handed steadfast love in place of disaster. Remember? *Should I not pity those people . . . who do not know their right hand from their left?"* Bethie grabbed Hannah's hand. "Nineveh wasn't full of deserving prophets. It was full of people like you. Hannah, you don't know your right hand from your left."

Hannah shook her head gently, her eyes lowered to the ground.

Bethie watched her, and her mind raced with all the ways she had failed to help her sister. "There's a true bridge," Bethie whispered. "And like something only you would dream, sister, redemption began with a newborn baby."

Static pierced the room and the intercom buzzed. "Visitation time is up. The door will open shortly. Please refrain from further conversation. This topic clearly violates the agreed boundaries."

"I was not ruined," Bethie whispered in Hannah's ear. "I was empty, I didn't know my left hand from my right. But I believed in the bridge. I became a miracle canvas."

"Silence, please. Bethlehem, you have signed a contract guaranteeing your cooperation."

The door opened. The nurse stood on the other side and waited for Bethie to join her. Bethie saw the look on Hannah's face, the sweet, sad look as she struggled to hope on the miracles that Bethie declared. And though she promised herself she would not, though she promised Mother she would never, she could not stop herself. In that moment, when she knew she would leave Hannah in that white cage, when she knew Legion would never allow her to visit Hannah again, Bethie knew she had to do more than just *back up Hannah*. She had to bring her the waterfall. She had to bring her the miracle on the mountain.

"Visiting time is over," the nurse said. "Please exit the room."

Bethie threw her arms around her sister. The crashing, desperate embrace of her dreams.

"Your miracle is happening *right now*, on our mountain," she gushed as tears, held back so long, suddenly poured down her face. "Look at me, Hannah. Even as we speak, your miracle is—"

The nurse put her arms around Bethie's shoulders and pulled her back. As the white door slammed and Hannah's face disappeared, Bethie sank to the floor and screamed, "*She's* your miracle!"

The doctors came running down the hall. Dr. Vaughn helped Bethie to her feet.

"Hannah will need sedation," one of the doctors said to the nurse. He looked at Bethie. "You have no idea what you've done," he said angrily. "All the work, everything we've done to make her feel safe, to encourage her mind to focus on reality. And then you come along with your waterfalls and your promise of miracles." He shook his head with disgust. "There are no miracles for a woman like Hannah. There's only reality, with all its pain and sadness. And it's one she must deal with, whether you like it or not."

Dr. Vaughn led Bethie back to the chair where she had waited earlier. Then she walked to the nurses' counter and asked for a cup of water. The doctor that yelled at Bethie came and stood by her. "Susan, this was all your idea," he said to her. "They've had to give her two injections to calm her down. Ten bucks says she won't speak a word to us tomorrow. You wanted it too much. You've lost all sense of professional boundaries."

Another doctor joined them. "Let's calm down. It's not entirely Susan's fault. Having to call Hannah 'Mother' over the intercom as she talked to that empty chair. Having to sit across from her for so long without any sign of progress. Of course you want her well more than any of us. But it's compromising your decisions. Your desire is becoming risky to the patient, Susan." He jerked his head in Bethie's direction. "And she was a very bad choice."

Dr. Vaughn returned to Bethie, carrying the cup of water.

"I'm sorry," Bethie said. "I had to tell her the truth."

Dr. Vaughn sighed. "It wasn't *all* terrible. She saw you as real, Bethie. You were able to convince her of that." She shrugged her shoulders, shook her head. "If there's a setback..." Her voice trailed off. She looked away, down the long hall that held Hannah at its end. "Tell me about this miracle."

ANGEL

I

I found it. After years of searching, after years of fighting the call of Momma's gun, I finally found sweet peace.

It wasn't what I thought it would be. There were no singing stars. No bacca or moonlit mountain. There was no light at all. Only darkness, heavy and thick, like the smoke from an old trailer fire, the kind filled with too many dead things to ever rise.

Darkness wrapped around me like a first fall breeze. A beautiful coolness swept over my body. Broke the heat that had burned for so long inside me. I looked around and saw Nothing. Every star had fallen. Every light had turned off. The whole world had burned down, and all that was left was a giant pile of ash.

Darkness filled my ears. At first, I heard the *shhhh shhhh* noise from my dreams. The ones where I remember the ocean and the sound of waves rushing up to me. The ones where I'm so little and Janie's still with me and we're running down the beach while Momma and Daddy decide whether to kiss or yell.

Darkness grew, and soon I was hearing more than the *shhhh* of Carolina. I was hearing Janie, too. The way she would laugh as we ran down the beach. The way she'd stand, just nine or ten years old, and yell cusswords into the waves. She'd giggle about how loud she screamed them. She'd giggle about how she shocked the tourists. I'd stand, baby that I was, in awe. At the way she narrowed her eyes when she yelled them. At the way even her laughter sounded tough.

But I wasn't a baby anymore. And in my perfect darkness, Janie suddenly didn't sound so tough. She didn't sound like the gook family taught her anything special. No grit or skill to help her survive all that she must.

Laugh again, Janie, I thought. And she did. And then she cussed for me, too. I wanted to cry when I heard her. I knew then only a baby would have mistaken that sound for toughness. Only a baby would have thought Janie was strong. The truth was, Janie knew better than to care. Janie knew better than to hope. She was just a baby, too, but she'd already given up.

Shut your trap, Janie, I thought. It was a favorite expression of Daddy's.

"Angel?" she called.

"Yes."

"Hot damn! What are you doin' here?"

"Same as before. Runnin' as fast as I can. Tryin' to git away."

"We're supposed to go in the water this time, Angel," she said.

"No."

I had never been in the ocean. Sure, I'd stuck my toes in. I'd run up to my knees and then run back as the waves tried to catch me. But I was too young to go out farther when we lived in Carolina. And Momma and Daddy didn't swim.

"I can't swim, Janie. You know that."

"Got to. Listen. Hear that?"

She was right. The darkness had a new sound. I listened close and heard the sound of weeping. The gasps and the sobs and the begging, "Oh. Please. No." I heard the sound of prayer. Like at Grandma's grave. Like from my baby mouth, inside

Black Snake trailer. And when I heard *Please* and *Please* and *Amen* and *Amen*, I knew this much. Trouble was close.

"Awright then," I whispered.

We stepped in the water. And instead of pushing me out of it, like the waves had always done before, I felt the water grab me. Lift me. Pull me hard and quick, until I was caught inside its grasp. It was colder than I remembered. Soon, darkness turned to something else entirely. I was freezing. Shaking with cold. Desperately wanting out of that icy water.

"Damn them Swarms," Janie said. "They're all the same. They think they can tell people like us what to do. Even here, in our last darkness."

I listened again. Someone cried, "Stay." Someone begged, "Please." I felt a rope. It slid around my wrists. It wrapped around my legs. It pulled tight against my skin.

"Gonna have to fight to go now," Janie said. "Gonna have to fight like I taught you."

I pulled against the rope, deeper into the icy water.

"But you didn't teach me, Janie. You weren't tough. You were just lost, same as me."

"Shut your trap," she hissed.

"I got somethin' else that might work. Treasure."

I cried out as loud as I could. "Hey! You know those two silver spoons that went missin'? The heavy kind from the china cabinet, right next to the Great Room archway? I stole 'em. I still have one, too, here in my pocket. I lost the other, but you can have this one back. Just let me go."

I threw that silver spoon as hard as I could and listened for any response. But the rope pulled tighter.

"I can't stay with you, don't you know? We don't belong together. I pretended once that we did. That day we were sewin' aprons, and you were tellin' me pretty stories. I closed my eyes and imagined you young. Imagined you were her and we belonged together. It was a lie, but lies can be a gift sometimes."

The ocean seemed colder than ever before. My skin was numb. My legs were stiff and could barely move. But through the perfect black of a whole world burned to ash, I saw it. The tiniest sparkle, through the water, there on the bottom of the ocean floor.

"Look," I whispered. "The missin' spoon. Maybe if I sink down low I can git it. Maybe if I sink down low I won't ever come back. See them marks across the handle? That's our name."

I sank down to my shoulders. The spoon was so close, its light so clear.

"Grandmother," I whispered. "Where's my green baby blanket? The one you wrapped me in on the day I was born. I could use it now. I'm cold. I'm so very, very cold."

II

When I opened my eyes, I was surrounded by cinder blocks. The same dull gray as the ones of my childhood. But this time, they were high above my head on every side. Who would have thought cinder-block towers could rise higher than I'd ever climb?

I didn't know where I was; there was no window to look out. Just four walls of gray and a black door. My first thought was to rip the IV out of my arm so I could escape. But then I realized my arms were tied tightly to the bed.

I could see, though, with a quick raise of my head, that I was badly hurt. Bandages wrapped around my arms and legs. Red circles stained through the white cloth. That's when I remembered the room at Red Castle. The *click*, like the sound of fingers snapping. The heat and the gagging. The check I signed over to Tabby. The window that lied, just like everyone else. Promised sweet peace but left me bleeding and hurt, tied down inside a gray cinder-block tower. If I had only known what to cry for, I would have screamed out the panic that swelled inside me. But I couldn't cry *Mother* anymore. You were dead. I couldn't cry *Money* anymore. I had it but gave it away.

The thought occurred to me to cry *Whiskey*. After everything, the blood and bandages that covered my body, that word still sat greedy on my tongue. And it made me sad. It took away the hope that Janie's letter once gave. That sweet letter she wrote before she ran away:

Angel,

I'm getting away. Sorry I can't take you with me. But I'm not your momma and I can't always be taking care of you. You'll figure out how to do it yourself one of these days. I hope to see you again.

Love,
Janie

P.S. I wasn't pretending when I called you princess at night. I know I'm one of them. But they say you ain't. You could be anybody Angel. Even a princess.

The letter gave me hope. But the day I woke up tied down—cut and hurt all over and still craving whiskey—I learned a new lesson. One Momma and Daddy never taught me. In the end, I was theirs, too. As much as I liked to deny it, as much as they fought against it, it was true. Maybe we didn't share any blood in our veins. But as it turned out, blood wasn't nearly as important as I'd always believed. Wasn't nearly as important as Janie believed the day she wrote that letter. The thing we shared, the thing that flowed in all of our veins, was stronger than a family name. Stronger than any drop of blood. Whiskey flowed through us. Made us kin, made us family, in a way that nothing else ever would.

I sucked in my breath and wished that my hands weren't tied down so that I could try again to end the pain. That horrible pain that twisted inside me. Not from the cuts or the fall. Not from the bits of glass that were surely still stuck to my skin, but from the truth. That after all the running, all the fighting against it, *I* was the drunk woman passed out sloppy on the couch. *I* was the drunk woman demanding whiskey prizes. I was Momma, and though I hated her, she was all mine.

"You're awake," the old woman whispered. "Do you hurt?" She leaned over me with a tissue and gently tapped at the tears that spilled down my face. "I'll call the nurse.

"Just a bit to help her relax," she said to a lady who walked in with a tray of needles. "She's been asleep so long already, no need to make her sleep again so soon."

Something dripped down into my IV and soon I felt things start to slip away. The gray walls, the blood seeping up through white bandages, the shame of being Momma. I was drunk again. Tied down and drunk.

The old woman reached over me, tried to remove a tiny bit of blue glass still stuck to my skin. Still cutting me.

"This isn't what I wanted," she said. "I never dreamed I would end up holding you prisoner. Never dreamed you'd nearly die in my arms. What I always wanted, what I always prayed for, was something different. I have seen you thousands of times in my dreams. Where you grew up happy. Where you were gifted in music. Sometimes you were even valedictorian. Sometimes you marry well and I have great-grandchildren. Each of them with white hair, just like your mother's. When I fall asleep at night and fear wakes me up, there are two things I do. I whisper the carving above my door and then I whisper prayers. That you grew up well. That you grew up safe and happy. Do you know when I carved those words above the doors?"

I tried to shake my head.

"When I tried for the last time to find you and couldn't. It was a sort of rebellion, I suppose, on my part. My own way of screaming at God, saying, *Fine. You won't bring her back to me, I'll stop wanting.*" She laughed softly. "Like a two-year-old throwing a tantrum. Doesn't work, though. That whole 'raise the fist to heaven' thing."

She reached out and gently touched the top of my hand. There was one unbandaged spot, about two inches of spared skin. She stroked it with her fingertips, back and forth, one of the only places she could touch me without causing more pain. She pulled her hand back quickly, sucked in her breath, and whispered, "How I wish she could see this."

She covered her face with her hands. I looked away.

"Let me tell you something I've learned," she whispered. "Death is a slow, slow thing, child. Death isn't something instant and easy, like a fast bullet or a jump through a second-story window. You start to die long before you breathe your last. Looking at you here, at the pain in your eyes, I imagine you started to die the day I first handed you over to that woman. Hannah started to die that day, too. We all did."

I knew your name. Finally. You were Hannah Rey.

"During your birth, as she screamed and Cora prayed, I stood and faced the wall. Not because I didn't want to see you. Not because I hated Hannah, but because I couldn't bear the pain. Hannah was the love child of my old age, and there she was, wretched in blood and misery. Once you were born and I heard your cry, I went to Hannah and pulled you from her chest. Weak as she was, I still felt her hands tighten around you. Weak as she was, I still saw the panic in her eyes. I remember I had my hand on the doorknob when she cried 'Wait' the first time. 'Wait,' she said again."

The old woman stood and stepped away from my bed. She turned her back to me, but I could still see her shiver as she whispered, "Even now I dream of it, over and over. In my dreams I always stop and ask, *Why?* Hannah's answer keeps changing. Sometimes she says, *I want to hold her again.* Sometimes she says, *Let me look at her once more.* Sometimes she just screams loud and crazy, like a mother whose child has gone missing."

Even through the numbness of good drugs, I could feel tears pouring from my eyes. She misunderstood. Thought I was crying about my cuts. "Don't worry. They are many, but most aren't deep. The doctor said you won't have too many scars. It was the ones on your arms that were the most dangerous. We had a hard time getting those to stop bleeding. He had to give you a few pints of blood."

I closed my eyes to try and stop my tears, but I couldn't. I didn't know how to stop *that* kind of tears. The old woman's words pounded inside my mind like a victory chant. Like the last bell in a great boxing round. She started talking again, but I didn't listen. I closed my eyes and savored the joy of finally knowing for certain.

You wanted me. Your hands tightened around me as she pulled me away. Your face went wild with panic as she pulled me from you. You cried, *Wait.* And then you cried it again: *Wait!*

And I knew the answer. The one the old woman didn't. The one from her dreams, when she asked, *Why?* I knew what you were trying to say. Not, *I want to hold her again,* and not, *Let me look at her once more.*

I knew your answer. It went like this:

Wait! you screamed, your face wild with panic, your arms reaching for me, even as your mother walked away. *Wait!*

Why? she asked coolly.

You look at her and you say the truest thing you'll ever speak. You say the one thing, the only thing, that either of us will ever be certain of.

We belong together.

III

Days later, I finally began to wake up from the fog of my new friend Morphine. My body throbbed with the jagged cuts, the hundred stitches that covered my skin. I tried to sit up but discovered that I was still tied down. I pulled against the restraints.

"Untie me!" I demanded.

The old woman was sleeping in a chair next to my bed. She startled awake, looked at me steadily, and shook her head. I tried again. "You can't keep me tied up like an animal. I'll tell the nurse when she comes back. Untie me!"

"I can't believe it," she said bitterly. "You really still want to leave?"

"Yes!" I screamed. "I'm well enough now."

"Look at you, Angel. Look at your body, back from the brink of death. Look at the miserable choices you've made, for whiskey, for that window. And now, after all the time I've poured into you, grooming you, teaching you, *saving* you, you still want to run? You are alive because of me. Only a fool would want to leave."

I screamed for help. I screamed for somebody, for anybody, that might hear. "Somebody please help me!"

The old woman sat in the chair, studying me. "Foolish girl! No one can hear you. No one can help you."

"I hate you," I moaned. "I hate you so much."

She nodded her head. "I know."

"Just let me go. You don't have to pay me anymore. I just want to go."

She shook her head. "Never."

I screamed for help again. I pulled against the restraints with all my might. I promised her as I fought, "I'll find a way out of here. When you're not lookin', I'll find a way. But before I go, you can bet I'll git you first, I'll show you just how mean a girl from Black Snake trailer can be."

My body was throbbing with exhaustion and pain. The old woman sat in her chair, disgust smeared across her face. I turned to the wall to hide my defeat. I whispered, "Why?"

"Because," she said, "I made a promise. I always keep my promises."

"I'm hurtin' again," I cried. "Call the nurse."

She stood over my bed and looked down on me. "Remember, Angel. *I'm* the one who calls the nurse. *I'm* the one who makes your pain go away. Or not."

"I'll never forgive you. If that's what you're wantin'."

"No," she said, and shrugged. "I want to raise the dead."

"Call the nurse," I begged.

"In time, child. But now that you feel well enough to want to leave, I'd like to explain why that wouldn't be wise."

She told me again about what it was like to find me in that hospital room. What it was like to have me, at last, safe under her roof.

"You were supposed to love it in my home. You were supposed to find peace and healing and realize you had no need for anything else. You were supposed to make everything better, like any miracle would."

"Just call the nurse."

"But you tried to leave me. Over such a thing as whiskey. You jumped out of a second-story glass window. You nearly ruined everything, the entire plan."

"Lady, I didn't know there was a plan," I cried.

"There's *always* a plan," she said lowly. "And I will not allow you to mess it up. I will not allow you to run away. I will not allow you to die. There's a reason you are here, Angel. You have been chosen. You have been sent to me."

"I have a thousand cuts across my body," I whispered.

"Nurse!" she called out. She leaned across the bed, until her face was just inches from mine. "I sold you, beautiful as you were, to try and save my daughter. There is *nothing* I won't do to save her. If you try to leave again, if you try anything like before, believe me, I will make you wish there was a window nearby. Do you understand?"

The nurse held the morphine injection up to my IV line. "No, not yet," the old woman told her. "Do you understand?"

I nodded my head.

"Then here is your peace."

Warmth slid through the needle in my arm and crept its way throughout my entire body. The room grew softer. The lights no longer glared, but glowed like a Tennessee moon.

"She cried, 'Wait,'" I mumbled.

"Yes." The old woman stood up and walked to a table that had been placed by the wall sometime during the night. There was a pitcher of ice water on it. She poured herself a glass and slowly took a sip. She brought the water to me, held it to my lips. I felt the coolness trickle into my mouth. I forced myself to swallow.

"When I was a child," she said, as she sat back down, "my father was a hard man. He had this line he'd say, before he whipped us, about beating the Devil away. I remember thinking sometimes, when he'd stare at me in such anger, *Beat me harder*. Whatever it was he saw, whatever clung to me and made me bad, I wanted it gone. Sometimes at night, I'd sneak his belt out. Hit the back of my legs until they were bruised.

"My mother was so different. Gentle and easy to crush like my sister, Leah. She only spanked me twice in my whole childhood. And she cried as she did it. She said, 'I don't do this to hurt you, child. I do it because I love you. Because I want better for you.' Who do you think I was more like, the day I took you away? My mother or my father? I know what Hannah thought. She thought I saw the Devil in her. She thought I was trying to beat the Devil away. But I swear to you, I wasn't thinking *Devil*. I was only thinking of Hannah. How she was just seventeen. My own child, having a baby. I didn't sell you to hurt Hannah. I did it because I loved her. Because I wanted better for her."

"I wasn't somethin' bad," I mumbled. "I was just a baby."

"No you weren't bad. You were *perfect*. So tiny, both your feet fit inside the palm of my hand. And your little ears, they looked like pink seashells. But Hannah had this great sin. This black mark that would ruin her life. And I didn't want to face it. I couldn't deal with it. I wanted to hide it, make it like it never happened. The thing is, I *knew* it couldn't be done. I had studied too many scriptures to ever believe that I could hide sin. But in my panic, I still tried. I still thought *maybe* I could get away with something Eve couldn't. *Maybe* I could avoid Achan's curse. Do you know any of those stories?"

I shook my head.

"I'll call the nurse to feed you some broth and I'll be back shortly. There's something I want to read to you. It'd be a good place for us to start. A nice first step in our work together."

When she returned, I was dozing in a perfect haze. She patted my hand until I opened my eyes.

"This is part of our story, too. *Your* story."

She read about Adam and Eve. How they ate the wrong fruit and tried to hide it from God. How they lost the love garden. Their easy, carefree lives. How they lost the face of God himself.

"What do you think about it all?" she stopped and asked. "I've always wondered what it must be like to hear these stories for the first time. I've never had a first time. They were whispered to me from birth."

"I like the part about the serpent."

"Why?"

"Makes me think of Black Snake." I wanted to tell her

about the first night in the trailer. But the words were spinning inside my head. And the only thing I could get to come out right was "Maybe the serpent just wanted the garden to himself. Maybe he thought Adam would come after him with a hoe."

She laughed softly. "Believe it or not, this story gave me hope. Even as I sold you, I thought of it. Adam and Eve hid their sin. They were found out and they lost the garden. It was a hard punishment, to be sure. They had to work to live, could no longer see God's face, but they still had each other. They were still whole. They still had a chance in this world, to live and grow and love. That's all I wanted for Hannah."

"Wait," I whispered.

"What?"

"She didn't?" I asked. "No chance?"

"No."

"Why?"

"There's a different story." She turned pages and started reading again. About the Israelite named Achan, and how he hid stolen treasure beneath the floor of his tent. He was found out and they stoned him. And his children. All of them destroyed, over that hidden sin.

The old woman's voice shook as she read the story. I looked at her, saw how the lines in her forehead creased deeper with her effort to control her emotion. It was only then that I started to realize what *you* must have been through. All this time I had wanted to tell you about what had happened to me. About what I had seen and felt. I had longed, for so many years, to hold up the ruins of my childhood before you and whisper, *This is why* . . .

But as she read about Achan and his children, *I knew*. You

had a story, too. Your very own right words about what happened to you. About all the things you've seen and felt.

"What happened to her?" I struggled to whisper.

"I hid our sin. I thought I was doing the right thing, I thought I was saving her. I promised her."

"But what happened to her?" I demanded.

"Like Achan," she sobbed. "I put stones over my people. Stones over my children."

IV

Days continued to pass inside the basement. A nurse attended my slow-healing wounds. She poured soothing drugs and powerful antibiotics into my IV. The old woman promised I wouldn't feel whiskey withdrawal ever again, as long as I didn't fight the slow wean of addiction. As long as I didn't try and escape, try and do something drastic, like before.

But I still fought. I pulled against the restraints and yelled all the curse words Janie ever taught me. I screamed hate for the old woman. When my screams didn't work, I begged. And then night would come. Night *always* changed my mind. The heat began to swarm over my body. The pain, the gagging, and the shaking returned. I remembered the feel of that ocean and its icy water, the one I found after I jumped through the window. "You win," I'd whisper. "I won't fight you."

In the mornings, the nurse brought a walker and I practiced taking steps. The record of my last desperate run marked in scars across my body. I hated to look, even though the nurse promised the wounds would fade.

The old woman came to me nearly every day. She spoon-fed me soups and stews as she told me your story, bit by bit.

"I did all I could to save her. I wasn't ignorant of her descent. I found a clay baby that she made. I held it in my hands, stared at that blank mud face. I shivered to imagine what she must've felt, what hunger she must've suffered, to have formed such a thing. I wrote letters. I made calls. I went back to the place I gave you away. No one knew where you could be."

"Black Snake trailer," I whispered. "I burned it down."

"That's what the police told me at the hospital."

"They didn't know for sure it was me," I said. "I wouldn't give them my name."

"Oh, they knew it was you. They came here for you, just after your first week of work."

"Why didn't they arrest me?"

"I made arrangements on your behalf."

"Why?"

"I couldn't let them get in the way."

"What was the arrangement?"

"I am making restitution. And in return, the Swarm family will drop the charges. They will agree it was an accident."

I laughed softly. "Where would we be without your money?"

"You'd be in jail," she said dryly.

"No. I'd of been with you, with her, all along. Momma never would have taken me if it hadn't been for your money."

She nodded. "Perhaps."

"So they don't care I burned it down anymore. Just like that. You write a check and they don't care."

"I'm paying your debt," she said. "And now you'll pay mine."

"How?" I whispered. "Just tell me. Why are you keepin' me prisoner?"

"You have an important job to do."

"What is it?"

"This basement, Angel. It's about more than you recovering, becoming sober. The nurse has already reduced your morphine to half of what it was. You didn't know, did you? You didn't know that you are only half as addicted as you once were. It was that easy. And now you're ready for the next step. We don't have time to waste."

The old woman stood and leaned over me. Her eyes searched mine, as she spoke again. "You must learn your story."

"My story?"

"The story I'm going to teach you. The story that will bring your mother peace. That will set her free from the pain and guilt she's been plagued with since the day you were born."

I sucked in my breath and held it till my lungs throbbed for relief. "She's alive?" I cried.

The old woman nodded.

"But you said—"

"Death has many forms."

I repeated her words to myself, over and over. But I couldn't think what to ask. I couldn't think anything, except this: *You were alive. I'd lost you,* twice, *but you were alive again.* Alive!

"I'll explain it all, in time," she said.

"Where is she?"

"I'll take you to her. But first, you must earn the right to see her."

"What must I do?" I begged.

"Start by learning your name."

"What?"

The old woman stood up, leaned over me. "The name you will give your mother when she first sees you."

"I've dreamed it a thousand times," I said. "I always say this: *You can call me Angel.*"

She shook her head. "This is my last chance to fix her. This is my last chance to keep the promise. I can't afford mistakes."

"My name's not a mistake."

"For my sweet Hannah, your name is Lily Adams. A nice, polished name. A name I wouldn't mind giving a third daughter, if I'd been blessed with one."

"What's wrong with Angel?"

"It sounds like a vision. It sounds like something that would speak to Hannah through the hum of a baby monitor. And that's exactly what Hannah will think if you call yourself Angel."

"But that's my name. I've always wanted her to know that. There was this one time, I got home from school and walked into the trailer to find Momma passed out on the couch. She'd been that way for days. I stared at her, wondered if she was dead. I let the door slam behind me. She opened her eyes. She said, 'Who in the hell are you? You come in here to steal my prizes?' I tried to act easy, tried to act sweet. I said, 'It's me, Momma.' But she shook her head, all confused. 'Who are you?' she asked. So I tried again. 'It's Angel, I've come home from school.' She pointed at the door. 'Git outta here 'fore I call the cops. I don't know no Angel. I only got one girl, and she's out with the farmhands. Go on, git!' I ran outside. Sat in the middle of the empty fields and cried for someone that knows me, someone that won't forget my name. I cried out for her. My mother. So don't you dare tell me, now that I got my chance, she can't know my name."

The old woman reached over me, jerked the IV out of my arm. "I've planned this for years. From the first time I tried to find you, I've had a plan. I thought it would be easier. I didn't count on a fight. I thought you would come to love me, love this place. I didn't foresee your love of whiskey. Or your wanting to leave. I never imagined you'd try and kill yourself. Just think if she found out about that. Think of all the new guilt she'd feel. Knowing her baby jumped out of the window of her old bedroom. She can't *ever* know those things. She can't ever know how *right* she was about you. How lost you really were. She would never forgive herself."

She turned out the light and started to leave.

"You can give her life again. You can soothe her in a way that nothing else will. You can lay to rest all her dreams about you and the danger you were in. I'll teach you how. I'll give you the right story. I'll tell you every word that you need to say."

"I've got my right words," I said. "Found them long before I found you."

She shook her head. "You don't understand. You are an expensive criminal, and you burned down half a farm. I agreed to a payment plan. I have three months to either finish paying or hand you over. And it's up to me. Do you hear that? *It's up to me.*"

"Why are you doing this?" I cried, as she left the room.

"I made a promise once. I *always* keep my promises."

I sobbed in the darkness. And spent the night crying for you. Crying for my name. And hoping I'd be strong enough to keep it.

I wasn't. She didn't come to me the whole next day. She let me suffer without the hope of any relief. Just before the start of the second night without my IV, when my body felt every cut and a fever swept me up in a tight grip, she returned.

"Say your name, child. Say your name and I will end your pain."

"Lily," I sobbed, "Lily Adams."

"Good," she said, as she stroked the top of my hand. "Hannah will love that. It's so pure. So very *safe*."

I cried as she tried to comfort me. As she told me I was fulfilling my purpose.

"You didn't just come here. You were sent," she said. "And this isn't just for her, but for you, too. When it's over, you'll be sober and well. You'll have seen your mother. You'll have helped her heal. It's for you, too, that I do this.

"Nurse," she called. "Lily needs a full dose, please." She leaned over me and kissed my forehead. "There, there, sweet child. Our sweet baby girl. It's all going to be okay. I promise."

Soon, a new IV was in my arm, dripping fresh magic into my veins. The blur, the sweet numbness, crashed down on me heavier than before.

"I've a gift for you, Lily," she said. "Something you've never had or seen. Something of your mother's."

I shook my head, heavy as it was, back and forth. "I had somethin' of hers," I mumbled. "Green blanket. It burned, though. I kept things less precious. But I burned the only thing I had of my mother's."

"I'm sorry it burned."

"No, I meant to. So I could find her, look at her, and say, *I've got nothin' of you.*"

"Well here's something new," she said, as she reached down to the floor. She lay a copy paper box across my lap. She pulled the newspaper stuffing out of the top. Underneath lay something red. It was the bottom of a plate. A clay one.

She picked it up and held it before me. Turned it so that I could see all the paint that you once swirled across its surface. She placed it under my tied-down hands so that I could run my fingers across the surface.

"What do you see in her art?"

"The bacca," I whispered, my eyes following the broad strokes of green and gold.

She lifted the plate from my lap and placed it by my bed. My tired eyes closed, and the colors of your paint danced behind them. I forced them open and saw the old woman staring down at me.

"What do you see in her art?" I mumbled.

She laughed softly and stroked my forehead. "Clay baby, come to life."

The room was a fuzzy rainbow. I felt all my pain, all my fear and misery, float up to the pulsing colors above me. "Ain't afraid of you," I whispered, and enjoyed the lie.

"Reconsider," she said bitterly. "It just took twenty minutes to give you away. I remember thinking as I walked back into the shack to check on Hannah, that it should've taken longer. To give away something so beautiful. It should've taken time, to kiss you, such a sweet baby, the way you deserved. Time to worry over whether it was the right thing or not. But I was gone and back in twenty minutes. I didn't pause to pray or worry."

"Ain't afraid," I repeated. "You're one of us."

"Who?"

"Sycamore people. You're broken. You're scared. You can never be allowed inside. You can never be trusted."

"Go to sleep," she whispered, as she left the room.

Later, I stirred in the night and called out for a new dose. It was brought quickly, and soon I saw sycamore leaves, scattered in the darkness. I felt my body float out of bed. I picked up the leaves, one by one. Lined them up, like straight rows of bacca and read them.

Go to sleep, Clay Baby. Go to sleep, and rest well. You've got a promise to keep.

V

"Good morning, Lily," the old woman sang over my bed. I pretended to sleep.

"We don't have time to waste," she said, as she jostled me. "Wake up. Are you awake?"

I blinked my eyes open and nodded.

"Good. I have your breakfast here. Eat, then I'll have the nurse take you for a walk around the room to stretch. No meds this morning; you need to be completely alert today. You have so much to learn." She looked at me and smiled. "You'll do fine, though. You're very smart. Remember when I asked you, in the library, whether you could learn? You thought I meant sewing. You said, 'I taught myself how to read.'" She laughed softly, then sighed. "You know, your mother was the smartest girl in school. On track for valedictorian until she met your father."

"Did he know about me?"

She shook her head. "He could barely admit to knowing Hannah. There's no way he would have accepted responsibility for you, too. We never told him, and she never spoke to him again." She leaned over and held a spoon of eggs out to me. I opened my mouth. "It's not like if we kept you, everything would have been ideal. I know you've told yourself that all these years. It's just not so. You would have had a seventeen-year-old child for a mother. You would've never had a father."

I finished the eggs and waited for the nurse to come. She undid my restraints and pulled me from bed. I leaned against the walker and scooted around the room with her, wincing with pain.

"Help me," I whispered to the nurse when we turned our backs and started walking the other direction.

"Sorry, no meds this morning."

"She's holdin' me prisoner down here."

"Oh, honey," she replied, loud enough for the old woman to hear. "You're her precious grandchild. If only more grand-mothers cared the way she did. I work in a clinic downtown. I've seen so many lost girls your age come in. Hooked on all sorts of things. Be glad you got a grandma that will help you out. That cares enough to get you healthy again. Weren't for her, you'd be dead."

"That's enough exercise for the day," the old woman called out. The nurse nodded and we turned and walked back to the bed. She helped me lay down. Gently wrapped the restraints around my wrists.

"Are you in pain?" the nurse asked me.

"Yes," I lied.

"She'll have to wait," the old woman said. "She has work to do. I'll call for you when we're ready." She waited for the nurse to leave the room. "Shall we begin?"

I nodded slowly; tears that I refused to cry sat in my eyes. "My name is Lily Adams," I whispered.

"Perfect," she said, smiling. "Now after introductions, Han-nah will wonder *why* you found her. Her natural assumption is going to be that you are in some kind of trouble. That you called out for her over the monitors. It's your job to prove that false. So you'll need to be prepared to explain why you've come. I've watched several of those daytime TV reunions lately. Oh, I see you're surprised. Yes, I bought a TV and hid it in the storage room for research purposes. The best reunions, the ones that made the audience smile, were when the child said, 'Thank you for giving me away.' It makes sense, doesn't it? How wonderful that would feel to have a child find you, just to say, 'You made the right decision. Thank you for your sacrifice.' Imagine what those words could do for Hannah. Try it, let's hear how it sounds."

I said it, the words catching in my throat and sounding as painful as they were. Lies, what used to be my one great mercy, suddenly hurt worse than anything. Suddenly wouldn't slide smooth and easy off my tongue.

"Try it again. Say it like you mean it."

"My name is Lily Adams. I'm your daughter, and I came here to tell you thank you. To tell you that you did right by me, when you gave me away."

She stared at me while I said it. Then she sighed loudly and shook her head. "It will be fine to cry when you see her. She is your mother, after all, so of course you will cry when you see her. But we have to make your tears seem like happy ones. Perhaps if you could just smile a bit as you say it. Let me get a mirror for you to see." She brought a hand mirror and held it before me. "Say it again. Watch your face. Keep your forehead smooth. Make your eyes a bit happier. Your voice a bit softer."

I tried again. And again. And then again.

"No, no, *no*," she said with frustration. "Hannah is so smart. . . . If we were dealing with Bethie, things would be different. But if you don't look believable, if you don't look grateful, Hannah will never buy it. Try again. We'll go all night if we must."

I took a deep breath. I closed my eyes and thought only of the bacca. I didn't think about the rest of it, about all the things that happened to me, all the things I saw and felt, after you gave me away. I didn't think about Black Snake trailer. Momma's couch. Daddy's sweet tooth. Or even Janie. I just thought about the bacca. And pretended that was it. That was all that waited for me on the day I was born.

"Thank you," I whispered. "I found real goodness after you gave me away."

The old woman clasped her hands to her chest, nodded, and smiled. She had me repeat it, over and over. Her effort to stamp the words in black-and-white letters behind the lids of my eyes.

"It's perfect," she said. "What an excellent beginning. Now we must create a history to prove such goodness."

"History?" I asked.

She nodded. "The details of your life. About your wonderful parents, your older sister that was always your best friend. About family vacations, childhood Christmases, family pets. The day your parents threw you a surprise birthday party. About all the funny times that still make you laugh."

She was pacing the room, talking loudly, her hands waving as she yelled out new ideas. She looked up at me and smiled. "Don't look so worried. The challenging part will be introducing yourself and explaining why you're there. But you've got that down pat." She threw her hands up in the air and nodded quickly. "I have an idea," she said. "*Maybe* we can use a bit of your own stories after all."

"My own stories?" I whispered, shaking my head.

"Yes. The good parts. You pick. Something from the list I just gave you. Perhaps a family vacation? Or a family pet? Did you have a dog you loved?"

I shook my head again.

"There must be something you can use. A favorite holiday tradition?"

"No."

"Oh, come on," she said. "All of it couldn't be bad. That's impossible. There must be some good memories."

"I had a good sister. But she done a lot of bad things. We did have this one vacation together, a weekend in Gatlinburg. It ended awful, but while we were there... it was perfect."

"What about laughter? Hannah would enjoy that. Did funny things ever happen? Did you ever laugh?"

Of all the questions I had prepared for during those nights out in the bacca, that one never crossed my mind. *Did I ever laugh?* I laid there for a moment, my mind searching. And then I remembered.

"Ever been to the races?" I asked her. "Not the big ones, but small local ones or anything?"

She shook her head.

"Daddy had this car, the coolest car. It was all power and when I was young, man that thing could move. We'd shine it up Friday nights during the winter, take it to a track a few miles up the road. It was farmland come spring and summer, of course. But during late fall an acre or so was turned into a dirt circle. People would come from miles around. They'd bring blankets and lawn chairs, chicken and beer. We'd all sit and watch the muscle cars line up. Half of 'em dinged up, missin' mufflers and roarin' so loud me and Janie would cover our ears and try and read each other's lips when we wanted to talk. Man, we loved race night. Momma would get so pretty. She'd spend all day frayin' the edges of her cutoffs *just so*. And she'd do this thing with her T-shirt, where she cut the collar out, not like it had been ripped out, but cut with purpose, you know? And then she'd wear a tank top underneath, a real thin one that made her tan show through. That T-shirt would go over top, but with the collar cut out it just sort of hung off her shoulders, the way those princess ball gowns do in all the fairy tales. She was the sexiest woman there. Daddy was so proud back then. He had the coolest car, the hottest woman.

"He won a lot, too, at first. It was good winter money for us. One night, Daddy bet big on his car. He had to win, or we wouldn't have money for the rest of the month. But when it came time to line up the cars, his radiator sprang a bad leak. He worked hard to fix it, but the race was gettin' close to start. The man he bet against came over. 'Looks like you need a new radiator,' he said. 'Good luck findin' one in the middle of these fields.' Daddy ran to me. 'Angel, you run git me an egg.' Momma cussed big. 'What in the hell you need an egg for? I fed you good 'fore we came. You just need to focus on fixin' that bucket of yours 'fore you lose all our money.' Daddy didn't have time to fight her then. He grabbed me by the shoulders. 'Farmhouse is over them hills. You can do it. Pretend it's Momma's treasure. Go git me an egg and I'll win this race for you.' I ran as fast as I could. Even though I knew farmhouse rules were the same everywhere. Girls like me don't belong in 'em. But I had to git that egg. Not just 'cause Daddy sent me and nobody told Daddy no. But because of what he said when he sent me. That he'd win the race *for me*. I walked around the house till I saw the door that led to the kitchen. I opened it. Held my breath and waited for someone to grab me and haul me down to the police. When it didn't happen, I took a step. Then another. Until I was standin' in front of the fridge. I grabbed the egg and ran. Let the door slam behind me and didn't stop runnin' till I was back to Daddy.

"He took that egg and then he did the funniest thing. He uncapped the radiator, cracked the egg, and poured it in. People that saw him thought he lost his mind. They pointed and laughed, and hollered out jokes at him. Momma joined in with 'em. 'This ain't no picnic. It's a race!' Daddy didn't pay them no mind, though. He hopped in that car and he drove it with all his might. That car never so much as sputtered on him. Can you guess why?"

The old woman shook her head.

"The egg." I laughed. "Daddy said that when the car heated up, it scrambled. The chunks plugged up the radiator leak. He won. And from then on folks at the track called his car the Eggmobile."

The old woman smiled.

"So yeah," I whispered, still smiling, "I guess I did laugh sometimes. Yeah, some things were funny. Like that egg."

"Good," she said, staring at the floor in concentration. "Yes. I think we can work with that. Perhaps we could say your family had been grocery shopping. Your car broke down on the highway. Your father used an egg to fix it. Nothing about stealing or gambling, of course. Nothing about T-shirts with the collars ripped out." She looked up and smiled victory. "I'm glad you have the egg memory. I'm glad that everything wasn't always bad. Sometimes you laughed."

I nodded. But I knew there was a deeper truth for people like me. For people like you, too. A truth that the old woman would never admit. Would certainly never allow me to tell you. *Laughter isn't free. Neither are smiles.* Sure, funny things happen. Good things occur every once in a while. But behind my smile, fear was waiting. Behind my laughter was a ready cry. Growing up, I could not escape hurt. And I knew this, I thought of it, even when I laughed.

"Okay," the old woman said, as she glanced at her watch. "That's it for the day. I'll call the nurse now. Oh, and Lily, I have something else for you. Another gift."

The nurse came in holding the shot that would make it all—the lies, the story, the old woman—go away. But behind her was something even more important. The old woman walked in, her hands filled with the most beautiful thing I'd ever seen. A birthday cake. Eighteen candles in a perfect row. Little pink rosebuds mounded on the corners.

"Happy birthday." She saw the look on my face. "Did you forget?" she asked. "You forgot it was your birthday?"

I nodded.

"I've never," she whispered. "I've never forgotten." She pulled a knife out of her apron and reached for the cake.

"Don't," I cried. "Don't cut it. I just wanna look at it."

She looked at me in surprise. I sighed. "I've never had one before."

"Very well," the old woman said, and slipped the knife back in her apron. She nodded to the nurse, and sweet dreams soon poured into my vein. "Just think, now you'll be able to tell your mother all about it. You'll be able to say you have a special birthday memory. And it won't be a lie."

I nodded.

"Happy birthday, dear Lily," she said, as she left the room. "The best is yet to come."

VI

It took us a month to craft our story. Each day, and into the night, the old woman sat across from me as I rehearsed. She twisted the details. Took my truth and tied it up in little happy knots. Until she was sure the story would bring you joy. Until she was sure the story would bring you back to her, wherever you were.

"Did you know," she asked me at the end of the month, "you haven't had morphine in three days? I told you the nurse was reducing your dose, but in fact I've had her only pretend to be giving you morphine injections. And you've slept. I've watched, I've made certain. Child, you are no longer an addict. You are healed."

I turned my face and stared at the wall.

"Whatever it was that made you drink before, this is your chance to escape it. Embrace your new story. Embrace your new life. You know, after you visit Hannah I still have plans for you. You will stay here as Lily—good, sober, happy Lily. You can see Hannah whenever she chooses to visit. The two of you will bloom again."

I nodded.

"I have to go away for a day or two. The nurse will be here to care for you. I've given her orders to allow you ibuprofen as needed. And a mild sedative if you can't sleep. I also want her to increase your exercise. I want you up and walking five times a day. You need to regain your strength. You'll be making a trip soon, and I want you looking healthy for it." She stood and leaned down to hug me.

"Where is she?" I asked. "If she died but is still alive, where is she?"

"You're right," she said. "You deserve to know her story. I'll tell you today. But first..."

She walked and picked up the hand mirror. She gave it to me, and I held it up to my face. The bandages were gone. Pink crooked lines, shiny and smooth, were stamped across my skin.

"Don't worry," she said. "The scars will fade, and we'll use a bit of makeup. Hannah will want you to be pretty. You see, I didn't understand this when I was raising her, but Hannah is a true artist. For some reason that I'll never understand, pretty is important to people like that. Shall we begin?"

I sighed as I remembered the words. The beginning to my new story. It sounded like a sweet book, like one I'd steal from the library as a girl and hide out in the bacca to read. I imagined, as I rehearsed it, that I was back in school. I pretended, as I stared in her mirror and practiced happiness, that I was giving another class report. It went like this:

My Story
by Lily Adams

I wish memories were like pockets. I wish I didn't have to choose what to tell you. I wish you could reach inside me and pull out everything I've saved. Then I could be quiet. You would know everything, and I could just sit here with you and nod in agreement.

But memories aren't like pockets. And it's up to me to show you what happened after I left your arms. To give you a piece of all the things that I saw and felt.

I could start by telling you about the music classes Momma sent me to. I learned how to dance pretty there. How to sing old, classic songs. Or I could tell you about Christmases. About trees so grand, so

beautiful, they proved that goodness was real. Goodness could sit in our front-room window.

But the story I really want you to hear is about my
birthday. The time when I turned five years old and
Momma surprised me with the prettiest cake. She put
a whole box of candles across the top, instead of just
five, because she knew that's how I liked it best. Pink
roses covered it, because she knew my favorite color
was pink. I wouldn't let her cut it. It was too pretty. I
took it to bed with me that night. Set it on my nightstand. More than any other present, all I wanted was
to go to sleep staring at that cake. To close my eyes to
darkness and remember the picture of something so
perfect, so pretty inside my mind. That cake was like
special treasure. Unlike anything a person could find
in a field. Unlike anything a person could ever steal.

Not that I would, though. I would *never* steal. I had
no need. Momma and Daddy were rich. I wore jeans
from a mail-order catalog, not the back of a candy
barrel store. I wore dresses to church, too. And I
learned a whole list of prayers to say there. One of
them was *Bless you*, and sometimes when I said it, I
thought of you. I thought of me, too.

One time we all went to Gatlinburg for the day. I
got to feed the black bears. I rode in this little bench
that was hooked to a wire. It carried me up the side
of the mountain. I went to the fudge shop. They had
more kinds of fudge in there than any place in the
world. Daddy bought me a slice of each one, too.
On the way home, our car, a brand new Oldsmobile,
sprung a leak in the radiator. Momma cried because

she was worried about all the good groceries we had just stopped to buy from the fancy new grocery store. She was worried they'd spoil before the car was fixed. "Don't you worry, sweetheart," Daddy said. "I'm gonna fix this car for you. I'll save our groceries."

He did the funniest thing. He took an egg from the groceries in the trunk. Popped the hood, cracked the egg, and poured it down into the radiator. We drove home no problem except for the smell of egg in the car. Daddy said it had scrambled, and the chunks had plugged the leak. We laughed the whole way home. And to this day, I can't eat eggs without smiling.

I bet you wonder where I grew up. It was inside a big farmhouse. We had so many rooms I could get lost if I wasn't paying attention. But my favorite was always outside. I loved to carry lemonade out to all our help-ers waiting in the hot sun. Momma always said it was good to be helpful to folks that got less.

So here I am. I've come to say *Thank you*. And if you ever wonder why I say it, if you ever wonder why I tell you that you made the right choice, just remember this story. Remember all the sweet things. All the funny things. And then you'll know, then you'll understand, *This is why.*

HANNAH

I

Hannah sat in the rocking chair, tired from a night with stronger-than-usual drugs. Legion was silent, content to watch her doze. Content to believe the drugs were working and Hannah's mind was calm. But Hannah's face lied. Thoughts tumbled inside her, like water off a mountain.

She thought of Bethie, and how much she had changed since she was a girl. With her swingy hair and her bright colors. With her babies. Oh yes, Hannah had noticed it all. And she wondered, who was that pretty sister that came to see her? How did she ever do it?

She thought about the look on Bethie's face as the white door slammed closed. She thought about Bethie's scream, loud enough to pierce into her room. *What was it she said?* Hannah's mind cried. *Why did her face pull tight with panic? Pull tight with hope?*

Hannah struggled to name Bethie's last words. To decide if what she heard was just Bethie repeating her earlier promise. *Your miracle.* That could mean anything. A waterfall that makes words slippery. A mother that loves in her old age like she didn't when she was young.

But the thing that made Hannah scream "Bring my sister back," the thing that kept her mind fighting through the fog of Legion's drugs—was the possibility, the hope, that she had heard something more than *Your miracle.* Something different, and worthy of the panic across Bethie's face. An extra word. The most important one. It sounded like freedom, but felt so much better.

And maybe Bethie said it. Maybe Bethie screamed it. "*She's your miracle.*"

Hannah could never know for certain. But she knew this much from the visit, from that secret swell inside her sister's belly, once again life had not stopped for her. People were growing, living, dying, outside her great white walls. Everything carried on, just as it always did before. Without her.

She wished she were mud. It had been ages since she'd remembered mud. But the sight of Bethie's colors, faded though they were, couldn't help but remind her. She wished she were mud so she could throw herself against the wall. Break herself into pieces and *try again*. Make something better centered. Make something more useful and understandable. Paint a common picture. Paint herself like a plate of ordinary flowers.

She wondered if anyone else would come. She wished she could see Mother. She'd ask her, *What's right?* Even though the answers were so often lies. She wished Daniel would show up and make everything seem possible like he once had, so long ago.

And Father—she wanted to ask him about the bridge. Bethie had obviously found it. Why couldn't she?

"The first rule is *Believe*," he once told her. "The second is *Love*."

Oh but the Love part cut her. Shut her up inside those white walls. Drove her to madness. She looked at the empty chair in the corner of the room and felt the truth sting the roof of her mouth. *She's not there.* She shook her head with disgust for herself. Disgust for Legion. *She's not there.*

She closed her eyes and pretended to sleep. But inside,

she stepped into the workroom of her mind. A place she had closed years ago. A place she hadn't visited since she'd arrived at the Great White Room.

She looked around the room. *We're all just mud,* she thought.

She saw Bethie, like a perfect vase, with her golden skin and soft smile. She was made to receive joy and beauty, to store it within. She saw Daniel, like a tray. Made for holding things up. And then she saw herself. An old, cracked plate. All this time, she thought she was the cradle. That perfect shrine to emptiness. But inside the mudroom of her mind, she saw the truth. *Pain is not special. I'm not that special. I need a new center.*

II

It was late. Hannah should have been asleep, but she'd only pretended to swallow her drugs that evening. She lay down as the nurse left, then spit the white pills onto her white pillow. Deep into the night she turned her head toward the camera. "Legion," she called, and waited.

It took a moment, but soon someone answered. "How are you feeling, Hannah? Aren't you tired?"

"I want to speak to the woman who calls out the questions."

Several minutes passed until the intercom buzzed. "I heard you wanted to speak to me. Can't sleep?"

Hannah shook her head.

"Why not?"

"What should I do?" Hannah asked.

"About what?"

"To fix this."

"This isn't about fixing things. I'm here to learn about you. I love hearing your stories. About when you had me, and when you were pregnant. Would you like to tell me one of those?"

Hannah sighed softly. She glanced back at that empty chair in the corner of the room. She stood up and walked to it. And though it pained her, she lowered herself into that chair. Even though it hurt, it wasn't the worst thing. She knew now, finally, what the worst thing was.

"You are not her," Hannah whispered. She closed her eyes. She ran her hands down the edge of her chair. "You are *not* her. Please, I know you. You come to me, here in the room. You sit on my bed and talk about memories and focusing. Tell me what to do."

No one spoke for several minutes. Hannah wondered if Legion was mad. She wondered if they'd take the chair away.

"Why now?" Dr. Vaughn asked, using her normal voice.

Hannah searched for the right answer. It wasn't because her eyes suddenly worked the way they were supposed to. She still knew that any moment she wanted, she could build her heart's desire. It wasn't because she'd finally had enough of white. Or even that she missed Bethie and couldn't go another year without her.

It was about that *thing*, that horrible thing that she did, that sent her to that room.

And how Hannah suddenly knew there was something even worse than remembering it. Even worse than speaking of it. It was the possibility—however small, however misguided she was about Bethie's words—of having a miracle occur, *her* miracle, just like everything else did. *Without her.*

"I'm just ready," she whispered to the camera. "I'll tell you now. I will. I'll tell you everything you want to know."

III

It started with dimples. Little crescent-moon creases. The kind you can only find in fat, running baby knees. Hannah was at the market when she saw them. Down the aisle a mother's mouth pulled tight, yelled the dreaded words *Time out*. A little boy ran to her, buried his body in his mother's legs until the only baby skin Hannah could see was one knee peeking out. Round and pink, a smudge of dirt across it. Hannah stared at those dimples, the truth swelling strong inside her like high tide. Baby would have had those knees.

Hannah left the market and went to a party. It was for a three-year-old girl, the daughter of one of Daniel's partners. The girl stared, wide-eyed, at a pile of gifts set before her. Everybody cooed over her, whispered "how sweet," except Hannah. She hated that little girl. And loved her, too. Those eyes, that joy, all of it should have been Baby's.

Hannah left the party and walked ahead of Daniel. She told him she needed fresh air. She glanced at an old woman, at least eighty, leaning against a wall. She expected exhaustion, but when their eyes met she saw only Baby. She saw peace.

She was building something new. A patchwork baby. And every day that followed she searched out new, stranger scraps to build with. It was the only thing she could do to distract herself from the truth that once Baby had been real. Even if she only held her for a moment. Even if she abandoned her.

It was a hard word, *abandon*. One that her mind sometimes

fought against. *Mother's the one that did it,* she'd tell herself. But the truth always found her. And the truth was, she didn't fight. She had broken every single one of Mother's rules. She was immodest. She was impure. And so she had no idea why, when it was finally *good* for her to break the rules, when it was finally the right thing to do, she didn't. She wouldn't fight anymore. She let Mother take her daughter because she was afraid. *If that's not abandonment,* she told herself, *nothing is.*

One morning, not too long after the dimples, she dropped Daniel off at his office and returned to the market. She was supposed to be working with him that day. He had insisted on it, told her he was desperately behind in client billing. She knew it was a lie. But it was easier to agree with him than offer an excuse.

She was supposed to run a quick errand to pick up coffee filters for the break room. But she found herself in the produce section. It would be the reason they said she planned it. They had the tape of her from the store security. It showed her standing there by the oranges going over each one. Looking around slowly. *Baby shopping,* that was what the prosecutor said she was doing. And, oh, there were so many babies that day. It seemed every woman in the world had one but her. They passed by in shiny carts. Babies with sippy cups of juice. Mothers singing, "Row Row Row," and counting out apples.

Hannah must have touched a hundred oranges that day. She held each one up to the light, pretending to inspect for flaws. "Watch her eyes," the prosecutor said. "She doesn't even see the orange. She's a predator. She's on the hunt." Around the aisle came Baby. Hannah had waited so long for her. Wrapped in a soft blanket. Hannah could ignore the little ducks stitched around the edge. She could ignore the pink stripe down the center. She blinked her eyes and saw everything she'd ever desired: Baby Girl, wrapped in soft green cotton.

Hannah followed her through the store. Always a safe distance behind. Baby started crying. And Hannah tried to name it. *Hungry? Sick?* The woman with her didn't even look at Baby, just reached into her purse and popped a pacifier in her mouth. Baby Girl cried more.

"Stop it," Hannah whispered. "You're not listening to her." The pacifier fell, and the woman picked it up and sighed. Wiped it off and put it back in Baby's mouth. Still she cried.

"Listen to her," Hannah whispered. "She doesn't want a pacifier. She wants her mother." The woman was sorting coupons. Searching for something on the shelf. She was too busy to listen. Too busy to hear what Baby was screaming: *Mother! Mother!*

Hannah looked around the store quickly. She stepped toward Baby Girl. Their eyes met. And Hannah told her, Hannah promised her. She wasn't too busy to listen. She wasn't too afraid to fight anymore. She'd never abandon her. They belonged together.

IV

Dr. Vaughn sat inside Hannah's room, not writing but listening. When Hannah finished, Dr. Vaughn smiled. "You did good."

Hannah sighed and dropped her head into her hands.

"I was just wondering about when they found you. The report says they found you at home later that day. Why did you go there?"

"I wanted to rock her. I wanted to feel what it would be like to have my nest full. To have a baby in my empty nursery."

"You were arrested and the baby was returned unharmed."

"Yes."

"And then your husband began his fight. Do you know how hard he fought to have you placed here instead of in a state prison?"

"He asked me over and over to tell him what happened. To tell him why." Hannah sighed. "I couldn't look at him."

"He made deal after deal, stacked favor upon favor, to get you to us."

"I do remember one thing, his last words," Hannah said. "He said he was going to find someone to fix me." She looked up at Dr. Vaughn. "So fix me."

"I'll do my best. But you've owned your crime tonight. Now you've got to find peace with it."

Hannah shivered. *Peace.* Had she ever known it? Even as a girl, a baby girl with her nose pressed up against a false bridge, there was always *something* off. Tiny cracks in the plate.

"Hannah," Doctor Vaughn said softly, "you had a baby when you were seventeen. She was adopted by another family. You do not know her. You may never know her. And that may not be the best thing. It may not be your dream or your vision. But that is your story. And when you own it, when you accept it, then you will begin to heal."

Hannah nodded slowly.

From then on, doctors came to her room every day to ask hard questions. About growing up as a Holy Roller. About Sam and then Daniel. About what it meant, what it felt like, to have a daughter. To never know her.

Hannah learned how to answer to the doctors' satisfaction, even as she wondered what good it could do. To pretend that a life like hers, an ache like hers, could be reduced to a few quick sentences. Say it dryly enough, fast enough, and the pain might disappear.

Flowers were brought to her room. A simple spring mix of soft colors. Hannah restrained herself around them. Her first thought, the one that worried her, the one that proved *crazy*, was to taste them.

It was because they were more than beautiful. They were excessive. So much color. So much perfume. It seemed wasteful to enjoy them with only one or two senses and not more. *Taste them*, her mind demanded. She snapped her mouth shut and sat on her bed and watched them. When the petals fell as the flowers died, she saw splashes of paint. Picked them up and arranged them into rainbow swirls across her white floor.

Next, came noise. The doctors turned the intercom on, even when they weren't speaking to her. She heard them talk about the coffee, how it tasted burnt. She heard them typing at their computers. She heard the radio playing in the background. The phone ringing. People arguing. People laughing.

Soon the man that carried the meal trays left a menu. When Hannah picked it up she didn't read *Grilled Chicken Sandwich* or *Baked Cod*. She rearranged letters. Searching out all the new words she could create. Her eyes saw the pencil on the tray. *Check off one entrée choice, please.* She picked it up and turned the menu over. Slowly, with careful marks, she drew a flower. A clear pencil design across vanilla cardstock.

Repetition was key. The doctors had Hannah repeat her story—what she did, why she did it—on a daily basis. They had her say, over and over, that she was a mother. That she might never know her daughter. She had to own it, they told her. She had to stop running from it. She had to be able to talk about it. To tell people, to allow people to know the real Hannah. *It was the hiding,* they told her. That was what drove her to take that baby. The pretending that everything was okay. She was simply trying to make her fantasy become reality.

She didn't ask them about going home. About freedom and being well. She already knew the answer. It was up to them. They could keep her as long as they wanted. They could keep her until they believed she was truly well.

So she read the menus. She marked off her entrée choice. She listened to the intercom, the flow of random noise that spilled into her room. She met with doctors every day. She answered the questions. She told the right story. And she waited.

"Have you thought of what it would be like to see Daniel?" Dr. Vaughn asked one day.

Hannah nodded slowly, careful to hide the pain and joy that surged together inside her.

"He's here today. I didn't tell you before because I want you to speak to him from your heart. I didn't want you to worry or practice."

Hannah turned to Dr. Vaughn. "Bring me a mirror."

As Daniel walked the hall toward her room, Hannah studied herself slowly. The white hair, hanging limp at her shoulders. The pale skin. The tiny lines around her eyes. She wished for mud to smear across her hands. She wished for paint to smear across her chin. She wished the whole room were yellow instead of white. So she could frame her body with her best color, with something almost heavenly.

When he walked in, Hannah stood in the middle of the room. Unsure of what she should do, just like old times, when she used to find him waiting for her in the Great Room. He hurried to her, hugged her tightly. His hand reached up to her head and pushed it against his shoulder.

"Hannah," he whispered. "Put your arms around me."

She slid her arms up and around his neck.

"Let me see your eyes," he said.

As he stared at her, she wished that she hadn't asked for the mirror. Wished she didn't know exactly what he saw.

"I'm different," she said. "They cut my hair."

He shrugged his shoulders. "I'm different, too."

Hannah saw the patches of gray above his temples. Had it really been three years since she'd seen him? *Three years?* She thought of all the nights they hadn't spent together. All the breakfasts she hadn't prepared for him.

"I'm sorry," she choked, as she laid her head against his shoulder.

"It's all right."

"No. It's not. Nothing is. Daniel, I had a baby when I was seventeen. I've spent every year after that trying to pretend it never happened. Trying to make up for the fact that it did. But I can't." Hannah sobbed against his shoulder. "And it doesn't feel all right. I should have told you the truth—"

"I knew," he interrupted. "Your mother told me."

"What?"

"She told me. About Sam. About when you were seventeen."

"*She told you?*"

"Yes."

"Mother?"

"Yes."

"I don't believe you. She wouldn't. Everything, every lie I've told since then has been because of her. She promised me—"

"I'd had some friends track down information on the family that called to offer us the baby. The trail led back to your mother's hotel. There was a worker there, a former prostitute she'd hired from a truck stop. She had a fifteen-year-old sister who was pregnant. Your mother found out. Offered the family twenty thousand dollars if they would give you that baby."

"Mother," Hannah whispered.

"Yes. I called the family myself and heard from them that the deal had been called off long ago. You hadn't told me. And you were still fixing up that nursery. I knew then something bad was wrong. So I went to her. Told her I needed answers. Asked her what she was fighting."

"Fighting?"

"There's a war inside you. I've known that from the beginning. She was still trying to fight it."

"All those years she groomed me to pretend it never happened. It's the reason we settled on the mountain, changed our name. So that I could start over. So we could all start over. And then she just tells you—"

"You could have told me, Hannah."

"It wouldn't have changed anything that happened."

"Might have. I would have at least known what to fight."

They sat on the edge of her bed together and Hannah told him about Baby Girl. How Mother staged a false reunion, shortly after the failed adoption. What Baby Girl looked like the day she was born. How sometimes it was hard to remember, and that was why Hannah had created her from the scraps of strangers. Daniel told her about the trial. Hannah, out of her mind, had missed much of it. Daniel told her about the doctors he hired. How Bethie testified on her behalf, and how he forced Mother to testify, too. She nearly went to jail for contempt when she wouldn't answer his questions.

"So the whole world knows, then," Hannah whispered.

"It had to come out. I had to prove that your motive was pain, not evil, if I was ever going to get you placed here instead of with the State."

Everyone knew. The judge. The newspapers. Guests at the hotel. Her customers at the artisan's fair. It was in all the records. Like the ones Hannah's parents had paid so much money to avoid. She'd never hide it from anyone ever again. There was nothing to pretend anymore. *Everyone already knew.*

"No more secrets," she said.

"There's still one," Daniel said lowly. "I've spent so many nights thinking about the pottery. Every single piece broken, Hannah...all my favorites. Was that message—was it meant for me?"

Hannah shook her head. "It happened the night before... when you were working late."

"But why?"

"Because I know what's in the mist. What nobody else could figure out. And I couldn't bear to see it anymore."

"What is it?"

"It's home." She turned from him, until her whole body faced the wall. "With every stroke of paint, with every layer of color, I was painting home. Not ours." She began to cry. "Hers. Sometimes I just painted myself. Because my body was the only home we ever shared. Other times, I painted the unknown. All the places she may have lived. All the somewheres she might be."

Daniel's arms slid around her, pulling her to him. They sat there together, until her whole body relaxed against him. He leaned down and kissed her forehead.

"You should know better," she whispered bitterly. "I'm not safe to love."

"No," he agreed. "But I knew that about you, I loved that about you, from the very beginning. *Love is an emergency.* Remember? If we have that, who needs safe?"

A five-minute warning was called out from the intercom. And it occurred to Hannah, for the first time since Daniel had walked into her room, that he would have to leave. It was up to Legion when she would see him again. It was up to Legion, *if* she would see him again. And as she started to cry, he told her to be strong. To fight the war with him. For him.

Hannah remembered her sister then, and how Bethie had screamed her good-byes. Screamed those magic last words.

"Have you seen Bethie?" Hannah asked. "She came here a few months ago. Have you seen her? Did she say anything?"

Daniel shook his head. "I haven't seen your family since the trial. But last week there was a message from Bethie on the machine."

"Did you call her back?"

"Not yet."

"Why not? What if she needed you?"

"No. It had something to do with your art, I think. A piece of yours she's found and thought I'd want. I'll call her back tonight, don't worry."

"Daniel," Hannah cried. "Tell me exactly what her message said."

He shrugged his shoulders. Tried his best to remember the right words. "*Hi, this is Bethie. I need to meet with you . . . There's something of Hannah's here . . . I can't describe it on the phone. You'll have to see it to believe it.*"

ANGEL

I

In the middle of the night I heard them, right outside the door. They were loud. Every once in a while they shushed each other and tried to be quiet. I couldn't make out their words, but their voices were new. And that was all that mattered.

"Hello?" I cried. "Is somebody there?"

It was quiet for a moment. And then a man answered.

"Who are you?"

It was a test. The old woman was testing me, to see if I would keep my end of the bargain. I sighed.

"I'm Lily."

"Lily who?"

"Adams."

"Are you her?" he called out. "Are you Hannah's daughter?"

"Yes."

"Can you let us in?" he asked.

"I'm tied to the bed."

They raised their voices again, and this time they didn't bother to shush one another. Someone tried to force the door open. It didn't work. I knew then, when I heard the boom of a shoulder against that door, they were coming to rescue me. I knew when I heard the knob rattle and shake in its socket, they weren't with the old woman.

"We'll be back, Lily," the man called out. "We'll be back for you."

I waited all night. I lay there in total darkness, my eyes playing tricks sometimes. Imagining I saw light coming from under the door. Imagining I heard them whisper. But they never came.

The old woman did, though. The next morning she walked in happy.

"Good morning, Lily. How have you been?"

I didn't answer.

"Well the nurse gave a good report. Said you've done your exercises and rested well." She sat down in the chair next to my bed. "I never dreamed things would turn out so well for us. Hannah is in prison. You are an addict. But in the end, you will both be well."

I turned my head and stared at the wall. It was the only rebellion left to me.

"A simple *thank you* would suffice, Lily. Doesn't it feel nice to sleep naturally? To take Tylenol for pain? To not *need* so much? When you first came here you were half starved. Standing on my porch in those awful cutoffs, and it wasn't more than fifty degrees outside. You were nothing but a skinny redneck. And now, look at you. You are healthy. " She stood up. "I went shopping for you."

"What did you say?" I whispered.

"I have some new clothes for you. You'll need to wear them when you go see Hannah."

"You called me redneck."

"I called Angel a redneck. But you, Lily, are nothing like her." She smiled sweetly and walked away. When she returned, she carried two shopping bags.

"These are for you. I bought them at the Gilded Lily. I thought it was fitting to purchase your new look from a store that shares your lovely new name. Have you ever shopped at one? Did they have one in Tennessee?"

I started to shake my head no. I started to tell her how me and Momma shopped for clothes at the general store. Where behind all the candy barrels stood a discount rack of clothes: T-shirts with beaded fringe, ribbed tank tops that said *Great Smokies,* jeans designed more for farm work than fashion. Nothing was ever more than a few dollars. But then I remembered what Lily would say. And I nodded. "Sure. Been there lots of times."

"Look here," the old woman said, as she pulled a sweater out of the bag. "The lady at the store told me this was a great deal. It had been eighty, but it was marked down to fifty."

She held it up to the light. It was a shade of green that reminded me of home. The same money shade of Daddy's car.

"Would you like to try it on?" she asked.

I nodded.

"Let's get you some pants to go with it. I imagine it's hard to judge a top unless you're wearing the right pants for it."

She pulled a pair of jeans from the bag, with little studs where the belt should be and a lacy stitch across the pockets. She undid my wrists and helped me dress.

I looked at the tags. I was wearing a hundred dollars' worth of clothes. Half the price of Black Snake trailer. More than Momma and Daddy would spend on a month of groceries.

"Lovely," the old woman said.

There wasn't a mirror, except for the small one that I used to practice my story for you. I looked down at myself. I'd never worn such a pretty color, or such thick soft cloth. Never worn jeans that weren't skintight or didn't have holes in them. I stared at myself and had no idea if I looked pretty or ugly. Or maybe something more strange: *decent.*

"Perfect," the old woman said softly. "I can't wait till Hannah sees you."

"Yeah," I answered.

"Is there...," she began, then stopped. "Did anything unusual happen while I was away?"

It might have been another test. Maybe she set me up after all. Sent people there to see what name I would give.

But then maybe she didn't. "No," I said, and shrugged.

She stared at me until I looked away. "Take off your clothes. You need to keep them fresh and pretty."

I was starting to undress when the door went *boom* again. We both jumped.

"Let me in," the man's voice called. "I know you're in there, Mrs. Reynolds."

"Daniel," the old woman said in a low voice. "This is a private part of my home, and I demand that you respect my privacy."

"I'll wait as long as I have to. Now open this door."

The old woman turned to me. "Sit down in the chair." She smoothed up the bed covers. Pulled the blankets over the wrist restraints. She walked to me and smoothed my hair down, tossed it over my shoulders a bit. Then she turned to me. "Remember Tennessee and what you did before you left. Remember you'll see your mother because of me. Don't mess it up. It's showtime, Lily."

She walked to the door and opened it. Daniel stepped inside. He looked around the room.

"Daniel, what on earth—," the old woman began.

"It's her," he said, as he looked at me. "Look at her. Look at her hair."

"Yes," the old woman said. "This is Lily."

He stepped toward me. "I'm Daniel."

I didn't know what to say yet, and so I stayed quiet. Was your Daniel safe? Could I whisper *help*? Would that one word send me to a Tennessee prison? And if it did, would it be worth it? Would I be Angel again? Would I meet Janie there?

"She took a fall, Daniel. She was working here as we slowly got to know one another, and she took a bad fall. She didn't have health insurance, so I thought it best to provide private care. She felt awkward, since she doesn't know us, so I agreed to keep the incident and the expense private."

"No, no," he said. "You don't owe any explanations, this is wonderful. I can't believe it. You found her." He hugged her warmly. "Good job."

"That's kind of you, Daniel," the old woman said, and smiled.

"Are you taking her to see Hannah?"

She nodded. "Of course. She has so much to tell her."

"Really? Like what?"

I looked at the old woman and she gave me a quick nod. I took a deep breath and wanted to cry. Because I knew then I wouldn't ask for help. Because I knew I *couldn't* ask him for help. "Thank you," I whispered. "I'm gonna say thank you."

II

I was out of the basement. Back in our room. I'd done so well with Daniel, the old woman set me free. Almost. The door clicked before she walked away.

But finally, I was back in your old room. The window was fixed. The bed was clean again. I opened the closet door. There was my bag. The one I'd hid beneath the bacca leaves.

The one I filled with just enough food and water to help me escape after I burned Black Snake trailer. I looked inside it and saw my cutoffs. I pulled them out and searched the pockets. Everything was still there.

I looked at the picture of me. I imagined new right words. Ones that would please the old woman. Ones that would heal you. "My name is Lily Adams. This is me and my daddy washin' the car. I'm doing all I can to help him and he's workin' hard so we'll have somethin' nice to be proud of. That's what good families are supposed to do."

I found the pocket watch next. "This doesn't tell time anymore, but that don't matter much. Even though it's broken, even though it's old, its message is the same. It says *Love*."

Next was the milk cap. I sighed. I couldn't think of any words that would make it all better. "This is nothin'," I whispered. "A person like me, with the good life you sent me to, has no reason to hold on to trash."

I pulled out the soap. "I used to want to live in a hotel when I was a kid. And because of you, because of your mother, I've done that now."

"Lily?" a voice whispered.

I turned to the breakfast slot. I saw someone had pushed it open slightly.

"Yes?"

"It's Bethie. Hannah's sister. I was the volunteer that helped you at the hospital. Can you break the window?"

"What?"

"There's not much time and I can't find a key to this door. Can you break the window? Is there a chair or something? We have a ladder outside you can climb down. I'll meet you there."

"I don't…," I started to say, then stopped. "Why are you doing this?"

"I'll tell you everything later, but if you want to get away, we need to go now. Break the window, Lily."

I picked up the chair by the desk. I threw it as hard as I could, turned my back to the familiar sound of everything breaking. Large pieces of jagged glass remained. I picked up the chair and knocked at each of them. Over and over, until the glass was nearly gone. Until I could safely stick my head outside and see the ladder propped against the house. I took a deep breath. It had been so long since I had smelled the mountain. I went and grabbed my backpack, the one with my cutoffs and pocket treasure, and threw it out the window. I pulled the quilt from the bed and laid it over the bottom of the window to protect my skin from any further hurt.

As I climbed down the ladder, Bethie came running through the woods. "This way!"

I grabbed my bag and followed her until we came to a road. Daniel was inside a car, waiting for us. I jumped in the backseat, Bethie in the front.

"Let's go!" she said, and then turned to me and started talking fast and loud. "We knew she was holding you prisoner. Daniel came today because he didn't believe me. He had to see for himself that it wasn't another lie. That you really are Hannah's daughter."

"How did you know?" I asked. But she misunderstood, and thought I meant about being held prisoner.

"After you left the hospital, Mother asked me to keep my distance. You didn't know us, who we were yet, and she said she wanted to introduce you slowly to our family, to who you really are. She was afraid if you saw me again, if you found out I was her daughter, you'd remember me from the hospital and get suspicious. So I stayed away. And it all seemed to be going well. Every time I called, she said she was going to tell you soon. But then one day she said you disappeared; without warning, you ran away. At first I believed her. I mean, the first time I met you, you were a runaway. Why wouldn't you do it again? But then things didn't add up. Like the way she closed the hotel down. Peak season, and she closed it down. And the way she sent all the workers away, without notice or warning. Just one day cleared house. I tried to talk to Father, but he couldn't help. He can barely walk down the hall now, let alone know what his wife is up to. I noticed the nurse, of course. Mother said she was for Father. That he needed full-time care. Mother said the nurse had a room in the basement. That she stayed there when she wasn't needed. And I started thinking why? Why wouldn't the nurse stay on Bedroom Hall? With all the workers away? All those empty rooms? So one night, I stayed there. I told her my husband was painting, and I couldn't be near the fumes. I snuck down to the basement and saw the nurse sitting in a chair outside the door. I showed her my hospital badge. Told her I was there to see the patient, that I'd been called in to offer counseling. She looked at my badge closely. Saw that it was official, and she let me in. I didn't know what I'd find as I stepped through those doors. But there you were, sleeping and tied down. I knew something bad was wrong. I knew you needed help." She turned back toward the front. "Daniel!" she screamed.

He slammed on his brakes. Through the bit of moon that peaked through the clouds we all saw her. She was standing in the middle of the road. We couldn't see her face. We just saw her dark shape, her long black skirt, her long gray hair.

The outline of her was a shade darker than the night. Just like Momma's gun. Just like any other lie about sweet peace.

"What's she doing?" Bethie whispered.

"Stay in the car," he said to her. "I'll talk to her." But before he could get out, she stepped toward us.

"You can't have her," she screamed to Daniel. "She's mine. I bought her." She pointed her finger at me. "You...I've already called the Swarms...already called the police."

"Get out of the road," Daniel yelled.

"Don't do this," she cried. "Lily is our last chance. She can fix everything. I've taught her how."

"Get out of the road," Daniel repeated.

She leaned down and looked in the window at me. "Think of all our hard work, Lily. Think of all the things you've studied and practiced. All the hours we've poured into you. Think of how I've helped you. You don't cry for whiskey anymore because of me. Think of your mother. Think of how you can help her. Get out of the car, Lily. Get out of the car and keep the promise. I'll forgive you, if you'll just get out of the car."

"Don't, Mother," Bethie said.

"They're coming for you," the old woman hissed at me. "I'll make certain of it. The Swarms will come for you. Get out of the car and I'll stop them again. Get out of the car, Lily!"

I took a deep breath, put my hand on the doorknob to pull it, and thought of you. I thought of you in prison, wanting me but needing Lily. I thought of you on the day I was born and how you cried, *Wait.* And then I thought of you, and the choice that you made once, the man that you trusted. I thought of you, and who you'd want me to pick. Who you'd tell me to pick, in all your mother's wisdom.

"Go," I whispered to Daniel. "Go."

III

Daniel reversed the car and steered into a ditch. The car jerked and threw me back into the seat. As he pulled up onto the road again, I saw that the old woman was behind us. I could hear her screaming long after the darkness swallowed her.

Daniel drove to Bethie's house.

"I should come with you," she said.

"You've got the new baby to look after. We'll be fine."

"You think Mother really called the cops?" she asked, as she stepped out of the car.

I answered before he could. "Yeah. I'm sure she did."

"I'll get to the bottom of everything," Daniel said to Bethie. "Don't worry. She's safe."

Bethie looked back at me one last time. "I'm sorry," she said.

I didn't answer, but my eyes must have asked, *What for?*

"For everything my family's done," she said. "I would have loved to watch you grow up."

She went inside and Daniel looked back at me. "You wanna move up front?" he asked. I shook my head. He started the car again. We were driving down the mountain now. Even though the darkness hid it well, I could feel us sinking low.

"So," he said. "Why'd she call the cops?"

I shook my head, shrugged my shoulders.

"She lies a lot, that old woman," he said. "But if there's anything to it, if you're in some kind of trouble, I can help. It's kind of what I do."

I shook my head again, stared out the window. "I'm in bigger trouble than you can fix."

"Oh, I doubt that." He laughed dryly. "What'd you do? Kill somebody?"

"No."

"Nearly kill somebody?"

"No."

"Oh, please," he said, and laughed again. "Please tell me you didn't kidnap anybody's baby. 'Cause that one actually is hard to fix."

"I burned my home down. Black Snake trailer. And on accident, half the farm went with it."

He nodded slowly. "Okay. How old were you?"

"Seventeen."

"Who was with you?"

"What d'you mean?"

"I mean, where were your parents? At work? At church? Did they know what you planned?"

"They'd runned off."

"Without you?"

I nodded.

"Were they coming back for you?"

I shook my head. And fought the tears that wanted to escape. *It was wrong of them*, he told me with that look of his.

"They weren't a preacher's family, like they were supposed to be, were they?" he asked lowly.

I shook my head. "Momma cleaned for the preacher's wife. Old woman paid her to take me."

"Mercy," he whispered to the window. "Hannah was right."

We drove in silence the rest of the way. The car slowed and Daniel turned down a long paved drive. "This is it," he said.

It was a clear night the first time I saw your house. Stars, all of them, sat right on top of it to light the way. To lead me to your farmhouse, a big one, like all farmhouses should be. Daniel started talking to me about burning Black Snake trailer. About how he could handle it.

I wasn't really listening. I was busy looking at your house. I was thinking about what it was going to feel like to step inside it. *Finally*. I was thinking about what Momma and Daddy would have said, if they could've seen me.

Daddy would have said he felt like saluting, the way he was taught the month he was in the army. Momma would say she felt like praying, the way the preacher did over Grandma's grave. Janie would mumble a cussword for me, because for her that's as big as it gets. And me. What would I have said all those years ago, all those hot days out under the sycamore? If I had known one day I'd make it inside the big house? *Your big house*. I'd say it was the end. I'd say I'd reached the heaven preached at Grandma's grave. I'd say, *Let me in*.

"It's only a few hours till morning," Daniel said. "I'll take you to the guest room and you can rest. We'll figure everything out after you've slept some."

I nodded and followed him. I saw the way you arranged your furniture. With the couches laid out in perfect lines. I saw the way you hung pictures of the desert down the hallway walls. I saw the paint colors you chose. How you painted your ceilings a different shade than the rest of the room. I saw the pretty curtains you hung in your windows, the way they let in just enough starlight. I lay across a bed that you picked out, covered in sheets and blankets that you shopped for. I went to sleep in your nice house. Its details, all of them chosen by you, surrounded me.

I woke up to a knock at the door. I blinked my eyes, sat up quickly, as the memory of the night before returned to me.

"Lily," he said. "If you wanna wake up, I've made some lunch downstairs. Bethie's gonna come over later this afternoon."

"Yeah," I said.

Downstairs I sat at a table across from him. He had made ham sandwiches, cokes, and chips. We ate in silence. Then he pushed his plate back and sighed.

"What do you wanna do?" he asked me.

"I don't know. I came here to find my mother. She's in a prison for crazy people. And she doesn't need me."

"What do you mean?"

"The old woman told me my story would hurt her more."

"She doesn't have the right—"

"No," I said. "It's not a pretty one. It won't heal her. And..." I stopped.

"And?"

"She might change her mind about me once she hears it."

He shook his head. "You don't know how much—"

"Mister," I interrupted, "you don't know what kind of people I come from. What kinda girl I was raised to be."

"Doesn't matter." He stood up and walked to the window. "There's a rose garden just down the path there. When Hannah was here, and those roses were in bloom, there wasn't a day that she didn't cut a few, bring them to the house and set them somewhere. A table, or a desk. Sometimes in the window where she does the dishes. One night, it stormed so bad it took down a couple trees. The next morning, when we were looking at all the damage, I noticed the roses had taken a beating. Not a single petal was left on them. Just a bunch of thorny stems."

He looked at me. "She still cut them, Lily. Still carried them into our home. Still filled vases with water for them and put them in the center of our table. I pulled one out, held it up to her. Teased her about it."

He turned back to the window. "She said, 'It's still a rose. The storm hurt it, but it's still a rose.'" He cleared his throat quickly and started gathering our dishes. He carried them to the sink and rinsed them off.

"Will you just let her see you?" he asked lowly. "She's imagined you for so long."

I nodded and stared toward the rose garden you loved. How I wished I'd been planted there.

IV

"What's she doing here?" Bethie cried as we walked through the big metal doors.

I looked up and saw for myself. The old woman. She was standing with a group of men in white coats.

"That's her," the old woman said, and pointed at me. "The impostor. Daniel is paying this girl, because she looks like Hannah, to pretend she's her lost daughter. What will happen when Hannah finds out the truth?"

"You," Daniel said through gritted teeth. "You were holding her prisoner in your basement, and we—"

"Sir," one of the men in white coats said, and stepped toward us. "I know you care for the patient, but I think it's best to remember—"

"She's my wife!"

"Yes, I understand, but—"

"I've brought her daughter." He turned to the old woman. "It's what Hannah's wanted from the moment you first paid the maid to take her baby away."

"I never," the old woman started. She pointed a finger at me. "Is this what she told you?"

"Listen," another man in a white coat said. "Before *anyone* sees Hannah, we'll have to do a thorough screening." He looked at Bethie. "Cooperation of all visitors is of the utmost importance. Otherwise, years of therapy can be compromised." He turned to me. "We'd like to take some information from you. We'd like to ask you some questions. And if you are who you say you are, then maybe, if it's appropriate and the risk is not too great, maybe one day we'll let you see her."

"I can't see her?" I cried.

"Not today."

"Where's your boss?" Daniel asked. "Who do you report to?"

"That'd be the new director. But she's not available right now."

"Where is she?" he demanded.

"She's resting. But I promise you, this is her new protocol. We all learned the hard way, didn't we, Bethlehem?"

We left. The old woman's face was like stone, and that's how I knew she was gloating. We walked out the double metal doors. We left you behind them.

"I'll keep you from her forever," the old woman hissed. "You won't hurt her. Not my daughter."

Bethie was crying. Maybe I was, too.

"C'mon," Daniel said. "Let's go home. We'll think of something."

He stepped toward the car. He pulled on my arm, trying to get me to move. But I wouldn't. I wanted to stand a minute and look at the building you were in. We were so close, you and me.

Then the doors swung open, and out stepped a woman wearing a white coat. She had messy gray hair and glasses.

"Wait!" she cried. I turned to Daniel, but she was looking at me. "My name is Dr. Vaughn, and I need you to wait."

Someone was behind her. I couldn't see who yet. But the old woman did. The old woman cried, "No," as she ran to my side.

"What will you say?" she hissed, as she grabbed my elbow and held on to me. "Your story can hurt or heal. You have the power. What will you say?"

Daniel stepped forward. He took me by the hand and pulled me from the old woman. "Hannah," he cried, and choked over the words. "This is your Lily."

And out of my stars, out of your paint and my dreams, out of your faceless clay babies, there we were together. You stood very still against the door. For a moment, I lost courage and tried to look away. But I couldn't. Because that pull, the one I always hoped for, was there. My blood was made from yours, and drawn to it.

You said something then. About me, and how I was something close to holy. You stepped toward me, and I never had to move again. You found me there. You whispered *Lily* as you reached for my hand.

I shook my head. "You can call me Angel."

"I've been waiting for you," you said.

"I've been whisperin' to you my whole life," I cried.

"Well, tell me everything again. Tell me everything you said."

I didn't think about the old woman then. I didn't think about being locked in that basement, about the story she made me practice. I just felt right words, pure and strong, pour into my mouth. I didn't have to search for them anymore. They were there, inside me all along. Just waiting for you.

"*Thank you,*" I said, as I let you put your arms around me, hold me for the second time ever. "Some other day, I'll tell you about the fire. And how it burned up my childhood. I'll tell you about the smoke. And how it was too heavy, filled with too many dead things to ever rise. Like dirty ashtrays and broken dishes. Like my sister's letter, the one she wrote before she ran away. I'll tell you these things, not to hurt you more or to make you sad again. But to show you how a sycamore grows. How a good black snake sheds. To show you just how high a tower can rise."

I pulled back from you. I saw your white hair, like an angel. I saw your brown eyes, like a baby calf.

"But today I just want to say thank you," I whispered. "For wantin' me when nobody else did. Thank you for going crazy because you didn't have me. For knowin' that we belonged together. Thank you for all of that. Because I know now—now that I'm finally here with you—more than anything else, more than any other right words . . . this will be my story."

Acknowledgments

I am forever grateful to my agent, Andrea Somberg. Without her commitment, my books would just be old files stored on my laptop. They are read because of her.

Thanks to Christina Boys, my brave editor. Her sharp insight into the rhythms of this story kept it from being choked by the weeds. Christina, you helped this book bloom the way it was meant to. I have learned so much from you.

Thanks to Shanon Stowe and Laura Troup for their diligence in spreading the word. And to all the members of the Hachette Book Group team who have worked behind the scenes to make my writing printable.

Thanks to my parents, Joe and Sue Blankenship. When I was seven years old, they fought for me to have full check-out privileges in the elementary library rather than being limited to the children's section. They didn't laugh when the first thing I checked out was the biggest book I could find, a thousand-page volume about King Arthur. "Looks like a good story," Momma said, smiling.

And finally, thanks to my husband, Kip, who told me inside a law-school library that I should be a writer. He embraced the dream long before I did and set about to prove himself right. He is my first reader, my first editor, and my champion. Kip, you have polished me.

Reading Group Guide

1. Angel avoids the advances of men, describing them as "sideways lines" that don't lead anywhere, while Hannah is easily charmed by the first boy that pays her any attention. What are the reasons for this difference?

2. Angel believes being pretty is "useful," to help her get what she needs. Hannah finds beauty seductive and craves affirmation of her own beauty. Mother believes beauty is unnecessary and dangerous. Whom do you agree with most? Do you think Mother is right that beauty is particularly important to Hannah because she is a "true artist"?

3. Why does *wanting* scare Mother? Is it just because of Leah, or is there something else that troubles her? Does Angel get what she wanted? Does Hannah? Does Mother?

4. Angel believes that lies are mercy. Is she right?

5. Why doesn't Father's drawn bridge work for Hannah? Why does Father say they've worn themselves out trying to build their own bridge?

6. Why, even though Hannah was taught so differently, was it easy for her to let Sam pull her close under that live oak tree? Why did the alarms she was taught to hear not work for her?

7. Why is Bethie able to escape Mother's hold on her, form her own beliefs, and enjoy a normal adulthood? Why isn't Hannah able to do the same?

8. Did Hannah abandon Angel because she didn't fight Mother to keep her?

9. Bethie says "emptiness is the miracle canvas." Do you agree?

10. At first glance, Angel and Hannah have very different childhoods. But as their stories develop, shared themes emerge. In what ways were their childhoods similar? Do you think one of them had a worse childhood than the other?

11. Do you agree with Daniel that "love is an emergency"? How was love an emergency in this novel?

12. Mother cries that she put "stones over [her] children." What were those stones? Were they ever lifted off, or did her children simply learn to live in spite of them?

13. Why was it so important to Angel to tell her story? Why wasn't it enough just to be reunited with her mother?

14. When Angel wakes up tied down in the basement, she decides that "blood isn't nearly as important" as she always thought when it comes to defining a family. What makes a family? Is it shared beliefs, like a bridge? Is it shared desires, like whiskey? How much does "blood" matter?

15. Who is the memory thief? Are there multiple memory thieves in this novel?

16. Angel believes there are only two kinds of people in this world: Swarms, and those stuck waiting beneath the sycamore tree. Which category does Mother belong to? Father? Bethie? What do you think the future holds for Angel? Does she make it out from under the sycamore tree? What about Hannah?

If you enjoyed *The Memory Thief,*
look for Rachel Keener's first novel, *The Killing Tree.*

"[A]n intensely lyrical, emotional debut." —*Publishers Weekly*

Mercy Heron spends her days working at the local diner, but unlike her wild best friend, Della, she's never considered leaving the insulated community on Crooked Top Mountain. Not until the summer when she meets Trout, a man who opens Mercy's eyes to a world beyond what she's known. Their relationship must be kept secret, because Father Heron won't approve of his granddaughter's being involved with a migrant worker. But when Mercy tries to escape, she'll learn just how powerful—and ruthless—her grandfather can be. And the truth of her past will threaten to forever bind her to the mountain.

Available from Center Street wherever books are sold.

CENTER
STREET.